PURSUIT

by

John McAllister

For Trish
And
Daniel who acts as unpaid researcher
And
Lucie, my publicist

Published by Glenlish Publications

Copyright: John McAllister, 2016

The right of John McAllister to be identified as the author of this work has been asserted by him in accordance with the Copyright, Designs and Patents Act 1988 Sections 77 & 78

All rights reserved. No part of this publication may be transmitted in any form or by any means, electronic or mechanical, including photography, recording or any information storage or retrieval system, without the permission, in writing, of the author.

The work is sold subject to the condition that it shall not, by way of trade or otherwise, be lent, resold or otherwise circulated, without the author's prior consent in writing, in any form or binding or cover other than that in which it is published.

ISBN: 9781071186510

All characters in this novel are fictional. Any resemblance to real persons, alive or dead, is coincidental.

Photograph by JohnBellArt
Cover design and formatting by Caligraphics

PURSUIT

Chapter 1

Killing RM seemed like a good idea.

Doc felt his blood sizzle at the thought. All the same the killing gave him no pleasure. In his opinion, a killing needed an element of subtlety, of creativity about it. Sitting in a car, at the top of a tree-lined avenue with houses on either side, required something quiet and fast. *Basic tactics*. The only problem was DNA. He'd have to torch the car and the body, and he was wearing his good suit. He daren't risk it smelling of petrol.

Doc thought he should first double-check with RM, whose Acne clusters shone with greasy sweat.

'You did steal this car?'

'Yes, I said.'

'A car with the key in the ignition?'

RM's knuckles went white on the steering wheel. 'I got lucky.'

He's lying.

A quick chop to the throat seemed too good an ending for the scrawny youth. Any man who worked for Ronnie Fetherton deserved something more inventive. There again, this RM had lasted longer than most and probably knew too much. All the previous RMs (Ronnie's Man) had ended up in jail or dead – and maybe skinflint Ronnie was hoping Doc would do the job for him on the cheap. A sort of discount on the day's work.

'I don't think he's coming,' RM said, attempting to change the subject.

Still undecided about killing him or not, Doc brought himself back to that day's task. *He's right*. Today of all days, the man they were waiting for was running late.

RM said, 'He's not coming, maybe we should go on home?'

Doc shrugged, more to dismiss the memory of the instructions given by his own boss, as anything else. "No waves," Jimmy had said, and driving around a strange town in an allegedly stolen car with a body in the back could cause complications.

All the same…

RM said, 'I think we should give up. What do you think?'

I don't like that, he sounds nervous.

Doc checked himself and the car. He'd worn surgical gloves right from

5

the start and there was no obvious grot or grime to stain his suit. That suit, he again realized, was the main reason why he hesitated. It was the only one he had until he did something about replacing his wardrobe. Lazenbatt, the tailor he used, had to know that the wife had left him. The slightest smirk, no matter how innocent, and he'd kill the man.

A final check around. *No cars on the avenue, no one walking to work.* Doc flexed his shoulders for the blow even as a British Telecom van turned off the main road into Mullough Avenue. Sunlight and shadows flickered across its grey paint as it came up the hill towards them.

RM pounded the steering wheel in his excitement. 'It's him. It's him.'

And it's not you... This time.

Chapter 2

The British Telecom van turned into a driveway near where they sat. Doc got out of the car and checked that his surgical gloves hadn't torn anywhere. RM pulled up his hood and put on wrap-around sunglasses. Doc looked but said nothing. He walked down the pavement, not rushing, and turned into the driveway. RM joined him, breathless with excitement.

The van driver, Nelson, had his key in the lock and the front door open. He saw them come around the side of the van, and waited. Only his face turned their way. His body swayed into the hallway and his feet followed. Nelson's skin, Doc noted, was grey and stretched after a week of nightshifts.

'Can I help you?' asked Nelson.

In spite of his obvious tiredness he sounded pleasant and willing to oblige.

Without speaking, Doc put his shoulder to Nelson's bulk and bullied him further into the house.

'What the hell?' said Nelson.

Doc closed the door behind them.

RM produced a gun, an old Smith and Wesson .38 revolver. Doc twitched at the sight of it.

I should have come on my own.

Nelson backed hard against a wall and held his hands at shoulder height. 'No harm, boys, no harm.'

This was no time to discuss tactics in front of a victim, so Doc told Nelson, 'We would like you to do us a favor.'

Nelson swallowed, dry mouthed. 'A favor?'

RM jabbed the muzzle into the bulge of Nelson's stomach. 'And we're not asking.'

He cracked the gun against Nelson's face as he doubled over, sending him sprawling. A Yucca plant went flying across the floor.

Doc nudged RM off-balance as he went to put the boot in. 'Enough.'

He left them and went into the over-furnished sitting room. He was hardly in the door when he heard a *crack* and a cry from Nelson. He looked back. There was now a welt on Nelson's other cheekbone. RM was crouched over Nelson, gun up, ready to hit him again.

'I said "enough".'

RM's sunglasses stopped Doc from seeing his eyes clearly. All the same, RM had better obey or more than Nelson would have a marked face.

Amateurs.

In the sitting room, every level surface was given over to plants in pots. The thought of all that greenfly made Doc uneasy. He saw what he was looking for among the vegetation and scooped them up. Back in the hall, he found that RM had Nelson pinned to the floor, the gun-barrel resting between his eyes.

Doc crouched over Nelson and used a finger to push the gun away. RM retreated but kept the revolver trained on them both. Doc stared at RM until the gun was lowered, then he turned again to Nelson. 'We don't mean you any harm.' He stopped and let his words register. 'Honest to God,' he added, reassuringly. 'But we're going to give you a phone number, and we want you to tell us who calls that number and from where.'

'I can't.'

Doc unbundled his arms. A lifetime of family photographs cascaded onto Nelson's stomach and poured over his thighs. The point of a heavy frame dug into the floor and the glass shattered. 'For your family's sake.'

He read the note pasted on the back of the broken frame. 'Elizabeth, age 9.' It was a faded black and white photograph of a little girl clutching a corgi. He rummaged through the other frames until he found a colored miniature of another little girl. He held it up. 'Her daughter?'

Nelson shook his head. 'Richard's.'

'There you are then,' said Doc. 'You spend your life worrying about them. Even when they're parents themselves they're still your kids.' His voice dropped as if letting Nelson in on a secret. 'You'd do anything to keep them safe.' He raised his voice again. 'Isn't that right?'

Nelson's nod was hard enough to make his jowls vibrate.

Doc removed the two pictures from their frames. Then he said, 'I can't understand a man who puts his kids at risk. Can you?'

The jowls swung to and fro.

He patted Nelson on the shoulder, confident that the man would comply, and straightened up. 'My friend will give you the number. Someone will call every night about midnight for your report.' He had a good look at the two photographs before putting them in his pocket. 'Nice kids.'

Doc noticed that Nelson's face had gone pasty, the skin under his lips now edged with blue. *Not a good sign.* He cut off RM's bluster and kept staring until RM thought to put the revolver away. They handed over the number and left.

Chapter 3

Doc and RM went back to their car, the one allegedly stolen with the key still in the ignition. RM was cock-a-hoop. 'Easy peasy,' he crowed.

Doc was puzzled at Nelson's attitude. The worse they could have done in there was kill Nelson himself. Anything else and Nelson's screams would have alerted the neighborhood and the man obviously would happily die for his kids. *So why not get on with it and save everyone a lot of bother?*

Just then a wreck of a Peugeot 309 came down the hill towards them. RM was on the road, on the driver's side. He stood tight against the door. Doc ducked into the passenger seat.

The Peugeot was two hedges and a shady tree past them before RM reacted. 'Hi hi, look look,' he shouted.

'I see them,' said Doc. His opinion of RM and of his boss, Ronnie Fetherton, dropping even further. They should have known that the Bradleys now lived at the top of the hill, in Sperrin Manor, so naturally they'd use Mullough Avenue to get into town.

He checked in the rear-view mirror. He didn't think it necessary to kill a distant pedestrian, who must have heard RM make a fool of himself, but it left things... *untidy*.

The Peugeot 309 stopped near the bottom of the hill. A youth jumped out and raced across the road, holding something in his hand. He stabbed at a red object, then ran back to the car.

Nothing in his hand now, Doc noted.

RM jumped about in his seat with excitement. 'Bet you that's a letter for Bradley.'

'Could be,' said Doc in a dismissive voice. *All the same....*

RM persisted, 'We get the letter, we've got Bradley.'

'Maybe.'

RM said, 'When the postman comes....'

Doc looked at him, wide-eyed and full of false enthusiasm. 'We threaten him with your gun and steal all the letters and....'

'Yeah, yeah yeah.'

RM reached for his revolver.

Doc pushed it down and out of sight as a car passed. 'All that with people coming and going around us? No backup car and the road out of town like a hill-climb. In this thing?'

'It was the best I could get.'

'From a mate?'

'Naw!'

The denial came too quickly but Doc let it pass. 'And if the letter's not for Bradley?'

RM thumped the steering wheel for emphasis. 'It's bound to be for him. Mrs. Bradley works in a bank. She'll pay all her bills direct.'

Doc blinked, surprised at this sudden burst of intelligence. *He's right.* All the same the chances of robbing the postman and getting away with it was remote. Nelson and the phone tap was a safer bet. A man like Bradley was bound to phone home almost daily.

'Not without Jimmy's okay,' said Doc.

RM looked at him in disbelief.

'Jimmy,' repeated Doc.

'Ring him.'

Doc held up his hands to show them empty. 'We don't use mobiles.'

'I heard you lot were Stone Age.' RM swapped his revolver for a mobile. 'What's the number?' Doc told him and he keyed it in. The phone rang out but no one picked up. RM gave up after three attempts, drove down the hill and parked at the post box.

Chapter 4

Doc turned his head towards RM and the pavement as two cars passed them. He noted the flush of excitement on RM's face and the way his clenched fists shook as he psyched himself up for the robbery.

Doc put his hand on the door handle. He said, 'Good luck.'

'Are you not helping?'

'Not without Jimmy's say-so.'

'Did you never hear of using your loaf?'

Doc made himself sound supportive. 'You should check with Ronnie first, and you want to stay out of sight until the postman is due.'

'Where?' asked RM, suddenly not so confident.

Doc shrugged. He didn't know the town and had no intention of ever returning to Glenlish. Nature and trees looked fine when they were halfway across the city on Cave Hill. Here the stuff came right down to the roadside. Even so, some of RM's nervous excitement was feeding into him. *There's a thrill about taking risks.*

'So what's your plan?' he asked.

'Wait for the postman.'

'Wait where?'

'Somewhere. Anyway, steal the bag of post and getaway.'

'And what if the postman puts up a fight?'

The revolver was waved about in Doc's face, as if he hadn't seen it before. 'If postie has any sense he'll back off.'

'He'll give the police your registration number.'

'I'll steal a new car then.'

'Where and when will you steal this car? And now you have more witnesses who will tell the police the way you're headed.'

'I'll shoot them. No witnesses and all that.' RM still sounded confident, but he was beginning to frown at the increasing complications.

'What about roadblocks or if you get a puncture?'

'You worry too much. I'll be away before the police even know I'm in town – you'll see.'

Doc nodded as if in agreement, but he was thinking, clear away up a winding road onto a bare plateau, and miles from the next town?

'Check with Ronnie,' he said.

RM scowled. 'I'm sick and tired of being the messenger boy. This is my chance to step up into the big league.

'True,' said Doc and indicated the white plate on the post box, the enamel battered by the years and usage. 'When exactly is the postman due?'

RM took off his sunglasses and squinted at the numbers on the white plate. 'Nine.... Na, nine-thirty?'

Doc checked in the rear-mirror. *No traffic*. And one of the cars passing had picked up the stray pedestrian. There again they were close to the main road with its steady stream of rush-hour traffic. *There's always a risk of someone seeing*. The nearest house on RM's side had a high hedge. All the same, things could get *interesting* if the owner or one of his family suddenly appeared.

He said, 'Stick your head out the window. Make doubly sure of the time.'

RM sighed to show his annoyance. He buzzed the window down and glanced again at the white plate. 'Yeah, nine-thirty.'

Doc braced shoved the head out further.

'Hey!' said RM.

'Have a good look.'

'I'm telling you. Nine-thirty.'

Doc held firm against RM straining to get back into the car. A quick glance: up, down and around. No traffic in sight, no people passing. No one coming out of the nearest houses.

He hit the button to buzz the window up again.

RM tried to push Doc's hand off the button. 'Don't. That's dangerous.'

Doc kept RM's head out the window and the finger on the button.

'Look mate, stop it. It's not funny.'

'I'm not your mate.'

RM froze momentarily when he realized what was happening to him. He said, 'Oh, God.' Tried to look back. Pleaded, 'No, please.'

The window kept rising.

Panicking, RM elbowed back at Doc, but couldn't get any power in the blow. He grabbed at Doc's finger and tried to force it off the button, slashing back with his Doc Martins as he did so. The kick was blocked by the gear-stick. RM's breath came in quick gulps. Doc breathed nice and steady. He kept his head turning, watching for any possible witness and saw none.

RM pounded at the glass with his hands. When it didn't break he grasped the top of the glass and tried to force it back down, to tear it out of its setting.

Then the rim of the glass made contact with RM's throat. Doc eased the pressure on the button and the glass stopped rising. RM gave a sigh of relief.

'Not funny,' he said. It came out choked.

Doc again pressed the button. RM's larynx crumpled with a satisfactory crackle. His body spasmed and went still.

Doc had a quick look around. *All clear.* And got out of the car. He felt reasonably elated. Not one of his better killings, but for an ad hoc situation, *not bad.*

He walked away from the car, then turned quickly to check something on the rear bumper. An old "VOTE FETHERTON" sticker.

I was right to kill him.

Chapter 5

Doc walked back up Mullough Avenue like he'd all the time in the world. On the way he looked for but didn't see Nelson's face at a window.

No anxious face, no emergency call to the police.

The Bradleys were gone, presumably for the day: the wife to work and the boys to school. The way things were, Mrs. Bradley could barely make ends meet, let alone employ cleaners and gardeners.

It's worth the risk.

Doc crested the hill and turned into Sperrin Manor, where the detached houses of Mullough Avenue gave way to cramped bungalows with unkempt gardens and panoramic windows. The sort of window retirees watched out of for hours on end and noted strangers. The Bradley house was No5, a rectangular bungalow. Doc recognized it from Google Earth.

He rang the bell and glanced around while he waited for someone to come to the door. *No nosey neighbors watching.* He rang the bell a second time then, satisfied that the house was empty, he used a strip of plastic to force the simple Yale lock. Inside the house, with the door shut, Doc checked his watch. *After nine already.* He could risk five minutes at most, preferably three. He sniffed and got the smell of perfume. Chanel No5, he thought. His own wife's taste ran more to Bvlgari.

Suddenly his breath came in quick, hard wheezes. Someday he'd find the bitch and kill her. Let her savor every bitter last second.

Doc put a hand over his racing heart and forced himself to breathe slowly and deeply. *She can wait. Stick to the job in hand.*

He stood on until he felt fully recovered, and then looked around. He stood in a rectangular hallway, the stubby section of an L shaped corridor. The telephone sat on top of a one-drawer table. He looked in the drawer and found the telephone directory, but no book of personal numbers. The directory's "Useful Numbers" page was solid with names and contact details. Some written painstakingly neatly, others merely scribbled. He ran his finger down the nines and found none for a "Paul" or a "P Bradley" or "dad". He put the directory back in the drawer, exactly the way he'd found it.

Two hurley sticks sat blade-up in an umbrella stand. He touched them. According to rumor, the curved inner edge could take a man's head off his shoulders. Doc stroked the grain of the wood. *Pure exaggeration.* The one time he'd tried it, the men never moved again but their heads stayed on their shoulders.

He stepped into the kitchen, nothing there of interest, followed by the sitting-room. He recognized the suite of furniture, green brocade, from the Bradley's old house, and now totally out of keeping. It clashed and dominated where once it had mounded in.

Doc searched swiftly, opening any envelope he came across, looking for a letter from Bradley that would give his current address. Replaced things neatly. Shuddered at the mess in the boys' room where a stir-about of clothes and DVDs littered the floor. Lifted a sardonic eyebrow at the framed newspapers on the wall. "Bradley by a landslide" and "Anti Sleaze Candidate Gains Cross-Party Support". Decided to give that room a miss.

In the sterile main bedroom he found a packet of school photographs lying on the dressing table, and selected one to take with him. Checked his watch again, *seven and a half minutes*, and was annoyed at himself for the fit of temper that had cost him time. He left. Once outside he found everything still quiet outside: no neighbors at their windows, no one walking the family pet. Confident he hadn't been seen he headed down the far slope of Mullough Avenue to the main road and from there to the Glenlish Enterprise Centre.

Once at the Enterprise Centre he followed the signs for the reception area. Stripped off his gloves and threw them into a rubbish bin, grabbed a newspaper from the shop and headed for the restaurant. By his watch it was nine twenty.

The restaurant was quiet. Doc talked to the girl, varying the basic fried breakfast on offer, wanting two eggs instead of one, more toast and less sausages. Opted for a cup of tea while she cooked it fresh and managed to stumble and spill the tea as he left the counter. The girl was very kind. She gave him a fresh cup free of charge and told him to use a handful of napkins to dry his shoes.

While he waited for his breakfast to come Doc slipped out to the public phones. He dialed a different number from the one he'd given RM.

Chapter 6

Jimmy Terence answered Doc on the first ring and identified himself with an, 'Mmm.'

Jimmy was in his "office", the old kitchen of his terrace house. He preferred it to the office proper across the yard, being closer to the scullery for quick cups of tea and more private for making phone calls. The old scullery had long since been knocked down and replaced with a state-of-the-art kitchen – the wife took this notion, he would explain – and the old kitchen was now a sitting room.

Jimmy sat in the corner near the fire. The voices of his taxi drivers calling in and the Dispatcher acknowledging, via the speaker high on the wall, was like a trickle of ghostly voices.

Jimmy was looking at a muted television on the sideboard. It showed a taped off crime scene in an alleyway. Police in white plastic coveralls worked around a body.

'Tell me,' he asked Doc, 'where were you last night?'

'Walking.'

Yeah, but where to?

Fear turned Jimmy's breakfast to acid. Doc out of control was a nightmare, and the old restlessness had been in the man for weeks. *Even before that bitch did a runner.*

Doc said, 'Delivered package. No sign of spare part. Taxi had a puncture.'

'What do you mean…?'

Doc hung up.

Jimmy flung down the phone and kicked at it. 'Bastarding man. Could he not make it two paragraphs?'

He looked again at the television and his unease grew. Especially when he thought of Doc's report. "Delivered package" was fine, Nelson had agreed to cooperate. "No sign of spare part", nothing in the house giving Bradley's location. But "Taxi had a puncture"?

Was there a spare wheel, someone else to drive? *A witness*? And what would happen to that "spare wheel" when they got back to Belfast.

Why didn't Doc stick to "Alighted taxi"? Stick to making the remaining

17

calls on his own? Two, *at least*, dead already? The mood Doc was in it could be a slaughtering match.

Jimmy grabbed the cable and hauled the telephone back. He should ring someone. Ronnie maybe, and ask him? *Waste of time*. Ronnie would be all hot air and unfounded optimism.

And why does Ronnie want Bradley dead? *Almost slavering to do it*. It's me Bradley made a fool of.

The Man in London might tell me something?

Even thinking about either man made Jimmy want to snarl. He found himself staring at ghostly faces taking shape on the far wall. Men Doc had "punctured". Bad bastards the lot, but they'd started to come between Jimmy and his sleep.

Jimmy punched in The Man's number.

The Man's carefully modulated voice said, 'Good morning,' and waited.

'I'm worried about this booking,' said Jimmy.

'Do you wish to cancel?'

Jimmy glared at the phone. In his own way The Man was as bad as Doc. "The Man", whose name must never be spoken. The Man behind the men behind the politicians. The Man who knew everything and nothing. The Man who took no responsibility and exercised absolute control.

Jimmy said, 'No, but there's been a problem, a puncture.'

'That's unfortunate,' The Man said, an edge of anxiety to the modulated voice.

They talked around the subject and agreed that sending replacement "transport" was out of the question. Other than that The Man had no suggestions, gave nothing away. Doc was out on his own and one must not interfere.

Chapter 7

Doc enjoyed a leisurely breakfast, then he waited at the front door of the Enterprise Centre for a taxi. One came, Doc got in. 'Town center, please.'

'We'll have to take a detour, mate. The traffic on the main road's backed up.'

'Roadworks?' asked Doc.

'Some sort of accident.'

'Whatever,' said Doc. He sat back and appreciated the closed windows as they drove through leafy side streets. The only shading trees in his part of Belfast were on the television. Even looking at that made his hay fever twitch.

The Glenlish Arms was an old coaching house brutally modernized. The bar held a number of men washing a week's work out of their throats. Two drunks sat humped over a table, with several empty glasses in front of them. The rest of the men grouped around the bar.

Doc walked up to the bar, conscious of the sudden silence in the room.

The barman took his time coming over. 'What do you want?'

At least his shirt was fresh on and his fingernails clean. The rest of the place could have done with the same attention to detail. The shine on the mahogany counter had long since disappeared under scrapes and the acids from spilled drink.

'A shandy and go hard on the lemonade,' said Doc, giving the code sign.

'A shandy?' The barman made it sound like something out of the sewers.

Doc said nothing. He became aware of a subtle movement of the men beside him. Of chairs being pushed back and footsteps. Most unprofessional, but Doc wanted to smile. Today the old itch was getting a quare scratch.

In the mirror he watched the two drunks shamble towards him. Both of them at least six foot in height, broad shouldered and heavy with what had once been muscle. One of them knocked into Doc. The other drunk trod on his toes.

'Watch it,' said the first drunk. He put a shoulder to Doc and shoved him into the second drunk.

The second drunk asked, 'Are you trying to start a fight?'

'No.'

Doc still had his eyes on the mirror, watching the first drunk. He saw him turn away then swing back, elbow up. Doc couldn't jump clear, the second drunk had him blocked in. Instead he ducked under the swing, grabbed the wrist and twisted. Brought the man down to knee level. A quick bang and he'd shatter the elbow, was tempted to do it. Then he remembered Jimmy and his, "no waves" and settled for a dislocation at the shoulder. The drunk tried to scream and puke at the same time.

The second drunk's fist slammed into the back of Doc's head. He was already moving away from the blow so it was more push than slam. Even so he went down, rolling away from the group of men and their ready boots. The floor was old wood, one time treated but now worn down to raw. Stirred dust from between the planks irritated Doc's sinuses.

The second drunk came after him.

Annoyed now, because his suit needed cleaned, Doc reached up and grabbed the drunk's crotch. Dug his nails in hard. The drunk screamed and tried to pull away. Doc pulled harder in the opposite direction. Kept gripping as he climbed to his feet. Silenced the drunk with a slicing blow to the throat.

He checked the group of men at the bar. They were watching, not interfering. *Is this the best they can come up with?* Doc let the drunk go. The drunk slid to the floor and curled foetal.

Doc looked at the barman. 'Where's the toilets?'

The barman indicated a door in the far corner.

Doc said, 'I suggest no one follows me in.'

Chapter 8

When Doc came back from the toilet with his hands washed and his suit brushed down the drunks had been carted off. The group of men at the bar had dispersed, most now sat at tables with their drinks. A few of the older men waited at the bar. One stood out. He wore work clothes that had never seen a building site.

'I'm Mick,' he said and pushed a shandy Doc's way.

'Doc.'

'We were told to expect you. Well someone.' Mick looked almost embarrassed. 'Sorry about that, but the way I got the word … I mean I've a position to maintain.'

Doc said, 'Not from my boss. He talks quiet and he never forgets a favor.' He sipped at the shandy for politeness sake. 'I'm looking for information. What do you know about Bradley?'

Mick shrugged. 'He was in the mental for a while, then he took off.'

Doc pretended surprise. 'I thought he was in jail?'

'He got out months ago.'

Doc snorted. 'Wouldn't you know it, the politicians take care of their own.'

Mick said, 'He got involved in a prison riot.' He shouted over at one of the younger men. 'When that happened to you, you got time added instead of time off.'

The younger man imitated a spit. 'Bad luck to him anyway.'

Mick said, 'The man wasn't right; walking the streets at all hours, him and that dog.'

There's nothing to be got here, Doc decided. And thanks to RM and having to set up an alibi, he was already running late. 'Is there a car I can borrow for the day?'

'Take my Mercedes,' said Mick.

'Maybe something a bit quieter.'

Chapter 9

The driver brought the lorry over the crest of the hill. The valley opened up before him, with the town of Glenlish snuggled into its base. 'Thank the bugger for that,' he said, as he always did after miles of open moor, seeing only heather and wind-shriveled grass.

He dropped down a few gears, getting ready for the first tight bend. Anyway he needed to keep the speed down; the pull-in was just up ahead. He swung the lorry around the first bend, taking up all the road. He hated this part, with only his skill and a dry stonewall between him and the valley floor.

I'm bucked if the brakes fail in this old rig.

The boss had promised to put him on town deliveries, kept promising it, but the bastard couldn't keep his word if his life depended on it.

Annoyance and fear at the uncertain brakes popped beads of sweat on his face. He wiped at the sweat and dried his hands on his overalls. Bright orange overalls that the boss insisted all the lorry drivers wore.

It's not him going into Republican areas.

Another bend, then the road ran straight for a while. And there was the old quarry, its buildings crumbling into flakes of red rust. A blue car, a Ford Focus, was parked at the quarry gates. Dust hung around its wheels, as if it had just pulled in.

The driver indicated and stopped beside the car. A man got out. He was thin and wore a crumpled suit. The driver had a feeling that they'd met before. Way back at a time when you didn't ask questions.

'You're running late,' said the man as he climbed up into the passenger seat.

I know that voice, thought the driver, trying to place it. *More Cherry Valley than the docks.* He said, 'The traffic's gone mad for some reason.'

Nice suit but in need of a clean, he thought, examining the man out of the corner of his eye. *That tie's from one of them nobby grammar schools.* If he remembered right, years back, the man had been brought in to sort-out a police informer. Afterwards Kyle – *that's the name he used as cover* – afterwards Kyle had eaten a sandwich before leaving. He said little and didn't join the forced small talk around the table. Forced, because the tortured man might be dead but his screams still rang in their ears. You didn't dare let Kyle think you weak.

The driver said, 'I was told to meet you here.' Even all these years on, and a subcontractor now himself, *but not in Kyle's league*, he knew he had to appear tough. He looked pointedly at his watch. 'I've a schedule to keep. The boss doesn't like people running late.'

'Don't worry about Ronnie,' the man known as Kyle said. He tapped his pockets. 'I'm out; you wouldn't have a cigarette?'

'Sure.' The driver dug out his packet of fags. 'These okay?'

'Thank you.' He lit up.

A car came up the hill towards them. Kyle ducked down until it passed. Straightening up, he flicked open the glove compartment and caught a quarter bottle of whiskey as it fell out.

'It's for my indigestion,' said the driver, a bit too quickly.

Kyle shook the bottle; it was half full. Unscrewed the top and sniffed. 'If you say so.'

'What do you want me to do?' asked the driver, feeling he could afford to be rude back.

'Die,' said Kyle.

Suddenly a knife was in his hand. The driver's eyes widened in shock as the knife drove deep into his groin. Driven in and sliced across. Air whistled out of the driver as arterial blood spurted. He clamped his hands over his torn groin and screamed. Kyle cursed when blood went on his sleeve.

The driver doubled over the steering wheel. His hands forced the tear in his groin shut, trying to stop the blood. He whimpered in pain.

Kyle wiped the knife clean on the driver's overalls. He noticed another car coming and ducked down again. He wheezed with tension. The driver's throat rattled as he gasped for life.

The car passed. Kyle poured the whiskey over the driver's arms and thighs and lobbed the whiskey bottle into the foot-well. He opened his door, stood on the step and reached in. Knocked off the handbrake. Flicked his cigarette at the driver and jumped.

Chapter 10

Doc turned off the B class road onto a farm track and drove between two tumbled ditches until the track broadened out into a farmyard. An old house, faced with crumbling cement, took up one side of the yard, ancient outhousing the other. Blocking Doc's way ahead was a line of pollytunnels. The sun-bleached plastic on two of the tunnels had shredded and the tunnels abandoned. One tunnel remained in use. Inside it he could see lots of green vegetation safely contained and, thankfully, there were no trees near the house so his hay fever should be okay.

The man's still home, Doc thought with relief, because a battered Volvo estate sat in the yard. He looked at the clock and couldn't believe the time, *lunchtime already*. The front door bell didn't work so he knocked. A fawn greyhound slunk into sight and crouched. Doc kept an eye on the dog as he knocked again.

A faded woman in an equally worn lime-green skirt and a white blouse opened the door. Mud stained her clothes and her hair hung dank with sweat. She held a dishcloth in one hand. A fresh breeze caught the edge of the skirt. Doc watched her smooth the skirt straight. *Nice leg*.

'Good afternoon, Connie,' said Doc, as if they'd met before.

The woman's eyes were sharp and searching even as she shrugged her disinterest.

'I told you someone was there,' said a gruff voice from the living room.

Doc stretched to look for the man and could see only a big toe sticking out of thick grey socks and the apex of a considerable gut.

He said to Connie, 'I'm looking for Charlie.'

'Someone to see you, Charlie,' she called.

'Who is it?'

'A man about a dog,' said Doc.

Charlie grunted as he heaved himself out of the chair. In socks he stood inches taller than Doc and his stubble had gone beyond "designer" to "untidy". Connie edged back to make room for him.

Doc said, 'You gave a dog to Bradley, the politician. What did he call it?'

'Useless, like the rest of them.' Charlie went to close the door.

Doc stuck his foot in the door-jam. 'I'd be obliged.'

His foot was trapped. Charlie pushed until it hurt. Doc pulled a red metal ruler from his breast-pocket. He reached through the narrow opening and used its sharpened edge to slash at Charlie's forearm. Charlie screamed and backed off. Doc burst the door open.

Charlie's body shook from shock. Blood oozed from under the hand clutching the wound. *No danger there*. Doc checked Connie. She'd backed off against a hall table. Her eyes were like saucers.

Doc's breath came in quick wheezes. *All that green stuff.*

He turned again to Charlie. 'I asked you a civil question.'

Connie stayed at arms-length as she reached the dishcloth to Charlie. 'Don't get blood on the carpet.'

Doc thought, she's not as calm as she's pretending. All the same there was no screaming, no hysteria. He had a feeling it would take more than threats to keep her quiet about his visit. No "waves" Jimmy said. *He never warned me about this one.*

'Do I have to ask again?' Doc said.

He held the ruler up as a threat, more in Connie's direction than Charlie's. Right then Charlie looked only capable of having a heart attack.

Connie said, 'We don't know. I gave Mr. Bradley the naming form myself. It was up to him to fill it up and send it in.'

Doc waited a wheezed breath while he thought things through. Nothing was going the way he'd hoped. He didn't believe in luck as such, but sometimes things refused to fall his way.

He asked Charlie in a you-better-or-else voice, 'Can you find out for me?'

Charlie cringed away.

Again it was Connie who answered. 'Sometimes he rings the Irish Coursing Club in Clonmel and they tell him things.' She looked at the pendulum clock on the wall. 'They're closed for lunch right now.'

This woman is trouble. His heartbeat quickened at the thought of a double puncture.

Double puncture? I'm getting as bad as Jimmy.

He checked his watch. *Lunchtime, that means waiting until two o'clock.* Better that than reporting failure to Jimmy. He kicked Charlie to keep the cycle of violence going. Used his crushed foot by mistake, and it hurt him as much as it hurt Charlie. He reversed feet and did it again. 'Get up.'

Charlie had the dishcloth wrapped around his slashed arm. He moaned and groaned and used the handrail to crawl to his feet.

'You'd better help him, Connie,' said Doc.

He'd never slashed a woman before and rather liked the thought of the new experience. But she did as she was told and linked Charlie's arm to help him along. For some reason that he couldn't understand, Doc felt relieved.

Chapter 11

With Connie's help, Charlie made it to the sitting room and collapsed into his chair. A mobile phone sat on the arm of the chair. Doc switched it off and put it in his pocket.

Connie gave Doc an appraising look. Then she headed for the far end of the room and the door into the kitchen.

Maybe I should just kill her?

'Where do you think you're going?'

'For the First Aid kit.'

He followed her and stood in the doorway, watching her carefully. *She's bound to have a mobile phone.* The kitchen units were chipped and battered. He reckoned them even older than the ones they dumped when they rebuilt Jimmy's kitchen.

He sensed movement behind him. Turned and saw Charlie making a bolt for the door.

Doc was onto Charlie before he was out of the room. Charlie took a swing as him. Doc caught him in a headlock and banged his head off the wall. Threw him back into his seat. Then Doc spun around, not knowing what Connie was up to.

She stood holding an impressive looking First Aid box. Was it his imagination or, *did I see her smiling*?

He stood by and watched Connie bandage Charlie's arm. *Very professional.*

'I nurse part time, it gets me out of the house,' she said as if sensing his surprise.

The blouse gaped and closed with the movement of her arms. It didn't seem to bother her. Doc's focus was on the way she handled the scissors. He could only guess what sort of relationship he'd walked into. He didn't want her killing Charlie and putting all the blame on him.

The scissors safely put down, Doc studied the family photographs on the mantle-piece. They were faded with age, and showed two boys: the younger in a school blazer.

'Nice kids,' he said, wishing they were there. A threat to her children always kept a woman in check.

'Gone,' she said. 'They couldn't wait to leave.' She threw the blood-stained tea cloth into the fireplace.

Something about the way she stood up put Doc on guard.

He asked, 'Now what?'

She used her hands to indicate the state of her clothes. 'I was working in the tunnel all morning. I'm going for a shower.'

'Stay here.'

She shook her head. 'I'll keep singing so you know I'm not up to anything.' She walked past him.

Jimmy had said "no waves", so no killing and no maiming. And she'd stared him straight in the eye. People who did that usually looked away quickly. She hadn't. He found that unsettling. Annoyed, he glared at Charlie. *If he moves, I'll kill him.* But Charlie seemed to read his thoughts and only gave the occasional shudder of pain.

Connie sang: on the stairs, in the bedroom while she collected her clothes, and continued to sing over the pound of water in the shower. She had a nice voice, with little vibrato.

At one point she called down, 'Do you want Loyalist songs or Republican?'

He didn't reply and got a medley of both. She had left the bathroom door open and the oil-laden steam seeped down the stairs and worked on his imagination.

Connie came back wearing a best dress, and ignored them both as she towelled her hair dry. Cleaned up she looked surprisingly good. She hadn't the body to be slim but her shoulders were full of muscle and her stomach flat. She stood on tiptoe at the mirror. Doc was able to confirm his earlier impression of a nice leg.

Doc was disgusted with himself. Why hadn't he thought of tying her up? *And gagging her.*

Chapter 12

At two o'clock Doc ordered Charlie to try Clonmel. Eventually a woman answered the phone. 'Charlie, I haven't even put my shopping away yet.'

Charlie told her what he wanted.

'Why don't you buy the studbook? It's in that.'

Doc had the phone switched to "conference" so he could hear both sides. He pulled his ruler out to empathize that he needed this information.

A greasy sweat poured off Charlie. 'Please, it's important.'

'And what about the money you owe us?' asked the voice on the phone. 'Did you send it by way of Timbuktu?'

'It'll be in the post today.'

'You say that every time.'

Doc put the ruler near Charlie's eye and twisted it threateningly.

'Please,' begged Charlie.

He was talking to Doc but the woman in Clonmel misunderstood. 'Oh, all right if it's that important.'

Clicks of a keyboard came down the line. After a delay she said, 'There it is, the mating of Masie Dotes to Mullinure. Five pups, only one named: a fawn bitch, Labonga. L A B O N G A.'

Doc whispered, 'The owner's name and address.'

Charlie asked her.

'What else do you want for nothing?' she replied and hung up.

Doc drove the edge of the ruler at Charlie's throat. Charlie jumped back, fell over a chair and crashed to the floor, screaming, 'No no no no no.'

Doc spun around to face Connie. She hadn't moved. He rubbed the ruler's flat edge against her jaw-line. 'Ring them back.'

She was breathing quickly, but quietly compared to the wheeze in his lungs. *That vegetation.* At least there was none in the house.

'If you want,' she said. She picked up the phone and dialed the number. The phone rang forever at the other end. Eventually Connie said, 'Sometimes they don't answer if they know it's Charlie. They can read the number of the incoming calls, you see.'

Her voice shook.

Doc thought, that's the first time she'd showed fear. He put the ruler away. He had the dog's name, Labonga. Surely Jimmy could make something of that?

All the same?

He picked up the phone and flung it against the wall. It crunched and tinkled nicely, the plastic casing shattered.

'That's your head if you don't do exactly as you're told,' he informed Charlie.

Charlie was to go straight to the bank and do an electronic transfer of whatever money he owed to the Irish Coursing Club. Pay them extra if need-be to get the rest of the information. If he even thought of going to the police there'd be no house or wife left to come home to. Then he'd find Charlie and salami him toe joint by toe joint until he was walking on his ankles.

Connie, Doc saw, didn't seem unduly concerned at that threat. *She should.* When Charlie got back he'd have to kill them both. He might threaten Charlie into silence but Connie was a different matter. Now showered and changed, with her hair brushed and wearing a touch of makeup, the faded look had gone. Her face had character and resolve, and her eyes the look of someone who would do the right thing regardless of consequences.

And she kept staring him straight back. No one had done that in years except Jimmy and his family.

Connie hurried Charlie into a coat and out the door. Doc stayed close in case she made a bolt for it as well. She came back in closing and locking the door behind her, and headed up the stairs.

Doc asked, 'Where do you think you're going?'

'Upstairs.' She sounded surprised that he'd asked.

The only way to control this woman is to kill her.

Doc started up the stairs after her.

Chapter 13

Doc watched from the doorway of the bedroom as Connie stripped the double bed down to the mattress. The covers that came off were worn thin with age. They'd barely do for rope, he thought, and had to step clear as she pushed past him and delved deep in the hot-press. The replacement sheets were starched linens, hand stitched and glaring white.

She said, 'I promised myself these the day Charlie left.'

'What do you mean "left"?'

Connie laughed at him, at some expression on his face. A red haze blocked Doc's vision. The wife had been the same. *Treated me like dirt in the end.*

The red haze cleared. Connie turned away as he crossed the room. She smoothed a crease out of the fresh pillow covers. To reach her neck Doc had to put his hips against the curve of her buttocks and pull on her shoulders to straighten her up. He ached to snap her upright but did it gently so as not to frighten her. *If she struggles I could get clawed.*

She straightened slowly and settled her head and neck into his encircling arms. 'I want to thank you,' she said.

For killing her? That was a new one.

'That's too tight,' she whispered, and he eased his grip. Anyway, his arms were in the wrong position to snap the C2 vertebra.

She said, 'Charlie won't be back; he hasn't the guts. Or rather he's got too many in the wrong place.'

'Damnation!' It was the nearest word Doc ever got to a curse.

He was now in damage control. Kill the woman, burn the house and hope no one saw him drive out of the farmyard. Charlie couldn't have reached the town yet. His alibi of a man threatening to kill him if he didn't get the name of a dog would be laughed out of court.

She said, 'Don't worry, Charlie will phone with the information, but he won't come anywhere near the house again until he knows it's safe.'

Kill her and run, or wait and trust her instincts that Charlie will deliver?

He needed to be sure. 'But you said "left" like he'd never be back?'

She laughed. Now he found it a lovely laugh. 'He won't dare, not when people with Belfast accents keep ringing to see if he's home.'

She'd all the angles covered to make Charlie too terrified to return. *She's missed one trick.* He couldn't trust her to keep quiet. All the same he was enjoying her warm closeness, and the musk of the countryside off her that even scented shower gel couldn't conceal.

'He's your husband. How come you hate him so much?'

She said in almost a whisper, 'On our first date, Charlie raped me.'

Doc let her talk. He caressed her jawline to get her used to his hand on the spot where the jerk would come. The more relaxed she was the easier to snap her neck.

'Our first date. I didn't mind a bit of something, you know what I mean, but he wouldn't stop. He was all apologetic afterwards and promised he'd swear off the drink. I was stupid enough to believe him, desperate to when I missed my next period. Once we were married...' Her voice shook. 'Since then he's treated me like a slab of meat.'

If she starts crying things will get complicated.

He slid his arms down to waist level and held her to him in a gentle hug. Stopped himself from whispering cusha, cusha into her ear, the way he used to do with Jimmy's children when they were upset.

Her hips rubbed against his groin.

His arousal at a victim's closeness seemed indecent. *Unprofessional.*

There again he always needed sex to calm himself after a good kill and his wife hadn't been available the last couple of times.

Made herself unavailable more like.

Surprisingly, instead of the red mist coming down at the thought of his wife his body hardened against Connie. He would give her an orgasm, *probably the only one ever*, even as she died.

He tried to think back to the early days of his marriage, what had turned on his wife then. Lately the only thing to turn her on was screaming abuse at him.

Stomach and thighs.

Connie groaned to show her pleasure at his caresses. He found his breathing speeding up, the wheeze had gone. Taking his time he unzipped her dress the length of her spine and eased it off her. She wore fresh underwear. Underwear that, he guessed, Charlie had never seen. Underwear with just enough see-through to heighten the senses but not enough give everything away.

She's done this before.

All those doctors and orderlies in the hospital, he supposed. Flexible shifts, unexpected overtime. Revenge more than desire, because he hadn't sensed anything of the cheap tart off her.

He wished he had done something the same with his wife but the fear of disease had always kept him faithful. Which is more than he could say for her and the local ne'er-do-well she'd fallen for.

He eased Connie onto the bed. She tried to turn over but he held her face down by massaging her neck and back, especially her neck around the carotid artery. When the time came the bedclothes would stifle her screams. *Not that anyone's likely to hear in this bog hole of nowhere.* Still it didn't hurt to take precautions against the unlikely.

Doc threw off his jacket and kicked off his shoes. He let Connie squirm around in the bed until she could help him undress. By then she was lying on her back. That didn't matter, he decided, nor his DNA. The fire would take care of that. When he kissed her he got the taste of jasmine. Why jasmine, something earthy and sweet, he didn't know, but his sister-in-law kept it in pots at the back door and it didn't irritate his sinuses.

Doc wasn't used to a woman who ached for him instead of being merely forbearing, and came down on Connie with slow, careful movements. He didn't want to risk her changing her mind and scream in panic.

Her hands caressed his back and flanks. The calloused skin from gardening reached something in him, something so deep he could hardly concentrate on what he had to do. Slowly he brought his hands up along her sides, used them to circle and tease her nipples, then the neck. His thumbs reached the carotid artery and began to press.

Connie's eyes opened wide, then wider again. Her mouth gulped air and she still couldn't get enough for the screams tearing out of her throat.

'Cusha, cusha,' he said and brought his mouth against hers to stifle the screams. His gasps for air were as fierce as hers.

She bucked hard under him.

A last gasp of air sighed out and she lay still.

Chapter 14

Doc finally forced himself out of bed, anxious that the day was slipping away from him.

He collected his clothes, went into the bathroom and stepped into the shower. There was no hot water. The cold water pounding his hot body drove away the languidness. Stupidly enough he felt guilty at being unfaithful to his wife. All the same the sex had been fantastic, it reminded him of the early days of his marriage, but unprofessional, *and must never happen again.*

He used Connie's shower gel and stayed longer under the shower than he needed to. Dried and dressed again he looked in on her. The way she lay she could have been asleep, her lips curved in a smile. He found himself tip-toeing down the stairs.

In the kitchen he helped himself to a glass of water and went into the sitting room. He drank the water while rooting though drawers in a display cabinet. The drawers contained a mixture of family life and business records. Connie had recently renewed her driving license and had two passport-size photographs leftover.

Doc slipped the photographs into his pocket, put a match to piled paper and kindling, and left.

Chapter 15

Jimmy spent the day by the phone, hoping Doc would ring again. The airwaves were going mad about fires and violent deaths in Glenlish. Half the television crews in the country seemed to be heading that way.

Jimmy had his hand on the phone a dozen times, thinking to ring the Glenlish Arms and always drew back, not knowing who would be at the other end. Times like this he understood Doc's urge to kill people. *Starting with Doc.*

Jimmy had been called to a meeting, not to be consulted but to be given his orders. People higher up in the Organization had already made the decisions. Jimmy knew what the Organization wanted to do to Bradley when they got their hands on him, but not why. *And why the sudden urgency?* Why hadn't they sorted the man when he was in jail or in the months afterwards when he staggered around Glenlish, a raving lunatic with drug-fried brains? If Jimmy had even thought that Bradley could remember him, he'd have gone down and kicked the man's head in.

Letting himself be caught in a newspaper sting. The stupid plonker!

'I told you "no waves",' he snarled at the television screen. 'Do I have to put every order in writing – in triplicate?'

To give himself something to do Jimmy went across the yard to the office proper. The public office was thick with cigarette smoke from resting drivers, the television tuned to Channel 4 racing. The Dispatcher had his head in a sports page. He was writing names onto a betting slip. He waved a hand at Jimmy.

'I'm glad someone's got something to do,' said Jimmy.

Some of the younger drivers slipped out. The older ones sat on and puffed contentedly at their cigarettes. Their afternoon shift started with the school run.

Still writing, the Dispatcher slid open a drawer and handed over a thick sheaf of invoices. 'Would you okay these for payment?'

'That's why I never come here,' said Jimmy. 'You always give me paperwork to do.'

'If you don't check them today, I'll tell Eleanor.'

35

'She's off shopping so there's no money left.' He looked at the resting drivers. 'And that includes your wages.'

'So what?' asked one of the drivers. He pointed to the screen, at horses circling the parade ground. 'Number five there is going to make my fortune.'

'Don't hold your breath,' said the Dispatcher.

Jimmy stumped into his private office. It stank of stale air and polish. *Eleanor and her flaming duster.* He threw a window open and breathed deeply of diesel oil and the throbbing life of the city. Sat down at his desk and started to flick through the invoices. Something caught his eye, something not there.

He put his head around the office door. 'The telephone bill, all I've got is the top sheet?'

The Dispatcher looked up, puzzled. 'Doc took them a few days ago. He said you wanted to check something.'

'Oh, aye, right,' said Jimmy, trying to cover.

What the hell's going on, he wondered, as ice crawled up his spine. He waved the top sheet at the Dispatcher. 'These telephone bills, they come by computer now, don't they?'

'I'm surprised you know that,' said the Dispatcher.

'Run us another copy, would you.'

He ignored the Dispatcher's puzzled stare and went back into the room. Sat at the desk and had a good worry to himself. *Those telephone printouts showed…?*

The copies came. He went through them, yellow marker in hand. The first time he marked a number, his jaw tightened. By the bottom of the last page his jaw ached and he had the start of a migraine.

He picked up the phone and dialed a number.

A voice replied, 'Far and Wide Travel, how can we help you?'

'JP, listen son. If your uncle Doc books a flight to England, let me know straight away.'

Chapter 16

Doc rang the doorbell of No5 Sperrin Manor. No one came to the door though he could hear a television blaring from a bedroom and the sound of an air extractor churning at the side of house. He sniffed and got the odor of burnt fat. A ruined tea, he guessed, and rang again.

This time Barbara Bradley answered the door. She still wore the uniform of the Regional Bank, a muted crimson jacket and skirt. A good height for a woman, thought Doc, though her broad build made her appear shorter. Shoulder-length dark hair tumbled around her face after a long day.

'Yes?' she asked.

'May I speak to your husband?' asked Doc.

'And you are?'

'Ronnie Fetherton,' said Doc.

Her eyes flicked past him. He could tell she was studying the Mercedes at the gate. Hopefully she wouldn't recognize Mick waiting to take him to Belfast.

'Would he be home yet?' asked Doc. He touched his tie as if checking that it was on straight. The movement drew her eyes to the tie and he could see her register the school it represented, Inst: The Royal Belfast Academical Institution.

She opened the door wider. 'Please come in for a minute.' And led him into the sitting room. On the way she waved despairingly at the three plates abandoned on the kitchen table. Two sat untouched, one had an edge of food missing. 'I was late home and the boys never thought to turn down the oven. The tea's ruined. Completely inedible.'

'Kids,' sympathized Doc. He sat on the out-of-place settee and looked around him. 'You've got some nice things.'

'Yes.'

That came through tight lips, he noticed, and he went dry, not knowing what to say next. There'll be no casual chitchat out of this one. This *social* call was a mistake.

'I'll not waste your time, missus,' he said, anxious to finish and get away. 'I need to speak to Mr. Bradley about a dog.'

She perched on the edge of an armchair near the open door. A hint, he realized, not to stay too long.

She said, 'He's away at present.'

'Could you give me his number?'

'I'm afraid that's not possible. What do you want to see to Mr. Bradley about?'

That tone's frosty, he thought. She'll not tell me anything.

If only she was a man. He could threaten to take out her larynx and put it back a different way if she didn't talk.

Doc ploughed on with the story about a dog, feeling he'd nothing to lose. 'I'm out of time, missus. If I can't contact Mr. Bradley, then it's bad luck on him.'

One of the boys appeared in the doorway. Rory, Doc thought, remembering Jimmy's description: red hair, age sixteen and shooting up.

Rory asked, 'What sort of dog?'

Doc said, 'A dog, a pup, a sapling.' Jimmy had used all three descriptions and seemed to know what he was talking about.

Doc couldn't understand it but the old restless itch in him had eased, and with it the intensity that made people anxious to keep on his good side. More than that, he'd lain on in Connie's bed when he should have been gone, and afterwards he'd wandered around the shops in Glenlish instead of door-stepping Mrs. Bradley when she arrived home from work.

He blamed it on his eventful day. He found he wanted to be nice to this woman, *you can't blame her for her husband.* Still he needed the information.

Maybe she'll talk if I threaten to wring Rory's neck?

'Look, missus, your husband did me a favor. The tax people had me screwed and he sorted things. I promised him a pup out of my good bitch. Nearly six months old he is now and it's time Mr. Bradley took him. Overtime, missus, if you see what I mean.'

She said, 'Just sell it and send us the money.'

Doc stood up and moved towards Rory. 'I couldn't do that, not without Mr. Bradley's okay.'

Footsteps sounded in the hallway. Shane, the dark haired one, appeared. He was finer and taller than Rory. Seventeen or thereabouts, Doc thought, and very like his brother.

Shane asked, 'What's the breeding?'

Doc stopped his advance on Rory. One against two. One against three, if you counted the mother, took planning, and car doors were banging outside. That meant people were around to hear any disturbance.

Jimmy said "no waves". He didn't want the Bradleys alerted in any way.

Frustrated at not getting his hands on Rory, Doc's mind went blank. 'It's an old bitch, she never did anything.' It sounded unconvincing even to him.

'And the sire?'

Barbara opened the sitting room door wider, making it quite plain that he was to leave.

He rushed his answer, remembering there'd been talk about it on the news way back. 'That English dog, the one that nearly won the Derby but got done for drugs.'

Barbara went red, then white, then red again. The boys jerked as if struck. Doc could think of nothing to say. Could do nothing to stop Barbara from storming to the front door, other than threaten one of the boys.

Maybe I should?

She flung the front door open. 'Get out!'

A police inspector stood on the doorstep, his hand up to ring the bell.

Doc slid past the policeman and walked down the drive, half expecting to be called back to show some ID. Saw police cars parked all over the estate and police going from door to door, clipboards in hand.

Mick was looking out for him and visibly sweating.

Chapter 17

Station Inspector Ian Patterson was tall, inclined to plumpness and well built at the shoulders from playing golf. He watched Doc get into the Mercedes and be driven off. 'Was that man bothering you, Mrs. Bradley?'

'A reporter,' spat Barbara. 'At least I think so, and a nasty little one at that.'

She held the door open for him. Ian Patterson stepped in, surprised at her cordiality. The last time he'd called she'd interviewed him on the doorstep. Then it was about her husband rampaging through the garden, slashing at little green men with a kitchen knife. Luckily for himself, Bradley dropped the knife when the patrol appeared or they would have done more than run him down to the Sanatorium.

Ian said, 'Hopefully I'll only keep you for a minute. I suppose you heard about the death?'

'Yes, the poor man.'

Patterson kept his eyes on the clipboard rather than risk being caught looking around him. The house was basic, minimum spec, with paper-thin partitions. Someone had painted the walls, not too well. Barbara, he supposed. In the Bradley's last house the dogs had better kennels.

He looked at Barbara's face and saw ageing. Hard experience, he realized, but surprisingly not bitterness. *Always it's the families that pay.* Paul might have got three years but they've been given life.

He said, 'It happened about nine o'clock this morning. I presume you were at work by then and the boys at school?'

'We were.'

He'd thought so but the call had to be made. And by himself personally rather than risk a subordinate being ham-fisted or downright ignorant, because Bradley had let the whole town down with his drug taking and the rape. *There's no other word for it.*

The atmosphere in the Bradley house he found surprisingly good. *That reporter must have really annoyed them when they prefer me.*

Two more questions and he'd be away. 'Did you go by Mullough Avenue?'

'We did,' she said, then answered the second question before he could ask it. 'But we didn't see anything.'

Rory's head tilted up and sideways in puzzlement. 'It was supposed to be an accident, the window caught his throat or something?'

Shane said, 'Sliced his head half-off.' He was still at an age where he liked gooey.

Rory pointed out the still open door. 'Yet you've got men going from house to house?'

'Maybe they're looking for the window,' said Shane.

'Boys!' snapped Barbara.

'It's all right,' said Ian Patterson, and it mostly was, though the boys were being politely insulting. Of course their father was innocent and didn't deserve jail. It was all the police's fault for getting it wrong. *How many times have I heard that?*

And like their father they were quick on the uptake. The accidental death of a Belfast hood had become something else when the ambulance men found a revolver in his pocket. A Hood coming all the way from Belfast armed with a revolver had all the indications of a planned killing. *But who and why?* By sitting parked in Mullough Avenue he had to be waiting for someone nearby.

Stretched as his force was that day, Patterson had to find the "who" quickly, otherwise the "who" could still end up dead.

I'll get nothing here. The whole house-to-house thing was a shot in the dark anyway.

He made to take his leave. 'Well thank you anyway, and sorry for any inconvenience.'

Rory said, 'There were two men in a car parked halfway down the hill.'

'What car?' asked Barbara and Ian together.

Shane said, 'The one with the "Vote Fetherton" sticker on the back.'

Ian opted for the kitchen rather than the sitting room. 'I like to be near the kettle,' he said by way of a gentle hint. Two cups of tea and several biscuits later he sat back and looked with satisfaction at the three statements in his hand, two of them useful. The boys' vague description of the hooded youth standing at the driver's door matched the dead man. But nothing for the second man, he thought with regret. *Now who was he, what was he here for and where did he go?*

One thing puzzled him. The Bradleys had seen the car parked halfway up the hill but the man had died at the bottom. *Why move? Why stick his head out the window when the only thing of interest there is the post box?*

'You've had a busy day,' said Barbara, interrupting his thoughts.

'Tell me about it,' said Ian. 'This death, then that lorry coming off the road and half the hillside on fire.'

'We saw it from the school,' said Shane, like it was a fun thing to watch.

'A man died in it,' said Ian more sharply that he'd intended. He stood up and collected his hat. 'This is a stupid question. When you passed the post box, did you notice anyone or anything there?'

'Definitely not,' said Shane.

'You're sure?'

'Yeah, I'd a letter to post.' He looked at his mother. 'Meanie here made me send it second class.'

Barbara said, 'He wanted something out of the Liverpool Supporters' Shop. I had to send them a check.'

Chapter 18

That morning Doc had left Jimmy sitting in his corner chair. When he arrived back in the evening, Jimmy was still in the corner chair. In the morning Jimmy had leaned forward, a pointing figure metronoming up and down as he emphasized what was and what wasn't to happen in Glenlish. Now he sat back in the chair, arms folded. Silent.

What now? thought Doc.

'I'm glad someone had a nice day,' said Jimmy.

Doc set down the carrier bag he carried. 'My suit needs cleaned.'

'I'm not surprised. Going by the news, you got up to all sorts of fun.' His glare focused in on Doc's new outfit of clothes: a Harris Tweed sports jacket, tan flannels, a check shirt and yellow tie. 'Most kids make do with a stick of rock saying "A present from Blackpool".'

'I took off all the local labels.'

'And paid for them by…?'

'Cash.'

Jimmy picked up the phone and asked the Dispatcher to send a driver over. They waited in silence for the driver to come and pick up the suit and take it to the dry cleaners, where Jimmy's wife was still working. The driver left with instructions for the suit to be cleaned and returned ASAP.

Doc watched as the frustrated Jimmy heaved himself out of the chair and went into the new working kitchen. Frustrated because no matter how mad his big brother got, Doc never fought back.

Jimmy's muttered complaint trailed after him. 'Half of Glenlish on fire, bodies everywhere and he goes shopping.'

Instead of following Jimmy, Doc stood on, his ear cocked to catch the mood of the house and the yard. *There's something in the air.* What he couldn't say, almost as if someone had stuck a wrong note with a tuning fork.

After a while he pulled down the blinds in the sitting room, went through and did the same in the working kitchen.

Jimmy stopped what he was doing and asked, 'Do you think there's danger out there?'

Doc didn't bother shrugging. He washed his hands at the sink. Jimmy set out the plated-up the tea that Eleanor, Jimmy's wife, had left ready for Doc:

roast beef and a potato salad. The table already held bread and butter, sauces and pickles. Doc ate sparingly.

Jimmy sat across from him nursing a cup of tea. Eventually he said, 'Have you anything to tell me?'

'Labonga by Mullinure out of Maisie Dotes. Fawn bitch, registered in the name of Paul Bradley, 5 Sperrin Manor, Glenlish.'

'And that took all day?'

'Charlie phoned as soon as he got the information.'

'You let him go looking on his own?'

Doc kept his voice neutral. 'The wife stayed with me.' Could sense Jimmy ache to know more so he caught his eye and glanced at the ceiling, reminding him that the place could be bugged. You never knew with the police these days.

Jimmy reached across and turned on a radio. Doc shuddered as music from Radio 1 blared out. Jimmy leaned over the table. Doc put down his knife and fork and did the same.

Jimmy said, 'There's dead bodies turning up all over Glenlish, fires burning at every turn. Did you have a busy day?'

'Things took longer than I thought.'

'I suppose you called at the Bradley house?'

'You told me too.'

'After the… death of RM, did it ever occur to you to ask if that order still stood?'

Their heads were about two foot apart. Doc gave Jimmy one of his cold looks. 'I was on a public phone in a public place. Now if you allowed us to use mobile phones…'

Jimmy looked at him in astonishment. Doc realized that he was arguing back and went silent.

Jimmy asked, 'So what did Mrs. Bradley tell you?'

It seemed safer to say, 'Nothing,' than get into a complicated explanation of his visit with the Bradleys.

'Great, wonderful.' Jimmy snorted in disgust. 'You're useless around women.' He lobbed a copy of the *NewsLetter* across the table. 'Look for a Labonga in there.'

Doc held the paper up so Jimmy could see the photograph on the front page.

Jimmy said, 'I've seen it. Ronnie with our MPs in London and a broad hint that he might be joining them soon.'

Doc kept holding up the newspaper.

'Okay, okay, I get the message.' Jimmy pushed the paper down. 'That left our Ronnie at a deniable distance if things went wrong today.'

Jimmy delved into the "Greyhound" section of the *Irish News*. Doc kept leaning over the table, he knew his big brother, knew he wasn't finished yet with the questions.

Jimmy's head came out of the paper. 'What's up with you tonight? You're not only talking, you're arguing back.' Doc said nothing, so he continued, 'And that new outfit of yours, all countrified. You'll be taking up hunting and fishing next.'

Doc could see himself standing at a river's edge, casting a line – in-between sneezing and blowing his nose. City pollution suited him better. Rather than reply he opened the *NewsLetter* at the sports section.

One by one the newspapers landed back on the table. No Labonga was listed as running.

Jimmy indicated for Doc to lean even closer.

Now what?

'Last night?' asked Jimmy, failing to sound casual.

'Last night was last night.'

'Had you anything to do with that?'

'Why would I?'

'That wasn't the question.'

Doc's ears were vibrating from a high-pitched song screaming out of the radio. He turned it off, sat back and stared at Jimmy, expressionless. Jimmy scowled, now he couldn't ask any more leading questions. Instead he cleared the table and put the dishes in the sink.

The next question was casual in tone. 'And you think there's danger out there?'

'Don't you?'

'Aye,' said Jimmy slowly. 'I think I know where and I'm beginning to wonder why.'

They drank the last of the tea. Doc watched Jimmy flick glances his way, anxious to know exactly what he'd been up to in the last twenty-four hours.

Doc glanced at the clock. It had been a long day and he had things to do before he got back to his other life.

Eventually Jimmy drained his mug and slapped it down on the table. 'The sale of your house completes next week.'

'Fine,' said Doc.

'House and contents.'

Doc said nothing.

'Contents don't normally include a fortune in suits and shoes.'

Again Doc kept quiet.

'For God's sake it's not logical.' Jimmy got up and stood restless. 'Let the woman go. When they're at the change they're not right in the head.'

Doc said, 'Tell me about insanity.'

Chapter 19

The evening was drawing to a close. Mick was back in the Glenlish Arms, still in the *Baumler* suit he had put on for the drive to Belfast. *No good looking like a culchie even if the city people see you as one.* Especially when Doc took him into the Windsor Bar for a thank-you drink. *The Windsor Bar!* During the worst of the Troubles you might walk into the Windsor Bar but you didn't get to walk out of it if they didn't know you.

Right then Mick was sitting at a table with a beer in front of him. For appearances sake he took the occasional sip. Knowing when to stop was one reason why he was boss. People trusted him to keep his head.

People?

He looked at the men who made up his "gang". The men who shared his table had reached the stage where they were slobbering over their drinks. A few days ago he'd thought them a bunch of hard men, well able to take care of business anywhere. *Layabouts and drunks more like.* No more than corner boys grouped together for strength.

He shook his head to clear it. If only it was the drink and not a feeling of failure. Sure he could thump people into doing what he wanted and the builders in the area paid him a thousand pounds a house to avoid any "trouble", but…

It was Doc. The way he talked quiet and yet he'd taken those two bouncers apart without making anything off it. And then there was the other man, the voice on the phone…

Doc was fine, not talkative but he'd thanked Mick politely for his help and for the lift to Belfast. Mick could only hope that Doc never found out the truth otherwise he'd end up thinking that those bouncers had got off lightly.

Suddenly Mick felt more like the tough kid in kindergarten being bullied in turn by sixth-formers.

As if on cue his mobile rang, the number withheld.

Mick took a deep breath and answered it politely. 'Hello.'

A voice, a man's, cold as a bed laced with broken glass – said, 'You're not on your own.'

'I'm in the bar.'

'Go somewhere else.'

Sweat beaded Mick's body. Going outside could mean stepping into trouble. 'There's a private room.'

'Use it.'

Mick was almost grateful to get staying inside. What it was about this particular voice that made him panic, he couldn't say.

'Give me a minute, it's upstairs,' Mick said and got no reply.

The men grouped around his table had gone silent and were giving him odd looks.

Let them look.

Pride made Mick walk across the bar where people could see him but once out of their sight he ran the stairs to the back room. He tried to sound confident, someone the voice on the phone could rely on, as he said, 'It's okay now, sorry for keeping you.'

The voice said, 'Tell me.'

'You were right, he came here.'

'This isn't questions and answers. Get on with it.'

Mick had met the man behind the voice once before, years back. Had driven him to a factory, picked up the factory owner and taken him to the bank. The owner looked almost grateful to hand over a bag of money and being able to walk away. Mick had never dared tell of what he knew, not even to his best friend. A cocked gun against Mick's head and the threat of the trigger being pulled if he even hinted anything bought his silence. It wasn't the threat. It was the look in the man's eyes. He wanted to pull the trigger.

Chapter 20

The next morning Doc was waiting for Jimmy when he arrived downstairs from freshening himself up. Doc was wearing his suit, now freshly cleaned. Jimmy looked strained. From worry, Doc realized, and wondered why Jimmy bothered getting uptight over a few bodies.

Jimmy went out to No16, his personal taxi. Doc pushed ahead of him.

Jimmy frowned. 'Aren't we being a bit paranoid?'

'You do the same run every week.'

'With Kids? No one would dare… not with kids?'

Doc said nothing but got into the taxi. Jimmy got in as well and they drove off to collect his regulars: two little boys for a Special Needs School. Doc got into the back with the boys. He had a pound coin hidden in a hand. If they picked the right hand they could keep the money. But this pound coin could make itself invisible and jump from hand to hand like a kangaroo. They found one coin then a second as the taxi pulled up outside their school.

Jimmy muttered, 'I thought you were supposed to be guarding me?' He had a smile on his face for the first time that day. 'I told you long ago, Doc. You should have adopted.'

Doc shrugged and got back into the front passenger seat. He sensed unease in Jimmy, who checked in with the Dispatcher then switched off the radio. They stayed silent but alert as Jimmy took the taxi in a restless wandering around the city.

'Things are changing,' said Jimmy, finally breaking the silence. 'People are taking up positions, and I don't know which people and what positions, or why.'

Doc nodded, knowing Jimmy was putting words to what he himself felt. But where Jimmy saw changing loyalties and power play, he saw it in terms of gun smoke.

Their first stop was in the mean little streets across from a shopping center. The taxis parked opposite them belonged not only to another company but to the other 'side'. Catholics who ran their taxis up and down the Falls, whereas Jimmy and his men stayed on the Shankill Road.

No16 was spotted immediately because its number was on a yellow shield above the windscreen. Some of the younger drivers straightened up and stubbed out their cigarettes. One of the older men drew his finger across his throat, but was smiling as he did it.

Jimmy nodded and drove on and headed straight up the Falls Road itself.

'Wing mirrors,' said Doc.

Jimmy adjusted their angle so that Doc could watch the pavements on either side. They got as far as Chapel Lane, leading to St Mary's Catholic Church, before a pedestrian did a double take.

'He's got old and soft,' said Jimmy referring to the pedestrian. He twisted sideways in his seat until he could see out the rear view mirror on his own side. The pedestrian had stopped walking and was turned their way, mobile phone in hand. 'And he still knows the right numbers.'

That was the one thing Doc knew he could rely on, Jimmy stating the obvious. His eyes continued to sweep to and fro in an arc that took in: side window, mirror on his side, straight ahead, and finally the mirror and window on Jimmy' side – then back again.

The early mean streets of the Falls Road opened up into something more spacious, with parks and the odd line of trees. Doc used his little finger to put a trace of Vic in his nostrils to catch any stray pollen.

A couple of men waited for them outside a newsagent's shop. The shop had a bright window display. The men were both about Jimmy's age and wore suits, no ties. A tall, lean man with untidy hair going grey, waited further up the road. The man stood beside a post box, handy cover if shooting started.

Jimmy said, 'Trusting sods, they've brought Mick.'

Neither of Mick's hands showed. Doc concentrated on the hand held out of sight around the Mick's back. The other hand, the one that appeared to hold a threat in the jacket pocket, had been shot off years before by the army.

Jimmy pulled up beside the two men and rolled down the window. The men leaned in and nodded though there was no offer of a handshake. Their eyes flickered to see where Doc's hands were, then they ignored him.

Doc kept watching Mick, trusting Jimmy to make sure the hands of the two men stayed in sight.

Jimmy said, 'I was thinking of expanding into the Falls.'

The thinner of the two men said, 'And I was thinking of starting the Third World War.'

'How's the kids?' asked Jimmy.

The man laughed. 'They've got their own families now to keep them off the streets.'

'My lot haven't got that far yet,' said Jimmy.

'And your lot are still voting for the men who've screwed this country for generations.'

'No Surrender,' said Jimmy.

'Chuckie ar La,' said the man.

'It's been and gone and never was,' said Jimmy.

They drove away. Doc and Mick jerked a nod at each other as they passed. Doc noticing how pain had deepened the lines on Mick's face. He remembered the rumor that Mick's wife had thrown him out and wondered if they might solve each other's problem. And knew that wouldn't work, Mick still loved his wife.

Some of the tension seemed to have gone out of Jimmy.

'No trouble there,' said Jimmy, again stating the obvious.

Doc said nothing. The danger was from their own side, but he supposed Jimmy had to check.

Chapter 21

They ended up, as Doc knew they would, at an alleyway cordoned off by blue and white incident tape. An armored police Land Rover sat jammed across half the road, backing up traffic on both sides. The body had gone from the alleyway. Bright arc lights to brighten the dull day, flooded the area. A forensic team still hunted for clues. Doc noted the size of the bloodstains and the overturned bins.

He took the stubby red ruler out of his pocket and threw it onto the dashboard.

Jimmy said, 'He was only a mouthy drunk. Nothing more than that.'

He looked at Doc. Doc stared him back without blinking.

The traffic moved forward in fits and starts. At the bottleneck, official faces turned in their direction. The policeman directing traffic brought them to a halt. A sergeant loosened the gun in his holster and blocked their way.

A detective in civilian clothes bulled out of the ruck of officialdom. 'Out.'

Leary's got fatter, Doc noted as Jimmy asked, 'Why?'

'You think I don't know your brother's signature when I see it?'

'When did Doc ever write to you?'

Leary hawked and spat on the windshield. 'The knife smartass.' He drew his own gun, a hefty Browning automatic, and pointed it at Doc. 'Please try to escape.'

The car finally tidied, Doc swung into the passenger seat. The barrier at the front gate stayed down for several minutes.

Jimmy asked, 'Did you tell them anything?'

'Nothing,' said Doc.

'Nothing at all?'

'I admitted to knowing the name of my solicitor and his phone number.'

Instead of laughing Jimmy frowned. 'That's the second joke you've made recently. Who lit your fire?'

Doc said, 'Women, I can't be doing with them when I'm working.'

The barrier came up and they drove on.

Chapter 23

They arrived back at Jimmy's house. Doc saw that Gunner Smith had kept himself busy tidying an outhouse while he waited for him. Doc went into the house and changed into his flannels and jacket, and again left the suit for cleaning. He refused the offer of supper because he didn't want to keep Gunner waiting.

Gunner was an old man, he wouldn't deny eighty, and a widower with no grandchildren to spoil. He happily spent his days doing odd jobs for Jimmy, driving Eleanor here and there and tidying up around the yard.

Gunner saw Doc coming and locked the shed. He asked, 'Botanic, Central or Great Victoria Street?'

Doc said, 'The old Tech building,' and noted that Gunner didn't register a flicker of surprise at his new outfit, or where he wanted dropped off. Almost invariably Doc started his other life from one of the train stations or the bus depot. As a salesman with a history of epilepsy he was of course dependent on public transport or taxis to get around. "The old Tech building" was a first.

They got into Gunner's car, an ageing Ford Fiesta with bucket seats that had subsided down to the metal supports and more than 300,000 miles on the clock. Gunner was forever taking time off to see old friends and he hated flying. He also drove with some music CD playing. Today it was Anya and *The Celts*. With Anya at the top of her range and the sound turned up full-blast, Doc's head vibrated.

Doc twisted his hips into the least uncomfortable position. He shouted 'You should think of changing cars.'

Gunner shouted back, 'And give God a laugh at me wasting money when he's other plans for me?'

Doc was surprised at himself for making an unnecessary comment. *What's wrong with me today?*

Gunner took pity on Doc and reduced the volume. They finished the journey in silence. Doc got out at the disused Belfast Tech building. He walked past the lawns of Inst, his old school, and on up the street to the brick-fronted Jury's Inn.

He ordered a gin and tonic and sat where he could watch people coming through the front door. People came in and met up with friends, or disappeared into the lifts. Satisfied that he hadn't been followed, at least not into the hotel itself, he went to the public phones. His heartbeat heightened as he did a final check around before dialing a number from memory. The phone rang a few times then was answered.

'It's me,' he said.

'Hello Me.'

He hadn't given her a name. Hadn't known which one to give her, or whether to make one up on the wing, so "Me" is all she had to go on.'

'Is everything okay?'

'Why wouldn't it be?'

That's what he was ringing to find out. 'I mean...'

She interrupted him. 'I know what you mean.'

She hasn't gone to the police. At least she doesn't sound like she has.

He said, 'Yesterday was wonderful. You were wonderful.'

'You're not bad yourself.' She tried to make the words casual, but he heard a rise in tone. 'If you're ever back this way again...'

He didn't want to make commitments he couldn't keep. He interrupted her. 'And your husband?'

'Heading for Tralee.'

The next town after Tralee was New York. *Charlie's really running scared.*

'If he ever bothers you again I could...'

What he could do was nothing he dared voice. She might be wired up by the police and leading him on, or have her telephone bugged by them, or perhaps someone was listening in at his end. One of his "Paranoids" was about security. *People fear my other one.*

Connie seemed to realize what he was offering. There was a distinct pause before she said, 'He is the father of my children.'

Again he didn't dare comment.

Connie continued in a bright voice. 'As I was saying, before I was rudely interrupted...'

'Sorry about that.'

'You're doing it again.'

He found himself smiling and hugged the receiver to his ear until the pressure hurt.

He voice came tart. 'As I was saying, if you're ever this way again, that neck thing...' She rushed the words, embarrassed. 'Don't get me wrong, it was fantastic. I thought I'd died and gone to heaven. But afterwards... it's not me, it didn't feel right somehow.'

'No more neck thing,' agreed Doc. Autoerotic asphyxiation wasn't for everyone.

Rather than make a promise he couldn't keep about seeing her again, he made excuses about being in a public place and unable to talk.

Before he could hang up she said, 'A piece of advice, don't become an arsonist.'

'What?'

'That fire in the sitting room I asked you to light, it didn't catch.'

She hung up on him.

Chapter 24

When Doc exited the Jury's Inn it was past midnight. He walked up Great Victoria Street and crossed with the lights at the junction with the Donegall Road. From there he walked the length of Botanic Avenue and cut through the quadrangle of Queens University onto the Malone Road. There were a lot of trees around Methody College, but he thought them too polluted by traffic fumes to be a danger to his sinuses. By the time he had passed the Bot and the near-by chippie, he was on his own.

Happy that no one tailed him, he turned right down a side street, then left down another. Without being aware of it, his stride changed once he left the main road. Where before it had been purposeful, now it became the carefree walk of a man who has enjoyed a long but stimulating day at work.

He went through the gateway of a modern block of flats and walked up a short drive to the front door. He opened the door with his key and ran up the stairs and into his apartment on the first floor. A vibration-activated alarm began to beep. Doc typed a pass code into the keypad on the wall and the beeps stopped. He reset the alarm to sound if it detected anyone in the hallway or in the spare bedroom and went into the sitting room.

Doc's apartment looked out over the back garden of the building. From his sitting room window he had a view of the back lawn and the high security fencing that circled the apartment block. He closed the curtains before switching on the lights.

As well as the spacious sitting room, Doc's apartment had two *en suite* bedrooms. The kitchen units, like the rest of the furniture, came from IKEA. The walls were white, the furniture white and black, with red throws and cushions for contrast. A corner of the sitting room was given over to a workstation flanked by bookcases. On the wall above the fireplace was and original Lowry painting of children in a playground.

Doc went straight to the workstation and switched on the computer. While it was powering up he went into his bedroom and changed into casual slacks and a black polo-neck jumper, trainers instead of the leather shoes.

Back at the computer he pulled a strip of Sellotape from a dispenser and stretched it over the video lens before going into Skype TM. He clicked on a name. After the usual clicks and buzzes an aged but serene face appeared on the screen.

'Good evening, Professor Flaubard, is it too late to call?'

'Monsieur Robinson, if I had not wanted to speak I would not have answered.'

They shared smiles over the Internet.

'You are looking particularly well this evening, Professor.'

'And you, Monsieur Robinson, are looking particularly fuzzy.' The professor put on a scowl. 'But I have a bone to pick with you. Twice you disturb me.'

The computer was swung around until Doc could see the Seine at the Pont Neuf Bridge, with a Bateaux-Mouches boat drifting by. By squinting at the screen Doc could make out people dining on the upper deck. For a moment he could imagine himself and Connie…

The Professor continued. 'You disturb my quiet contemplation of one of the finer things in life.' The computer was swung round again to show the professor gently swirling an amber liquid in a brandy goblet. 'And I give you a 5,000 word assignment, yet you send me 10,000. Have you no consideration of your old professor's eyes?'

'You make everything so interesting,' said Doc. He didn't even try to sound apologetic.

'And so do you, my friend. Forget the Masters. Expand the assignment into a thesis for a PhD.'

'I'll think about it,' said Doc, though he'd no intention of ever going that far. A Masters from the Sorbonne was one thing, assignments got buried in the vaults, but a thesis for a PhD was available for everyone to read. *Partition and Conflict, Ireland and the Middle East* was the sort of thing likely to be commented on by one of the newspapers. The reporters would want to know something of the author, Frederick Robinson, and that would be highly embarrassing.

The real Frederick Robinson was reported to have died in questionable circumstances somewhere in South America. The report was never confirmed, no body ever recovered, so a Coroner's Inquest had never been held. To all intents and purposes Frederick Robinson was still alive and well and working as a janitor/handyman for a property company. Doc and Jimmy paid the taxes and Gunner Smith drew the wages.

Doc and the professor chatted for a while, then they got down to a critique of Doc's latest assignment.

Chapter 25

On Monday morning Jimmy didn't wait to be invited. There was a separate VIP entrance into Ronnie Fetherton's office but Jimmy always took the shortcut through the secretary's office. The secretary wanted to announce him. He gestured her away and stormed on, slamming the door in her face. Doc delayed in the cluttered outer office to watch the security cameras.

First he had to move a pile of un-filed letters blocking the monitor. At least they were dust free, as was the whole room. Dusting was the only thing the secretary ever put real effort into. The secretary was a girl in her twenties with dark curling hair and a permanent bored expression.

She'd told Doc once, 'It ruins my clothes and gets in my hair and makes me stink.'

Doc pretended to hesitate, wondering where to put the filing.

The secretary said, 'Throw them anywhere.'

Doc made room for them on her desk. The girl's face tightened in annoyance. She dumped the invoices on the floor behind her. Doc had palmed a fifty-pound note under the invoices. While bending down the girl slipped the fifty-pounds into her handbag. She straightened up, stared at the security camera aimed at her and continued to look annoyed. The bending down had popped open buttons in her orange blouse. She didn't seem to realize that.

Doc moved so that he was between her and the camera. Now Ronnie couldn't see them talk. The girl's breasts bulged out of a gossamer bra. Doc got the smell of a perfume nearly as strong as body odor. Her annoyed look disappeared. His sinuses burned.

She whispered, 'Ronnie's got a new RM.'

No surprise there.

'And?'

'Nothing.' She made a face. 'They come, they go: dead or jail, who cares, but they all think shagging me is part of the perks.'

'Never,' said Doc.

'Now me, I like the older man. You know, experienced, not all over you like a rash.'

She fluttered her eyelashes at him. Somehow in re-buttoning her blouse it gaped even wider.

Cheap, Doc thought, looking at the bra, which displayed more flesh than latticed material.

He glanced back at the security monitor. When he and Jimmy arrived there'd been only the security man at the front door. The security man had now been joined by two yardmen, with others approaching. They were all wore their street clothes. The men talked among themselves. One of them was a youth wearing a mock-leather jacket. He was taller and thinner and had more acne than the RM who had died in Glenlish. He also seemed to have a lot to say. Goaded on by the others he undid his flies and urinated against Jimmy's taxi.

Doc watched the men laughing and high-fiving each other in their enjoyment. One of the older men glanced up at the security camera as if to say, 'I know you're watching, Doc.'

'You're right there, Arthur,' said Doc into himself.

He followed Jimmy into Ronnie's office.

Chapter 26

Ronnie Fetherton glanced in Doc's direction as he went in the door. Ronnie smiled and looked quickly away.

Doc knew what Ronnie was thinking. "You can't be that tough if the wife made a fool of you." Which was why he had to kill the wife and her lover. People might begin to think that he'd gone soft. That he and Jimmy were now vulnerable.

Other than the look and the smile, Ronnie tried to ignore Doc, just as Ronnie was ignoring Jimmy. Ronnie was pointedly updating his on-line diary, making Jimmy wait. Jimmy didn't seem to notice the implied insult. He had his earphones in and his eyes closed, listening to a tune on his Walkman.

Doc settled himself against the wall of Ronnie's office, on the hinge side of the door. Well enough along so that the door couldn't be smashed open in his face. The spot he'd chosen kept him out of Ronnie's line of sight, something Ronnie didn't like, going by his twitch of unease.

In between using Ronnie's security monitor to assess the gathering of men at the front door Doc checked the pictures on the wall. There were a couple of new photographs since they'd last been there. A photograph of Ronnie shaking hands with the Prime Minister outside 10 Downing Street, now took pride of place. There were other changes too. Ronnie's men might still sport orange overalls but the orange walls of the office – emphasizing Ronnie's Loyalist credentials – had become a conservative blue.

Eventually Ronnie sat back in his chair. 'I can only give you a minute, I've a funeral to attend.'

'What?' asked Jimmy, his eyes opening.

Ronnie sighed and pointed at the Walkman. Jimmy pulled off the earphones and left them hanging around his neck. Music seeped out until he thought to turn it off.

Ronnie pointed again at the monitor and the men at the front door. 'Funeral.'

Jimmy said, 'I heard you lost a lorry in Glenlish.'

'Luckily one of the older ones.'

'Doubtless well insured, as usual.'

Ronnie didn't rise to the bait. Instead he said, 'I take it you're not for the funeral?'

'For that fat bastard? No. I've better things to do, people to see.'

Doc caught the look of distain on Ronnie's face as he assessed Jimmy's idea of dressing up to go visiting: a sports coat and trousers. Good quality at a time but now worn to the bone. No label showed when the coat flapped open. Probably stolen, he could feel Ronnie think.

Ronnie himself wore a pinstripe suit and a white, double-cuffed shirt that flashed solid gold cufflinks and stretched over Ronnie's extending waistline. *Those political lunches are starting to show.* That day Ronnie's chosen tie was black because he was going to the funeral of his driver.

What happened to RM in Glenlish had already been covered in a cryptic phone call. No one mentioned having to attend his funeral. As the girl said, RM's came and they went: young would-be hard men, impatient to make a name for themselves.

In the early days they'd turned over so quickly that Jimmy had stopped trying to remember their names and called them all RM – Ronnie's Man. The nickname stuck. The poor idiots wore it as a badge of honor, not realizing that it implied an early demise.

Ronnie pulled a padded A5 envelope out of a drawer and held it out for Doc to take. 'For services rendered.' He held onto it for an extra moment before allowing Doc to slip it into his pocket. 'Compliments of the Ulster Resistance.'

'Is that lot still going?' asked Jimmy.

Ronnie looked him up and down coldly. 'We were always willing to dig deep to fund our Protestant brethren in their struggle against the forces of evil.'

'Aye, cheaper than paying protection money and you got added advantages. On the house, so to speak.'

'What do you mean by that?'

'Competition discouraged or eliminated. People willing to pay dear or sell cheap.'

'I deny that.'

'Well you would.'

Ronnie said, 'I suppose you heard about Winston Shaw in that alleyway?' He gave a false smile of bonhomie. 'Maybe you knew about the killing before it happened?'

'I was in my bed.'

'Oh, you're an armchair general now?'

Jimmy shrugged. 'Have you heard anything?'

'A castration, other than that it was a regular kicking.'

Jimmy said, 'Using a knife on Winston was a mistake.'

He didn't look Doc's way as he said it.

But Ronnie did as he replied. 'That's the problem with Doc, he likes to leave his calling card.'

Doc stared him back.

Jimmy said, 'Allegedly.'

Ronnie looked away from Doc's stare, started to type again.

Jimmy leaned against the computer monitor. It creaked under his weight. 'That RM you sent was as thick as champ. A total dickhead.'

'Stealing the letters? It was a good risk. We could've had Bradley in one.' Ronnie looked up from the computer towards Doc. 'Why didn't you back him up?'

Doc stared out the window at the disused linen factory across the way and ignored the question.

Jimmy said, 'Doc likes step-by-step instructions. It can turn your head at times but at least I know what he's up to.'

'Robbing a man doesn't take much planning.'

'Apparently it does. The idiot managed to kill himself in the process.' Jimmy jerked upright as a machine whirred behind him. 'What's that?'

Ronnie smiled, his teeth showing a whiteness they'd never got on the National Health. 'The printer.'

Jimmy watched, apparently fascinated, as a hard copy of Ronnie's appointments for the next week printed out.

He said, 'That car RM was supposed to nick. He borrowed it off a mate.' He kicked the printer stand. 'You and your half-assed planning.'

Ronnie jumped to his feet, trembling with rage. 'I think you've said enough.'

'I haven't even started yet.'

Doc watched the two egos square up to each other. Wondered, if the men clashed, should he separate them? Ronnie had the height and weight to take Jimmy apart. There again Jimmy's fingers were as thick as chisels and his knuckles had the stopping power of a four-by-two piece of wood. Doc decided not to interfere and enjoy the contest, and was disappointed when tempers cooled and the two men backed off.

Jimmy said, 'If the police decide to question the owner of that car he'll land us in it.'

'They won't.'

'On your head be it,' replied Jimmy and they got down to the real business of the day. Tracing Bradley and keeping an eye on Nelson in case he got brave and went to the police.

Chapter 27

Their meeting finished, Jimmy stalked out of Ronnie's office. Doc followed at his heels. The secretary looked up. She smiled and flexed her shoulders until her generous breasts strained the buttons on her blouse.

Jimmy leaned over the desk. He ran fingers over her breasts and down into the V. 'Assets like that, love, you should keep covered up. You don't want them catching cold.'

The secretary's hand came up to conceal the second fifty-pound note he had just slipped into her bra. 'Doc saw me all right,' she said.

Jimmy gave the breasts a final pat. 'That's for balance.'

Doc opened the outer office door. No one waited in the corridor and the other doors leading onto the corridor remained closed. He held the door open for Jimmy who walked on, his stride gradually turning into a strut of temper.

Doc tried to get ahead of him at the front door but Jimmy bulled out onto the street. Doc slid out quickly and checked. The group of older men waiting to go to the funeral had grown. They stood close-by, eyes hard on him and Jimmy but not threatening. With the exception of the youth in the mock-leather jacket the younger men were out on the road doing the usual Monday deliveries.

The side of the taxi was still damp from the urine. Doc turned as if to speak to Jimmy, then he spun back, his elbow coming up. The youth went down, blood pumping out of his nose.

Doc nodded to the rest of the men and got into the car. This time he drove.

Once they were safely on their way Jimmy snarled, 'That stupid plonker Ronnie, he'll get us hung one of these days.' He snatched off the Walkman and threw it into the glove compartment.

Doc said nothing, his mind busy with impressions and overheard half-statements, nuances of people and what they were up to. It seemed too easy to blame Ronnie for everything.

Jimmy interrupted his thoughts by asking, 'Why is Bradley so important and why does The Man want us to work with Ronnie?'

Doc glanced his way but remained silent.

'We have to,' said Jimmy. 'And that's the frustrating thing about it. The threat was there. They've enough on you to put you away for life.'

He seemed annoyed when Doc ignored the accusation and continued to worm his way through the city, homeward bound. On Peter's Hill they passed one of their drivers taking an unauthorized tea-break. Someone, Doc reckoned, was in line for a bollocking, especially with opposition cabs flying past, full of paying customers.

Nearing home, Jimmy sat upright. 'What do you think of Ronnie?'

Doc took his time about replying. 'He never thinks things through.'

'So you agree with me?'

Doc shrugged.

'Don't overdo it,' snapped Jimmy. 'I can't stand it when you argue back.' He stretched to ease some of the compressed irritations he felt. 'Bradley was worse than you. You'd tell him things you shouldn't, just to get a reaction. You never did. The bugger sat there drinking his watered down whiskey – my watered down whiskey – saying little. Then when you'd talked yourself done he'd latch onto something you'd said and hook opinions out of your guts you never knew you had.'

Doc remained silent.

'Ah fuck!' said Jimmy.

Chapter 28

Dear Barbara,

I've got a job. It's not much, working in kennels, but if I can stick it for a few weeks I feel I can start putting my life back together again.

The owner is a nice fellow, but the wife is the greatest bitch. She doesn't want me around and couldn't make it more obvious.

Paul Bradley sat on, pen poised over the page, undecided. The fingers of his left hand worked at a scar on his forehead. Barbara didn't like him even mentioning the name of another woman. Eventually he scored out the last two lines, but continued to work at the scar. She'd be suspicious if he didn't say something about the wife.

Finally he gave up and hurried away from the unfinished letter. He pulled the living room door shut behind him. Immediately the narrow corridor of the granny flat closed in on him. The door to the stairs and the outside lay open. He ran down the stairs into the yard. Drew two deep breaths to get the ghosts of claustrophobia out of his system.

Old single-story outhouses boxed-in the yard on two sides. Large as they were they were dwarfed by the dwelling house, a manor house with wings added during the Victorian period. The recess between the two wings had been turned into a patio, pointedly separated from the rest of the yard by raised, pink hexagonal slabs. All the out-buildings were painted white, their doors picked out in different pastel shades. The fourth side had a high wall cut by an archway that led onto an oasis of grass and trees.

Paul walked through the archway, intending to spend the rest of his lunch hour under a tree. Everything in the garden was quiet, even the treetops were still. A couple of greyhound saplings lifted their heads to look at him, one even wandered over to the gate. He ignored them because Kristi Stockdale, the owner's wife, lay stretched out on the grass. He couldn't help but notice how well the cream towel she lay on set off her gold-tanned body. Kristi looked his way and stretched languorously. If she wore a bikini it was the exact shade of her suntan. Paul went back into the yard, feeling restless. The thought of Kristi lying there naked didn't help.

He crossed to the outbuilding that held a block of kennels. Even with the temperature in the seventies it felt cool. Two-foot thick walls and small windows kept it that way. He opened the door and his greyhound bitch, Girl, scrambled off her bench.

'Coming for a walk?' he asked, massaging her between the ears. She arched her neck under his touch and pressed so close he had trouble putting on the lead. The only other dog in that block of kennels, a scrawny brindle, stood at his door, waiting hopefully. 'Sorry, big fellow,' said Paul and led Girl out into the yard.

He headed towards the nearby town of Marston. A faint breeze got up and swirled in and out of the shading trees. He walked slowly, forcing himself to relax, letting Girl stop and sniff where she wanted. Coming to a phone box, he decided to phone Barbara at the bank.

Rather than be enclosed in the kiosk, he stood with his foot against the door to keep it open while he fed a pound coin into the slot. Once the phone at the other end started to ring he backed out of the kiosk as far as he could and still use the telephone. The fierce springs of the door pressed hard against him.

A lorry hammered past. The swirl of dust from its tires enveloped him. He held his breath and closed his eyes. Girl lay panting in the shade of a hedge. She sneezed. On the phone, a man's voice answered.

'May I speak to Barbara, please?'

He cleared a nervous husk out of his throat, fingers again working the scar on his forehead. Barbara came to the phone, sounding cautious. He wasn't surprised, he'd heard the man say, 'I think it's your husband.'

'It's me,' he said.

'Is anything wrong?'

How could he explain about the owner's wife, Kristi, and needing the reassurance of her voice?

'Nothing. I was out getting some messages and I thought I'd give you a ring.'

'It's not very convenient.'

'How are the boys?'

'Fine.'

'How are you?'

'Fine.'

Barbara always had some little plague to bother her. *Now all she ever says is "fine".* His back and side were hurting from the stretch to the receiver and the press of the door. He thought he shouldn't mention that.

She broke the silence they'd let gather around them. 'I'd better go; we're busy. Did you want something?'

'Just to say hello and to tell you about the job.' Even as he spoke he knew she wouldn't approve and he rushed his explanation, finishing with, 'I called to give Girl a run and the owner and I got to talking.'

'I suppose it's a start,' she said, echoing the words in his unfinished letter.

The tension eased out of him. 'Yes.'

He looked down at Girl. She panted back and rested her muzzle on his foot while they said their goodbyes. Then Barbara called out, 'Wait.'

'Yes,' he asked, grateful for the reprieve.

'When will you be home?'

He couldn't find the words to say, 'When I can trust myself not to kill you.'

Chapter 29

Paul's employer, Ken Stockdale, was back at the kennels before him. Ken was a tall man, in his fifties, one of those men whom premature greying suits.

Ken was walking the scrawny brindle under the trees, his footsteps slow and unguided. He nodded vaguely to Paul as he approached and held out his hand. They shook. Ken's grip was firm and he'd a habit of giving an extra, friendly squeeze.

Ken started out of his abstraction and his mouth crinkled into its usual smile. 'We were waiting for you. I thought you'd like to give Girl another run.'

Paul smiled back. It disappeared when Kristi joined them from the house. The jeans and blouse she now wore had a good round shape to them. Paul felt the sobriquet "bitch" justified because, like any good dog, she walked well-up on her toes. Kristi was considerably younger than Ken, could give even Paul himself a few years.

She asked. 'Where have you been?'

'Giving Girl a walk.'

'Who said you could?' She came even closer, until her scents invaded his senses. 'I certainly didn't and Ken wasn't here.'

Explaining his absence, Paul felt, was beyond him. How could he explain the occasional tension that flared in his chest like a dry pain? The inability to cope with pressure and of his need to get away from things? He stepped back from her, and was grateful, when Ken said, 'I was only at the bank. I was hardly gone an hour.'

'And so was he, and he left the door into the granny flat open. Again. Next thing we'll have mice in the house.'

'I'm sorry,' said Paul

She said, 'If you're not going to work, you're not going to be here.'

They walked over to the schooling track. Paul allowed himself to fall behind, even then Kristi's voice carried. 'We know nothing about him, and for all we're paying him he'd be better off on the dole. He's a fighter, look at that scar on his forehead. Even a drunk would've got it stitched.'

Ken shushed her down and the argument continued. Paul prayed to get staying, to get talking about things other than the weather with shop assistants.

Eventually Kristi raised her voice in exasperation. 'Damn it Ken, so what if he comes cheap. You're worrying about pennies when we're bankrupt anyway.'

At the track, Ken trailed over to the 500-metre box. When Paul joined him Ken said, 'Your wee bitch is starting to bend well so I thought I'd put her in with the brindle.'

'Fine,' said Paul, not sure if Girl was ready for company.

The scrawny brindle only needed an encouraging pat to make him step quietly into trap 4. Paul eased Girl into trap 2, using his knee against her rump to stop her from backing off. Annoyingly, she still fought that part. The hare came rattling past and the lid snapped up.

The brindle blasted out of trap 4 and hammered down the home straight for the first time. Girl took one uncertain step, then another before exploding down the track after him.

'Stupid bitch,' said Paul.

'She's greener than grass,' said Ken'

Paul was too busy swinging the traps out of the way to watch much after that. He got the impression that the brindle ran wide while Girl shaved the bends, pulling back lengths. The brindle faded on the home straight and they were neck and neck at the escape.

Chapter 30

Paul made himself busy in the Feed-house preparing the evening meal for the dogs. So many scoops of nuts per bowl, according to a list on the wall. Be generous with water in this heat. He chomped the minced beef in the fridge, with a wooden spoon. Defrosting nicely. It would be added only at feed time, to keep it fresh. This sort of routine he could cope with.

A shadow thrown across the bench from the open doorway alerted him to Kristi's arrival. Her eyes, he noticed, looked everywhere but at him. Checking, he thought, to make sure every bag of dog-meal was stacked neatly and every work-surface scrubbed clean.

'Ken wants a word,' she said, and left.

She's won. She'd got her way and he was out of a job. He'd been a fool to hope. There was no way he'd get staying-on when Kristie didn't want him around.

He rinsed his hands clean under the tap and found they were shaking. He'd signed off the dole and it would be weeks before they put him back on benefits: no money for petrol, no money for food. That meant subbing off Barbara and things had to be tight enough there as it was.

He expected to be given his marching orders at the back door. On his way there he had to pass the patio. Ken was in the sitting room. He waved Paul in through the French doors, which lay open against the summer heat. Paul had never been in that part of the house before. Had never got beyond the utility room.

Paul looked for a mat wipe his feet on. There wasn't one and he checked the soles of his shoes carefully before daring to step onto the highly polished mahogany floor.

Ken was slumped in the settee. Beaten, Paul decided, from the stretch of despair in his face. Beaten by Kristie, the relentless heatwave and a lot of other things Paul didn't know about. He hadn't forgotten Kristie's impatient "we're bankrupt anyway".

Ken motioned again, this time for Paul to sit in the chair across from him. *Kristie's ordered him to do it the American way.* Tell me he's doing me a favor by letting me go.

The floor was strewn with cardinal-red mats. Paul curved around them in case he had missed something on his shoes. He sat across from Ken, upright and tense.

Newspapers and studbooks lay heaped on the floor beside Ken. A wine bottle sat on the casual table between them. Ken gave him a half-dopey smile. *He's been drinking.* Paul looked away, embarrassed.

A mirror on the wall reflected the room behind Paul. The mirror was large, but he noticed a picture stain on the wallpaper behind it. Has that mirror replaced something, he wondered, maybe a larger painting? And now he thought about it some of the furniture wasn't quite right either. Modern reproduction mixed haphazardly with the definitely old.

That realization triggered memories in Paul's mind. Of looking across the table in his office and seeing the despairing faces of clients with crushing money worries. All the same signs of failure were in Ken's exhausted face and in the way the kennels were being run. Paul realized he'd been so bound up in his own problems that he'd missed all the signs. He felt guilty at letting a client down. Then he remembered that Ken wasn't a client. Ken was the boss who was about to fire him. He bore Ken no ill will but wouldn't mind seeing Kristie on the street.

In the circumstances, there was no good arguing against being sacked. He'd cope somehow, but maybe Ken would give him a sack of feed for Girl.

Ken reached for the bottle of wine. 'You'll take a drink?' He examined the bottle carefully, mouth slightly agape. 'Empty.' He called, 'Woman, more wine.'

Kristi shouted from the kitchen, 'You've had enough.'

Ken rattled the bottle onto the table and kept his hand on it to stop it from falling over. Embarrassed at his employer's drunken state, Paul looked away.

'The point is,' said Ken, as if continuing a conversation. 'Girl nearly headed the big brindle over 500 meters, and he's gone nine consecutive runs without a defeat. There again, he isn't fully fit. He's four pounds underweight and only starting to run into shape.'

'None of them are,' said Kristi bringing in a tray of tea things. 'That kennel cough tore the guts out of every dog in the kennel.'

Paul's eyes locked on the tray. *Three cups?* Did Kristie plan to throw a cup of tea in his face? He didn't think so because the cups were venerable bone china and so thin he could nearly read a newspaper through them.

What the hell's going on here?

Kristie produced napkins and asked Paul if he took milk with green tea – he said no – and poured him English Breakfast. Offered him the bowl of lump sugar. He looked at the bowl. He didn't take sugar, *but sod it*. He picked up the sugar tongs from the tray and helped himself to one lump. Accepted a plate of gooey chocolate cake and waited. Smiled his thanks when Kristi thought to fetch dessert forks. *Thank God Barbara harped on about table manners*. He was so unused now to sweet stuff that the cake tasted almost disgusting. He smiled again and nodded like it was delicious.

'The point is,' said Ken, stabbing at Paul with a fork as if they were in the middle of an argument. 'The point is Mr. Know-it-all, did you check the time?'

Am I being fired or not? 'No.'

It's Girl, he realized, they want to buy her. He put the cake down and the teacup. *No way!*

Ken's stab became a wag. 'Well I did.' He settled back in his chair. 'The equivalent time in Wimbledon is 29.87.'

Deadpan Paul asked, 'Is that fast?'

29.87, and with a green pup? That made Girl worth…. *The sort of money Barbara could be doing with.*

Ken insisted on shaking hands before flinging his arms wide in salutation. '29.87. We've got a runner in the Rosebowl.'

Paul felt relief that Ken wasn't offering to buy Girl, an offer he could hardly refuse. Then he said a flat, 'No.'

'Why not?'

There was no way he could answer that, *at least not honestly*. If Girl got to even the semi-finals the media would take an interest and he'd have to move on. 'It's too expensive when she hasn't any real chance.'

The coffee table groaned under the weight of Ken's elbows. 'I'm sorry, I should have asked first.'

Oh shit! He hadn't money for anything, let alone the entrance fees into a minor classic.

Kristi said, 'We had to reregister the bitch with the English greyhound board. They've already got a Labonga on their books.'

Ken tapped the studbooks beside him. 'I looked it up. She's was a brood bitch so they can't give it to you.'

'So what's Girl's racing name now?' asked Paul.

'Arrant Beauty.'

It could be worse, he thought, eying Kristi, and sliced nervously at the cake. Eventually he looked up and saw Ken slumped forward, a plaintive look in his big brown eyes. Found he had to smile. They were greyhound men and greyhound men only came properly alive when their dogs were on the track.

'What the hell,' he said.

Ken straightened up, his face flushed with excitement. 'I'll give you a toast.' He raised his cup. 'Every year the Stockdale Kennels put out a runner with a chance. This year's no exception; that wee darling can only improve.' He drank the toast, then shouted, 'The sky's the limit.'

The saplings in the paddock took up the call and the challenge spread to all the kennels.

Chapter 31

It was getting late and evening kennels were over. Paul's body ached from a long day working in the heatwave, but his mind remained sharp and restless. He wanted Barbara, wanted to hear her voice, have a normal conversation with her.

Ken had long since been poured into bed and Kristi was having a last look around before heading into the house. Probably making sure I haven't skimped anywhere, he thought, too tired to feel bitter.

Even the thought of walking to the public phone made his body ache harder. 'Make the bitch refuse,' he said to himself. He searched his pockets for a pound coin and held it out to her. 'If I pay, may I use the phone?'

'Landline or mobile?' she asked.

He registered her tone as neutral, she'd been that way since teatime. 'Landline, I want to phone home.'

She said, 'Keep your money. Use the phone in the kitchen.' Started to walk off then turned back. 'Ken needs to have Girl here for the next few weeks, but don't push your luck.'

She stood on, hands on hips, and stared openly at his groin. 'This afternoon in the garden, you had a good look at me lying naked.' She pointed. 'There was no movement down there.'

He said, 'Drink and drugs, missus,' and wished her to hell.

Chapter 32

Barbara took the call.

It's wrong for Paul to ring so late, she thought. He knows I have to get up early for work. She lay on in bed, curled in under the duvet with the receiver snuggled up to her ear. Missing him, knowing that she would cry herself to sleep as soon as he hung up. He sounded thrillingly different. Full of things to talk about, with none of the usual awkward silences between them. And excited too about a useless dog in a stupid race.

She felt guilty for not calling the boys to speak to their father, but they tended to hog the phone. Things were nice the way they were. In the old days, evenings like this, once talk lagged the bodies took over. She tried not to think about that.

Barbara enjoyed telling him about the youth who had killed himself in the car. 'It was terrible, that poor young man. You would have been proud of the boys, they were really helpful. Inspector Patterson asked them if they'd ever thought of the police as a career, and do you know what they said?'

'What?' asked Paul.

'They've got it all worked out. Shane wants to be a policeman.' She stopped, sorry she'd started this line of conversation. Realized she had to go through with it. 'He wants to find evidence to prove you innocent, and Rory is going to be a lawyer and fight your case through the courts.'

'They're not bad kids.' His voice shook.

Is that emotion or embarrassed guilt in his voice? Bile gathered and she wanted to spit. *That two-faced whore of a secretary.*

She rushed on, not wanting to hear any more lies. 'The boys are loyal. It's dad through thick and thin.' Desperate to change the subject she remembered the visitor. 'I'm glad Inspector Patterson called when he did because that nasty little man was here at the time.'

'What nasty little man?'

'A newspaper reporter, Ronnie someone or other. He pretended you'd done work for him at a time and he'd promised you a pup in return. All he wanted was your address.'

'You didn't give it to him?'

'I didn't know it, did I?' she said, aching for it to be 5 Sperrin Manor.

Chapter 33

Nelson, the British Telecom engineer, listened into the conversation. He was on duty again that night having called in every favor to get it. And every night, near midnight, came the call. Any time he slept the disbelieving voice and its threats replayed itself in his mind and woke him up. Rheumatism in his wrist caused it to ache, he massaged it constantly.

I'm so tired.

The number those men wanted flickered on the screen before him. But the person they were looking for was no longer a number to be exchanged for the safety of his own family. Paul Bradley was now a man with his own problems and someone he'd voted for. Respected in the town and always pleasant even before he became a politician, and never seemed to go anywhere without those two boys. But if the wife was anything like his own he couldn't blame Bradley for being caught in bed with his secretary. The woman was getting on a bit, but still a good looking bird.

Nelson looked at the clock, *nearly time for their call.* Well tonight would get them off his back. He'd got hell at home for that broken photograph frame and the plant pot. 'What did you think you were doing?' and 'Could you not leave well enough alone?' The authority that the wife brought to her job as a ward sister tended to rub off on family life. It never seemed to occur to her that his job had its own stresses.

The manager understood the pressures he was under and would occasionally move shifts to suit him. That's how he'd got the extra nightshift, by pretending that she was in one of her moods and he wanted to keep clear.

The office phone rang. The pulse in his throat caught his breathing. He answered it quickly to get it over with.

A Belfast voice, but not one of the two men who had threatened him, asked, 'Nelson?'

He swallowed. 'Yes.'

'Well?'

He looked at the screen, he felt light-headed. Said, 'No.'

'Nothing?'

They don't believe me!

His body spasmed in fear and he knocked his wrist on the edge of the desk. The pain was hell.

Maybe I should give them the number?

He said, 'Honestly, local calls. Nothing from England.' The silence that followed was worse than threats. He rushed on, feeling he must be mad to risk all for a man he hardly knew. 'I can only get so much night-duty. After this week it will be another month. They won't give it to me. Honest. Honest.'

There was conferring at the other end. A hand placed over the mouthpiece blocked the words and he could make nothing out. Sweat bubbled until his clothes clung to him. He hunted a tissue out of his pocket and wiped at his forehead. Wished he could get to the door to let in some fresh air.

Eventually the voice said, 'Keep the tap going. Check once a day and we'll phone you at home.'

'It's too dangerous, someone will notice.'

'It's too dangerous not to.'

The receiver clicked down.

Nelson wilted over the desk, it was all he could do not to vomit. Eventually he straightened himself up and zapped Paul's number from the screen.

Chapter 34

Ronnie Fetherton, CEO and chief shareholder of Fetherton Haulage cursed Nelson: seed, breed and gender. He wanted to hurt someone, break something, but office desks and computer screens cost money. Eventually he remembered the replacement RM and swung around, fists up. RM jumped well clear of the threat and sidled towards the door.

On reflection, Ronnie thought it best not to take it out on the creep. He needed RM fit and active. Also he could get blood from that acned face on his silk shirt.

He asked, 'What time does Nelson get off duty?'

'Don't know, boss.' RM did a bit of quick thinking, he knew something about the previous RM's trip. 'Eight or so, about then.'

'Well be there when he does and kick his head in a couple of times.'

RM looked frightened, Ronnie realized. Scared of going anywhere near Glenlish. *You'd think it was Mars or somewhere.*

RM stuttered, 'That man Nelson might be telling the truth. When I'm away I only ring home when I want something.'

Ronnie jerked to his feet and RM backed off rapidly. Held up his hands defensively. 'I'm going, I'm going.'

Before he could escape Ronnie had him by the throat and pinned to the wall. 'You tell Nelson from me. If he doesn't get that number, he's dead, and he won't like the way I do it.'

RM edged along the wall, searching for a crack of an opening to slither through. 'Yes, boss.'

'You tell him.'

'Yes, boss.'

His sliding progress threatened to knock pictures off the wall: Parliamentary hopeful Ronnie meeting the Speaker of the House of Commons, Councillor Ronnie Fetherton hosting a reception at City Hall.

Ronnie used his knuckles on RM's chest to bounce him off the wall. Cursed when he skinned a knuckle on the stud of the mock-leather jacket. Got his own back by hacking at RM's legs. Ronnie went back to his chair and sat staring at the security screens. No one moved in the street outside or in the recesses between the parked-up lorries. Somehow he'd this feeling that Doc…

He swung around to face RM. 'Do you know where you're going?'

'Glenlish, the telephone exchange.'

Ronnie asked with studied patience, 'And do you know where to find the telephone exchange in Glenlish?'

'I'll Google it, boss.'

Sweet lord, intelligence.

He motioned for RM to leave.

RM had the door open before he dared ask. 'How do you know Bradley phoned?'

'Where's Bradley hiding out?'

'Don't know, boss.'

'So how does Nelson know we're looking for a call from England?' Ronnie switched off the computer monitors. It was long past home time and he was weary after a frustrating day. 'Bradley phoned, and he's holding out on us.' He looked at RM wondering if he dared trust him on his own. 'Do you want Doc to go with you?'

RM grinned. 'From what they're saying on the street, the wife's a better man than him.'

'Well do you?'

'Who needs Doc?' asked RM, his voice rough with pretend bravado.

Ronnie said, thoughtfully, 'That's a good question.'

That question put him in a good mood as he dealt with another annoying problem. The increase in shipping fares to the mainland. He rang a private number.

A voice dull with sleep answered on the fourth ring. 'Hello.'

Ronnie said, without introduction, 'These new shipping rates for lorries going to the mainland,'

The voice became more alert and tinged with fear. 'It's the prices, they're going up. Fuel and whatever.

'Not for me, they're not. It's the old rates or someone will be round.'

He slammed the phone down and began to plan an answer to RM's question. "Who needed Jimmy and Doc?"

Chapter 35

RM stepped out from behind the BT van. He emphasized his Belfast accent, made it as harsh as possible. 'Nelson?'

Nelson froze in the search for his keys. Nelson's mouth worked soundless words and his hands started to shake. He found the keys, found the right one and rattled it into the lock.

'You are Nelson?'

'Yeeees.'

'Turd,' said RM and drove his heel into the van door, slamming it shut again.

'Please, no. There's been nothing.'

RM hitched a fist into Nelson's stomach knocking him against the van and held him there while he pounded face and ribs. Nelson could only flap his arms about and cry, 'Stop, stop.'

RM worked himself in a nifty one-two-three rhythm: guts, ribs, face; guts, ribs face. *If the boys at the club could see me now.*

His hands started to hurt and blood spurted onto his mock-leather jacket. *That won't come out.* It made him mad. He kicked at Nelson's legs until he fell onto his hands and knees, then RM stepped back and measured the distance. A kick to the right place would take the head off Nelson's shoulders. Then he remembered Ronnie. Ronnie needed Nelson alive and active.

He kept his right foot poised ready for the kick. 'Did Bradley call?'

Nelson spat blood. 'No.'

RM raked the boot along Nelson's ribs.

'Yes,' screamed Nelson. 'Yes he did.'

'When?'

'Last night.'

This time RM used his heel and aimed for the base of the spine. Nelson curled into the ground and lay with his hands over his head. RM kicked him in the stomach. The feeling of flesh enfolding his Doc Martins gave him a sensuous pleasure, and he did it again. After that he had to wait for his victim to get his breath back and to stop vomiting. From the smell Nelson had dirtied himself.

RM asked, 'What's the number?'

84

Nelson's words were all breath and no voice. 'Don't know... didn't... write down.'

RM ground Nelson's face into the tarmac. 'Get back in there and switch on whatever you have to switch on. We want that number monitored day and night.'

He was tempted. Another boot to the guts would round off things properly.

A voice called from an upper window. 'Hey, you. What the hell's going on down there?'

RM jumped back and stabbed a finger at Nelson. 'You get that number, mate, or you're dead.'

He would have liked to walk away. The last RM would have, he reckoned, but his nerve broke and he took to his heels.

Chapter 36

Nelson wanted to lie on and die. His chest hurt like hell and a punch had caught his bad wrist. Fear got him moving. If he didn't someone would call an ambulance and if the hospital kept him in he was dead anyway. He used the van's bumper to get started and the ridge of the drainage channel on the roof to straighten himself as best he could. He was on his feet and feeling for broken bones when help arrived.

'Are you all right? I thought I was dreaming. A mugging and in broad daylight?'

Nelson only had breath for a, 'Yeah.' His ribs hurt, God did they hurt, but they felt intact.

The engineer said, 'Hang on, I'll call an ambulance.'

'No.' He grabbed the engineer to stop him from rushing off. 'Get me inside.'

They started for the building and he heard the engineer sniff. 'Sorry,' he said. 'A bloody mugger and he scares the....' He stopped, too embarrassed to continue.

The few steps to the front door tore at every nerve-ending in his body. Luckily the toilets were on the ground floor. The engineer left him there on the excuse of getting old work clothes out of Nelson's locker.

They kept big plastic bags in the toilets for towel waste. Nelson emptied his pockets and dumped all his clothes into one. The face that stared back at him from the mirror looked grey and sagging. He was crying when he stumbled into the shower. Stood with his eyes closed so that he couldn't see the flow of discolored water.

He didn't dare stay long. The other engineer would get anxious and he had to be away before anyone else arrived. He dried himself with paper towels, dressed in clothes that had been left out for him and went into the control room. He still felt bad, his chest and shoulders hurt where he had taken the kicks and his bad hand couldn't do up a button.

He straightened himself at the door and pretended to be fine. The engineer looked relieved, especially when he said he would call with the police on his way home and report the attack. He said he could murder for a cup of tea and shuddered at his choice of words. The engineer rushed off to make him one.

Nelson went to the computer console and typed in the instructions. Day and night, any call to Mrs. Bradley's number would be logged, and this time he would give it to them.

Chapter 37

Ronnie had his feet on the desk. Past mid-morning and time for a relaxing can of beer. A couple of phone calls to London, a vague reminder of favors owed and things were going his way again.

Finish the beer, he thought, then get the secretary in. He glared at the girl showing on a monitor aimed to look down the V in her blouse. She'd let Jimmy stroke her for nothing but charged him a tenner for not much more. This time he wanted a freebee, would insist on it.

The last thing Ronnie needed was RM arriving back, full of his own importance at a job well done.

'Well?' asked Ronnie, suddenly anxious. He couldn't afford another cock-up with Jimmy making waves.

'Went like a dream, boss.'

'You didn't overdo it?'

RM put thumb and forefinger together. 'Judged it to a T. Nelson will be like putty from now on.'

Tension oozed out of Ronnie. He felt generous enough to toe the six-pack on the floor. 'Help yourself.'

RM took a can and gabbled on about doing this and saying that, about someone shouting at him, and him giving them the finger and walking away. Ronnie pretended to listen and wondered just how far RM's blind confidence would take him. *As far as…?*

He shushed RM down at the point where the getaway car started to burn fiercely, and said, 'There's a bonus for this morning's work.' Saw RM's eyes light up and added, hastily, 'Not much.' He leaned closer and stared him in the eye. 'The big money's for the big work, if you see what I mean.'

RM sprawled in his chair, arms and legs akimbo, his face glowing from self-adulation. 'Any time, boss, I'm your man.'

Prick, thought Ronnie, and dropped his voice to a whisper as if the wall had ears. 'There's changes coming at the top. Some people are out and some are in. They're looking for new… members. I'm….' He decided not to boast about his coming promotion to the inner circle. Jimmy might hear and take it as a warning. 'You're in. As for some others, arrangements will be made to terminate their… association.'

He let seconds tick by, trying to judge RM's reaction. It seems good, he thought, seeing RM's jaw harden. The idiot's taking the hint.

Just to be sure he added, 'For instance, Jimmy and Doc, who needs them?'

RM sat upright. 'That's big work. Big enough for a car?'

'A nearly new one,' said Ronnie, laughing inwardly at his greed. Whoever killed Jimmy and Doc would end up dead. Their friends would see to that. He'd only be out the price of three wreaths.

Jimmy had arranged to call again on Friday to discuss what they should do about Nelson. Ronnie's whole body bubbled with excitement. What if RM was waiting – Ronnie glanced at the disused factory across the way – waiting to take his shot the minute Jimmy and Doc stepped out of their car? He could see the shock on their faces as the first bullet hit, then their bodies jerking this way and that as bullet after bullet tore through them.

Dumdums, he thought. After years of Jimmy fighting him at every turn and being ignored – *why shouldn't people pay protection money?* – he didn't want Jimmy dead. He wanted his body so torn that all they could do was hose it down the nearest drain.

Of course he'd have to be careful because some people in the Organization wouldn't like it. He'd claim that he'd planned to warn Jimmy about RM. That RM blamed Doc for the death of his predecessor and friend, and was threatening to do something about it. There was no way that he, Ronnie, could know that things would happen so quickly and so violently.

RM of course wouldn't be there to say otherwise. This was one time he could use his legally held pistol to bring down a rabid gunman. *They might even give me a medal.*

Afterwards, the place would be crawling with police. *Better make sure there's nothing on the premises they would take exception to.* As for the media, he'd have to work on some suitable platitudes about the loss of a respected colleague.

In fact, he could bleed all over the television about how the killing of RM, no matter how justified, still haunted his dreams. Maybe front a "Mother's Against Guns" movement? Make himself famous nationally as well as locally.

He glanced over at RM who had gone quiet. Dreaming of his new car, he assumed, and was surprised when RM said, 'I prefer the AK-47. It's sweeter than the Armalite and there's less chance of a blockage.'

'I can get you one, no problem,' said Ronnie.

Together, they worked out the details of the planned hit. If Jimmy came alone, fine. But if Doc came with him, RM would have to be sure of them both. Even a winging would allow a few good men on the ground to terminate their association.

A neat phrase, Ronnie noted it for future use. He got rid of RM and told the secretary to come in.

Chapter 38

Jimmy had told Ronnie that he'd call again on Friday if they still hadn't heard from Nelson. Ronnie planned things accordingly. Even with a nod of approval from his friends in the Organization, he still felt nervous and went about things circumspectly. Certain of his drivers were detailed for runs that would have them back to the yard before Jimmy was due. He told them nothing, but they were experienced men and would know what to do when the time came.

Ronnie rated Arthur Anderson the pick of the bunch. Arthur was tall and thickly built, all muscle from decades of humping packages on and off lorries. Arthur could hurt a man or beat him to death, depending on his orders and the money on offer. Arthur was scheduled for an exceptionally short run on the Friday morning, then told to stay handy. For sending two bastards to hell, thought Ronnie.

Arthur nodded his understanding that his special talents might be needed and was casual about the whole thing. Ronnie gritted his teeth. Even on stand-by Arthur would expect a bonus and Arthur didn't come cheap, which was why he tended to use RM.

Ronnie spent Thursday evening with a group trying to raise funds for a community center. The committee was concerned because twenty-five percent of the total cost was for *protection* to prevent vandalism during the build. Ronnie put a fifty-pound note in the collection box, safe in the knowledge that an acceptable percentage of the protection money would come his way.

Once home he phoned Nelson and got the usual negative report. He rang Jimmy straight away and confirmed that Jimmy intended to call about noon. Ronnie didn't even bother going to bed. He knew he wouldn't sleep and his wife would give him hell if he tossed and turned.

As early as he dared, he grabbed fresh clothes from the hot-press and drove down to the depot. Saw the lorries off and made sure the drivers on short runs knew to get back by eleven at the latest.

RM staggered in late, his breath stinking of stale booze. He still wore yesterday's clothes. They looked like they'd been dragged through a hedge backwards. Ronnie made him hold his hands out in front of him. They shook.

'Oh for god's sake,' he exploded.

RM shoved them deep in his pockets. 'The hair of the dog and they'll be fine.'

Ronnie grabbed him by the shirt and gouged knuckles into his chest. 'You touch another drop and I'll kill you myself.'

'Just kidding, boss,' gasped RM. 'Just kidding.'

'See that you are,' said Ronnie, sourly.

He dragged RM to the window and pointed to the factory across the way. 'Third floor, fourth window over, that's the place you want.' He made himself sound confident, though now, when it was too late, he realized he should have got Arthur to do the job. He nervously checked the time on his watch, as if that would help. Negotiating Arthur down to a reasonable sum usually took days, time he didn't have. He sighed and glanced across at the factory. Even with the shakes RM could hardly miss at that distance.

He said, to be encouraging, 'Remember, wait until they're both well clear of the car before you fire.'

He told the secretary to make himself and RM a cup of coffee. It steadied RM who slipped away to get ready. Left on his own Ronnie moved restlessly about the office. Had a whiskey poured before he realized that he didn't dare drink. He needed a clear head for later. He poured the alcohol back into the bottle and called the secretary in. They played about for a while but he couldn't build up any real enthusiasm. Felt she'd only given him five-pounds worth when she held out for twenty. He gritted his teeth and paid up.

Once he had the room to himself he unlocked the safe, lifted out a chamois package and unrolled it to reveal a pistol: A Smith & Weston, Model 27 .357in Magnum. A gun he'd chosen carefully. It had a short, 9cm barrel and wooden contoured grips. Deadly at close quarters and easy to conceal.

He pulled out the ammunition clip and checked the firing action a few times. It worked perfectly. He reloaded the gun, slipped it into his jacket pocket and tried on the jacket on for comfort. The bulk of the gun made the coat bulge, but he intended to keep his hand in the pocket for a quick draw.

The thought of a wounded Jimmy or Doc coming at him gave him the shivers. He'd shoot if necessary, then claim they'd staggered into his sights just as he shot at the gunman. He'd never forgive himself, he'd tell the police, because Jimmy was a friend from way back. One of the best. The Smith & Weston was a legally held handgun, so no problem there. *But it would cost me that medal.*

Getting nearer the time he made a couple of trips to the front door to make sure that the men were in position. In between trips, he fiddled with the computer. Found himself preparing a eulogy for Jimmy – and hastily deleted it.

At long last he saw Jimmy's taxi turn into the street.

Over anxious, Ronnie pulled the gun from his pocket and checked the load. He hurried to the front door and couldn't resist looking up at the old factory as he came into the daylight. He could see nothing, but RM should be able to see him and know that they were coming. Hopefully the stupid bugger hadn't nodded off.

Chapter 39

Doc was driving. He saw Ronnie standing on the front step, and frowned. Ronnie hadn't greeted Jimmy at the front door in a long time. *If ever.* He couldn't see RM's slim shape among the group of men waiting with Ronnie, *not that he rates in that company.* The men there were the sort he didn't turn his back on and it wasn't like Ronnie to let men hang around doing nothing. He took a good look at Ronnie himself. *There's more than a hand in that jacket pocket.*

Doc slowed the taxi, by-the-way steadying himself for the turn. The men were relaxed, their hands busy with cigarettes.

If anything was planned, he thought, those fags would be underfoot by now. The men were looking in his direction, their mouths open. They were laughing at him and Jimmy, good-humored stuff, knocking the opposition.

Still? He slowed further.

'What's up?' asked Jimmy. He wound down the window and held the Walkman up to adjust the sound.

Doc's eyes scoured the area restlessly looking for who, what and where. The why he left to Jimmy. He reckoned any attack would come from across the street.

'Window up,' he said.

Jimmy wound it up immediately.

Doc drove past Ronnie and the group of men. Instead of reversing into the yard gateway to turn, he nosed in and reversed out. Hated having his back to trouble, even for a moment. Drove back down the street and stopped beside Ronnie.

Jimmy was on the pavement side. He unbuckled his seat belt. Doc unbuckled his as well, but sat on with the engine running.

'That's right,' Jimmy said. 'Keep yourself nice and safe and bugger me.'

'I don't have to get out,' said Doc.

Jimmy put a hand on the door handle, then looked over at him. 'Normal rules apply. Okay?'

'Got you.'

Doc watched Jimmy ease himself among the men. A word here, a joke there. The men closed around him, all keeping a respectful distance: no one threatening, all hands in sight.

Ronnie approached the taxi. The windows were up and the doors locked, even so Doc's hand rested on the breast pocket of his jacket.

Ronnie said, 'It's too hot to be sitting in there.'

'Leave him, he's in one of his moods,' said Jimmy and walked on into the building. He was now too far away for a quick retreat. Even so Doc kept the engine running.

The men grouped at the front door tried to bring him into their conversation, but they were used to Doc being antisocial and quickly ignored him. He sat stiff in his seat. His eyes the only part of him that moved. They went from mirror to mirror, constantly watching his back. The rest of him focused on his senses. Sound, sight, smell were fine. He went deeper, following his instincts. Sweat stood on him in the hot, sealed taxi but he felt a chill on his right side. The across-the-street side. More than that, high up on the point of his shoulder. Knew now where to go looking.

Jimmy was back in a couple of minutes, swinging his jacket as if he hadn't a worry in the world. Doc leaned across and unlocked the door to let him in. Ronnie stood in the doorway of his offices, hand still in his jacket pocket, politely waiting to see them off.

He hasn't done that in a long time either, noted Doc.

'Total a waste of time,' said Jimmy as he pulled on his seatbelt. 'Nothing to report. No phone calls from Bradley, or so Nelson says. Ronnie is talking about taking him out. I told him to give it another week.'

They stayed tense until they were out of the narrow streets of crumbling houses, and onto a broad link road.

Jimmy settled himself back with a sigh of relief and wiped at his forehead. 'What now?'

'Don't know.' Doc indicated and pulled in. 'I'll take a shufti around.'

They crossed at the boot of the taxi: Doc heading for the pavement, Jimmy the driving seat.

Doc said, 'You're safe enough for the weekend anyway. They'll have to rethink things.'

'So?'

'So I'll be away for a couple of days.'

Jimmy put a hand on Doc's arm. 'Don't do anything I wouldn't.'

Chapter 40

Access to the factory Doc found easy. There were more breaks in the security fencing at the back than gaps in a crone's teeth. He slid into the recess of an alley and kept an eye on an old red Fiat parked in the shadow of the factory. He was hardly in the recess when RM scurried out of the building carrying a wrapped package in his hands. Something long and thin, noted Doc, and stayed perfectly still as RM took a quick look around. Apparently satisfied that no one was watching, RM shoved the package into the boot of the car.

The old lust for a kill was in Doc again. And with it a sense of freedom he hadn't felt since the ceasefire years back. Ronnie and his cronies had tried to kill Jimmy, and failed. *Now it's my turn.*

Doc shook off that sense of freedom – *emotion can get you killed* – as RM drove off. RM travelled fast and bumped over rough ground rather than follow the old paths to the gates. Doc backed into a doorway and stayed there until the red car was out of sight. It gave him time to work out who and what.

The men at the door into Ronnie's offices had been relaxed and RM was disposing of the gun. Therefore, almost certainly, only the two of them, Ronnie and RM, were involved in the assassination attempt. Next time would be different.

Satisfied that RM had gone, he crossed the road at a brisk pace and entered the factory grounds through a gap in the fencing. RM had left a side door swinging open. Doc slipped into the building and stood, getting the feel of things. Heard the sound of drips and bits crumbling away, the filtered noise of the world outside and the grating of old hinges in the constant breeze that snaked through the building.

Once his eyes adjusted to the gloom he moved on. He didn't really expect booby-traps, too many children played there from time to time. Even so he stepped cautiously and avoided all heaps of rubbish and loose debris. He climbed the stairs, keeping close to the handrail, and always inspected the underneath of the next flight before trusting himself on it.

On the fourth floor he moved into the workrooms proper. The factory had been stripped down to its fundamental rawness and lay exposed to the elements. The floor was wooden, ripped up in places and covered in grit from the crumbling lime plaster. Iron pillars acted as Acrow Props to support the ceiling. The pillars were thin, too thin to conceal a man. Even so Doc's eyes and head twisted and turned as he exposed himself to ambush. He stayed tight against the wall and stepped quietly as he eased along until he got to the first of the windows.

He checked height and angle. He could see the roof and part of the wall of Ronnie's building, but not the street. He left the way he had come and went down to the third floor.

The third floor felt right. Old wooden crates lay scattered about. One had been dragged through the grit towards a window and its top was smeared from a rough dusting. At the window, cobwebs had been broken down as if someone had leaned against the widow frame to get the right angle.

Doc checked the angle of fire from each window and then went back to the fourth window for final confirmation.

He was smiling as he went home to pack. He had a flight to catch.

Chapter 41

RM was hardly in the door of the office before Ronnie had him by the throat. Ronnie's words were a torrent of expletives as he bashed RM repeatedly against the door. Finally he threw him to the ground and kicked.

RM lay groaning. Ronnie hauled him to his feet and shook him until blood trickled from his nose. 'Why the hell didn't you shoot? We had them.' Blood dripped onto his hands. He cursed, wiped them clean on RM's shirt and shoved him clear.

RM propped himself up against the door. Ronnie hoped he'd go down again. He'd kick him back to his feet.

RM said, 'Boss, Doc never got out. He always does.'

'You're a moron,' shouted Ronnie. 'All you had to do was get Jimmy. I could've shot Doc through the car window.'

RM hunted for a tissue and held it against his nose. 'You never said.' Ronnie lashed out at him again, but he twisted away and managed to avoid the worst of the blow. 'Boss, go easy.' Ronnie was between him and the door. He backed off towards the window as Ronnie came at him, fists already up.

The phone rang. Not the ordinary office phone but a direct line, the one Ronnie used for private calls. Ronnie stopped in mid-stride, drawn to answer the call but still wanting to beat RM to pulp. That call could be from anybody, the sort of people who took it as an insult if they weren't answered first ring, and could do something about it.

Ronnie rushed to answer the phone, shouting at RM as he went. 'I pay you to use your loaf.'

He snapped up the receiver. 'Yes?'

A hesitant voice said, 'Mr. Fetherton, this is Yeovil at the agency.'

'What the hell do you want?'

'You said anything unusual….'

'What about the shipping rates to the mainland?'

'Sssssorted,' stuttered Yeovil. 'But sssomeone booked a flight to England. I I I thought you should know.'

RM was already at the door, opening it a crack to slide through. Ronnie ached to get at his throat. 'We had them. We had them,' he raged.

'Pardon?' said Yeovil.

98

'We'll get them the next time,' said RM and added by way of mitigation. 'I could do with a bit of backup. It's not easy doing it all…'

The door clicked shut behind him.

Ronnie felt the worst of his temper subside as he watched RM flee. He nodded in agreement but his words were still bitter. 'Aye, someone who knows what they're doing instead of a stupid plonker like you.'

He listened with half an ear to the rest of what Yeovil had to say. Jimmy would be back on Tuesday. He'd arrange things for then. Maybe talk to someone first.

Chapter 42

Doc caught the 18.30 flight out of Belfast City Airport to Birmingham, flight time one hour. Even with carrying only hand luggage it still took him half-hour to clear the airport terminal. Mainly because he went on a long curving stroll that brought him to the rear of the taxi rank.

He walked the length of the parked-up taxis, glancing in at the drivers as he passed. Nodded back to any man that looked at him but recognized none, and finally joined the long taxi queue. When his turn came he got a driver from Lithuania. The man had good English but had been on the job for only one week. 'I first postman. Birmingham I know,' he reassured Doc.

Doc nodded, said, 'Holiday Inn, Coventry Road,' and busied himself reading a file of conference papers. After a while he looked up. Checked behind as if to see where they'd come from and tapped the driver on the shoulder. 'Where are you going?'

'Holiday Inn Express, Coventry Road. You say.'

Doc tapped his forehead in pretend disgust. 'I did, I did. This time it's a Holiday Inn in the city center, the Smallbook.'

'No problem,' said the driver and indicated off to the left. 'That way, but much extra cost.'

'My fault,' said Doc. After that he paid attention to where they were going, sitting comfortably in the corner of the back seat with a good view out the rear window. No following cars or taxis copied their unexpected change in direction.

Birmingham, to Doc, looked like every other city: concrete through-ways and backed-up traffic. The city center choked with cloned multi-national shops. If Liverpool was the second capital of Ireland then, Doc reckoned, Birmingham was an important city of the Indian Subcontinent. White skin would tend to stand out, at least be more noticeable. Something he'd have to remain aware off.

Eventually they reached the Holiday Inn in the city center. Reception was straight across from the glass entrance. Much more open than Doc would have liked, but they already had his reservation under the name of Frederick Robinson.

'Second floor, room to the rear as requested, Sir,' said the smiling receptionist.

They'd given him a double room with a king size bed and acres of space to walk around. The dominant colors were brown and white, and the room had an air of lightness about it. Doc put down his bag and drew the curtains before he put on the light. Consulted the menu and rang Room Service. Ordered steak and chips, with tiramisu to follow. Had a quick shower and shave while he waited for his early dinner to arrive.

Once the meal had been delivered he pulled on a pair of surgical gloves. Fingerprints and DNA in the room were irrelevant because the bill of "Frederick Robinson" would be honored. What he didn't want was to leave proof that he'd even touched the local telephone directory.

He took the directory out of the drawer, from under the Gideon bible, and read it while he ate. He kept his copy of Jimmy's telephone bill beside him for reference even though he had two numbers memorized. Both began with 0121, the Birmingham area code. He consulted "Taxis and Private Hire Vehicles" and quickly found one number. He memorized the firm's address and traced it on a local street directory. Quite a distance away, he discovered, and he'd be walking. The other number remained elusive though he consulted the index and tried "Limousine Hire" and a number of categories under "vehicle". Did the man he was looking for have a HGV license? He thought so and tried "Road Haulage". After that pages and pages of hotels and guesthouses. Still no sign of the number.

He had a think about it while he ate his tiramisu. He could always ring the number from a phone box but, now with mobile phones on the go, phone boxes were hard to come by except in public areas like train stations and bus stations where there was CCTV.

Whatever it took, his wife had to be found and dealt with. Her running off with the local waster had made him look foolish and vulnerable. *Otherwise Ronnie wouldn't have dared try it on.*

A spot of cream fell onto his trousers. It made him wonder if he was mad leaving all his other clothes in the old house. Perhaps madder than usual, he conceded. This was the suit he'd worn the day his wife ran out on him. Any more than that he couldn't bear to take with him.

The house! He slapped his forehead in disgust. Houses being sold and bought needed solicitors. A quick scan of local solicitors in Yellow Pages and he had a match for the second number.

He put the telephone directory back in the drawer, took off his gloves and put them in his pocket for later use. Slipped out of the hotel as unobtrusively as possible. He did consider taking the steak knife with him. His main reason for ordering a steak was to have a weapon handy. Unfortunately the staff might notice the knife missing and the police get lucky and trace it back to the hotel. He'd just have to use what came to hand at the time.

He enjoyed the walk. The headquarters of the taxi firm was a long way from the hotel, but the night remained pleasant, dry with a hint of chill in the air. Then there was the anticipated pleasure of seeing the waster's fear when they came face to face. This is business, Doc reminded himself. If she has to die to make certain people back off, so be it.

The headquarters of the taxi firm was in a side street. A well-lit building with a front reception room for passengers. Doc took station in a dark doorway across the street and watched the drivers coming and going.

Few passengers actually called at the taxi firm. Mostly the drivers seemed to respond to telephoned requests for a lift, so they came and went on their own. Something useful that Doc noted for again. After midnight, he warmed himself with a cup of hot coffee bought from a nearby hot-food outlet and walked back to the hotel by a different route. On the way he had a look around the outside of the solicitor's premises.

Chapter 43

Kristi rang for Paul to come. She cried down the phone. Paul hauled on a pair of trousers, and ran barefooted across the yard and into the house through the never-locked back door. As he raced up the stairs, he had the impression of opulent furnishings set against a background of restful pastel colors.

He stopped on a landing as big as a small bungalow and shouted, 'Which room?' Kristi appeared in a doorway. Paul got a flash of thigh as she threw a red dressing gown around her and knotted the belt. An old one of Ken's, he guessed, worn shapeless and far too large for her.

She gulped. 'In here.'

"In here" was a bedroom that had cost more to furnish than all of Paul's old house. Doors led off it into dressing rooms and an *en suite*. The carpet was thick enough to trip over and the plasterwork on the ceiling above the bed had been replaced by a mirror.

Ken was pacing the bedroom floor, fully dressed down to one sock, no shoes.

'She needs the run,' he was saying and sounded angry. He didn't seem to think anything unusual about Paul appearing in his bedroom. 'There you are, get Girl out. We'll give her a trial on her own.'

'Now?' asked Paul.

'Yes, now,' said Ken. 'She still gets her feet in a muddle at that first bend.'

Paul knew that Girl needed work. Her lack of balance going into the bends cost her lengths. *But at half-three in the morning?* Pitch black outside and the track with no lights.

He made himself focus on the problem of Ken. Ken's eyes were wide and virtually unblinking. Right then he seemed to be hunting for the second sock. He held it in his hand. Kristie kept wiping at tears in her eyes.

'Doctor?' Paul said to her.

Kristie said, 'He's on his way.'

But Ken was already shouting over her reply, 'I already told you. The only thing I need around here is a bit of cooperation.'

He tried to push past Paul but Paul stood on, jamming his arms and elbows against the door frame as an additional help to keep his balance. He felt shaken. He'd put Barbara through worse than that the day he'd grabbed the kitchen knife. *Thank God she managed to get me out of the house.*

Ken's muscles were so bulged with tension that he appeared to have put on weight. If he turned on Kristie Paul didn't know if he'd the strength to save her from this madman.

Paul said, 'We should have our breakfast first.'

Having breakfast would buy them time until the doctor came. Eating tea and toast might help calm Ken.

Ken stopped trying to push past. He glared at Paul. 'That's typical of you, any excuse not to work.'

'Thanks,' said Paul.

'You're fired,' said Ken.

'I want my pay, my cards and a good reference,' said Paul.

Ken tried to push past him again. 'You'll get them.'

'Now, please,' said Paul, his shoulders starting to burn from the effort of holding Ken back. His arms and elbows had to be bruised.

'After I've galloped Girl.'

There was something annoying about Ken in this mood that made Paul want to snap back at him. Say something like, 'If I'm not here, Girl's not here.' But Ken needed calmed, not worked into a frenzy.

Paul played on Ken's innate decency. 'It's this fantastic new job I've been offered. I have to get the reference to them straight away or they'll give the job to someone else.'

'So you're leaving me?' said Ken.

'You just fired me.'

Ken looked around him, and seemed to register the sock in his hand and the fact that he was dressed. 'You burst into our bedroom in the middle of the night demanding a reference? Are you mad or something?'

'Totally,' said Paul, wondering if madness was a safe subject.

'And I'm even madder to think about doing it.' Ken sounded disgusted with himself. 'You'll get your reference in the morning – after breakfast.'

He undressed and got back into bed. Curled up into a fetal position and pulled the duvet over his head.

Paul watched Ken's shape in the ceiling mirror as it stretched out and appeared to relax. He tried not to imagine other images that that mirror had reflected over the years.

He was still standing wondering what to do next when Ken started to snore. Kristie motioned they should leave, so they tiptoed downstairs and drank coffee while they waited for the doctor. Paul sat at the kitchen table. Kristi stood with her elbows on the breakfast bar for support. Every minute or two she slipped up the stairs and listened to make sure that Ken still breathed.

She needed two hands to stop the mug rattling against her teeth. 'Will he be all right?' she asked.

'Give him a few days and he'll be fine.'

He didn't believe that. Ken was teetering on an edge of a nervous breakdown, and he still had to lose the house that had been in his family for countless generations. He'd talked of nothing else in the days following Girl's entry in the Rosebowl, endlessly repeating himself.

Paul had heard a lot of things, including intimate family details. How Ken had met Kristi. That she wasn't always faithful, but would always come back to him. Nothing in organized memories, just bits and pieces as they forced themselves, haphazard, to the surface.

Girl had kept Ken going. Bankruptcy procedures would be underway about the time of the Rosebowl final and he had become obsessed with the idea of going out on a high note.

Chapter 44

Finally the doctor came. 'The man needs to be hospitalized,' he said after a brief examination.

Paul had enough personal experience to know that for himself. However Kristie refused to sign the papers. If the bank heard that Ken was in a psychiatric hospital they'd foreclose straight away, and Kristie couldn't bring herself to let that happen.

The doctor was Ken's age and it was too early in the morning for him to be bothered with a surgery manner. If Kristie refused to sign, then on her own head be it. That and the bother that went with a patient who needed 24/7 supervision. Ken was in bed and he was staying there. If he wouldn't take his tablets Kristi was to ram them down his throat. She had done it often enough with the dogs to have the knack. If that didn't work then definitely hospital and no argument.

Paul knew that he couldn't cope with all the kennel work on his own but felt he had to try. Kristi said she'd help when she could.

By that time the day proper had started. Paul went straight through from morning feed to evening kennels with only a break in-between to grab some tea and toast.

In fits and starts, with breaks to sip tea or to answer the doctor's questions, Ken slept for two days. Kristie barely left his bedside. The second day for Paul was no better, with the sun beating down on his head and a million things to be done.

He felt restless and jaded when finally the last dog was locked up for the night. He was glad of the company when Kristi called him into the house. He sat at the kitchen table and wondered if he would be able to get his legs going again. The stairs into the granny flat seemed as steep as a mountain.

Kristie had supper for him, fine sliced ham and potato salad. She said, 'You can have a steak if you want, I thought you'd be too tired.'

He told her honestly that it was fine. The worst of his exhaustion disappeared as he ate. He hadn't taken time to eat properly in two days and had to fight an urge to bolt his food. Kristi stood and talked to him and was friendly.

She was blunt too. 'I was wrong about you at the start, I thought you were no good.' Paul could only shrug as she poured herself a mug of coffee and sat down across from him. She had her elbows on the table, definitely hair-down time. 'Greyhound people tend to look like escapees from a jumble sale, all talk and no work. If they can't do the double they're not interested, and anything not tied down is likely to disappear.' She smiled, remembering. 'You looked no better, Ken always was a sucker for strays.'

'Thanks,' said Paul, and raised a smile back.

'I missed that you were clean shaved, and that your van was spotless inside and out. Mind you, your clothes needed ironing. Still do.' He remained silent, sat back and sipped at his coffee. She said, 'I enjoy being a bitch, but I'm seldom vindictive.'

He assumed that was the nearest thing he'd ever get to an apology.

She stayed silent for a while before, hesitantly, broaching personal problems. 'It's not the dogs, or the kennel sickness, or whatever. We had bad runs before and survived. It's Ken, he let the debt frighten him. He seems to have forgotten the skills that made him king of the tracks.'

She poured Paul more coffee without asking. He sat quietly, waiting, aware she wanted to ask him something. She sat down again and popped up almost immediately to clear away his plate. Paul small-talked about the dogs. The only way he knew to make her relax and come to the point.

She poured herself a third cup of coffee. He refused a refill afraid it would put him past his sleep. Kristi perched herself against the sink as if to distance herself from him.

She said, 'I remember one night I went to the track with Ken. He looked at the dogs running in the second race. He knew nothing about the dogs, but he knew the owners and trainers. One of the runners, the kennel was out of form; another, the owner wasn't doing the dogs right; a third was having a bad run of luck; the fourth dog carried an injury, Ken spotted that when they were parading. The fifth, its breeding: sprinters not stayers, was totally wrong for a 550 race.' She smiled, remembering, obviously wishing that it were now. 'We won ten thousand that night.'

She used a tissue on her eyes.

'Don't you go sick,' warned Paul. 'There's only one of me.'

She came and sat down again, and asked. 'Were you ever in one of those places - He knew she meant a psychiatric hospital and couldn't bring herself to say it - did you ever see it happen to someone like Ken?'

'Me,' said Paul, shortly. 'About a year ago. It's not funny. If breathing wasn't on automatic you wouldn't be bothered.'

'What were they like?'

'Where I was they closed the doors.' He gave an involuntary shudder. 'I'll never be able to watch a prison film again.'

Kristi said,. 'If I didn't know better I might even feel sorry for you.'

He was in bed before he realized that he hadn't phoned Barbara in days. Which day he was too tired to remember.

Chapter 45

On Saturday morning, Doc enjoyed a lie-in. When he eventually got up he dressed in new cords and a zip-up jacket, and walked around the town center enjoying the bustle of people and, to him, their strange accents. He did the obligatory one-hour tour of the historic town hall. On the way back to the hotel he went into public toilets and dumped the packaging from various purchases.

Early evening he was again back in the dark doorway across from the taxi firm. The wind had got up and it was even colder than the first night. Even so he wore light clothes, bad-weather gear might restrict him if he had to act quickly. Gripping the metal of a newly purchased Stanley Knife transmitted some heat to chill fingers.

The feel of the Stanley Knife in his hand made him think clinically about the coming meeting with his wife and her lover. The slight tug on hand and wrist as the blade sliced flesh wouldn't do. Not in a strange city and not without backup. It had to be something relatively un-messy. He could force them to drink alcohol until they became totally inebriated and then help them choke on their own vomit. With alcohol in their system their bodies would burn better when he torched the house. Getting Hillary, his wife, to drink up might be a problem. She still thought sherry the drink of sophisticates.

Instead of the bitter nag who had driven him mad for years, an image came into his head of the bouncy young girl who had begged his help with her A Level studies and beyond.

The night she graduated Hillary called carrying a bottle of sherry and her certificate stating that she'd been awarded a First Class degree in Philosophy. He let her seduce him, each other really, and savored for the first time the heat of a woman.

Chapter 46

Being a Saturday night the taxi firm was busier than before. Drivers came and went in a steady stream, but the hours passed and the man Doc was looking for failed to show. At two in the morning he left and walked warmth into his body on the way to the solicitor's office.

The solicitor's office was in an old brick-built house with a heavy paneled front door. The windows were Georgian style, with six rectangles of glass in each frame. Doc hardly glanced in their direction as he passed. The only way through them, he knew, was either using a sledgehammer or forcing a catch and opening a window. Either of which would trigger the burglar alarm.

His way in lay to the back of the building, over a gate topped with six-inch spikes. He put on his gloves and zipped his jacket tight, grabbed the top of the gate and walked his feet up the wall until he could roll over the spikes and into the yard. The yard was clear of debris, being used during the working day to park cars. The properties on either side and in the street backing onto the yard were all commercial. Their windows all dark, little chance therefore of him being spotted.

The windows at the back of the solicitors' offices were sash frames with a large sheet of glass instead of the six smaller ones. Each sheet of glass was framed with a strip of metallic tape. Breaking that tape would interrupt the flow of electricity through it and again automatically trigger the burglar alarm. Doc produced a rubber sucker and a glass-cutter, bought that day from a large DIY store.

He stuck the rubber sucker to the center of the sheet of glass then cut around the sucker in a huge rectangle, keeping just clear of the metallic strip. A sharp tap and the whole sheet of glass came free. He lowered it gently to the ground and used a pencil torch to have a good look around the room. It was a staff rest room, with no furniture near the window, both good and bad for getting in. Doc removed the obligatory pot-plant from the window ledge, went back a few steps to gain momentum and dived through the opening. He rolled and came onto his feet, hand on a chair to steady himself.

He went from room to room looking for one file in particular. All the offices were like the staff rest room: functional, with good quality but aged furniture. The sort of parsimony that Jimmy would appreciate.

As he entered each room, especially rooms to the front, he held his pencil torch tight against his leg and aimed the beam towards the floor. That way the torch still gave enough reflected light to see around. A dim steady glow was unlikely to attract any attention, whereas a light flicking on and off or being flashed around a room was asking to be noticed.

Doc went into every room and searched every desk drawer and found no files. Not one left lying on a partner's desk or on the floor at a secretary's feet. Every file had been put into the vault over the weekend. The vault door had a quality lock, way beyond Doc's skills, and the key wasn't left lying around the office.

Neither did he find hard-copy address books for clients or unanswered correspondence. He fired up a secretary's computer and was immediately stymied by the demand for a password. "PASSWORD" didn't work, neither did the name of the firm. Frustrated he went back to the vault.

Failing a key, the easiest way into a vault was through one of the sidewalls. They were designed to keep fire out, not someone armed with a sledgehammer. Again he had to consider the noise factor. He'd come across less security in government offices and could see why Jimmy had picked this particular firm.

Time to go.

He'd seen a bundle of pound notes in a boss's office. A late payment of an account, he guessed. He went back and scooped the money into his pocket. He didn't like doing it but an ordinary burglar wouldn't hesitate, and that's what he wanted everyone to believe the break-in was about.

Bolts and an iron bar secured the backdoor, but it wasn't alarmed. Doc let himself out and stood for a time in the yard, undecided. Short of going back during working hours with a gun, there was no way he was going to get his wife's new address off that firm.

Her lover hadn't appeared at that taxi firm in two nights, so maybe he hadn't got the job. Maybe Jimmy was just booking a taxi to take them somewhere? Maybe he only worked days? Maybe he was happy to do as he did at home, slob around on the dole?

Starting first thing in the morning Doc had a lot of travelling to do up and down the country. Then a late flight back to Belfast. Sunday night into Monday was going to be another late night. He had things to do before Jimmy's visit to Ronnie on the Tuesday.

Still working out the logistics of the next day's travelling, Doc arrived at the gate topped with iron spikes. Again he grabbed the top bar and walked himself up the wall.

Four youths were leaning against the solicitor's front wall. They straightened up as Doc thudded onto the pavement beside them.

Chapter 47

The youths pushed themselves off the wall as Doc landed. They were "hoodie" types and had a street-awareness about them that Doc knew only too well. One of them held a Spliff. He couldn't understand why he hadn't smelled that if nothing else.

Stupid, stupid, he told himself, for planning ahead instead of concentrating on the job on hand.

'What you doing there, man?' asked one of the youths.

Doc mimicked a southern England accent. 'Just mind your own business, boys.'

The four youths moved to block his way. They were all about Doc's height, but of different ages. Two of them possibly the younger brothers of the one who appeared to be the leader. Doc envied them their thick tops against the biting wind even as they enclosed him in a tight semicircle.

Their leader was the broadest of the four if not the tallest. 'We'll take our share of what you got, man,'

Doc said nothing. Made sure the four stayed in his vision, and that one of them didn't try to sneak behind him.

A knife appeared in the leader's hand. The knife had a long, slim blade. He held it loosely, not expecting trouble, and winked at the two younger boys as if this was a game.

'Like all of it,' he said.

'Yeah,' said the second oldest youth. He reached under his thick top and produced a knife as well.

Even in the poor street lighting Doc could see that the younger brothers were impressed.

This, Doc decided, he could do without. The longer he hung around, the better their description of him. The thought of a multiple kill jangled in his system. There was bound to be a chase and a lot of blood. *I can't risk it.* Not in a strange city, with no safe house.

Anyway, the younger boys had still to be school age. They only deserved a lesson demonstrating that street crime had its downside.

The leader brought his knife up in a warning stab towards Doc's throat. 'Everything, man: money, wallet, keys to your wheels.'

Hand them his wallet with its plastic cards and driving license, and his carefully constructed other life of Fredrick Robinson would be compromised.

Now if it was only the money they wanted.

Doc caught the rising hand and twisted it, pulling the leader forward and sideways, blocking any retaliatory stab from the second knife. The leader's eyes widened in shock when the point of the knife rested on the hard gristle of his own windpipe. He tried to pull back.

It would have been nice to take his time but Doc had to think of the second youth and his knife. He increased the pressure. The blade slid into the leader's windpipe. Doc let go. The leader staggered back making sucking sounds, clawing at the knife.

The other youths were momentarily frozen in shock. Doc grabbed for his Stanley Knife, flicked the blade out and stabbed the second youth. The fine point sliced deep into his arm. Doc didn't have to be so wary of blood spatter this time, the thick material of the top would absorb most of the flow. The youth's arm flopped, the knife clattered onto the ground.

The youth fell to his knees. He kept trying to, but the fingers of the injured arm wouldn't grip the knife.

He sobbed, 'My arm won't work. My arm won't work.'

Doc said, 'It will when the doctors re-sow the tendons.'

If they could. Not that he cared.

The younger boys backed off from the threat of his Stanley Knife. Doc made a flicking motion with his fingers for them to go further. When they were at a safe distance he walked past the fallen youths and headed back to the hotel to rest up. On the way he dropped the Stanley Knife into an open culvert.

Ideally, he'd have liked to stay on in Birmingham until he could trace his wife and her lover, but Jimmy and his problems were more pressing.

And I complained about things being quiet!

Chapter 48

On Sunday morning the man known as Kyle headed to Luton. The house he was looking for lay in a pleasant area of the town but, unlike all the other houses around, it had been allowed to run down. The front garden was a mud patch and the focal point for much of the debris of the area.

A slatternly woman answered to his knock. She was red haired, blowzy and had a cigarette dangling from her fingers. Kyle stayed in the house for fifteen minutes and in that time she started two new ones.

He flashed a warrant card past her, giving her time to see what it was but not the name. 'Police,' he said.

She said, 'He didn't do nothing. He was here all night.'

'So was the Tom cat,' said Kyle. He tried to hold the woman's gaze but she wouldn't look at him. He said, 'I'm looking for Elaine Shaw.'

She said, 'This is a good house, this is. We don't want no trouble.'

He stepped forward and body pressured her back. He closed the door behind him. 'Elaine,' he repeated.

He looked in the living room door. A slob of a man with greasy hair and yesterday's food on his pullover, sat watching Grand Prix cars snarl around a circuit. He held a beer can in his hand, the crumpled remains of a six-pack lay at his feet.

The man said, 'I was here all night and I've got a solicitor.'

'I'm sure,' said Kyle. He turned away and raised his voice. "Elaine, Elaine Shaw.'

A young teenage girl appeared at the top of the stairs. She was white faced and her dress hung loose on her. Two young children joined her; they all stood silently watching.

'Come down,' he said.

She left the children and came down the stairs, sideways against the wall, trying to make little of herself.

The woman grabbed her and shook her. 'What have you been up to?'

'Nothing,' said the girl. 'Nothing.'

'This is a good house, this is. What are the neighbors going to say, the police calling and all?' She turned to Kyle. 'We're a good family, never in no trouble. You ask anybody.'

Her head jerked in the direction of the young girl. 'Her, she's from a bad lot, she is. Her mother, my sister, she was no good either.'

Kyle held out his hand to the girl. She flinched as if expecting a blow. He took her hand. Felt bone through skin that burned from an unhealthy heat. He said, gently, 'Elaine, do you remember me?'

She shook her head.

He said, 'I knew your mother, she was a good person.'

The woman snorted. 'You didn't know her then. I thought we'd have to move, the neighbors still throw it in our faces. On the game she was, her and the nobs. Though I suppose if you're going to do it you might as well get paid proper. Her and her hoity-toity ideas, too good for the likes of us she was.'

'I can imagine,' said Kyle. He said to the woman. 'I want to take Elaine into protective custody.'

'Is that what you call it these days? Have her, she's more trouble than she's worth.'

Elaine's big eyes filled with tears.

The woman grabbed her again. 'What did you do? What did you do?'

Kyle said, sharply, 'That's enough.'

The woman backed off.

Kyle looked at Elaine. 'Will you come with me?'

The woman said, 'You're going, whether you like it or not. And don't expect me to come visiting you in jail, I've got my good name to think about.'

'Go and pack,' said Kyle.

'And don't take nothing that don't belong to you,' said the woman.

Elaine hesitated. Kyle smiled encouragingly, the woman took a step forward as if to continue the assault. Elaine went up the stairs slowly. She was away two minutes and then came down the stairs even more slowly carrying a small picture in a frame and a koala bear.

'Is that it?' asked Kyle.

She nodded.

'Are you sure?'

She nodded again.

'Come on,' he said and took her to his car. He had parked it down the road in case the woman thought to note the registration number.

'Do you want to go back there?' he asked, when they were on their way.

She shook her head.

'Don't worry,' he said. 'They'll never hear from you again.'

Chapter 49

Doc rang from a payphone near Leytonstone Underground Station, and made sure the number was withheld.

The Man answered the call.

Doc said, 'This is Kyle.'

'Good afternoon, Mr. Kyle,' said The Man, the perennial note of caution in his voice.

'I thought we should meet,' said Doc.

'Where are you now?'

'I'm in London, at Heathrow.'

'The usual place. Would two hours from now be sufficient?'

'Yes.' Doc hung up and went back into the underground. Leytonstone was two stops down from Redbridge station. Doc was there in ten minutes.

He emerged from the underground into the middle of a giant roundabout. After the burnt-electricity stink of the dank tunnels the traffic fumes were almost pleasant. Doc had checked out Redbridge before he went back to Leytonstone and made the call to The Man. He checked it out again because The Man had to know he was in England. Ronnie would have informed him that he'd used Ronnie's contact to buy his airline tickets instead of Far And Away Travel.

Again he walked quietly, very aware that this was a usual route and therefore suspect. Satisfied that all was as it should be, he took up position in a side street. He checked that his knife remained easy to get at. It was stubby ceramic knife, easy to get through airport security but difficult to replace. He kept it strictly for emergencies.

When the wind swirled he got the kitchen smells from the Chinese restaurant across the way. His hurried continental breakfast had been hours before. Hunger kept the mind sharp, still…

At two hours almost to the minute a cream Mercedes 500 pulled up outside the Chinese restaurant. The Man got out and stretched as if at the end of a long journey. It could have been, because he told no one where he lived. All calls were made and taken on a mobile phone. The car taxed and insured using The Man's office address in Westminster.

The Man was tall and heavily built, rotund without the muscle being in

117

any way slack. His hair was thinning but still dark, and gelled into place. He disappeared into the restaurant, moving quickly and lightly for his bulk.

Doc headed back the way he had come to the underground station. Waited until he heard the rumble of an east-bound train. Waited another two minutes and then walked directly down the main street to the restaurant.

The restaurant lights were dimmed to add atmosphere. There were few diners at that early hour and The Man had a table to himself, well away from everyone else. Doc joined him, they nodded to each other and he chose a chair where he could sit with his back to the wall. The Man used a *Harrods* aftershave. Very subtle and equally expensive.

Doc knew the exact brand of aftershave. He also had made it his business to find out a lot of other, personal, things about The Man. Things that The Man didn't want people to know. *Like his home address.*

The waiter came. He handed Doc a menu and walked away without speaking. The Man was a regular and had made it known that he did not appreciate casual conversation.

They ordered before they spoke. The Man asked for poached egg on toast. It wasn't on the menu but the waiter didn't object. Doc ordered spare ribs and sweet chili chicken with fried rice. The spare ribs came almost immediately. Doc scraped one onto The Man's side plate and began to eat, concentrating on not tearing the meat off the bone.

'I liked a man who can eat,' said the Man, patting his stomach.

Doc said, 'Running around Westminster should keep you fit.'

'My dear Mr. Kyle, one never runs in Westminster, one proceeds.'

They waited for the plates to be tidied away and main courses served. In The Man's case the poached egg on toast. Both of them looked around casually, checking for listeners-in.

The Man said, 'We are concerned, Mr. Kyle. And when I say we, I mean we are concerned at two unnecessary deaths.'

Doc said, 'There's others. Jimmy was nearly the last one.'

The Man's eyebrows raised in surprise. 'So it's not you?'

'Did someone say it was?'

The Man shook his head, refusing to be drawn, and began to eat. 'Things are starting to look very untidy,' he said between mouthfuls. 'What with Jimmy and Ronnie at each other's throats and the police asking questions. It makes one concerned.'

Doc continued to eat, knowing that a reply wasn't expected.

'Concerned too that you felt we should meet.'

'You like me to keep in contact,' said Doc, and didn't mind when his eyes flickered a frown, signaling a slight evasion in his answer.

The Man nodded slowly as if working things out in his head. Acting as if he didn't know that Doc had flown into Birmingham on Friday. 'So I assume there was also a personal reason for your visit?'

'Yes,' said Doc.

'Unresolved, I assume.'

Doc didn't answer. *A safe assumption.* There'd been no reports of a woman disappearing in the Birmingham area over the weekend, nor of an unidentified body being found.

The Man continued, 'One is also concerned at various incidents. Take that young man in Glenlish, garroting himself.'

'Most unfortunate,' said Doc. He tore at gristle to remind himself of RM's last moments. Analyzing it afterwards, it hadn't been such a bad killing after all, *but not one of my classics.*

'Were you ever in Glenlish yourself?' asked The Man, using his napkin to wipe delicately at a stray bit of egg.

Doc said, 'Once. The fellow I went with had borrowed the car off a friend.'

The Man looked shocked and dropped his next mouthful of food back onto the plate. He recovered and they continued to eat.

'Jimmy and Ronnie,' mused The Man. 'Both are loyal but Jimmy is his own man and Ronnie has ambitions.' He started to spin his butter knife, this way and that.

Doc finished his chicken. He put down his knife and fork, wiped his lips and waited. Said nothing.

'You obey orders.' said The Man. It was a question.

'Have I ever let you down?'

'This time it may be personal.' He continued to spin the knife to and fro.

Doc said nothing.

'Very personal.'

Again Doc said nothing. He watched a couple coming into the restaurant, *they look okay*, but remained aware of the knife turning from one side to the other.

The Man settled the butter knife back on the plate and used the napkin to dab at his mouth. 'One must consult.'

He signaled for the bill, which Doc paid, as usual.

Chapter 50

Being the weekend and early afternoon, the city-bound train had plenty of empty seats. Doc sat well away from anyone else, his back to the outer windows.

He couldn't make up his mind if The Man was warning him that certain influential people wanted Jimmy – and by inference, himself – dead, or if The Man was testing his own personal loyalty. *Knowing The Man it could be both.* There was no good worrying about it.

He recited a prayer of Jimmy's, from way back in the early days when the taxi business teetered on the verge of bankruptcy. "Dear Lord, if you have any more problems, hold them for a few days. I've enough to be going on with".

Doc made himself concentrate on people coming and going at the stations where the train stopped. The Man would have covered his own position by letting people know that they were meeting up in Redbridge. Things could get *interesting* at any time.

Redbridge was way out, almost at the end of the Central Line and there were a lot of stops: some underground, some over, on the way into the city. People mostly got on, few off. Doc watched them all, men and women alike. Assumptions about gender and safety had cost people their lives. And another dangerous assumption, but one reasonable to make. With CCTV in trains and around stations, he kept a special lookout for people wearing big hats or hiding their faces.

At Leyton two hoodies with lowered heads took the seats on either side of him, their hands concealed inside their tops. They could be holding anything in there, he reckoned, and quietly moved to the far end of the carriage. Their glares and their voices followed him.

'White pig.'

'Stinks don't it.'

A young West Indian girl, dark haired and attractive, appeared nervous. Doc gave her a smile and nod as she moved away from him.

Doc stayed on his feet in case the hoodies came after him. At Stratford station they made a point of walking the length of the carriage and pushing against him as they got out. He let them off with it. Their hands were showing and they made no attempt to box him in as they passed.

As the train pulled into Liverpool Street he saw the sort of man he was looking for. He stood near the end of the platform, right where the train came out of the tunnel into the bright glare of the refurbished platform. He wore a thin waterproof and a dark cotton Boonie hat, and kept his head low. Doc felt his blood start to sing as the man's gaze lingered on him for that extra instant.

That lingering look should not have happened, which meant the spotter was an amateur. All the same, whoever was coming for him could be better, *much better*. Doc made sure he didn't flick as much as an eyebrow in anticipation of the confrontation to come.

At Liverpool Street, he had to change lines. He had chosen the carriage that would stop right at the exit stairs. Something he'd double-checked on his way out to Redbridge.

Doc followed a moderate press of people out of the train and up the stairs. A half-turn to allow rushing teenagers to pass, gave him the chance of a quick look back. The man in the cotton Boonie strode up the platform towards him, but not rushing. The tick of danger in Doc's head heightened. Had there been someone else there, someone he'd missed? Someone who wasn't getting on the train?

With the press of people moving round him now it was too late to be sure. He walked on, stayed with the crowd. Made himself aware of footsteps behind and their speed.

He followed the signs upstairs and along corridors to reach the main concourse. Stood and studied a wall chart of the underground as if unsure where to go next. He needed the black line on the map, the Northern Line, heading north. That meant going deep into the bowels of the underground complex, long corridors and empty stairwells. CCTV cameras everywhere so his little ceramic knife would have to stay in its sheath. He bought himself coffee to-go at the concession stand and started down.

All of a sudden, from being one of a crowd, he found himself on his own: his feet rattling loudly on the stone stairs, his footsteps echoing along empty corridors. A musician playing a violin, not badly, was almost a relief. Doc was tempted to give the man a pound for effort, but that would have meant leaving his fingerprints.

Around the next bend he heard running footsteps coming from the opposite direction. Away from the Northern Line – North platform, and not towards it. He loosened the lid of the coffee container.

The footsteps got louder, almost drowning out the music.

The two hoodies from the train appeared. They said something to each other and their speed increased. *Seeing who gets to me first?* Doc saw the knives pulled from beneath their jackets and felt a glow of satisfaction that he'd picked up on the danger earlier. The hoodies might have been sent by an enemy, they might be opportunists wanting to *stick* him for an implied insult. Either way they were coming at him fast, the lighter one a stride ahead of the other.

Doc kept walking as if unaware of the danger. Kept his look casual, measuring the closing distance between them. Saw his opponents tense for the attack, their eyes wide and fluorescent against their black skin. Very black, central Africa somewhere, he thought as he flung the coffee at the second hoodie and used the palm of his hand to push the leading hoodie's knifepoint away from his stomach and past his side.

The second hoodie still stumbled forward, wiping at his face with one hand, the other hand slashing the knife at where he thought Doc was. Doc spun the first hoodie round and forced him to hold knife arm out. Let his friend run into the knife. They went down, stabbing at the other in their pain and fear. Blood and screaming bodies mingled on the tiled ground.

Doc walked on, slightly breathless from the effort. Came to the northbound platform. The young West Indian girl was there, the one he'd nodded to on the train. She looked shocked to see him, panicked even, and hurried up the platform towards the 'Way Out' sign. He let her go. What was he going to do, break her neck in front of fifty people? Anyway she was only a spotter. The real danger lay...

He put his back against the curved wall and watched. Someone was hovering on the exit stairs, just around the first turn and out of sight. He could tell that from the way people suddenly stepped sideways as they went around the corner. *The Girl?* He didn't think so.

Then he spotted the dark Boonie hat about a hundred feet down. Now he knew his target and the next train was due in two minutes. In a way he was disappointed. *More like a Ronnie effort than one by The Man.*

Dry diesel-fumed air started to push along the platform. *The train's coming.* Doc eased himself off the wall. He wandered casually to the edge of the platform and stopped with his toes over the yellow safety line. Now the station vibrated from the approaching mass of metal. The train showed as a faint glow around a bend, then a spotlight that funneled everything into its beam. The train took form, its noise became deafening, a controlled tumbling of thunder.

A shadow came flying at Doc. The man in the dark Boonie hat, ready for a quick shunt that would send him off the platform into the path of the train. Doc grabbed the man by the shoulders, let his momentum swing them half way around until the push of air flicked the hat off the man's head. They were teetering on the edge of the platform. The blast of air had passed. Now they were being sucked into the vacuum created by the oncoming train. Doc dug his heels in. The man's mouth opened, he's screaming, Doc thought, but the train was on them. Doc let go.

Chapter 51

Monday morning, first thing, Doc walked into Far and Wide Travel. JP, his nephew, looked both surprised and anxious at seeing him. JP had Jimmy's short height and Doc's fine build. Nights when he wasn't out with the boys he held judo classes in the local Community Centre.

Doc said, 'Flights to and from England over the weekend. I want to know who was on them, who booked the seats and when.' He put his finger on the page for emphasis. 'Specifically, I need information on anyone who booked late: name, address, through which travel agency. Photographs from the security cameras would be nice, if they can be got.'

'You don't want much,' said JP.

He looked at Doc for a long time. Doc waited patiently

JP said, slowly, 'There's a guy in England.'

'Don't ring. Go and see him.'

'I'd need to,' said JP in an "I'm not that stupid" tone. He thought for a moment. 'It won't come cheap.'

'Whatever it takes.'

'That sort of money ... I'd have to square it with dad first.'

Doc put the envelope Ronnie had given him, still unopened, on the desk. 'Cash you've now got. I don't want your father worried.'

Chapter 52

On Monday night, Kristi had to take Girl to The Arena for the first round of the Rosebowl. Paul didn't know the way. They couldn't risk him getting lost and Ken still needed constant supervision.

Paul was glad of the excuse not to go. Girl's presence in the field hadn't been commented upon by the newspapers. In their minds she was just one of the hopeful outsiders and would only become newsworthy if she got through a few rounds. At that point someone was bound to make the connection.

He saw Kristi off in the Mercedes, with Girl whirling in circles in the back, too excited to be on the road again to settle down immediately.

He felt restless and jaded when he finally locked up the last dog for the night. He could have done with someone to talk to, to help quell the buzz of thoughts in his mind. Things were coming back to him, more shadows of events than actual memories.

He looked in on Ken hoping he would be awake, but he heard the snores from the turn in the stairs and didn't bother going any further in case he disturbed him.

He let the big brindle out into the garden. The big brindle was content to follow at his heels. Suddenly Paul found darkness creeping over the garden. The passage of time without him being aware of it panicked him slightly. The same thing had happened during the last winter, when days could go by and he had no memory of what he had done or why. Quite often in those moods, he didn't eat and Girl had fared little better.

Chapter 53

Kristi arrived back noisily. She couldn't burn rubber with a dog in the back, but she revved the guts out of the engine and the force she used to close the car door after her nearly took it off its hinges. She didn't answer Paul's question, 'How did she do?' but stormed off into the house. A light came on in the bedroom and she started to scream at Ken.

Girl was fine, Paul discovered. She came bouncing out of the car, her tail whipping with excitement. Paul let her and the big brindle run loose in the yard while he got her supper and put it down in the open. She growled the big dog away when he tried to share her dish. He hunched down nearby. Girl snapped up mouthfuls of food, growling all the while.

Paul scratched the big dog's head. 'Women,' he said, as if that explained all. Girl let the big brindle share the final licks. Paul followed Kristi into the house.

Kristi was in the living room with Ken. He was slumped in the corner of the settee and looked like the end product of a night on the tiles. In spite of the heat he had his dressing gown pulled tight around him. Kristi ignored Paul at the French windows and continued to bang up and down the room, shouting. 'Look at this mess of papers you leave lying around. You've got your own study; use the damn thing. And look at that dressing gown you're wearing. It's a rag. It's high time you spent some money on yourself.'

Ken was wearing the red dressing gown she had hugged round herself the morning he took ill, taking comfort from his scent embedded in the material.

'Hallo, Paul,' said Ken. He looked relieved to see him.

Kristi turned on him as well. 'The two of you make a fine pair. All talk! I was never so embarrassed in all my life.' She snatched up glass of gin from the sideboard. Some of it slopped over the edge. She cursed and ground it into the floor with her foot. 'If we're going to live like pigs, we might as well act like them.'

'How did the dog do?' Paul asked, hoping to change the subject.

'Do? Do? What did you expect her to do when she spent the last week lazing around the kennels? Did anybody ever think of putting some work into her or, God forbid, taking her to the Arena to give her a run there? Oh no! That was too much like trouble.'

Paul knew that. Every time he had broached the subject of a trial Ken always replied, 'Later.' Or snapped, 'I know what I'm doing.'

He said, 'So that's it?'

Ken shrugged. He didn't know either.

Kristie wouldn't tell them. She had stood over the cameraman at the track until he had given her a DVD of all the races, and she made them watch them one by one. Girl was in the seventh race. They could only hear the commentary in snatches because she talked right through every race. 'At least she looked the part thanks to my grooming. I told everyone she'd had training problems – Kid Carbine, the previous year's winner, won the third heat easily – Training problems? Huh! More like trainer problems. You should have heard them laugh at me.'

Ken looked brighter. He was enjoying the racing and, in a perverse way, Kristi's temper. It was all shout with no bite.

The disc got to the seventh race. Kristi sat on the chair arm beside Ken and pointed to the screen. 'Now shut up you two – they hadn't spoken in minutes – and just see what you put me through tonight.'

The camera showed the dogs parading before the race. Only four dogs instead of the usual six; two had been withdrawn because of injury. The men looked at each other.

Ken dared ask, 'Kristi, did she qualify?'

'Watch!'

The missing runners were from traps two and six. Girl had drawn trap four, the coffin. She fought her handler as he put her into the box and her tail kept sticking out every time he tried to close the door.

'See,' exclaimed Kristi. 'She doesn't know what she's doing.'

Paul said, 'She's just being thick.'

He got a "What would you know about it?" snort in reply.

They could only watch. Kristi's constant, 'Look! Look at that!' kept drowning out the commentary.

Girl was slow away and the dogs from traps three and five came together pincering her out of a clear run from Trap four. She had to check immediately and was five lengths adrift of the leader at the first bend. She tried to pass the third dog, a big fawn, on the inside but he moved in and she checked again. The fawn stumbled as they turned into the home straight and threw his head high in agony as his wrist snapped. Girl had to check a third time as she swerved around him before stretching out in a hopeless pursuit of the leaders. The lack of gallops became obvious in the home straight. She finished a good fifteen-lengths adrift of the winner.

'See what I mean?' exclaimed Kristi, but by now the temper had gone and it was all for effect.

'She's through,' said Ken. 'That bet's starting to look good.'

'What bet?' asked Kristi.

'Girl.' Ken sounded surprised that she'd asked. 'I put two thousand on her. It was all I could scrape together.'

Paul was horrified. Kristi seemed less so. She wanted to know, 'What price did you get?'

'Two thousand to win two hundred thousand.' Ken made it sound like it was only a matter of picking up the check.

'For God's sake,' said Paul. He could see the temptation. Two hundred thousand would keep the bank happy for quite a while, but the odds were against Girl getting through the second round, let alone winning. A hopeless gamble by a desperate man. Made worse because it was Paul's his own bitch.

Paul went off to bed-down the dogs and stayed out of the way until Kristi called him in for supper. When finished he dared ask if he could ring home.

'I'll pay,' he added hastily.

She dismissed that out of hand, wished him good night and went on to bed.

He didn't talk long, he was too tired and anyway he had talked to Barbara at work the day before. He was nervous of being overheard so he told Barbara that Ken had flu and that all the work had fallen on him. She sounded pleased for him, that he could obviously cope in an emergency. And that Girl had got through a round. Over the exhaustion, he felt pleasure that he could focus on things again.

Her voice echoed her loneliness. 'When will you be home?'

'Soon.'

Chapter 54

Nelson was on duty that night, filling in for a sick engineer. At first he listened into the call, wanting to be sure that it was Bradley. The relief he felt for his family made him dizzy. Gradually he got drawn in to the Bradleys' lives. He could feel their loneliness at being apart, and found himself smiling when they talked about the boys. They laughed at them and complained about them, but always with love.

Bradley became Paul.

Not a stranger, but a man he knew and admired afresh. They would kill him and he, Nelson, was going to point the finger.

God, he prayed, get me out of this.

The call came soon after; earlier than usual. They were anxious as well.

Nelson's chest was as tight as a drum. 'Yes,' he answered and prayed, 'God.'

The Belfast voice was delighted. 'Where?'

'The number... it's...'

The tightness eased. Nelson felt a hot warmth spread through his chest. There was no pain, just the dark wrapping itself around him like a comfortable coat on a cold day. He slumped across the desk.

Chapter 55

The most striking thing about the man, was the nervous way he dragged at the cigarette held in his cupped fingers. He was tall and broad shouldered, wearing faded jeans and a leather jacket. He had an air of menace, the dark and brooding type. The type of man who attracted certain women.

He was a stranger to that part of Belfast yet he moved confidently, using the presence of the old warehouse looming over the surrounding houses as a navigation beacon for his journey. He counted the streets and the turns, and reached the warehouse at a point across the road from a fresh gap in the fencing. From there he stepped onto a paved surface where his footprints wouldn't show on the mud. At the side door, he stubbed out his cigarette on the wall. Checked carefully that no heat remained before putting the butt into his breast pocket. He pulled on a pair of leather gloves and pushed at the door with one finger. It opened quietly, having recently been oiled.

He entered and moved swiftly to the second floor where he did a circuit of the windows, looking for trouble in the shape of off-white colored Land Rovers discretely parked in side streets. As he watched, one nosed across a distant street and moved on out of sight. He made himself relax and stilled the extra heartbeats. He would only be suspicious if no police vehicle showed. The sight of one going about its interfering business was normality. He climbed to the fourth floor and did another circuit, seeing further and deeper into the surrounding streets. Satisfied that all was as it should be, he went to the third floor where a package waited for him.

The package was long and reasonably slim, and lay, unattended, on top of a wooden box. He unpeeled the layers of material: first cloth then oiled wrapping, to disclose an old army .303 rifle with telescopic sight attached. He stroked its surface lovingly, his favorite weapon, and he had used this particular model once before. He recognized it from the whorls of grain on the wooden butt. It had done its job then, a clean shot at four hundred yards to take out a Supergrass, and had made his reputation.

He was embarrassed when he thought of how little he'd got for that job. Now he charged premium rates. If you want the best you've got to pay for it, and he took pleasure in seeing people like Ronnie squirm. Getting money out of Ronnie was like extracting a misfired round from the barrel of a gun.

He liked Jimmy, but business was business. Things had been slow recently, money tight and the girlfriend kept nagging about going to Turkey on holidays.

He pulled out the magazine, checked that it was filled with live rounds and slapped it back into place. Next he stepped closer to the window, sighted along the barrel and focused his sights on one of the men standing at Ronnie's door. Forty meters, he reckoned, so virtually zero adjustment for distance.

Jimmy was due at any time and he wanted to be ready. He checked all the windows, and reluctantly decided that Ronnie had picked the right one for depth of field. However, the long gun barrel of the .303 was too obvious sticking out of the window and his crouch to use the sill as a rest quickly became uncomfortable.

He thought, if I could use the box?

He shoved at the box with his foot. It didn't move and the force of the shove made him stumbled back a step. He tried again, more carefully this time, and it still sat solid. Even with his hands, and he was fit, it would neither move nor lift. With the lid nailed down he couldn't see what was inside. He reckoned it was worth investigating but hadn't the time just then.

He positioned himself at the window again and waited. When Ronnie appeared in the doorway of his offices he knew that the taxi was close. He crouched and settled himself against the sill, worked a round into the firing chamber and rechecked his focus on Ronnie's face.

The taxi appeared, moving slowly. He sighted on the driver, Jimmy. He could kill him there and then, but his instructions were to shoot Doc at the same time. And there was a large bonus for a double hit. The taxi pulled up at the front door. No passenger, therefore no Doc. He cursed himself for his greed.

Jimmy got out of the car. *A head shot?* He waited, wanting Jimmy to be in the open where he could be sure of a second shot. Jimmy went forward to greet Ronnie. Now he was clear from the waist up. He settled his sights on the side of Jimmy's head, just above the ear, and began his squeeze on the trigger.

The side of the box fell forward with a bang that echoed through the building. Doc launched out of it, knife in hand.

Chapter 56

Doc arrived back at the house, his hair damp from the shower. He found Jimmy in the old kitchen. In spite of the summer heat outside Jimmy had a fire going in the grate. He still looked cold. The earphones hung forgotten around his neck.

Doc sat down in his chair and listened to get a feel of the house. He watched Jimmy struggle not to twitch with nerves and wondered why. *It's over – for now. You're safe. What's the problem?* In a way he wished he was more like Jimmy, because he liked the man he'd just killed. They'd worked together more than once in the early days, but they'd chosen different paths. Killing purely for money tarnished what should be a pleasure.

'Ronnie?' asked Jimmy.

It was a rhetorical question, not needing a reply. Jimmy spoke slowly, his technique, Doc knew, of thinking things out even as he put them into words. 'There's more than him involved. There's talk of meetings. I need to find out who was there and who wasn't.'

The earphones suddenly annoyed him. He pulled them off. 'Either way, we must separate. Usual rules apply if something happens to one of us.' He moved his chair away from the fire as fight came back into his system. 'I'll give you the list later.'

Doc didn't bother nodding. He doubted if the list would have changed much from the last one, if at all. Old friends seldom changed sides, old enemies never did. The list was there to stop him from taking out the whole Organization if anything should happen to Jimmy. Him obeying Jimmy's last order "Kill only these ones".

They sat on. Doc listened to the house and the world outside the house until the backdoor opened and Eleanor, Jimmy's wife, bustled in. Eleanor was short and heavy framed. She wore a shop coat and smelled of cleaning fluids. Her hair hung dank with sweat.

She smiled at Doc. 'Do you want a cup of tea?' Her head jerked in the direction of Jimmy. 'He'd never think of making you one.' When Doc shook his head, she looked at Jimmy. 'What about you?'

'I'm okay.'

'You look it too.'

She pulled a mobile phone from her pocket, clicked on it and held it out for Jimmy to see. 'While you were out, your girlfriend texted. She says Ronnie's as nervous as a cat.' The phone buzzed in her hand. She looked at the new message. 'Now Ronnie's got diarrhea.'

'He needs a shot of Imodium,' said Jimmy and winked across at Doc.

After a bit more tonguing Eleanor put baking potatoes on to boil for tea and left, telling Doc to turn them off in a few minutes. She nodded across at Jimmy. 'He wouldn't remember his head if it wasn't screwed on.'

Doc watched her wind her way between the parked-up taxis going across the yard to the backdoor of the dry cleaners. He nodded to Jimmy that she had safely gone.

Jimmy ordered, 'Say something.'

Doc looked up at the light fitting and a possible police bug.

They got up and wandered through the working kitchen and out into the yard. The buzz of work around the place intensified when they were spotted. All except for one old driver who remained leaning against his car, finishing the last drags of a cigarette.

Jimmy asked, 'Are you smoking yourself to death on my time?'

'Who ate your wee bun?' said the old driver, Sam Gilliland.

'A better man than you.'

Jimmy forced himself out of his worries long enough to give Sam Gilliland a smile as he passed. Sam Gilliland had been like a father to him and Doc when it mattered. Their first employee, who in the early days willingly waited for his money when things were tight. A lot of Jimmy's men went back nearly as far.

And getting too old for the game, thought Doc.

They walked on until they were out of earshot. 'Winston Shaw?' asked Jimmy.

Doc said nothing.

'Dead in that alleyway,' added Jimmy. 'And that man of Ronnie's, the driver, who went off the road at Glenlish?'

Doc was conscious of Jimmy's eyes on him.

Jimmy kept pushing. 'The day you were there.'

Muscle for Ronnie, Doc knew of the driver.

'And fat,' added Jimmy, as if reading Doc's thoughts. 'According to reports, he burned nicely.'

Doc saw Jimmy look at him speculatively when he asked, 'Why Sam?'

Jimmy continued, 'His wife might have told him how pictures of her bonking an MP ended up in the newspapers. An MP who was coked to the eyebrows.' He kicked impatiently at a loose stone. It skidded across the concreted yard and bounced off the wall of store. 'Hearsay evidence, but damaging all the same.'

By now they were heading back to the house.

Jimmy asked, 'But why kick Winston to death and then knife him?'

He looked at Doc. 'Things have been quiet recently for you. Winston was an easy target, a bit of practice on the side.'

Jimmy could have been speculating, he could have been accusing.

Doc remembered the potatoes. *Time they were switched off.*

Chapter 57

Doc and Jimmy were back at the house, hesitating close to the doorway.

Jimmy said, 'We need to send Ronnie a warning to back off.' His head nodded to the left and right as he ran his mind down a mental list of names. 'RM? That would give Ronnie a message. Let him know what was coming.'

Jimmy moved restlessly into the new kitchen where he put on the kettle to boil. 'All the same it's not that easy.' His voice carried out to Doc. 'Defending ourselves is one thing. Starting a turf war is a completely different matter.'

He wandered back out, packet of biscuits in hand. 'RM then. But nothing permanent, his replacement might be stupid enough to be dangerous.'

Doc stared him back. *I don't warnings.*

Jimmy said, 'Sometimes I think you're two people. And I'm not that fond of either of them.'

Doc watched Jimmy go back in and make the tea he hadn't wanted minutes before when Eleanor offered. Jimmy was like that, he knew, thought best when hands-on. Doc drained the potatoes while the tea drew, then they sat on a windowsill outside and drank in silence. Neither touched the biscuits.

'Bloody Bradley,' said Jimmy. 'He did me a lot of damage.' He slapped his mug down. 'I believed in the man. He was right, the nobs and the factory owners had the politicians in their pockets and ran the country to suit themselves. Our father worked every day of his life and never had a penny to call his own.'

He'd gone red in the face with passion, Doc noted, and thought they needed people like Jimmy in politics. *But he's too honest; it would break his heart.*

'And they're still at it,' said Jimmy, almost shouting. 'We fought to replace the nobs, but the men who took over are even worse and the politicians are still bought.'

His voice toned down to disgust. 'A man, a van and a dog, you'd think they'd be easy got.' He counted the points off on his fingers. 'One, We know Bradley's in England. Two, Nelson was found dead at work this morning, heart attack or so your friend Mick says. Three…'

Jimmy's eyes closed as his back eased against the window and his breathing became deep and steady. He could have been asleep. Doc wasn't surprised when his eyes suddenly snapped open.

'Bloody Bradley,' Jimmy repeated. 'The sooner we get our hands on that man the better.'

He turned on Doc, almost snarled. 'Say something.'

After an enjoyable day Doc felt relaxed enough to humor Jimmy with talk.

Doc said, 'What if something happened to one of his kids?'

He got a cold stare back. 'I'd have to think about that one first.' Jimmy's fingers tapped a nervous message against the windowsill before he said, thoughtfully, 'Spotting the van is a matter of luck and that dog has never run.'

He looked at that day's pile of newspapers. 'Those English papers never mention the Irish Coursing Club. They always talk about the NGRC or something.'

He stabbed a finger at Doc. 'Go back to Glenlish and ask more questions.'

Doc nodded.

I'll bet she held something back on me.

He'd go and see her as soon as he could find the time. And he'd call as Doc, still hyped up from the fresh kill, and not softie Fredrick Robinson.

He watched the horror of that morning's dangers refreeze Jimmy's face into a mask.

Jimmy asked, 'How close did he get?'

Doc asked, 'Why did you have to go there in the first place? You know Ronnie's trying to kill you.'

'I daren't show weakness.'

'Then you should have let me kill him and gone to his funeral.'

Jimmy looked surprised at the anger and concern in Doc's voice. 'Much as I'd like to, it's not as easy as that.'

Doc said nothing. He had his emotions under control again.

Jimmy asked for a second time, 'How long?'

Jimmy would insist on pushing things too far, take unreasonable chances and expect him to cover. *Maybe if he knew the truth he mightn't be so foolhardy in future?*

'A second. I nearly delayed another two before I moved.'

'You are joking?'

'If you say so,' said Doc.

136

Chapter 58

Ronnie was furious and through his anger the first niggle of fear appeared. *Jimmy couldn't know, how could he? He's not a mind reader.'*

He looked up at the old warehouse as he paced the office floor, and stayed well clear of the window in case Jimmy had the same idea as himself. He measured the distance with his eye. A clean shot, he could have done it himself. Easy for a marksman. *Why didn't he fire and where's he got to? He'll regret the day he was born.*

The fears stayed with him and grew as the hours passed and the contract killer failed to surface. Tuesday eased into Wednesday and the days stretched forever until it was Friday morning and he faced the weekend, still not knowing.

He phoned around, no one had heard anything. He knew he had made a mistake. Initially it was going to be just him and RM and afterwards RM wouldn't be needed. *You don't keep people who have something on you and Jimmy has a lot of friends.* Now there were too many in on it. He didn't like that because when things started to go wrong even the trusted few tended to look after number one.

The warehouse obsessed him, he spent hours staring at it from the window. RM pretended not to pick up on veiled hints that he should go and have a look-see. In the end Ronnie went himself with RM and three beefy minders. Another carload of men kept watch outside.

He hadn't been near the place in years. Not bad condition, he thought. He could maybe do something with it - shops and flats and things - if it came at the right price. He smiled at the thought of paying anything near market value. *What are contacts for if you can't use them?* He made a show of interest in front of the men and got a former tradesman in the group to examine floors and walls while he made notes. He delayed on the second floor while he drew a floor plan and sent them on to third.

One of them came back shouting, 'Boss! Boss! Come quick.'

Ronnie's heart lurched. 'What?'

'There's blood on the floor, gallons of it, and a rifle.'

Ronnie raced up the steps after him and pushed ahead on the landing, acting the leader taking decisive action. He knew there was no booby-traps or the men would have triggered one already. They stood clustered round a packing case, examining a rifle. It was a .303, old but looked to be in immaculate condition.

Ronnie wrapped his hand in a handkerchief and snatched it off them. 'For God's sake, fingerprints, they'll be all over it.'

He glared at them and looked around. A large patch of blood stained the floor near the windows. Flies feasted on globs of matter lumping its surface. He shivered and felt cold.

His eyes were drawn to the box. 'What's in that?' he demanded.

Arthur Robinson said, 'The lid's nailed down, boss, but there has to be something in it, it won't move.'

RM said, 'It did the other day, I moved it myself.'

Ronnie could have killed him. RM quailed under his look.

Ronnie asked, quickly, to cover, 'Where did you find the rifle?'

'I did, boss,' said RM, eager to make amends. He indicated. 'It was lying there, on top of the box.'

'Open it,' replied Ronnie, roughly, and walked away from the sight and the smell, and the sound of the flies.

Someone had to go for a crowbar. Ronnie stayed close to the stairs as they worked on the lid. There had to be something disgusting in there. *A body?* It might even booby-trapped. Either way he had no intention of getting too close. He worried himself sick as he waited, and kept an eye on RM in case he said something else stupid.

The wood screamed as the nails tore loose and the lid came off. The men looked inside, at first cautiously and then with confidence.

'Well?' demanded Ronnie.

'Nothing, boss,' replied RM in a puzzled voice.

Ronnie went and looked for himself. The box was empty, spotless. Two nails stood proud of the wood where they'd been driven through the base into the floor to fix the box in position.

'Well, well,' said Arthur Robinson.

Ronnie glared at him. He tucked the rifle under his arm and walked off.

Chapter 59

Once back in his office Ronnie locked the door and made sure the venetian blinds were shut.

What now?

The hours passed and the cold shivers up his back eased. The computers and the security camera aimed at the secretary had no pull on him. He didn't dare stop now, Jimmy would never forgive nor forget, and the next time he'd better get it right. He'd talk to people who'd protect his back for a while. They had as much to lose as him. In the meantime he had the rifle to add to his collection.

To give himself something to do he picked the rifle up and examined it closely. There was a tackiness at the muzzle, when he touched it blood came off on his fingers. When he checked down the barrel he saw that it was blocked. He knew the blood would corrode the metal and spoil the value so he got out his cleaning kit and pushed the brush through from the chamber. Whatever it was had dried and set and it took him some time to work it free.

A penis fell onto the floor.

Chapter 60

The farm had changed in the few weeks since Doc had been there. The rusted machinery had gone. The yard scraped and power-hosed clean and the potholes filled in with cement. The rotten window frames of the house had been patched and repainted. The doorknocker polished until the brass shone. A fresh plastic cover now stretched the length of a second tunnel.

Doc got out of the car and flexed the stiffness of the journey out of his body. The butterfly feeling in his stomach persisted. He'd had them the whole way from Belfast. All he'd had eaten was his usual breakfast cereal. *Maybe the milk was off?*

The fawn greyhound bitch came running to greet him. It crawled the last few feet, head down and tense, ready to run if Doc threatened it.

He bent down and scratched it behind the ears. 'Somebody's been bad to you at a time, girl.'

He straightened up when a vague figure showed in the renovated plastic tunnel. The figure, Connie, came to the opening. She stood there, hands on hips, staring at him. She wore a green gardener's apron over a pink blouse and jeans.

She said, 'Thank you for the phone call you didn't make. A girl really loves the shag and never-hear-from-again type.'

Doc found himself feeling indignant instead of being impersonal. 'I did phone.'

'That was a business call,' she said. 'Has Charlie gone to the police? Has she gone to the police?'

He stayed silent rather than risk saying the wrong thing. Instead he reached into the car and pulled out a large bouquet. 'I thought I'd say it with flowers.'

She retreated back into the tunnel and he had follow her in. Part of the punishment he realized. Her scent was of fresh sweat and of the peat loam heaped on plastic sheeting. The tunnel itself held a muggy heat. He was wary of the country smells igniting his hay fever, but it seemed all right.

He asked, 'What are you doing?'

'Preparing a bed for seedlings.'

She tried to remain cool and distant but her hand caressed the bouquet.

She looked up, he leaned forward and their lips met. He held her carefully, so as not to destroy the bouquet, and teased her mouth open with his tongue. When they separated their breath was already coming in quick spurts.

Business first, Doc reminded himself, even as he tugged her apron loose and threw it onto the pile of peat.

He asked, 'What has the NGRC got to do with Bradley's dog?'

She was easing off his jacket. She paused. 'What?'

'The National Greyhound Racing Board. You never mentioned that the last time.'

'You never asked.'

She flushed. Temper or frustrated desire, he wasn't sure which.

'I'm asking now,' he said.

'You walk in here, and you expect me to ring Clonmel and ask them if Bradley's dog has been registered in England, and if so under what name?'

'Yes,' said Doc, relieved it was as simple as that.

She flung the bouquet at him. He juggled with it, trying not to let it touch the ground, and at the same time not damage the blooms.

What's got into her?

He balanced the bouquet in a wheelbarrow and turned in time to see her crouch and pull a Stanley Knife from a pocket in the apron. She flicked it open and held it to his jugular. 'What has that poor man ever done on you? Do you not think he's suffered enough?'

He said nothing when the blunt edge of the blade pressed against his skin. *Amateurs*! He'd never make that mistake.

The blade nudged against his carotid artery. 'What do you want him for anyway?'

She's beautiful when she's angry, he thought. Something about the firmness of her body coupled with her maturity excited him, made him want to bury himself in that emotion.

He said, 'Information.'

'And then what?'

'Other people just want to kill him.'

That puzzled her, made her back off while she tried to think why finding Bradley was so important. The pressure of the knife against his neck eased. He reached up, grabbed her wrist and twisted. Had the knife out of her hand in an instant.

The old need to kill sang in his body.

She tried to fight back but he hooked a leg around hers and threw her onto the mound of peat. Stood over her and held her down with a foot on her groin while he undressed. These were good clothes, Fredrick Robinson clothes. He didn't want them stained.

She scrambled to get up while he took off his trousers but he was too quick for her and pushed her down again. Stripped to the skin, he carefully put his clothes on clean plastic.

He dragged her to her feet and slashed at her with the knife. She squealed in protest, then fell to her knees and leaned into him. He slashed again, this time aiming for between the shoulder blades.

Chapter 61

Glenlish was buried at the wrong end of the hills from Belfast and was therefore doomed to remain small and insignificant in city terms. Inspector Patterson, the Station Inspector, had little on his desk to keep him occupied. The most interesting was the coincidence of two Belfast men killing themselves in the one day: a self-garroting and an incinerated body from a lorry accident. So far as he knew, no one local had been killed or threatened, so the gun in the dead man's pocket had to be a macho thing.

From where Ian sat, a five iron would put him on the second green of the golf course. He decided to give it another half hour then put in a bit of putting; there had been too many threes recently.

A WPC tapped the glass panel of his door and entered. 'There's a gentleman here to see you, Sir, a Mr. Clements.'

Patterson tried to appear resigned but was quite pleased at the interruption. 'Show him in.'

He recognized Clements when he saw him, knew him vaguely from the Golf Club and security meetings. Clements was the chief engineer at the telephone exchange, pushing retirement and putting on weight. And he was nervous.

Patterson did his best with Clements but the man couldn't settle so, to start the ball rolling, he asked, 'Has someone been at the petty cash?'

Clements's face creased in puzzlement. 'We don't have petty cash, at least not that much.'

'It was a joke,' explained Patterson.

Clements said, 'I feel such a fool. I talked it over with the bosses in Belfast and they told me to forget about it. They want to bury it with him.' He chewed at his lip.

'And?' prompted Patterson, gently.

'Now I'm here I think they're right.'

He got up to go.

Patterson soothed him down again. 'Whatever it is, it's worrying you. Just talk, I'm a good listener. If I think there's nothing in it I'll tell you and no harm done.'

Clements said, 'Nelson... he was forever complaining about that wrist, he said it was pains… I'd never heard of a silent coronary before.'

Patterson interrupted. 'Nelson, that's the man found dead at work the other day?'

'Yes.' Clements lost his hesitancy as he warmed to his story. 'He hated working nights; he said it was too much for a man of his age but lately he took as much as he could get. We assumed he and the wife... you know how it is.' He shook his head. 'The man wasn't right and the mugging didn't help.'

Patterson's eyes narrowed and he leaned closer. 'What mugging?'

Clements frowned, surprised. 'Last week, he reported it. At least he told me he did.'

Patterson buzzed the front desk. 'Sergeant.' He looked at Clements. 'When did this happen and where?'

'The Monday night shift, no, Tuesday morning when he was coming off duty.' Now into his story Clements relaxed and became garrulous. 'He claimed that he was hardly touched, but the man who saw it said the attacker put the boot in rightly. There's been a lot of talk since he died, things he'd done recently, odd things. I began to worry.' He laughed. 'I even searched the place for bombs.'

Patterson held up a finger for silence and talked to the Duty Sergeant. Then he waited and as he waited his fingers drummed the table. He didn't like the idea of bombs. The sergeant confirmed what he thought, Nelson had never reported the attack.

Patterson hung up and glanced at the clock. Forget golf, forget tea. Better ring the wife. He said, 'Something brought you here Mr. Clements. Not just suspicion but something concrete.' He waited.

Clements said, 'Things were wrong, I had this feeling, nothing added up.' His hands flapped in helpless confusion. 'As I said, I checked for bombs, and sabotage and things missing. Then I made myself stop and think.' His hand actions now became firm and emphasized his words. 'Having verified the material items I started a Procedural Audit, and there it was, the phone tap.'

Patterson said, urgently. 'How many numbers? Whose?'

Clements handed over a computer print-out out. 'Just one, Barbara Bradley.'

'The MP's wife?'

'Yes.' Now that he had reported the illegal tap Clements tried to minimize its importance. 'I'm sure it was something innocent. Reporters…'

Patterson's brain *pinged* when Clements said "reporter." He ignored him as he talked on and unfolded the print-out. It gave the dates and duration of the phone taps. The first date caught Patterson's breath. He could have sworn to it yet he checked a file in his drawers to be sure. The two Belfast men had died on the same day – and the self-garroting had happened on Mullough Avenue where Nelson lived.

He phoned the Duty Sergeant again. 'I want the duty DC to take a statement from Mr. Clements, tell him to see me first.' He thought fast. 'They did an autopsy on Nelson, find out who the pathologist was and get him on the phone. See what happened to his personal effects and... Oh, the Coroner, I'd better speak to him.'

He looked at the clock as if that would tell him. 'I suppose the man's buried by now?'

'This morning,' said Clements.

Patterson smiled his thanks rather than yell in frustration.

He let the smile drop after a constable had escorted Clements from the room. He had a million things to do and the first of those was to think.

Nelson lived in Mullough Avenue. Nelson was under pressure and it started the day of the murder. The Bradley kids saw two men at that car – funny how that name keeps cropping up – and an unusual death less than an hour later.

The two men beside the car. Were they were waiting to see Nelson when he left for work? No, they'd knock the door and state their business. Then coming off duty. Was he working that night? He made a note to ask Clements.

Let's say the men were waiting to see Nelson. They speak to him: Threaten? Bribe? Afterwards, why didn't they go back to Belfast? Why park down the road at the post box? And where did the second man go after his friend managed to kill himself?

Patterson doodled on the pad. He drew the shape of an envelope, blocked in the stamp and put B.R.A.D.L.E.Y. for the address. Mrs. Bradley had posted a letter that morning. Okay it was to the Liverpool Supporters Shop, but the men weren't to know that. That letter could easily have been to her husband. So if you're looking for Bradley, you get the letter and you've got the man.

Chapter 62

Police Inspector Ian Patterson could do little so late on a Friday afternoon, people had either gone home or were unavailable. Only the pathologist answered his phone, and that call stayed brief and to the point. Nelson had died of a coronary. He, the pathologist, was positive of that and, yes, he had found bruising on the body and a cracked rib. However, both were too old and too insignificant to be a direct cause of death.

The man was attacked on the sixteenth? Yes, he himself had estimated a week, so fine, eight days. The wife, widow rather, had reported an earlier fall in the house. A bad fall too, things were broken: a vase and a picture frame. He consulted his notes and confirmed that the reported fall had occurred on the day of the garroting. How sure could Nelson's wife be of that date? The widow was a ward sister in the hospital where her name was a byword for efficiency. Obviously he didn't like the woman and it had been a long day.

It was late teatime before Detective Constable Green arrived back from the hospital with Nelson's personal possessions.

'What kept you?' demanded Patterson.

He ignored the man's excuses as he poured the contents of the package onto a sterile sheet of plastic: keys, coin, wallet, tissues, petrol receipts, notebook. He pulled on a pair of gloves and flicked through the wallet, *nothing special though we'll have to request a copy of his Visa account*, then the notebook. Not a notebook, he realized when he looked carefully, a personal telephone directory.

What else would a telephone engineer carry?

He worked through the personal telephone numbers, page by page. Everything was entered neatly in various hues of blue: name, address, telephone number. He found a Belfast number scrawled across an otherwise blank page. It appeared to be a recent entry and was so out of keeping with the rest that he concentrated on it. The other entries could be checked later with the widow. *A nice job for some poor sod.* He sighed, he knew who the poor sod would be.

He told DC Green to trace the mysterious Belfast number. Rather than sit and wait for the answer, and impatient to be doing something, he tallied the contents of the package against the check-list while he waited. Everything was there and accounted for.

Green came flying back. 'Sir, that number, it's ex-directory, a private line.'

'And?'

'It belongs to Ronnie Fetherton of Fetherton Haulage. He's all over the papers. He's going to be an MP.'

Fetherton Haulage!

Patterson closed his eyes and felt a migraine pulse in his head. One of Fetherton's lorries had crashed and burned the same day, the driver burned to a crisp in the fire. And the car driven by the self-garrotter had a "Vote Fetherton" sticker on the bumper.

The same day in the same dead-end town?

He got DC Green out of the office on an excuse and built the nerve to ring police headquarters at Castlereagh. Found himself being gradually pushed up the line until he was put on hold for the ACC (Assistant Chief Constable) in charge of Special Branch.

Their last telephone conversation had been awkward enough to make Patterson doubly nervous. A couple of years back one of the local constables had lost his firearm during a disturbance and it hadn't been recovered. One reason why Patterson still ran a remote police station. Not that he wanted a posting. Not with the golf course outside his window and a Station Sergeant who did everything but sign the routine reports.

ACC Thomson's voice rumbled down the line, sounding friendly this time. 'Patterson, what the hell's going on down there?'

Right then Ian Patterson wished for the bad old days when a murder in Glenlish would only have been a statistic. 'Merely following enquiries, Sir.' A bit cheeky, he knew, but it did answer the question.

'Tell me.'

'We're investigating an apparently accidental death and we think there may be a link between that and an illegal phone tap in the area.'

'Go on.'

Patterson drew breath, his first proper one in minutes, and launched into his explanation.

'Not much to go on,' said Thomson, when he had finished.

'I don't like coincidences, Sir.'

'Nor me,' said the ACC. 'Maybe you should keep an eye on the Bradleys' house.'

Patterson frowned, not liking being told how to run his station, even if it was done by way of a suggestion.

Anyway, he thought, it's about time that I asked some questions. 'This man Fetherton, what's he like?'

Thomson said, 'He might be an up and coming politician but he's also one of the nastiest sharks in the Belfast rackets. Not that we can prove it.'

Patterson wanted to shout Bingo!

Thomson added, 'If you get anything on Fetherton, I'll make you liaison officer at St Andrews during the Open.'

Patterson's legs trembled and he thanked God he was sitting or he'd have fallen. St Andrews and all expenses paid? He felt he'd died and gone to heaven.

'Bradley, eh?' said Thomson, just before he hung up. 'I told Bradley he was playing a dangerous game but he wouldn't listen. No wonder his nerve cracked.'

The way the ACC spoke about Bradley puzzled Patterson. It was charitable, even friendly. That was a new way to look at it. They'd all done crazy things under pressure.

Chapter 63

'**We've met,' said Jimmy** as Doc walked in the door carrying large shopping bags. 'Vaguely and a long time ago.'

Doc said, 'It takes a surprisingly long time to move a trailer-load of peat and bed it down.' Doc was annoyed with himself. Normally he'd answer a question like that with a shrug.

Jimmy looked warningly at the center light fitting as if he could see a police bug there. That look had been out of habit, Doc realized, because Jimmy had recently had the place swept for bugs – not that he trusted the sweepers to pick up on everything.

Jimmy asked, 'This time, did you listen to the news or anything before you went charging in to cause mayhem?'

Doc said, 'Nelson got a nice obituary in the local paper.'

'And you'd time for a bit of shopping,' said Jimmy pointing to the bags.

'I picked up a couple of day-to-day suits. I bought them that first day but they needed adjusting.'

He was surprised at himself for saying so much. Jimmy looked almost shocked.

Doc took his seat and strained to catch the mood of the house and yard.

'So you had a nice day then, keeping yourself busy around Glenlish?' asked Jimmy in a teasing voice. 'Nothing to tell me about Bradley's dog for instance?'

Doc said, 'The dog's been registered with the NGRC as Arrant Beauty.'

Jimmy threw a *Sporting Press* at Doc. 'See if you can find an Arrant Beauty in there.' He himself delved into a *Sporting Life*.

They saw it at the same time.

Jimmy jumped to his feet. 'Bloody hell, she's on tonight.' He grabbed the phone and dialed. When JP answered he ordered, 'Get me on the first flight to London, Heathrow or Gatwick, it doesn't matter which.' Doc heard JP say something. Jimmy roared back, 'What the hell do you mean it's the holiday season? Tell them there's been a death in the family, they always find a seat for that.'

'Whose?' queried JP, his voice carrying clearly into the room.

'Yours, my favorite son, if you don't get me on that flight.'

Chapter 64

Doc waited until Jimmy had burned tires out of the yard, then he went home.

Before he did he left his new suits in the bedroom he now kept in Jimmy's house for his work clothes or if he needed to stay over for any reason. Only then did he wonder why he'd worn casual clothes, not work clothes, when calling to see Connie.

Connie!

He remembered her lying wide-eyed on the bed of peat. Him standing over her, watching the peat growing damp and darkening on her body...

He was anxious to get home so he had Gunner Smith drop him at the far side of the Botanic Gardens. Because of his hay fever he hadn't been there in years even though he passed its gates almost daily.

He walked through the gardens, setting a curving walk to keep well away from flowering plants, and kept sniffing for the first sign of pollen annoying his nasal passages. Encouraged by the absence of hay fever he detoured through the Palm House. There he made a mental note of exotic plants that might be grown in a plastic tunnel, *if there's a demand for them?*

Post waited for him in the entrance hall of the apartment block. He picked it up on the way past, ran up the stairs and let himself into his apartment. The working day wasn't over yet and he needed a few hours to himself before he had to go out again. He settled himself in front of the computer.

The parcel in the post held the reference books he needed for his next Assignment. Running his hands over their covers, imagining the discoveries to come, gave him a thrill. Even so he couldn't bring himself to open the books and begin the research. That had never happened before. The next Assignment for the Professor is starting to loom, he told himself, and yet...

The screen saver, drifting to and fro on his computer screen, was an image of Connie, scanned from her driving license photographs. Doc looked at the image for a long, long time. For some reason her image made him feel sad. His profession always alienated women because theirs was about life and procreation. Whereas he...

Retirement was not an option and he'd never make old bones. Too many important people were afraid he'd go soft in the head and start blabbing or, worse, be caught and negotiate a deal for clemency with the police.

He felt uneasy, as if the spirit of someone had invaded his apartment. He got up and checked that he had closed the outer door and had the alarm on. Even then he searched the apartment, looking in wardrobes and under beds.

Something's been here. Nothing's been here. No one's here.

Everything seemed the same and yet somehow the apartment wasn't the one he had walked out of that morning. He had a sense of something missing and yet not missing. Of an emptiness in the apartment. Me lonely? *Impossible.*

It seemed wrong to risk her being hurt, yet he reached for the phone.

Illogically, before he punched in the number, he again made sure that the inner hallway and bedrooms were empty. That the alarm was on. That in no way could he be overheard.

The phone was answered on the second ring.

'It's me,' said Doc.

'You're a bastard,' said Connie. 'I didn't mind the rest of my clothes but that bra was brand new. Sixty pounds it cost me in Dungannon, and you cut it to shreds.'

Doc found himself smiling. 'I'll buy you a new one.'

Connie said, 'When I was young and didn't know better, I dreamed of making love in a meadow of white and yellow spring flowers and the sun beating down. Not a plastic tunnel on a bed of dry peat.

They shared a comfortable silence. He thought of the afterwards: them, still naked, sneaking across the yard in case someone happened along. The shower, he washing the peat out of her hair, she slicking it off his body. The renewed, almost panicked coupling and the afterwards, lying in the gentleness of each other's arms.

'You're must be a Ballymena man,' she said, eventually. 'Short arms and long pockets.'

'So you're looking for dinner then?' he said, pleased he'd picked up on the hint.

'Something like that.'

'A Chinese takeaway?'

'You'll be lucky.'

He said, 'I've a lot on at the minute, but leave it with me.'

Doc found himself slouched comfortably in the chair as they talked. *I never do that.* He realized also that he hadn't keyed in the block to stop her from tracing his private number, and didn't mind.

Before they hung up she said, 'By the way, Clonmel rang back. They contacted the NGRC for me and got Bradley's address.'

Chapter 65

Ken Stockdale declared himself fit enough to go to the second round of the Rosebowl, and nothing would please him. He wanted a new lead for swank and the old one for comfort, something for Girl to lie on and why the hell didn't he, Paul, want to go? It was ridiculous to say that it might bring her bad luck. She ran well or she didn't, she won or she lost. She got hurt – God forbid – or she didn't. It was all up to her on the track and had nothing to do with who was watching.

Paul had no choice in the end but to go. Ken wasn't fit to drive and Kristie had no intention of going. 'After that last time?' she said, when he suggested it, and became even blunter with Ken.

The car was barely in gear when Ken screamed at Paul to stop. He'd forgotten his lucky rabbit's foot and couldn't possibly go without that.

Kristie ran up. 'It's in the glove compartment, you put it there this morning.' She leaned in and kissed him open mouthed. 'That's what you really want,' she said, watching Paul for a reaction. He pretended not to notice and drove on.

Ken's angst started to build as they neared the track. Girl was in Trap 2, with Kid Carbine, the previous year's winner, in Trap 1. He thought Girl had a good chance of qualifying because the rest of the field were fairly ordinary. Paul would have been happy to own any of the other dogs.

Ken was so busy convincing himself that the bitch's lack of training wouldn't count against her that he kept forgetting to navigate. Paul thought they were hopelessly lost when they eventually came upon the Arena track almost by default. It was on a T-junction at the edge of a wooded glen.

Men and dogs were fanned out over the car park. With the clock ticking away they started to converge on the weighing-in room. Ken ran a comb through his hair. He wore his best suit, a grey twist with a thread of green through it. 'Going down with all flags flying,' he told Paul, wryly, as he lifted Girl out of the car.

'Is that Speedy?' asked someone as they joined the queue. The speaker laughed until his gut wobbled under his shirt. He said to a companion, 'She was so far behind the last night, I thought she was waiting for the next race.'

'You wait and see,' said Ken, grandly. He nudged Paul and indicated the fawn dog with the heavy man. 'That's Bromide, Trap 3. He's well named. Sometimes he runs out and sometimes he runs in, and he's got the weight to take everything else with him.'

Paul looked at the dog closely. 'He must be ninety pounds. He makes Girl look like a whippet.'

'Ninety four,' said Ken. 'And don't let that build fool you. He's a cracking dog, but I don't think 550's his distance.'

'That's one less to worry about,' said Paul, hopefully.

Ken laughed. 'Now who's getting nervous?'

The people in front of them gradually shuffled on. Paul and Ken emerged from a dull, concrete-floored passageway, smelling strongly of dog and detergent, into the weighing-in room where things were basic and functional. The track owners kept the glamour and the slapped on white for the paying public in the stands.

When it was their turn, Paul lifted Girl onto the scales. The moving platform under her feet frightened her and she tried to jump off again. He held her and soothed her until one of the staff called out "sixty one pounds". Then he lifted her off and patted her to calm her further.

'You're getting fat,' he said, and followed Ken out into the stadium proper. Girl was up half a pound on the previous week.

They walked Girl around the center of the track to let her stretch. After a while Ken noticed that Paul kept turning to examine every new arrival. 'Expecting someone?'

Paul ignored the question. More people knew him to see than he cared to think.

A movement, little more than a flicker of memory stirred at the edge of his vision. Instinctively he looked that way, towards the stands, but a lot of people were coming and going and no one registered. That feeling persisted and drew him around again. Once slowly and casually as if looking for a missing friend, and once quickly, as if to ward off an attacker. He saw no one that he knew.

He headed for the toilets and locked himself in until Girl's race was called. Even then he waited until the bell rang for the last two minutes of betting. He left the toilet block, slipping into the milling punters, and went looking for Ken.

Ken was easy found, standing head and shoulders as he did above most of the crowd. Paul pushed through and touched his shoulder to catch his attention.

Ken tried to look annoyed. 'Where have you been, you've missed three races?'

'Toilet,' said Paul.

Ken laughed. 'What would you be like if this was the final?'

'I don't think I'd survive it,' Paul said, relieved Ken had put his absence down to nerves.

They watched the dogs parading in front of the stand. The kennel-boy leading Girl was an ex-employee of Ken's. Ken swore he was the best man he had ever seem gentle a nervous dog. Certainly, as Paul looked on, Girl nudged the kennel boy with her muzzle and her tail flicked to and fro under the answering pat.

The leading boy turned back at the end of the stand and the pace quickened as they approached the box. The box had already been swung out on to the track, the lid pulled down and held in place by firmly planted feet until the catch slotted home. The Race Marshal supervised the loading of the dogs into the traps. The kennel-boys, once released of their charges, headed for the pickup point. The keener, more anxious ones ran.

By the time they were in place the hare was already at the first bend and picking up speed. Paul and Ken were standing near the top of the home straight. The pressure of the crowd behind pressed them against the rails as latecomers crushed in.

The sound of the crowd was like waves over shingle on a beach. It softened into individual rattles of voices as they waited for the off and then surged upwards again as the lid snapped up.

The dogs came out more or less together. Girl was slow away and Bromide moved over into her place, effectively blocking her and causing her to check. The dogs thundered past for the first time, the noise of their going drowned by the roar of the crowd. Five were more or less in line. Kid Carbine had a slight advantage on the rail, with Girl two lengths behind the rest of the field. Paul's stomach twisted, the impossible dream was already over. He felt Ken sag beside him.

Kid Carbine held the bend as if glued to it but Bromide ran wide, taking dogs four and five out with him. Dog six swerved to avoid them and lost ground. The crowd's roar took on a note of disapproval. Ken straightened up as Girl took her chance.

Girl dived through the opening created by Bromide and charged on around the bend, three lengths in arrears of Kid Carbine. She held her line and slipstreamed behind him as they came out of the second bend. The rest of the dogs fell into line behind them. At that point the colors of the racing coats tended to merge with the yellow track lights and the setting sun, and Paul could only guess which dog was which from their respective sizes.

The roar of the crowd rose to a crescendo as Kid Carbine stretched out down the back straight. He pulled two lengths further ahead of Girl. She pegged him back one, and they stayed that way until they went into the third bend. She lost it there, running wide, almost to the hare rail, and Bromide was quick to whip in and take second place. The sixth dog joined them and they hammered up the home straight. Girl was fading but it was a short run to the winning line and she just held on to take third place, two lengths behind Bromide and the shortest of necks in front of a fast finishing number six.

The first three home went through to the semi-finals.

Chapter 66

Jimmy was running late. He missed one flight and had an hour's wait until the next. Heathrow was busy, with queues for everything. He was tempted to hot-wire something in the Long Stay car park but decided to play it honest, mainly because of the outside security cameras.

The traffic was heavy and he had trouble getting out of Heathrow, let-alone a run on the motorway. His first bit of luck came with a much earlier than expected sign for The Arena. He turned off the motorway, followed the directions and found himself outside a dance hall.

He tried to keep calm, but inside his system churned.

'I'll kill, Doc,' he said to himself. 'Where did he get to all day?'

He arrived at the track as they were calling the dogs for the eighth race and headed straight for the paddock. He counted the kennels; the fourth block of six up, number two. The door lay open so Bradley's dog was gone. The racing card gave the name of the trainer, K Stockdale,

I can trace Bradley through him.

Jimmy checked his watch, it was near ten o'clock at night and he had been on the go since early that morning.

Chapter 67

Paul excused himself from the Stockdales' supper table to phone home. It was getting late and he felt fuzzy from tiredness.

He dialed and waited. The phone rang and rang. He began to think that Barbara and the boys were in bed. He decided to hang up, then realized that he had disturbed them anyway.

The phone continued to ring unanswered. He redialed, convinced that he'd hit a wrong button the first time, and again got no reply.

'They're out for the night somewhere,' he told himself, and didn't believe it for one minute.

Chapter 68

Dank night had long spread itself over Belfast. The Friday night drinking had started to wind down as people paired off and telephoned for taxis. Doc wore a dark outfit, including a black polo-neck jumper. He snuggled into the neck of the jumper until it covered much of his lower face. A woolen cap pulled down over his ears was not out of place in a rising wind and the threat of rain in the air.

Doc stood at an unlit corner, watching people come and go from the pub across the way. The pub was small, not much more than a double-fronted house in a street of mean houses. His nose twitched and he constantly wanted to sneeze. Not from the bed of turf that he and Connie had made love on but from the ingrained pollution seeping out of the walls of the surrounding houses.

This is ridiculous, I'm now allergic to the city.

Whatever happened he didn't want to sneeze and leave his DNA all over RM's body. Neither did he want RM's DNA on him. All this modern technology meant that he had to destroy the clothes he wore during a killing. The plastic sheeting, covering the floor from the front door to the bathroom of the safe house, incinerated. Afterwards the room had to be saturated in antibacterial spray. The very sump in the shower doused in industrial antiseptic.

This whole precaution-thing nowadays took much of the pleasure away. In the old days he'd mull things over while sipping a whiskey, then head home to the wife and act like a stag in rut. She had to know what it was about, and didn't mind. *Not then.*

Somehow he couldn't see himself killing RM and then going to Connie's. Using the Stanley Knife on her clothes was fun. In spite of the moans about the ruined bra she had encouraged him on. The actual lovemaking she wanted gentle. After half a lifetime with Charlie she'd had enough of brutality.

Doc forced himself to focus on the job on hand. How his mind had jumped from his wife to Connie was beyond him. Connie wouldn't approve of him killing RM, but how else could he make Ronnie back off? The man would keep trying and maybe one day he'd get lucky.

He checked the time. *Near closing.* RM wouldn't be long. He was too mean to keep pouring drink down a woman's neck.

Eventually RM did come out of the pub, holding onto a tall blonde. His hands were all over her. She kept hers to herself.

'I'll get us a taxi,' Doc heard him say.

'Do,' said the tall blonde.

'Your place or mine?'

The tall blonde didn't answer but pointed to a taxi cruising with its "for hire" sign lit.

Some people have all the luck, thought Doc, preparing to slip back into the night. He decided to wait for the decision "your place or mine". It might make all the difference.

RM staggered into the street and waved his arms about. The taxi pulled up, a CarloCab. CarloCabs were supposed to respond to radio calls only. Something to tell Jimmy, thought Doc.

RM opened the door with a flourish. He could have been seeing the queen into the Irish State Coach.

The tall blonde paused in the doorway. 'I left my stole behind,' she told RM. 'Would you mind?'

'My pleasure,' said RM and went back into the pub.

The blonde got in and closed the car door, leaned forward and spoke to the driver. The taxi drove off. RM reappeared without the stole. The fresh air was getting to him and he stumbled around, blearily looking for the taxi. Saw its taillights in the distance and kicked out at it. Almost fell.

'Neither place,' muttered Doc and flexed muscles gone cold with the long stand in the dark. The flexing ran muscles the length of the knife sheath secured between his shoulder blades. The knife was made of the finest Toledo steel. The blade only three inches long, just within legal limits but, if discovered, would allow Detective Sergeant Leary the chance to build another dose of frustration.

Connie liked inventiveness, Doc remembered. He shook his head. *Focus. Focus.* For RM he favored something simple but memorable. What with DNA and blood splatters he had gone off using his knife. His old signature mark of castration, he now reserved for the more deserving.

RM staggered around in the middle of the street for a while then set off. Home, Doc guessed, and slipped away. He chose a street paralleling the one RM was on and walked quickly to get ahead of RM. He knew of one particularly quiet place that he could use without fear of interruption. An abandoned building site.

Arriving at the site, he walked through a smashed gateway onto a stoned area and became a shadow in the seeping darkness. Already he could hear RM's slurred voice. 'Bitch! Whore! Her and her gin and tonics. Leading me on all night. Bitch! Whore!'

The voice got closer, was right there. Doc pulled on surgical gloves, reached out of the darkness and hauled RM to him.

'Hey!' shouted RM.

Doc chopped him across the throat. RM's shout ended in a gurgle of sucked air. Doc struck again and RM went down, conscious but too bound up with pain to fight back.

Now Doc hesitated. They were in an open place where the body would be found quickly. So far, except for the hand chops, he hadn't harmed RM. The real warning to Ronnie was to kick every bone in RM's body to pulp, but that would set up all sorts of DNA problems. All the same he didn't want RM to die too quickly so the knife was out.

He looked around him. Surely on an abandoned building site there had to be something heavy he could drop on RM's chest, let him drown in his own blood.

He crunched a heel down on RM's testicles, *that way he won't move in a hurry*. RM's throat was so sore he could only wheeze a scream of pain. Doc left him and went searching through the skeleton of the building for a breezeblock or a lump of concrete. He moved carefully, wanting to minimize trace elements of the site getting onto his clothes. All this modern technology spoiled things for people like him. All the same, it quickly got rid of the amateurs. Now Doc specialized. RM was just a throwaway job: an idiot who had become a threat both to him and to Jimmy.

Doc walked carefully through the site, sliding his feet forward rather than take proper steps in the near darkness and trip over something. Finally he saw a darker mound, a pallet of broken concrete blocks. Behind him he heard RM roll over and be sick. He'd need to be quick.

He hefted one of the blocks. Good and heavy. Load-bearing, not one of those internal things they used nowadays. Not that Doc had ever worked on a building site but, in the early days, Jimmy and he had built, repaired and renovated their home because they hadn't the money to pay anyone.

He walked back carrying the concrete block. Found it easier this time because he was walking into the uncertain light of street lamps. He was also following the sound of RM's moans. As he got nearer he raised the block high over his head, ready to bring it smashing down. A dropped block might only damage ribs. He wanted to be sure that the lungs were punctured.

The image of himself, concrete block over his head, ready to kill, became one of Connie stretched out on the bed arms above her head. Somehow she liked that feeling of total submission as she came. What she didn't like, not that she ever voiced it, was his occupation: his enforcing, his extracting of information. She didn't know, probably hoped that killing people didn't come into it.

Doc hesitated and lowered the concrete block. He didn't like killing when Connie was on his mind. It tainted her somehow. Maybe if he did a warning this time, merely pulverize RM's ankles…?

I'm getting soft in my old age.

Lights sprayed over the site as a car came down the street. Doc stepped behind a partly built wall, waiting for it to go by. Instead of passing, the lights flared hard over the abandoned structure as the car turned onto the site. The lights died, then came on again and he heard a woman's voice say, 'I told you I saw someone.'

A man got out of the car, cursing. The woman followed him, saying, 'You're out of lick if anyone's watching.'

Moving carefully, knowing that the couple were blinded by their own car lights and couldn't see him, Doc set the block down and foot-slid towards the back of the site. He could imagine Connie, standing hands on hips, laughing at RM's escape. *That bugger's luckier than most of them.* And so, Doc knew, was himself. If he hadn't hesitated over what to do the car lights would have caught him in the act of killing RM.

Doc slipped through the back fence and disappeared into a side street.

Chapter 69

The youth was on foot and not pleased about it. RM had borrowed his car and hadn't brought it back. Okay, so he was dead, *the stupid plonker*. Worse than that, people were wanting to know why he kept calling into the Tennent Street police station.

Where else would he go to complain that the police in Glenlish hadn't yet released his car? And the last time he called there'd been questions. Why had RM gone to Glenlish? Who was going with him? Not that he'd said anything, of course, but there'd been hints dropped that his probation could be revoked if he didn't start cooperating.

He was aware of someone coming up behind him, and wasn't worried. This was neutral territory between two gangs and as safe as Belfast could get. An area where the mean streets gave way terrace houses with stubby front gardens. Admittedly most of the houses were empty at night, being used by solicitors and accountants, but the very name plates on the railings gave him a feeling of security.

He had a sense of the person behind getting closer and glanced back over his shoulder, just to be sure. It was a man with a small, neat build. Probably a Duty Solicitor, or someone like that, returning to his office for some reason. Either way the youth felt relieved and walked on. Didn't worry when he heard the footsteps get closer but angled his step to the inside of the pavement to let the man pass.

The blow to the head cracked his skull, starting a mild brain hemorrhage. He remained conscious and aware enough to grab at railings to stay on his feet. His attacker was slim, dark clothed, and strong. Not young, not old. *He even wears a tie.*

The youth felt himself being lifted up. Could see black shoes and shoe laces. Cracks in the pavement drifted in and out of his vision as he was pivoted sideways until he hung over the railings. Metal railings with long, sharp spikes on top. Bolted onto the railings was a sign that he could only partly read. Someone and Someone, solicitors.

Felt himself being dropped, crunching sounds and the hot of pain of death.

Chapter 70

It was way past closing time. The barman had the glasses washed and the chairs upturned on the tables, ready for the cleaning lady in the morning. No one in their right minds would dare rob the barman of the takings but Mick liked to escort him to the night safe at the Regional Bank. You never knew these days with all the drug addicts desperate for the next fix.

Mick's phone rang. It could be any unlisted number but the man with cold glass for a voice called every day or so. Always it was the same; he only wanted to know about Doc.

'Anything?'

'No.'

And he was gone until the next time. Each time Mick felt somehow that he'd done wrong and would be punished for it. Like the time he was up before his old headmaster for thieving out of the Staff Room.

Mick answered this new ring. 'Hello.'

'Anything.'

Mick said, 'Hold on, please.' He held the phone to that the voice could hear him as he spoke. He threw the barman the keys. 'Wait for me in the car.'

The barman snatched the keys out of mid-air, picked up the bag of money and walked out without speaking. He did it quickly but Mick was still tempted to kick him up the backside to speed his journey.

Mindful of the need for brevity Mick said, 'Doc rang this morning and asked if he could borrow the car again today so we'd plenty of time to re-install the tracking device.' For a moment he wondered if he dared digress to tell where they had hidden the device and decided against it. 'He was there for almost three hours, then he returned the car and caught the express back to Belfast.'

'The same co-ordinates?' queried the voice.

'The same.' Mick read out the GPS co-ordinates, which corresponded to Connie's farm, and added, 'Again we didn't dare follow him too close so we can only guess where he stopped.'

'Don't guess.'

The voice disconnected.

Mick poured himself a stiff whiskey and drank it neat.

Chapter 71

Station Inspector Ian Patterson was tired; he hadn't slept properly in days. Mrs. Nelson was giving him hell, using hysteria as the basis for a compensation claim for the loss of her husband. It was all he could do to wish the Duty Sergeant a good morning.

Patterson asked, 'I'm expecting a package from Headquarters. Do you know if it's arrived?'

'DC Green's got something.'

No Sir, no offer to fetch it.

Patterson stared the Duty Sergeant out. The Duty Sergeant tried to ignore the look, but eventually he creaked to his feet. 'I'll get it for you, Sir.'

'Do,' said Patterson, smiling even as he registered his displeasure. 'If I'd wanted to be a messenger boy I'd have stayed on in my father's firm.' He walked off thinking that that particular sergeant and his bulging stomach was going to spend a lot of time on foot-patrol.

Patterson hardly had his hat off before DC Green came bustling in with a package. 'Sorry, Sir.'

The package was already unsealed. Patterson slid out a batch of photographs. Mug shots of known or suspected killers: some retained by hard men to do their dirty work, some who worked on contract. Patterson leafed through the photographs. 'Show them to my people, you never...'

The next photograph up was one of Doc.

'Sir?' asked DC Green, but he was talking to himself.

Patterson arrived at the front desk before the shock of recognition eased. 'Sergeant, into my room and bring the duty roosters.'

He tried to remember. Who was on duty the day of the garroting? Easy, everybody. But who did the door-to-door in Sperrin Manor? There was a car waiting outside Bradleys.

The sergeant came puffing in with the folders. Patterson threw the photograph across the desk. 'I talked to this man myself on the day of the murder, at the Bradley house.' He paced up and down. 'There was someone else in a car, a local man.' His finger stabbed at the sergeant. 'Big Mick, it was Big Mick.'

Green asked, 'Are you sure?'

165

'I wish I was as sure of heaven.' Patterson paced again. 'The Bradleys, what about those patrols?'

The sergeant said, 'Passing regularly, Sir. Nothing unusual.'

Patterson stopped pacing and stared at a photograph of his wife, Imelda, and their children. *If it was them, what would I want?* He turned to the sergeant. 'Station a car outside their gate. Tell the officers to stay alert.'

Chapter 72

An hour later Big Mick was in custody and playing dumb. He had spoken only once, and then into the microphone, to say, 'I want my solicitor present.' The Station Sergeant thought they would never get him to talk, he and Patterson had bet a double whiskey on it. The Detective Sergeant conducting the interrogation was breaking sweat. His future career depended on Patterson not losing, that had been made quite plain.

DC Green sighed as he leafed through the photographs for the umpteenth time. 'Makes you wonder, doesn't it?' He looked at Patterson. 'Where do we go from here, Sir?'

Patterson had to acknowledge it as a good question. The car with the "Vote Fetherton" sticker was awash with fingerprints and DNA: the dead man's, the owner's, sundry other males and females. Nothing that could possibly be linked with Doc Terence. Based on the smears, Doc, if it was him that day, had worn gloves the whole time he was in the car.

Patterson said, 'Show the photographs around the Enterprise Centre.' Green looked puzzled so Patterson explained. 'Doc Terence was in Glenlish that day, probably to terrorize poor old Nelson. Once his mate killed himself, Doc Terence needed to get away and fast, so where better to hide than the Enterprise Centre.'

He pushed his chair back and stood up. 'It's more-or-less on the way to the Bradley house. It's a Saturday so Mrs. Bradley should be home.'

Green asked, 'What are we going to tell her?'

Patterson liked Green, even if he didn't always remember to say "Sir". The young detective was willing to share responsibility. He said, by way of reply, 'Tell her that her husband's a dead man, he just doesn't know it yet.'

At the Enterprise Centre Patterson headed straight for the restaurant.

'Why the restaurant?' asked Green.

'It's a long drive from Belfast.'

The Enterprise Centre only opened for a half-day on a Saturday. The women behind the counter were getting ready to close, but were more than willing to giggle over the photographs. They rated the men by their sex appeal and assigned them to each other as their ideal lover. Doc's photograph was deliberately the last one in the pile.

'Hey, Ann,' said one of the women, a blonde, to the girl on the till. 'That's your boyfriend, the one with the eyes.'

'Couldn't be.' She looked at it. 'Oh, oh.'

Patterson raised an eyebrow to Green.

'Just think,' said the blonde. 'He came back yesterday to see you.'

'He never was.'

Patterson closed his eyes in despair. There couldn't be another dead body lying somewhere, could there?

'Why else did he buy flowers?' asked the blonde.

Ann sniffed. 'Well they didn't come in this direction.'

Green interrupted the woman. 'Can you remember when you first saw him?'

Ann said, 'That was the day he spilled the tea.' She pointed at the blonde. 'You didn't put the mop away and the manager fell over it. He could have killed himself.'

'Well he didn't, did he?'

'The day?' pressed Patterson, gently, having decided that Doc and his flowers were an unnecessary distraction. *Unless they were for someone's grave.*

The blonde spoke to Ann, delivering a telling riposte. 'I'd just heard about that young fellow killing himself. I was all upset because it reminded me of our Alan.'

'Two Kilkenny cats,' sighed Patterson as they walked back into the open. He stopped and stretched. 'It's not far to the Bradleys. I could do with a walk.'

Green didn't look happy, but he told the driver to meet them at the Bradleys house and they walked on.

Patterson said, 'We know that this Doc character was in town on the day of the garroting. Soon after the garroting he was having breakfast in the Enterprise Centre.'

Green said, 'And making damn sure that people there remembered him.'

Patterson's shudder was supposed to be for effect, but Green's words had struck home. 'I don't even want to think that way.'

Green persisted, 'It could be murder, Sir.'

Patterson nodded. 'Get Forensics back on that car, the passenger's side. Take it apart if necessary.'

They were on the back hill, leading up to Sperrin Manor. The slope cost Patterson a lot more puff than he liked. He surreptitiously patted his stomach.

More golf needed there.

Meantime he used Green as a sounding board. 'If Doc Terence came to terrorize Nelson, why did he call with the Bradleys and pretend to be a newspaper reporter?'

Green kicked impatiently at a loose stone. 'Maybe he didn't just speak to Mrs. Bradley. Maybe he threatened her.'

Patterson said, 'I doubt it. When I saw her she was ready to spit chips.'

Green looked straight at Patterson. Patterson almost nodded in approval at the confidence of the young officer. Green knew when to say Sir and when not, when to be the obedient junior and when to claim parity. Like now when they were jointly investigating a murder case.

Green said, 'I'm new here, Sir, and you know your patch. Where would someone like Doc Terence find somewhere to hide out?'

'The Glenlish Arms.'

Green had obviously heard the rumors, but didn't know the details. 'What goes on there?'

'Mostly hot air, thank God.'

They turned into Sperrin Manor.

'Two things,' said Green. 'Why did Doc Terence come back again yesterday?'

'Ask me the other.'

'Sir, what's so special about Bradley?'

Patterson sighed. 'What do you want to know? A politician gone bad? The man the town loves to hate?'

Green shook his head. 'If criminal gangs are after him then there's something else we don't know about.'

Patterson said, 'He was a family man: loyal, honest, with a good name about the town. He knew how to work and he knew how to relax. Any friends he made he kept. Politics always interested him, not politics, people and making the best of a bad job.'

His pace and his voice slowed as he reopened memories he preferred to forget. 'You know what it was like. All that sleaze in Westminster. Our sitting MP was up to his neck in it and his main opponent in court for taking backhanders on government contracts. It came to the General Election and people were saying that someone should do something about it. Then one night at the golf club we found ourselves looking at Paul.'

'We?'

'We,' said Patterson, firmly.

They were nearing the house. Patterson said, 'I'll tell you something I never told anybody else. Paul's wife, Barbara, is a bit sharp but she's a good woman. She didn't like him getting into politics, but she supported him one hundred percent. He was overworking, trying to run his business and be a full-time politician at the same time. He was losing weight as well, so a few weeks before that night she ordered him to see the doctor. The doctor reckoned the weight loss was due to overwork but ran blood tests just in case: liver, hemoglobin; the works. They came back clear. If he was taking drugs it started after that.'

'You say *if?*'

Patterson spoke with more passion than intended. 'I knew Bradley. He wouldn't even take a paracetamol if he could avoid it.' He looked anywhere but at Green.

They were silent after that, steeling themselves for the interview with Mrs. Bradley.

The two constables on guard saw them coming and climbed out of their car. They saluted and the senior of the two said, 'Nothing to report, Sir. Everything quiet.'

Patterson looked at the bungalow. The blinds were drawn and the garage door down. He asked, 'Have they gone somewhere?'

The two constables looked at each other and wouldn't meet his gaze. Patterson's stomach churned. Had they been guarding an empty house?

Or worse!

Chapter 73

Ian Patterson found very little to do when he got back to the police station. Big Mick still held out. He said he couldn't remember a thing about the day the youth garroted himself. He was always running someone somewhere. 'A good Samaritan, that's me,' he claimed.

The Bradley boys' opportune arrival home had saved the police from the embarrassment of forcing an entry into an empty house. Barbara was away for the weekend – where the boys wouldn't say. The boys themselves had spent the evening at a friend's house playing on his computer and then crashed-out on the floor.

Happy at not making a fool of himself and that the Bradleys were all right, Patterson decided to download all his concerns for the Bradley family onto the ACC. Of course, being the weekend, Thomson was at home, but the Duty Officer took the call. They agreed that questioning either Jimmy or Doc would be a waste of time without something concrete to go on.

They knew, or at least were fairly, sure that Doc had been in Glenlish the day of the lorry crash. It was difficult to tell from the charred remains, but the pathologist was puzzled by an unexplained wound in the driver's lower abdomen. Doc had an unexplained bloodstain on his shoe. Not the driver's, not the youth who had garroted himself, and not a Winston Shaw who had been murdered in Belfast the night before. Someone else. Someone without a police record or at least not one since DNA profiling became the norm.

Patterson decided that once he got the Duty Officer off the phone he'd head home. With a bit of luck he might get there before the migraine started. There had to be another body lying around. *Probably on my patch.*

While they were at it, the Duty Officer insisted that they reel in Bradley for his own good. If the wife wouldn't tell them where he was, then they'd have to do it the hard way. Patterson and the Duty Officer agreed they should send an "All Points" bulletin to New Scotland Yard. They had to be careful with the wording, not a hint must get out that Bradley's life was in danger otherwise the press would have a field day with conspiracy theories.

Patterson suggested something vague.
WANTED FOR QUESTIONING:PAUL BRADLEY,
PRESENT WHEREABOUTS UNKNOWN.

The Duty Officer was more suspicious of a man with "form" A man who associated with known gangsters, and was connected in some way to a series of unsolved murders.

Chapter 74

Even though he was in England Jimmy had the usual Saturday morning feeling of relief. No schools open, no school runs and he didn't have to get up. Even so he rang Doc early – a bit of revenge there – because Doc's unexplained delay in Glenlish meant that he'd missed Bradley. Doc didn't answer.

Worried, Jimmy rang Eleanor and put up with her tonguing about being woken up. No she didn't know where Doc was but he had left a message. She grumbled her way downstairs to find the piece of paper.

'Everybody's fine at home,' she said, 'And thank you for not asking. JP has gone off somewhere for the weekend and wouldn't say where or who with, not that you care.'

The message was the address of the Stockdale kennels. Jimmy let Eleanor complain herself into a good mood, then he hung up and luxuriated in a big, comfortable double-bed all to himself. He planned to time his arrival at Stockdales for around lunchtime. People, he knew from experience, tended to be more talkative later rather than first thing in the morning.

Creepy-crawly feelings of unease ran up his spine. Doc had gone missing again. England probably and after that bitch of wife of his. Jimmy had never liked the woman. Manipulative was the nicest thing he could say about her, but there were always two sides to every marital breakup. If Doc killed her there'd be a hell of a job proving his innocence.

The worry about Doc spoiled his rest. He got up and went in search of a late breakfast.

Chapter 75

Connie saw the blue car turn off the road into her laneway. For a moment her heart spluttered joy, thinking that it was Doc coming on one of his surprise visits. Her hand went automatically to her hair. It hung in tatters and she hadn't showered yet. She'd planned to shower and wash her hair before she went into town for her appointment at the hairdressers.

As the car got closer, Connie threw off her leather apron and used a plastic naming tag to scrape the worst of the potting compost out from under her nails. *A call to say he was coming wouldn't go amiss.* At least, thanks to Doc and the Stanley Knife, she was wearing new jeans and blouse. The new brassiere was still in its box. That would go on to come off when they went out for the promised dinner. Even the thought of Doc's hands sliding between material and flesh made her breath quicken.

Then she saw that the car was a Ford Focus, and felt disappointed. The car stopped in the farmyard and a man got out. He was thin and wore a crumpled suit. His shirt was open at the collar. She got a sense of someone playing at being casual and felt... not fear exactly, more the natural caution of a woman who lived and worked on her own. She held the plastic naming tag pointed-end out. *Dare he try anything.*

'Good morning,' said the thin man.

'Can I help you?'

'I'm sorry to bother you.'

She noted that he had the accent of someone reared in the better parts of Belfast and that he didn't look particularly "bothered". His eyes, having done a quick sweep of the farmyard were now aimed straight at her. He'd know her again if they met. *And I'll know you, sunshine.* His jaw had a slight twist as if it had been broken at some time.

The man continued. 'I'm heading for Glenlish. I tried a shortcut and seem to have run out of signs.'

She made her lips shape a smile at his weak joke. He hadn't left the side of the car and she stayed well back. Even so she gripped the naming tag tighter. What was it about him that scared her? The way he stood, she realized. On his toes, balanced, ready to spring in any direction. And his voice had the demanding tone of someone used to getting their own way. Worse than that, the greyhound bitch had slunk out of sight when he got out of the car. Mostly it stayed clear of strangers, with Doc it wanted to be friends. And this man? Gone. *Not a good sign.*

She pointed to the right. 'Head that way until you come to a T junction on the main road. Turn left and follow the signs from there.'

'Thank you. Sorry for being a bother Ms...'

'Mrs. Mrs. Taylor,' said Connie, with emphasis on the "Mrs.".

He got back into the car, did a three-point turn and drove away.

Connie watched the car until it turned out of her laneway and disappeared up the county road. The greyhound bitch came crawling up, all apologetic for its cowardice.

Connie gave it a pat, as much to convince herself that everything was normal, as anything else. 'You were a great help.'

It was all in her imagination of course, but she'd keep the shotgun loaded and handy for the next few nights and be more particular about switching on the burglar alarm.

Chapter 76

Mick was in no mood to take calls from unknown numbers. *Reporters or somebody*. He kept it at that, expletives deleted, not even allowed in his mind, because he was home and he wanted his children reared properly: young ladies and gentlemen mixing with the best.

The unknown number came up for the third time. Mick had his hand drawn back, ready to shatter the phone against the wall. *A night in police cells and now this*. Reluctantly he brought his arm down. He couldn't smash the phone and he couldn't disconnect because he was expecting a call from his solicitor. *Sheer harassment the whole thing, Patterson and his thugs laying into me. Me!*

He pressed the "answer" key. 'Listen, friend, I don't know who you're looking for, but it's not me. Ring this number one more time and I'll make it my business to find out your name and come visit.'

The voice of cold glass gave the GPS co-ordinates for Connie's farm, then he said. 'That woman, Mrs. Taylor, keep an eye out. Use this number. Let me know in advance the next time Doc comes visiting or if she goes travelling.'

'How can I...?'

'Make it happen.'

'I'll...'

The caller had disconnected. Mick stood on in a cold sweat. The cold glass voice didn't have to say it, the implication was there. "Make it happen – or else".

Chapter 77

The Booking Agent that Doc and JP had come to Liverpool to meet was way beyond fat. His clothes concealed slabs of self-indulgent flesh and even walking made him breathe heavily. He'd already had his breakfast but said he'd take a bite for form's sake. He ordered bacon and egg, with toast on the side.

They were in a greasy-spoon café, his choice. The wonder, as Doc saw it, was that he hadn't come in a battered old overcoat, with a hat to cover his face. His whole attitude was that of someone on a covert operation rather than a betrayal of his company.

Doc settled for tea and toast. Enough fat floated in the air already, he reckoned, without any of it landing on his plate.

JP ordered a coffee, decided that the mug wasn't clean and didn't touch it. 'Did you get the information?' he asked the Booking Agent.

The man tried to look as if he'd crawled under barbed wire fences and evaded savage guard dogs. 'It wasn't easy.'

'That's why we came to you,' said JP smoothly. He touched the breast pocket that held his wallet.

The Booking Agent's eyes locked on the pocket. He palmed a memory stick onto the table. 'It's all there. Any basic Word programme will open it.'

Doc had expected sheets of paper he could look through. He trapped the Booking Agent's hand over the memory stick. 'If I'm paying you for nothing, I'll be back looking for my money… with interest.'

Not that he wanted too. There's too much blubber there, he thought. It's already messy before you get anywhere near doing real damage. *Bloody DNA.* He let the hand slide free. If felt contaminated from the Booking Agent's grease.

'It's there, it's there,' said the Booking Agent. He started to sweat and looked anxious to be away.

'It better be,' said JP.

Doc said nothing, he'd already issued his threat. He stood up and walked out, leaving the Booking Agent to his breakfast and that day's Belfast edition of the *Daily Mirror*. The newspaper had an envelope of money taped inside it. As if some trained watcher wouldn't notice the transfer, thought Doc. He hated the amateurs he had to deal with in his profession.

Chapter 78

JP followed Doc out of the Café, his ear to his mobile phone. 'Yes, mum. No, mum.' He mouthed at Doc, 'Three bags full, mum.' Then he said, 'I'll be back in time for work on Monday at the latest.' A pause to listen, then he added. 'Drink, drugs and loose women, you know how it is, mum.'

He held the phone out and Doc could hear the squawk of indignation come over the ether.

Doc waited patiently for the call to end. He'd no plans for the day except to find an internet café to see what was on the memory stick, then catch the first available plane back to Belfast.

Finally JP put the phone away. 'Mum says you're not to let me get into trouble and The Man was ringing. Something about an envelope you've got of his.'

'So what are your plans for the weekend?' asked Doc. His day had suddenly become busy.

JP smiled, which made Doc wonder who else had been booked onto that morning's flight.

'Good job,' said Doc, nodding back at the greasy spoon café where the Booking Agent worked manfully through his second breakfast.

'Thanks, Doc.' A bus turned the corner onto the road. Without appearing to will it, JP's body was already straining to reach the bus stop before the bus. 'Do you need me for anything else?'

'No.'

Doc walked off, aware of JP's flying footsteps heading away from him. Liverpool might have regenerated itself, he thought, but this part of the city is the same dirty old hole.

He headed towards Liverpool city center, walking slowly. With JP safely out of the way, he took out his wallet. A child's envelope lay folded into the compartment designed for business cards. Doc slid out the envelope and carefully peeled back the gummed flap. Written on the inside of the flap was a telephone number and two times: one in the morning and one in the afternoon. Doc made a mental note of the times and walked on until he reached an internet café.

He went in, ordered a cup of tea and a pastry, produced identification for a Ronnie Fetherton and bought computer time, paying cash.

The memory stick held a satisfactory number of files, and spreadsheets, and the security video of passengers as they went through the departure gates. The spreadsheets gave the names and addresses of all the passengers on all the flights, together with their Travel Agency where they hadn't booked on line themselves.

The tickets for three passengers had been booked onto Doc's flight by the Travel Agency Ronnie controlled: Doc and a middle-aged couple. To be doubly sure he looked at the videos of passengers on the Friday evening and Saturday morning flights. There was no way to tell from the security footage who was whom. Several men appeared to be travelling on their own: workers or business men going home for the weekend or heading off for a weekend away.

Doc wasn't so much disappointed as slightly frustrated. The man – and knowing macho Ronnie it had to be a man – could have taken a different flight or booked online direct or be England based.

He studied all likely faces, hoping to sense in one the shadow of the unseen watcher, the orchestrator of the attacks on him in the London underground. Again no one stood out.

He's good.

At long last business was no longer routine. Doc sensed a real battle ahead as he sent a copy of the files to an email address not even "known" by Fredrick Robinson. Then he deleted the files from the memory stick and left it in the computer for the next user to make a lucky find.

On his way out he checked his watch. Nicely timed to make the morning call, he thought. He flagged down a taxi and told the driver to take him to Lime Street Railway Station. The station had banks of public phones and the constant public announcements would prevent any eavesdroppers from listening in.

Chapter 79

The Man picked up on the first ring.

'It's Kyle,' said Doc.

'The contract we discussed,' said The Man without preamble.

Doc waited.

'Payment for a successful outcome would be... generous on this occasion.'

A sound came down the telephone, as if The Man was swinging something metallic to and fro.

'Which product?' Doc asked.

'Ah!' said The Man. 'One is tried and tested, nothing exciting but dependable. The other is a next generation product and holds great promise. The problem is, they are totally incompatible. Bottlenecks could occur, accidents happen.'

'There have been casualties already,' said Doc.

'One of the expected risks in the development of a new product,' said The Man.

'Health and Safety at Castlereagh might think differently,' said Doc, referring to the headquarters of the Police Service Northern Ireland.

The something metallic, probably a pen, was still swinging to and fro so he added, 'When I got your message I assumed you had decided which product to go with.'

The Man sighed. 'Opinions are more one way than the other. The minority wish me to... conduct further tests. The majority insist on instant action.'

'Your call then,' said Doc.

'Have you an opinion?' asked The Man.

'I'm only the facilitator,' said Doc.

'Either way?'

'Whatever,' said Doc.

'You have a way of focusing my mind,' said The Man. 'Also, we are afraid that the missing part may be somewhat noisy in operation.'

Doc said nothing. Bradley wasn't his problem. He waited for The Man to continue.

'The current field trial. I think we should base our final decision on the ultimate outcome.' The sense of a shrug came down the line. 'Perhaps we will find that neither product is suitable for our purposes.'

Again Doc waited The Man out.

'The missing part required by both products, has it been sourced yet?'

'Yes.'

Doc gave the Stockdales' name and address.

'Thank you,' said The Man. 'There will be a consultation fee.'

He hung up. Doc walked across to the Starbucks café and ordered an early lunch of bagel and bacon with cheese on top. He thought about the phone call while he ate. Mostly the Man's remark about the "missing part being noisy in operation". That translated it into "We are afraid Bradley might talk".

Talk about what?

Chapter 80

It was after one o'clock when Jimmy reached Marston and the Stockdale kennels. He drove into the yard to find a couple, a tall grey haired man and a younger woman, fussing over a fawn dog. The woman held the dog on a lead while the man examined it for injuries. Jimmy liked the way the woman stood. He thought her pouting breasts went with a spiky temperament. *A challenge that one.* Made himself think again of business.

He got out of the car and turned casually, as if looking the place over, but really keeping an eye out for his quarry. He didn't want Bradley to bolt unseen.

He said, 'I'm looking to get in touch with Paul Bradley.'

Ken said, 'He's not here. But if you've come about the bitch, we're authorized to sell her.'

Jimmy shook his head. 'It's Bradley himself I'm looking for.'

Ken said, 'He's taken the weekend off.'

Taken the weekend off? Jimmy smacked the palm of a hand against his forehead. *Bradley's working at the kennels.*

All this time he'd been thinking of Bradley as the successful accountant who could easily afford to keep a dog at professional kennels. Of course he wouldn't, not with the wife and kids at home struggling to make ends meet.

'Monday?' he asked to be saying something because the couple were giving him strange looks.

Kristie said, 'He told us he'd be back Monday morning at the latest, but I don't think we'll ever see him again.'

Chapter 81

Back down the road Jimmy parked up at a remote call-box and phoned home. His wife answered on the first ring. She seemed relieved to hear from him.

'Jimmy, be careful. I've just got a text from your girlfriend. Ronnie Fetherton is catching the evening boat to England with some of the worst men he's got about the place. He knows about Bradley and Marston.'

'Bad news travels fast,' said Jimmy. *Ronnie and his men heading for England?* Which left him on his own, without even a paper knife for protection. 'I need Doc and some of the boys.'

She said, 'I've the boys booked on the evening flight to Heathrow, but Jimmy...'

'What?'

'They're away home to pack their beta blockers and statins.'

She didn't have to spell it out. They'd all grown old.

He said, 'I'll order up wheelchairs at this end.'

Which left him with a problem. Ronnie's men were of the new breed, younger and fitter, and more vicious. If it came to a straight fight there could only be one winner.

Jimmy couldn't stop himself from looking over his shoulder for a shadow that wasn't there. With Doc around he always felt safe. 'What flight is Doc getting?'

'He's away somewhere and The Man's been looking for him as well.' She sounded worried.

'This is turning into a fun weekend,' said Jimmy, and talked about other things while he planned what weapons and transport he needed for his men when they arrived.

First thing he rang Far and Wide Travel to speed the travel arrangements along. A girl answered.

Jimmy asked, 'Can I speak to JP?'

She said, 'JP and his uncle have gone to England for the weekend.'

'Have they?' said Jimmy and hung up.

JP in England for the weekend? That he could understand. JP was over twenty-one and he had a girlfriend somewhere. But why hadn't he warned him about Doc going as well? Maybe JP didn't like his aunt but that was no reason to help Doc kill the woman.

Jimmy drove on until he found a Starbucks. He ordered a latte and sipped it down while he had a good think to himself. Doc was in England to kill his wife. There was nothing he could do to prevent that. Even if he stopped him this weekend he'd get her sometime.

On top of that, The Man was looking for Doc. That could only mean a special job, *but who's in the firing line*? Things had been peaceful recently, with only himself and Ronnie at each other's throat.

Jimmy found a public booth, consulted his diary for a number and rang it. The Booking Agent answered and went all panicky when he realized who was on the phone.

'It was all on that memory stick, honest to God. It should have worked.'

'Aye,' said Jimmy, wondering what he was talking about. Someone had wanted to know something about flights and it had to be Doc to generate that sort of panic. 'Remind me again.'

'Just the passengers on those flights.'

'Tell you what,' said Jimmy. 'Just email the information to me at Far and Wide Travel. Mark it for my attention.'

'I will... I will.' The Booking Agent was breathing deeply in panic. 'Is there anything else I can get you while I'm at it?'

Jimmy asked, 'Is there a Paul or Barbara Bradley booked onto a Belfast flight anytime this weekend?'

He heard the rattle as the Booking Agent tripped over himself in his haste to supply the information. Barbara was booked on the first flight out on Monday morning. He also confirmed that the other information was already on its way to Far and Wide Travel.

Jimmy had seen an internet café somewhere nearby. He went looking for it, feeling out of place in a chrome and plastic atmosphere of teenage hormones and the faint trace of marijuana. This time he consulted his diary line by line as he initiated a remote access to the travel company's computer and called up the Booking Agent's email. He spent a long time looking at the list of names and the photographs of people going through security. The only one he recognized was Doc.

Doc had booked his flight through Ronnie's firm so Doc was up to something other than killing his poor bitch of a wife. Bradley was on the run again and how had Ronnie found out about Bradley being at Stockdales? That was something only he and Doc knew.

Jimmy had another look over his shoulder, this time wary of any shadow.

Chapter 82

That Saturday morning, soon after eleven o'clock, Barbara walked into the Stockdale's yard. She wore light blue jeans and a buttermilk blouse, and carried a small grip. A black handbag was slung over her shoulder. She stopped as she turned the corner from the drive. She looked uncertain and half inclined to run.

Paul saw her through the Feed-house window. Kristi was saying something at the time but he brushed past her and walked, stiff with shock, across to meet Barbara.

He said, 'Hallo.'

She said, 'Hallo.'

An unreasonable fear niggled at him. 'Are the boys... has anything happened?'

'They're fine.'

He thought she looked, not older, that was there as well, but something else. Her face bore a wisdom born of bitter experience and her eyes were assessing him, measuring his reaction to her sudden appearance. They looked from him to somewhere over his shoulder and hardness came into her face. He glanced around. Kristi was leaning against the Feed-house doorway, arms folded. Watching.

He knew what Barbara was there about. He couldn't go home. He still wasn't fit to deal with the contempt of people who once believed in him. *Yet Barbara and the boys have to deal with it every day.* The very thought of going home made his stomach twist with nerves.

'Come up to the granny flat,' he said, rather than have Kristi overhear.

For once, closing the outer door created a refuge from the world rather than a barrier keeping him in.

Barbara followed him up the stairs. She stood in the sitting room looking awkward. She put her bags down.

They hadn't touched yet.

Needing time to think, he said, 'I'll put the kettle on.'

She nodded. She followed him into the hallway. 'Where's the...'

He pointed. 'At the bottom, the door's open.'

He filled the kettle and hunted out the best mugs. He heard her come out of the bathroom and her footsteps stop as she peaked into his bedroom, then pass the kitchen to look in at the spare bedroom. It's not that she was suspicious, he knew. She just had to reassure herself that he lived alone.

He realized that absolute trust had gone, that he'd always have to be careful around other women. He couldn't blame her, felt frustrated. If only he could remember what had happened that night. Could he have taken the head-staggers or something? But didn't think that likely.

He was wondering if he should put milk in the jug or just use the carton when she came in.

'May I have a drink of water?' she asked.

'Sure.' He was in the middle of spooning coffee into the cafeteria. 'I'll get you a glass in a minute.'

She lifted a mug from the drainer. It said, Liverpool-The Greatest. 'This will do.'

The mug rattled against the tap when she swilled it out and water jibbled as she drank. It rattled again as she put it down.

Paul dared touch her arm with his fingertips. 'Are you that frightened of me?'

'Frightened?' she said. 'Frightened?' She gripped his body to hers trying to make them one again. 'Of you? Don't be daft!'

Paul hardly gripped her back. If only he could believe that as well. *If not her, what was I doing that time with the knife?*

The internal phone rang.

Paul almost sighed in relief. Now he could step back from Barbara before he found his hands around her throat.

The phone rang again. He fumbled for the receiver. In turning he leaned on Barbara's shoulder.

She grabbed it. 'Easy, I've a touch of neuralgia there.'

The normality of her little plague made him smile. Her first complaint since their troubles had started.

Maybe things are normal again. Maybe I'm normal.

'Yes?' he said, into the phone.

It was Kristi ringing. She said, 'Brunch. It's a bit early but we thought your good lady might be hungry from travelling.'

He was equally polite. 'Thank you, we'll be down in ten minutes.'

'Take your time, it's cold anyway.'

He had a cool shower to wash away the sweat and doggy smells and dressed again in fresh clothes from the hot-press. He knew he had lost before the argument could even start. His days at the kennels were numbered. Barbara had come to remind him of his responsibilities.

The kennels and a job, home and the dole. They would have to move. Glenlish was no place for him now, people there had long memories. That meant that Barbara would be out of a job as well.

Going downstairs was like walking into the unknown. At least Barbara's hand held his, so that bit was all right again.

The Stockdales were waiting for them on the patio. Kristi had changed out of jeans into a discrete dress and put on make-up. Paul made the introductions.

'You work, I believe,' said Kristi. She made it sound like something she had never tried.

'Yes, in a bank.'

'Manager?'

'Cashier.'

'Salad,' asked Ken, hastily, and monopolized Barbara for the rest of the meal. Paul didn't dare be more than formally polite to Kristi and help her clear up between courses.

She tackled him in the kitchen. She stood looking at him with her hands on her hips. 'You need a real woman.'

It could have been a nasty dig at Barbara. He chose to take it as a tease and tried to take the battle into her court. 'I'd only be exercise for you.'

She snorted. 'You overrate yourself.'

He found himself laughing as she chasséd out of the kitchen.

Chapter 83

Ken gave Paul the rest of the weekend off. He quickly packed his good clothes and wash-bag and had a last look around. All of a sudden the granny flat was no longer home.

Barbara didn't even make a face as she got into the old van. From the outside it looked like nothing, inside was factory clean and the engine ran as sweet as Paul's amateur mechanics could make it. A gap came in the traffic and he pulled out on to the road.

Barbara relaxed in her seat and breathed a sigh of relief. 'I thought I'd never get away from that bitch.'

He felt embarrassed at defending Kristi. 'She's all right when you get to know her.'

'She's a cow!'

He kept his face straight.

The traffic had slowed so he tucked in behind an eight-wheeled rig, content to follow. Jimmy passed them without one seeing the other.

Barbara's hand came over to hold his. 'I love your letters. The boys keep them in a shoebox in their bedroom. They laugh at me when I want to read them, they call it mother's weepy period.'

Bitter memories started to surface in their heads.

He said, to break the cycle of thought. 'Girl's only worth a few hundred pounds at this point.'

Barbara said, 'I know you'd like to keep her but...'

He finished it for her. 'But a dog in training costs money that we don't have.'

She was smiling at him so it wasn't such a hard wrench. He and Girl had gone through a lot together. They'd talked, well he'd talked and she listened, right through the worst of the hallucinations. He smiled to himself. Repeat that to the wrong person and he'd find himself back in the funny farm.

The motorway was taking them somewhere when he didn't want to go anywhere. He took the first turn-off and headed for a stand of trees on the horizon. They came across a truckers' motel there. It was neat and functional and impersonal, but well within their price range so they booked in.

The bedroom had chipped and worn furniture, a wafer-thin mattress and nylon sheeting, the sort that made him sweat in the heat. However the room was spotless and the bath big enough wallow in.

Paul put the bags on the bed and turned to see Barbara at the mirror. She was flicking her hair into place with her fingers as she watched him. It jiggled a memory and his smile at having her with him again slipped.

'Enjoy the dogs last night?' he asked.

She blushed.

'Forget it,' he said, quickly. Any explanation would involve shadowy other women and they were past that stage.

She searched her suitcase and handed over a handful of envelopes. 'I nearly forgot, post.'

She busied herself at the hospitality tray making coffee.

There was barely half a dozen envelopes. The others: the bills, the tax demands, the anonymous letters, had all been weeded out. He read them and appreciated the normality they represented.

She came back without the coffee and chose a chair rather than join him on the bed. She sat stiff and awkward. He assumed because of the attempted lovemaking that would come with the night. He dreaded it as well.

Barbara said, in a clipped voice. 'There's another one.'

'Yes?'

Her hands shook as she fistled a crumpled white envelope out of her bag. She couldn't even hand it to him, but slid it across the bed with the tips of her fingernails, face down. He saw that she'd had it for a while, for its surface was shiny with usage.

Barbara wouldn't meet his gaze.

Eventually, after a long silence, while he waited for an explanation that wasn't offered, he picked it up. The recognition of the handwriting was like a blow to the face. He dropped the envelope and wiped his fingers on his shirt as if reacting to a burn.

'Destroy the damn thing,' he ordered, suddenly angry, but she shook her head.

He wanted to tear it to shreds in front of her to prove... He closed his eyes in despair. That would prove nothing.

The letter was from Olive Shaw, his former secretary. Barbara had carried it with her for weeks, too frightened to open it and even more frightened of telling him that she had it. He looked at it carefully, delaying the inevitable. The envelope had a nick at the top as if she had started to tear it up. Not the whole way, not enough to pull the contents clear and then replace them. The date stamp was blurred.

It took him a while before he dared touch the envelope again, and when he did it was in a sudden move. He used both hands to rip the envelope apart and had to read the first page twice before he could even start to focus in on the words.

Chapter 84

Paul,

    I saw you the other day but you didn't see me. I'd gone to you, even now I thought if I could explain you would help. But I hadn't the nerve to go to the house and then I saw you in the street. I couldn't believe it was you at first because you had changed so much. You looked so down, so beaten, and I destroyed you.

    Paul, they gave us no choice. It was either you or Elaine. "You can't keep an eye on her all the time" they said. "You never know what might happen to a young girl on her own".

    I lied. For Elaine I lied. You never touched me, yet I had to say you forced me to have sex with you if I wanted to keep my job. They were smart, getting us to book the room, then not turning up for the first two meetings. It set up a pattern. They always meant to do for you.

    I'm telling you this because it doesn't matter anymore. Winston has taken Elaine over to Luton. She thinks she's going for a holiday with my sister.

    Perhaps sometime you can explain to Elaine how much Winston and I love her and what we did to protect her even though it cost us everything.

    Please forgive me. Please understand.

Olive

Chapter 85

Paul held Olive's letter for a long time, reluctant to finish with it, to say goodbye to an old friend. In the end he shoved the letter at Barbara and jerked to his feet. The confines of the room, the closed door, choking him.

The early part of that night was suddenly there in his mind in all its clarity. Olive had been acting funny for a day or two: unusually quiet: no tonguing, no gossip. He thought it was a family problem, she hinted that things weren't right at home, and he left it at that, not liking to interfere.

The sunlight in the room made the liquid in Barbara's eyes sparkle like stars. 'Forced? Her? Get real, Paul.'

Paul wasn't listening. In his mind the sparkle in Barbara's eyes was expanding to include every light in the room. It seemed the funniest thing.

He remembered he couldn't understand why Olive looked so hangdog serious. 'Lighten up,' he'd said to her.

Then the lights grew in intensity, glaring his eyes, fading, then glaring again. Olive straddled him. She was naked. Disembodied arms lifted his hands up until his thumb rested on the birthmark in the inside of her left breast. He'd only ever seen the top of birthmark before and had tried not to wonder at its shape and length. Now he knew. And he couldn't understand why Olive was crying even as he…

He fought down bile and shame. 'God forgive me, but I think I raped her.'

Barbara registered shock, as if he'd back-handed her across the face.

He tried to explain about the lights and the disembodied arms. Had the sense not to mention the birthmark.

His tears trickled between his fingers. He had to force himself to look at Barbara. She stood over him snarling, wanting details of whose arms and what lights. How had they ended up in bed together?

NAKED?

That was the bit she dwelt on.

'You must remember.'

'I can't. No I don't.'

'Were you drinking?'

'We were waiting for people to arrive. It was work.'

193

'Some bloody work.'

Still snarling she asked, 'Coffee then?'

He didn't know, couldn't remember. Felt so inadequate because he knew what she was thinking. That Olive had drugged his drink. And was grateful she was giving him some benefit of the doubt.

Yes, they'd flasks of coffee and tea laid on. They'd done the same the previous nights. And, yes, he'd have a cup or two while waiting for the people who never turned up. Olive only drank green tea. But that night? He could only suppose yes.

Barbara was standing so close. He wished she go back a couple of steps. Somehow he felt still contaminated by what had gone on between him and Olive. *She must get the smell.*

Finally Barbara backed off. She waved Olive's letter at him like a flag. 'All that stuff about being forced? Huh! She was one of them right from the start.'

He couldn't defend Olive. He couldn't defend himself. She'll want a divorce. *Deserves it.*

Words echoed in his head, words he remembered saying to Olive through the glaring lights, 'Why are you doing this to me, we're friends?'

And Olive's reply, 'I'm sorry. Forgive me.'

Now this letter.

He said to Barbara, fear making him speak more sharply than he intended, 'When did this come? Why didn't you say?'

Barbara said, 'I'll wipe the floor with that bitch for what she put me through.'

'When... did... you... get... the... letter?' repeated Paul.

Barbara gave ground first. She buried her face in her hands. Feeling daring at even touching his wife, he pulled her onto the bed beside him and put an arm around her shoulders.

'When?' he asked, more gently this time.

She couldn't or wouldn't reply and while he waited he looked again at the first page of the letter. It was undated. Then at the envelope, he couldn't even guess the month. He pressed the creases out of the pages with his thumb, feeling very sad.

At long last she said, in almost a whisper, 'It was the day after you went into hospital. She was found in some hotel room. Valium and whiskey.'

'Dead?'

She nodded.

Paul burned with impotent anger. Olive had battled with him for justice for the ordinary people and they had lost. He knew he would grieve for her later. In the meantime she must be forgotten because Barbara's hate and suspicions wouldn't allow him to talk of her and to remember the good times. The having it off together jokes that blew up in their faces, and maybe gave the gangsters the idea in the first place.

Barbara suddenly grabbed him. 'That's it,' she said, all excited. 'Olive's letter, you did see her. You weren't trying to kill me; you were protecting me. You thought her friends were coming to harm us and that's why you went rampaging…' She couldn't finish it.

She dug a tissue out of her bag and blew her nose, fussed with her makeup and hair. He watched her calm herself and wished he could do the same.

She turned from the mirror. 'Have you any idea what I've gone through? All those old bitches and their condescending sympathy "what a pity the house had to go, my dear". And "how do you manage?". I want to spit it back in their faces.' She held up the letter. 'I'm going to ram this down their throats.'

'Give me a day or two,' he pleaded. 'Let me sort things out in my head first.'

'I suppose you'll go back to the kennels.'

There was malice in her voice.

He knew she was thinking of Kristi and kept his fingers away from the scar in case she would take that as a sign of guilt.

Some sort of word association between Kristi and Olive made him ask, 'What about Olive's husband, Sam, have you heard anything?'

Her anger faded to be replaced with wariness. She fiddled with the kettle and cups. 'Murdered somewhere off Sandy Row.'

His anger came boiling up again. 'They'll pay. They'll pay with their own blood, even if I have to do it myself.' He paced the room, wanting to kick holes in the wall. As suddenly as it had come the anger drained away leaving his insides feeling like jelly. He realized that he still wasn't a hundred percent right and lay down on the bed so that Barbara wouldn't see the nervous shake in his body.

She came over and stood, white faced, looking down at him. He curled a hand around the back of her knee. 'It's okay, I'm not going to touch you.'

'You couldn't,' she said, and burst into tears. He pulled her down onto his chest and comforted her while she cried for them both. They slept after that. He woke to find her fingering the scar on his forehead.

He kissed her fingertips one by one and said, 'That was some row: you and me, and the boys trying to come between us.'

'I broke our loving cup,' she said.

'I never saw it coming.'

The memories they were sharing at that point made them quiet. After a time their bodies eased into a familiar entwining and they kissed and caressed gently, not rushing things. Barbara became concerned at crushing her good dress. Paul added to the rucking with an exploring hand.

Barbara swung out of bed and insisted that they undress. Paul watched while pretending not to, as her body appeared from beneath the layers of clothes. All the curves and soft bits, and the appendix scar, were still there.

He was relieved when she slipped under the sheets still wearing her bra and pants. Now he could keep on his underpants. Hide the fact that the lust was only in his head.

They lay for a time, brushing breasts and chest. Her fingers furrowed his stomach and slid to well below his belly button.

'Are you not in the mood?' she asked.

Again the old suspicions were there, that he was getting his fill at the kennels.

'I'm still impotent.'

Felt less than half a man for that admission.

The suspicions drained away. The smile returned as she unsnapped her bra and slid the pants enticingly low.

She said, 'Be inventive.'

Chapter 86

Paul found Barbara waiting for him in the far corner of the motel restaurant. She sat eased back in her chair, watching the place come alive with the first of the evening customers. Kitchen sounds that normally wouldn't be heard echoed through the cavernous room.

He slipped into the chair beside her and put two envelopes on the table. They were held together by an elastic band. 'No problem, they let me use the photocopier myself.'

She nodded in reply.

They ordered and were waiting for the first course to arrive when he asked, 'If this isn't a daft question. At my trial, how long did I get?'

'You don't know?'

He shook his head.

'Three years,' she said. 'Three years.'

The old hurt lines were suddenly there as deep as ever.

He put his hand on hers. 'I must have got out early?'

She nodded. 'There was a riot. Apparently you did something very brave.'

'Did I?'

She started to laugh. 'Oh, God, you're hopeless.'

'I remember,' he said. 'I remember being home again, not home, the new house, and just sitting or taking Girl for long walks.' He smiled at her. 'Why didn't you sell Girl with the rest of the dogs?'

She said, 'I felt safe at night with her running about the garden and she was great for the boys.'

'You didn't bring them?' he asked and had to stop himself from looking around for the boys. Not jumpiness from the illness, he assured himself. Just the number of intimate moments they'd interrupted over the years.

Barbara said, 'They're at home. They promised faithfully they wouldn't leave the house.'

Her mind must have skipped onto the same track as Paul's because she looked around as well. 'While you were... away... Shane and Rory walked Girl and took her rabbiting to have her right for Dad when he got home again.'

He pressed against her, from ankle to shoulder. 'And what they got was a gruff, moronic, ungrateful twit.'

'And that was the good days,' she said, trying to make light of it. She shook her head. 'The boys kept saying there was something wrong with their Dad. I should have listened to them.' She looked into his eyes as if trying to find the answer there. 'When did you start feeling normal?'

He said, 'In the Sanatorium. One morning I woke up and there it was.' He touched his head. 'Firing on all cylinders again. You, bless you, wanted me to come home but I didn't dare until I was sure it was permanent.'

The starters came and they shared them: vegetable rolls and spare ribs. He wanted to know and she refused to say where she had found the money to buy the van or how she could run the household and pay off the debts on her small salary.

'We manage,' she said and would give no more details.

On their way back to the room they stopped at the post-box in Reception. One of the envelopes was already stamped and addressed. He held it to the opening of the post-box. 'If I keep it, I'll burn it. If I let you have it, you'll give it to a newspaper.'

She nodded. 'So what are you going to do, King Solomon?'

He said, 'I'm sending it to the only politically sensitive yet fiercely independent person I know. The Speaker of the House of Commons.'

Chapter 87

Jimmy built up a head of steam. Bradley wasn't on the run, everyone was looking for him. 'And he can't be got,' Jimmy shouted at the sky. The next time he wanted to talk to someone, to hell with the psychology approach. He'd grab the bugger by the balls and then talk quiet.

He knew the make, color and registration number of Paul's van, and he looked for it in every carpark in Marston, without any luck. They've gone to London, he decided, and tried all the service stations on the way. He gave up the chase on the outskirts of London and checked into the Strand Palace hotel on the edge of Leicester Square. In the evening, he tried to second-guess which stage show the Bradleys would go to. Spent all of Sunday morning tramping Oxford Street without any luck. I'm daft, he decided in the end. Mrs. Bradley is a Harrods sort of woman. She'll look even if she can't afford to buy.

He caught the tube to Knightsbridge and went into the store. Tramped the floors until he was sick, sore and tired of shops and shopping. His last call was in "Menswear". Bradley might need a pair of socks.

The supervisor was straight over. 'Mr. Terence, so pleased to see you again.'

'You remember me?' asked Jimmy.

He got a smile. 'Sir, you are the only gentleman ever to want the Harrods label taken off their purchases.'

Jimmy said, 'It's my customers. They bitch about the fares as it is without letting them see where I buy my gear.'

The supervisor fingered Jimmy's jacket. 'Perhaps…'

An hour later Jimmy limped back to his hotel ladened down with Harrods bags. He wouldn't use public transport on principle and he thought the taxi prices sheer extortion. He wouldn't mind charging them, but damned if he was going to pay.

He rang home and got Eleanor, they talked for a while. She wanted to join him. 'It's business,' he said, hastily, and had to promise her a trip to London.

'I'd love to see the Christmas lights,' she said.

Jimmy rubbed his feet and groaned.

He rang The Man to give him an update on the search for Bradley. The Man informed him that Ronnie and his men were on their way to England. Jimmy expressed surprise and suggested that he and Ronnie should rendezvous first thing Monday morning at a service station near Marston. That would keep that lot of troublemakers well out of the way while he, Jimmy, collared Bradley at Heathrow. Surely to goodness the man would see his wife to the airport?

On Monday morning Jimmy arrived at the airport early and took up position at "Arrivals". He saw the van at last and couldn't believe that Mrs. Bradley would be seen dead in anything like it. He moved forward to intercept. It pulled up well short of him and he increased his pace.

Barbara got out and slammed the door. She was half laughing, half crying.

'Next week,' shouted Paul through the open window and pulled away.

He's not stopping. He's not coming in.

Jimmy ran forward to attract Paul's attention, but Paul's eyes were on the image of Barbara in the rear-view mirror and he never saw him.

Barbara walked into the terminal. Jimmy ran for his car, pushing past people and cutting across the traffic. He was in his car and out of the car park in no time and had a clear run on the motorway. He reckoned he had to be going half as fast again as the van and yet, twenty minutes down the road there was still no sign of it.

Chapter 88

Everything about Paul felt gritty. He shifted uncomfortably in his seat and told himself that the kennels and a constant stream of hot water was only two hours away. The shower would pound him clean, but in the bath he could stretch out and doze. *Which? Maybe both.* He felt alive in a way that he hadn't in years, and ashamed at his own cowardice.

Having decided, at the very last moment, that Olive's letter was too important to trust to the post he had decided to hand-deliver it. His nerve failed him within sight of Westminster Palace. He'd spent the whole of Sunday afternoon nervously pacing up and down Parliament Square before delivering the letter in a rush. Now all he could do was sit wait at the kennels, hoping for a reply. *Or something. Anything.*

A police car crawled into the space behind him.

His eyes automatically sought the reassurance of the speedometer needle. *Inside the limit.* The lights were working, and anyway it was daylight and he wasn't using them.

The white prowl car stayed on his tail.

A coincidence? He decided to find out.

He reduced his speed from sixty to fifty to forty-five. The police car slowed and held its place. The motorway traffic bunched up behind them. One driver in a crimson Jaguar gave them a raspberry on his horn as he bombed past. Paul shivered, wondering what it was all about. He knew he had done nothing wrong. *Maybe the Speaker...* Olive's revelation wouldn't embarrass the Speaker's Office. At least, he couldn't see how.

The police might come out of it looking bad.

The glare of the sun from behind meant that the police driver and his passenger were invisible to Paul in the rear-view mirror. Occasionally, as the road moved in relation to the sun, he could make out vague dark shapes behind the tinted windscreen. Illogically, that vagueness lent fear to his concern. A vague monolith loomed, that of the Civil Service out to "get" him to save their own embarrassment.

It was almost a relief when he spotted a perfectly normal elbow sticking out a side window of the police car.

He was afraid of being arrested for driving at variable speeds so he stayed at forty-five miles an hour while the traffic sorted itself out, and then sank the boot. The van gained twenty yards before the police car reacted. It came back on his tail again in seconds, and so close he wished he dared touch his brakes and give them a scare. Get a bit of his own back.

Miles on down the road another squad car joined in. He first saw it parked on the bridge ahead. The two men were leaning on the railings watching the traffic pass beneath. Its blue lights were already flashing as he drove under the flyover and it followed him down the slip road. The first police car dropped back and made room for it then accelerated up the fast lane until it came level with Paul. The men in the car gave him hard faced looks before pulling contemptuously away.

For the first time Paul felt real fear in the face of such orchestrated pressure. He drove on; there was nothing else he could do.

He had the copy of Olive's letter in his pocket. If the police searched him they'd find it, and he knew there was no greater gossip than a policeman. He loosened his seat belt and was virtually standing before he could pull the photocopy from his pocket because the wallet was jammed in on top of it. He looked around for somewhere to hide the letter and could find nowhere. Knew that the police would tear the van apart, looking for drugs, or anything else they could hold against him.

In the end he pushed his sock down and rammed the letter as deep into his shoe as he could. Pulled the sock up again and secured it with the elastic band. In his haste he snagged the elastic on the heel of his shoe and had to correct a drift in the van's direction before he could untangle it. Not much of a hidey-hole, he realized, but the best he could think of in the circumstances.

Later, at another invisible boundary of responsibility, a third and fourth police car replaced the second and he again got the hard faced stares. The line of cars gradually extended as drivers with nothing better to do tucked in behind to see what would happen next. Usually they got bored after a while and went on. However the two vehicles that came down the slip road with the last police cars, stayed stubbornly in place. One drove parallel with him for a few minutes while someone operated a shoulder-held camera. The type used by television companies. Paul watched them from the corner of his eye. His anger started to build.

The next service station was thirty miles up the road, Ken's place fifty and Paul didn't think he had enough petrol to get there. The service station came up. He was tempted to try and stretch the petrol, but decided not to risk it. He waited until the very last instant before pulling onto the slip road, hoping that the police would over-shoot and have to go on. Their tires squealed and they had to bump over the inverted arrow signs, but they stayed with him.

Chapter 89

Paul drove up to a petrol pump and waited. One police car pulled up tight behind him, the other blocked his exit. Passers-by started to take an interest. They slowed their walk or blatantly hung around to see what would happen next.

Paul wound the window up and pushed the locking pin down with his elbow. The policemen got out of their cars and stretched to display their beefed-up muscles. Another squad car came hammering across the forecourt. The newcomers got out and positioned themselves in front of the van. They were armed and wearing flak jackets. Paul's stomach twisted. That sort of response he hadn't expected. He slid his hands up until they were resting on top of the steering wheel and clearly visible from the outside. Some of the onlookers hurried away, others pulled back a little. The man with the TV camera was again in action. Another man stood beside him, talking into a microphone.

The driver of the rear police car approached Paul, his companion eased around to the passenger door. The armed policemen aimed their weapons.

The policeman on the driver's side tapped Paul's window to attract his attention. 'Would you get out please, Sir.'

Paul dragged his eyes away from the guns. The policeman stayed slightly to the rear of the door, his hand level with the handle. Paul could see that his blue shirt was two-toned with sweat and that both policemen stood poised, ready to throw themselves clear if he moved suddenly.

Paul wound the window down a crack. 'What am I supposed to have done?'

'You know.'

'Tell me.'

The policeman at the passenger door said, 'We don't want any trouble, do we, Sir?'

Paul shook his head. He heard the door handles creak as they tried them.

Anger surged up through his fear. He said, 'If those stupid bastards don't put their guns away, I'll ram them down their throat and pull the trigger.'

'Issuing threats against police officers...'

'Go to hell!' said Paul. He didn't know his legal rights but he had no

204

intention of being intimidated.

The handle on the passenger door creaked as it was tried for a second time. The shape there disappeared and the back door creaked in its turn. The shadow reappeared at the window.

'You're not doing yourself any good, Sir,' the policeman continued. 'It'll be added to the charges: wasting police time and resisting arrest.'

Paul said, 'You tell me what I'm wanted for and I'll open the door.'

The policeman was silent. Paul settled back in the seat and folded his arms. Immediately the guns were pushed out that bit further and aimed even more carefully. He glared back at the guns and, starting with his toes, began to unwind the knot of fear in his stomach.

The two policemen went into their tough guy / friend routine. The first one made threats and warned of dire retribution. The other acted conciliatory, trying to do his best by Paul and asking him to help his case by being more co-operative. The one playing the tough guy demanded to see his driving license.

Has he a right? Paul wasn't sure so he reached for the license in the glove compartment. A bullet tore through the window. It whipped past his ear and exited through the rear door. Paul dived into the footwell and stayed down.

There was only the one shot. Over the screams of the onlookers he could hear the policemen shouting at each other. 'Don't shoot. Who the hell did that?'

He thought he'd choke on his own fear.

It seemed to be an eternity before the window was tapped again. Paul looked up, expecting to see a gun pointed at him. A policeman stood boldly in front of the window. He had to be an officer because he wore pips on his shoulder.

'Mr. Bradley, you may sit up. Please sit up, Sir, you are in no danger.'

Paul came up slowly and reluctantly. The crowd had gone; cars were pulling out of the service station at a rate of knots. Bad for business, he thought, illogically. The policemen who had first accosted him were standing in line while a sergeant examined their weapons.

Paul sat up further and saw a small, neat hole punched in the van's windscreen. The hole appeared to be equidistance between his eyes and at the same level.

Frigging hell!

If the policeman hadn't asked for his driving license? If he hadn't reached for it at that instance? Maybe a policeman had fired because he moved?

He had a definite headache starting.

'Well done, Sir,' said the policeman, encouraging Paul to remain upright. He was an inspector, and painfully young for his rank. The few lines that showed on his fresh skin only emphasized his youth.

He bent forward and saluted. 'Mr. Bradley, I would like to apologies for any inconvenience or distress caused by this incident. It should never have happened.'

'Inconvenience!' It came out high and squeaky. Paul clamped his mouth shut.

The Inspector said, 'You have my word, Sir, the officer who fired that shot will be disciplined.' He phrased the next bit very carefully. 'In view of the serious nature of the incident, I must ask you to accompany me to the station for the purpose of making a statement.'

'You've got to be joking.'

The Sergeant pulled his superior aside and spoke urgently. The younger man said, 'That's impossible,' in an angry tone and listened again. Eventually he said, 'Bag them, we'll let Forensics sort it out.' When he returned to Paul some of his calm had evaporated. 'Mr. Bradley, things would appear to be more serious than we first thought.'

'Why, am I dead?'

'Sir, all my men deny firing that shot.'

'Cover up's starting early, isn't it?' said Paul.

Color popped into the Inspector's cheeks. 'One of my officers reports that the shot came from behind him. When he turned to defend himself the crowd panicked and broke in all directions. Because of that he was unable identify and apprehend the assailant.'

The television crew dared approach. Paul found a microphone shoved against the window opening.

'Mr. Bradley,' the well-fed reporter wanted to know. 'Are you facing more drugs and sex charges, and why did the police fire?'

'No and don't know,' said Paul, shortly.

The Inspector interjected smoothly, the microphone quickly swung in his direction. 'Mr. Bradley is not wanted in connection with any crime or misdemeanor. He is free to leave at his own convenience.'

The reporter was quick to attack. 'Then what was this all about? And why were you armed in the first place?'

The Inspector stepped back a bit, the reporter and the cameraman automatically followed. Paul found himself ignored. The Inspector had said that he was free to go. He started the engine.

The Inspector whipped around immediately. 'Mr. Bradley, where are you going?'

'Marston,' said Paul, unhelpfully, and drove forward until his bumper touched the police car in front. All the time he watched for guns to reappear, ready to cut the engine if they did. Too late he remembered the petrol, the needle hovered at the bottom end of the red warning mark.

The Inspector nodded to the sergeant and the car was moved. Paul drove on, past the line of waiting police officers and the new crowd, down the exit ramp and onto the motorway. One police car followed him at a discrete distance and a red Granada followed the police car.

Paul was well down the motorway before he dared open the window and let the reek of fear wash out of the van.

Chapter 90

At the edge of Marston a local police car took over the tail. When the traffic started to build up, it pulled out past Paul with its light flashing. The policeman in the passenger seat waved at him to follow.

Paul was shivering, chill in spite of the summer heat. Partly from the shock of the near miss from the bullet. Partly from the thought of a police station with its windowless rooms and closed doors. That's where they wanted him to go and that was where they were taking him.

'Frig it,' he shouted, trying anger and frustration to build something other than fear.

He pulled out of the line of traffic and followed the police car down a side road. A few other drivers tagged along as well, but these gradually peeled off until only the red Granada and another car, a muted-blue Lexus were left. They maintained a respectful distance.

The rout led him out of the clog of cars, down side streets and through the industrial zone into the inner ring of the town itself. The van engine coughed twice and died. There was nowhere to park; cars were bumper to bumper along both pavements. Paul flashed his lights at the police car and braked to a halt.

The red Granada rolled quietly towards them.

The police car reversed back. The officers got out: a large constable and an even larger sergeant. They had been handpicked to intimidate and were poised, ready to grab him if he attempted to run.

Paul didn't fancy being taken down in a rugby tackle by either man. He stood waiting for them. 'Sorry, I'm out of petrol.'

From the looks he got he could have done it deliberately. At least they weren't producing handcuffs.

He heard the Granada coming up and stepped in-between the van and the police car to give it room to pass, the policemen held their ground. The Granada pulled up.

Prison life had taught Paul to be wary of the unusual. He was already reacting, turning to check, as four men wearing black balaclavas came storming out of the Granada.

Things were happening so fast that Paul's fear was only a tightening of his chest and a quickening of breath. The policemen were quickly immobilized. Caught flat-footed, they were held at bay with guns until Mace was sprayed into their faces. They went down, clawing at their eyes. The sergeant tried to give the alarm on his radio and got a boot to the head for his trouble.

Paul ran, there was nothing left to do.

A Belfast voice called, 'Get the bastard.'

They tried to cut him off as his path twisted and turned round them. He was all but caught when someone fired a squirt of liquid at him, but hit another of his attackers instead. Paul kept going, pounded down the pavement.

I'm not fit for this, I'm too old.

A bullet cracked off the wall near his head and he hurled himself across the road. Oncoming cars swerved and braked to avoid him. A second bullet screamed through the air.

He reached a side street; took it. Another to the right; took that, then a third turn down an ally. The space between his shoulder blades felt draughty, hollow.

Paul was running now, stretched out in a way he hadn't attempted to in years. The ally was long, and before he got to the bottom of it he heard the shouts of his pursuers. He glanced back. There were two of them, they were well behind and would never catch him unless...

Oh Dear God I want to live.

There were no turn-offs and he couldn't run any faster. He tried to pull dustbins down behind him but they wouldn't tip unless he actually stopped and gave them a heave. He burst out of the dull of the ally into the brightness of a main street.

The Granada was there, cruising slowly. Two men in it. Its tires burned as it accelerated towards him. He spotted a railing across the way. Hurdled it and found himself falling feet first into a shallow stream. It was two steps to the far side and a long way up. He ran under a footbridge, back-tracking against the Granada. The way he had seen hard-pressed rabbits do in the field when his dogs were after them. It had worked then and it worked now, his pursuers looked for him across the stream and up the way.

The indignant quack of the ducks and the flapping of terns as they took flight betrayed him as he used a half drowned shopping trolley as a springboard onto the far railings. Paul swung himself up and over the railing and rolled until he hit metal.

He found himself in the large open-air car park of a shopping center. He knew the police station was at the far end, through the trees and up a bit. He could see the radio aerials on its roof from where he crouched. There was no time to stop; the footbridge was too handy for the gunmen. He exploded out of cover and ran ducked-over between the lines of cars. He didn't dare take the time to look behind. His chest hurt now, the burning started at the bottom ribs and worked up until his shoulders were on fire.

Why me?

He made it to the trees and, using one as cover, checked behind. There was no one following, no one rushing after him. He relaxed and drew breath.

Something rammed against his neck. He turned instinctively and caught the spray open-eyed; it was like a naked flame searing his eyeballs. He screamed and would have fallen if rough hands hadn't grabbed him and held him up.

'Get the bastard into the car,' ordered a Belfast voice.

He struggled against them, he knew his best chance for life was now, and shouted for help as loudly as he could. They gripped his arms. He twisted and fought and lashed out with feet. He kept struggling, knew he was panicking, losing out.

The Belfast voice spoke again. 'Hit the bastard!'

A fist slammed into his stomach. His arms almost tore from their sockets as he doubled over. A second blow to the chin knocked him backwards and into a deep red mist. He was aware of being pushed forward. His shoulder hit something and he was hauled sideways, his head hit something else and he fell into darkness.

Chapter 91

Doc settled himself in the passenger seat of the blue Lexus with a quiet sigh of satisfaction. He was having a thoroughly enjoyable day; right from the moment the radio station had issued a news flash of the pursuit of Bradley on the motorway.

Jimmy had bombed up the road in his car, until he was close enough to listen in on the police radios. Doc had followed in a stolen Lexus, the men in the Granada. Mobile phones kept them in contact with each other.

Jimmy using a mobile phone?

Jimmy risking his carefully nurtured reputation of being stupid, and for a disgraced politician? What made Bradley that important, Doc couldn't work out.

Doc sighed again. This time because of Jimmy. Sometimes he wondered if Jimmy knew why he did things, like having Ronnie position his men at the last service station before the turn-off to Marston.

That shot had only missed Bradley by a splinter. He'd have to analyze later how that had happened. He supposed, for an opportunistic shot in a crowded area with plenty of potential witnesses, it had to be treated as a good try.

Bradley's death would have solved a lot of problems even though Jimmy would have blamed him. His job, according to Jimmy, was to stop Ronnie or his men from killing Bradley. Jimmy wanted to sort the man personally, or so he said.

Sometimes my real job is protecting Jimmy from himself.

A voice in the rear of the Lexus snarled, 'Don't you try nothing.'

Doc looked around. Bradley was stretched across the floor with the men's legs perched uncomfortably on his body. Bradley moved and groaned, but couldn't do much with his arms secured with plastic ties. 'Keep him quiet,' he ordered.

A foot thumped down on Bradley. 'Lie still.'

Doc looked forward again, they were on the home stretch and not a police car in sight. He couldn't wait to get the Lexus into the garage and the door down. The police must be swamping the town, trying to find Bradley.

'Are you sure of the house?' he asked the driver. It was one of many detached red-bricked houses in the row.

'The one with the two laburnum trees,' the driver said, indicating for the turn.

The car bumped over the pavement and ran along smooth tarmac into the garage. The garage was detached from house, which made it awkward for transferring a prisoner, but the best Jimmy could rent in the time available.

Chapter 92

Paul cried out in pain as they dragged him from the car.

A fist cracked against his cheek. 'Shut your gob if you know what's good for you.'

His eyes were filled with tears from the Mace spray but he managed to force them open. The men had taken their masks off without blindfolding him first. He knew they would only do that if they intended to kill him.

Two men held him up. They were about his age, *older*, with guts overhanging their trousers. He had outrun them once, he could do it again.

He twisted until his shoulder jumped in its socket, and kneed one of the men. The man released his hold and stumbled away. The other man pulled at Paul. Paul used the momentum of that pull to bring his foot down sharply. The edge of the heel caught the man square on his instep.

Paul squirmed free of the man's grip and ran for the light of the entrance. A third man was closing the garage door. Paul slammed into him and was a step away from sunlight and freedom when Doc stretched out a hand and grabbed him by the collar.

Doc slammed Paul against the boot of the car and ground a gun into his jaw. 'Listen friend, you're dead if you so much as breathe.'

Paul knew Doc, who he was and what he did for a living. He looked into his cold eyes and lost all hope. He wanted to be sick. *If only I could*. Right down Doc's shirt and over his pristine Inst tie.

The injured men sorted themselves out with a lot of cursing, then they boxed Paul in for the walk across the open yard. Paul's sight was almost normal again and he could see an estate of houses overlooking the yard. He tried to drag his feet, tried to twist and turn in their grip. Hopefully someone in the overlooking houses would see them and realize that something was wrong and call the police. The men held his arms tighter and hurried him along.

They went into the house via a lean-to utility room. Dragged him through the kitchen and up narrow stairs. Threw him onto a double bed. The pain of their rough handling came almost as a relief. It meant that he was still alive. If he was still alive it meant that they wanted information out of him. That meant more pain.

He didn't think the pain could get any worse, and knew it could.

Chapter 93

The various travelers came together and like any gathering tended to stay in their own clans and groups.

Jimmy arrived. First he stowed his hire car in a lock-up garage. Then he circled the area on foot until he was sure that neither he nor the house was being watched. He went in by the back door, greeted the men and took a bottle of beer with him into the living room. The settee looked inviting. He stretched out on it.

Doc joined him for a few minutes. Jimmy had the pleasure of bollocking Doc for that near miss at the filling station. Then he sent Doc off to rest, he'd be needed that night. Jimmy settled the Walkman on his stomach and drifted off to sleep.

Ronnie and his men came crushed into the Granada. They used the front door, laid claim to half the beer and congregated in the front hall and on the stairs. Arthur Anderson, Ronnie's strong-arm man, took over the guarding of Paul. Doc joined him and sat with his back against a wall where he could watch door, window and bed at the same time. They seldom spoke.

Ronnie went into the living room and wasn't overly concerned about disturbing the sleeping Jimmy. RM dared keep him company. Ronnie was basking in the glow of a job well done and was prepared to be magnanimous. The rest of his men took it in turns to tramp up the stairs to see their prisoner. Ronnie didn't want to see Bradley; he merely wanted him dead.

He made himself comfortable in an armchair and said, to RM, 'Get me a drink.' While he waited he looked around the room, a sitting / dining room. He thought the colors alone made it look tatty. He preferred colors that made a positive statement.

RM came back with two beers.

Ronnie scowled. 'I said a drink.'

'That's it, boss.'

'I see Jimmy's economizing,' said Ronnie, who had only been out travelling expenses. He took the beer anyway. RM stood hesitating. 'Sit down, for god's sake,' he said.

RM looked pleased at the invitation. The other armchair was at the far side of Jimmy so he fetched a dining room chair and placed it close enough to invite confidences.

Ronnie said, 'That was a good thing one of the boys did today. I'm only sorry it wasn't you.'

RM shifted uncomfortably. 'Without you there I had to stay back and keep an eye on things generally.'

It came out smoothly. Ronnie didn't believe a word of it, but nodded as if he did. Just like he didn't believe RM's story about being attacked by three men in that building site. *Got pissed and fell over his own feet, more like.* He asked, 'Who actually fired that shot?'

'Don't know, boss. Whoever did isn't saying.'

That puzzled Ronnie. Why not admit taking the shot at Bradley. There again, why admit to attempted murder? Missed opportunities didn't earn a bonus and it gave someone a name to pass onto the police when that someone was short of drinking money. It had to be one of his men. If not them, then Doc, he'd been there as well but he wasn't known to miss.

He tapped RM's leg to get his full attention. 'Things are starting to stack up against you. Nelson's death, the police are looking for someone to blame.'

RM quivered. 'Can't you protect me?'

Ronnie shook his head. 'It's not looking good.'

'But I was only obeying...'

Ronnie's head whipped around and his eyes burned holes in RM's confidence. 'I told you to go talk to Nelson, not beat him to death.'

'But...'

Ronnie patted his leg reassuringly. 'But you've got me fighting your corner.' He relaxed back and felt content. The police could look all they wanted. Once Bradley was dealt with he'd negotiate a price with Anderson to make RM disappear permanently. Ronnie looked over at Jimmy, little bubbles of snores were coming out of his mouth. He motioned RM closer and whispered. 'You've got to become so important that the politicians in London have to protect you.'

'How, boss? Anything, boss.'

'Kill Bradley.' RM immediately jumped to his feet. 'Not now you fool. Later, after The Man's been.'

RM's eyes widened. 'You mean...'

'No names. Not now, not ever. Not for him. But you do it as soon as he goes.'

'Yeah, yeah.'

Ronnie's finger brought him even closer. 'And after that...' He nodded in the direction of the sleeping Jimmy.

Now RM was bursting with confidence, as if he already believed himself to be the new hit man for the faceless men in London. He said, 'Doc's mine.'

A lorry's air-horn blared outside the gate. Jimmy shot awake, cursing.

Chapter 94

Paul lay on his side facing the wall. He couldn't understand how he had managed to sleep with a stream of people coming in and looking at him, and leaving again. Everything about him hurt, even his legs from the unaccustomed running. He tried to wipe at his burning eyes but his arms wouldn't reach, they were still tied behind his back.

The effort made trying to wipe his eyes focused his mind on the pain. He hadn't known that numb hands could hurt so much. He flexed and stretched his fingers to keep the blood flowing. His eyes followed the wallpaper pattern of delicately stemmed cornflowers on a forget-me-not background. It gave him something to think about other than why they wanted him alive. The tears in his eyes weren't all from the spray.

Two men had talked through his sleep, one a lot more than the other. A third man came into the room, RM a deep voice called him. The same deep voice told RM, 'Piss off, and give my head peace,' but RM stayed and from then on he did most of the talking.

Paul knew that the quietest man in the room was Doc. There was no mistaking his voice, they'd talked sometimes when he was visiting Jimmy, and he knew Doc's reputation. He prayed because God was his last hope. With the Our Father he got as far as *"Thy kingdom come"* but couldn't bring himself to tell a lie with the words *"Thy will be done"*. He wanted home and unharmed.

Long after dark the front door bell rang. Paul heard voices as more people arrived; someone below seemed to be permanently on their mobile.

There was a heavy tread of feet on the stairs and the room door opened. Doc and his companions stood up. Paul was aware of a figure standing over him. He continued to stare at the wall until hands gripped his shoulders and forced him on to his back. His own weight crushed his wrists against the restraining ties. He arched his body to relieve the pressure.

Jimmy said, 'You've caused me a lot of grief.'

He gave Paul another haul and left him on his side, but facing out this time. The change of position took away a lot of Paul's discomfort and he was almost grateful.

The man with the deep voice, said, 'You expect politicians to be slippery with their tongues but this one's like an eel, he nearly got away twice.'

Jimmy nodded. 'That's why you're watching him.' He straightened the collar of his new sports coat. It was unbuttoned and Paul could see where the maker's label had been cut out.

Jimmy said, 'Untie him and bring him down.' He poked Paul with his stubby fingers. 'One lie and you'll regret it.' He walked out.

With Jimmy turning him over Paul could now see who else was in the bedroom. He didn't know for sure who the man with the deep voice was, no one had called him by name. The man was in his fifties, with dirty-grey hair and a body still bulky from softening muscles. The unwanted RM had to be the younger man in the mock-leather jacket and tight jeans.

Knowing what they looked like, knowing some of their names was like a death sentence. Paul screwed his eyes shut and wished he still faced the wall.

Rough hands reached over him and cut the plastic ties. His arms flopped useless.

Paul only realized how numb his hands had become when the blood started to flow again. The ties had dug deep groves in his skin, some of which seeped blood. Doc ordered him to stand up. He found movement, any movement, agony. The worst of the pain seemed to be centered on his ribs and back. Everything creaked and protested as he levered himself to his feet. He became light-headed and overbalanced. Doc's restraining hand stopped him from falling.

Paul exaggerated his weakness. He might get away from three men. Once downstairs in a crowded house he hadn't a chance. And he had this idea…

RM seemed to sense Paul's determination to escape. He drew a gun.

'Put that away,' said Doc.

RM hesitated.

'Do as you're told,' said Arthur, and RM obeyed.

'Toilet,' said Paul as they guided him to the door. They ignored him. 'I'll do it in my pants,' he warned.

They took him into the bathroom, which, as he hoped, overlooked the flat roof of the utility room. The window was held shut by a light catch. Five seconds and he could be through. He started to work at the top button of his trousers, then stopped and looked at the three men. Doc and RM were in the bathroom with him; Arthur waited outside.

Paul's heart pounded in hope and fear. 'Do you mind?'

He was banking on the Irish embarrassment with sexuality. Doc and RM turned away and moved towards the door.

Paul tensed, unsure whether to jump or try to lock the door first, then he heard a metallic click. Doc was pointing a Browning automatic at him over his shoulder. His head was turned far enough to keep Paul in the periphery of his vision. RM drew his gun and, again, Arthur told him to put it away. Paul gave up, slumped onto the toilet seat and buried his face in his hands.

When he was ready they went downstairs in single file. Arthur and RM first, Paul in the middle and Doc bringing up the rear. Doc's gun rested on Paul's neck, pressing against a bruise. It hurt.

Arthur asked a question, Paul was too wrapped up in his own fears to hear what the question was but Arthur seemed to answer himself. 'There's not the same piecework there used to be.'

Paul gagged and nearly missed his step. He was now part of that piecework.

Chapter 95

Men crowded the hallway, blocking all but the door into the living room. None of them would meet Paul's eye. Doc and RM followed him into the room and leaned against the door. The rest waited outside.

A kitchen stool had been set in the center of the floor. Behind the dining-room table sat a tribunal of three masked men in combat jackets, and behind them, on the wall, an icon of the crucifixion.

Jimmy was on the left, Paul recognized his shape, and thought the man in the middle vaguely familiar. The man, whoever he was, never spoke, but played with a knife, twisting and turning it while he listened. That too rang a bell somewhere. The third man's shoulders were rolled forward and his hands were bunched. Without knowing who he was, Paul feared Ronnie.

He knew better than to sit without an invitation and tried to stand still, but his legs were shaking. He didn't know what to expect, but knew they couldn't torture him in a housing estate in Middle England so his death would have to be quick. His heart was hammering hard. He really did need the toilet.

Jimmy asked Doc, 'Did you search him?'

'Sorry, no.'

Doc stepped forward and held out his hand. Paul emptied his pockets: wallet, tissue, a few coins and, from the back pocket, his comb. Doc placed then on the table for the Tribunal to see.

Jimmy asked, 'Is that it?'

'Yes,' said Paul.

Jimmy nodded to Doc who began a body search: arms, chest and sides, small of back, hips and inner leg. Paul thought he was clear when the searching hands stopped at his knees. He'd forgotten that Doc was a knife man who knew the importance of a good hiding place. Doc hunkered down to search around the ankles and found the letter.

'Jimmy,' he said, and produced a knife to cut the elastic band. Nothing ostentatious, merely a Swiss army knife with a black handle and carbon steel blade. The elastic parted at the touch.

The man in the center sat on, the other two got to their feet. Jimmy reached Paul first and slammed a fist into his chest. Paul hit the wall and bounced back. Jimmy waited for him, with his arm drawn back.

He said, 'I warned you, no lies.'

His fist, the size of a small sledge broadened from years of humping steel, pistoned into Paul's face.

Paul's eyes cleared for a moment after the second flash of pain. His body was spread-eagled, splattered against the wall. It slithered down into darkness.

Chapter 96

Paul was at home, in bed trying for a lie-in and the boys were teasing him awake with a damp facecloth. He swiped vaguely at them. 'Go 'way, go 'way.' But they kept rubbing.

'Go 'way,' he muttered a last time, and came awake.

It wasn't the boys with the facecloth. It was Doc. Paul's eyes snapped wide open.

'Good morning, sleepy head,' said Doc. 'Or should I say, good evening.'

Paul twisted away from Doc's rough ablutions. He couldn't turn far because his neck hurt and there seemed to be a growth on his face near his left eye. He had a headache.

Doc stepped back, the facecloth bunched in his hand and stained with blood.

He asked, 'Can you hear me?'

It was easier to speak than nod. 'Uh.'

Paul looked around him. He was lying on the living room carpet. The two hooded men were back sitting at the table and other men crowded the doorway, watching.

Doc leaned over him again. 'That's better, your eyes are focused this time.'

Pain lanced through Paul's ribs as Doc heaved him bodily onto his feet. He couldn't get a breath. He sat humped over on the stool with his hands locked against his chest and wished he had one to spare for his neck or to hold his spinning head.

Jimmy held up the photocopy of Olive's letter. 'Is this kosher?'

Paul gulped in air and started to breathe normally again. 'Yes.'

'Where's the original?'

He swallowed and wished he dared ask for a drink. 'I gave it to the Speaker of the House of Commons.'

'What did you tell him?' asked the man on the right. He sounded anxious.

'Nothing. I didn't see him. I gave it to a messenger in the House.'

'What day?'

'Today... Sunday... yesterday...' He didn't know which day it was.

'What did you do over the weekend? Where did you go, who did you see?'

Paul shook his head and regretted it. His brain seemed to move with the shake. 'No one, nothing.' He sensed Jimmy's fury and flinched away from it. He added quickly, 'Westminster. People there know me. It took me a long time...'

The man in the middle nudged Jimmy and tapped his watch. Jimmy nodded and said, 'We're on a tight time schedule. The countryside's gone mad looking for you.'

Paul nearly said, 'Sorry for your trouble.' But bit it back. He felt hope, a little glimmer somewhere in the pit of his stomach. Then he looked at the three masked faces before him and it disappeared.

Olive's letter was put down. Something small was lifted off the table and held up for Paul to see. He had to blink his eyes hard to get the focus right. It was a photograph of his two boys. They looked more mature than he remembered, filled out, their faces stretching into adulthood. Jimmy tore the photograph down the middle, placed the halves face down on the table and swilled them around with his finger. On his nod, Doc walked over, chose one and put it in his pocket.

Jimmy said, 'Rory and Shane. Inseparable, aren't they?' Paul could only nod. 'That depends on you. Doc has a photograph of one of them. One more lie and he dies.'

Fear crept over Paul's body like an itch. 'You'll never believe the truth,' he blurted out.

'We'll never believe your lies either.'

Ronnie gripped Olive's letter and shook it at him. 'When did you get this?'

Would they believe that Barbara had never read it? Rory and Shane? Which one? Would Doc stop at one?

He opened his mouth to say, 'Months,' and heard himself say, 'A few days ago.' His words croaked out into a cold silence and he continued hurriedly, 'Olive sent it to the house, but Barbara never read it. She gave it to me unopened. You've got to believe me, she never read it, and I sent it on to the Speaker.'

It was Jimmy's turn again. 'Why now?'

'I was talking of going home.' Home! He ached for it, for that caravan of a house after what they'd had. 'She wanted... If I didn't dare show her the letter... then she would know. I wouldn't have to keep on lying about Olive and me and we could start again from there.'

Jimmy said, 'Let's start with Olive. Why did you employ her? Was it deliberate?'

He nodded, and then wished he hadn't when his brain thudded against his skull. 'I needed someone who had been reared in Belfast and was street wise. Olive had the contacts. It was only a question of getting her confidence and starting from there.'

'Why did you want to get involved with the rackets?'

Paul said, 'Because there can be no real peace in Ireland until all organized crime as such has been eliminated. It's destroying what little the people have.' He took a deep breath. The honest truth couldn't make things any worse for him. 'You three are part of the reason why there's more people in Northern Ireland on benefits than in a job.'

Ronnie made to rise again. The man in the middle stopped him. The three man tribunal looked at their watches again; one did it and the rest followed automatically.

Jimmy moved the half photograph remaining on the table to remind Paul of the threat, as if he needed reminding. 'You met us in Belfast and the politicians in London.' He leaned over the table towards Paul and spoke slowly and distinctly. 'Did you ever hold anything back? Betray a confidence to the other side? To the police?'

'No.' Paul wiped at his eyes. His mind had started to clear and he realized that there was something important about that question. He added, 'That's not the way I operated.'

A chill of tension filled the air.

'On the life of your child?'

'Yes.'

The mangled photograph was held up.

'Yes, for God's sake, yes.'

Was lowered and the threat receded.

Ronnie said, 'Our men say the meeting broke up early and they went on leaving you and the Shaw woman alone together. They say it was a useful night.'

'I don't know, I can't remember,' said Paul.

Jimmy had the photograph trapped under his hand. Ronnie stretched across but couldn't reach it. Instead, he tapped the table in warning. 'So what happened?'

'I think we went to the hotel in a taxi. I needed to keep a clear head so I opted for coffee. After that - nothing.'

'Come on,' said Ronnie, 'A bit of booze, a shot of something; we've all had it.' From the way Jimmy stiffened, he hadn't. 'None of us were ever the worse of it and you claim to remember nothing?'

Paul appealed to Jimmy. 'It's true. Look, I drank the odd one, but how often did I take more than a watered down whiskey? You threatened often enough to throw a brandy into my coffee when I wasn't looking. And the drug, cocaine or whatever the hell it was, exploded my mind.'

Which one is it, Rory or Shane? Oh God!

He cried even as he appealed to be believed. 'My doctors have only ever seen three cases as bad as mine: one is institutionalized and will never be out; one killed himself. The third is me.' He dragged his eyes back to the cross and tried to do something with his ragged breathing. Sweat poured out of him, he didn't wipe his face. Don't show fear, he told himself.

Jimmy asked, 'Who was there that night, the letter doesn't say?'

Paul gave the names of the men he was expecting. One of the names was Ronnie Fetherton.

Jimmy nodded at the names. There wasn't one among them that he would count as friend. His voice became softer. 'Did you ever try your luck with Olive? There or anywhere else?'

'No,' said Paul firmly.

'He's a bloody saint,' said Ronnie.

'So what can you remember?' asked Jimmy.

Paul shook his head, his brain felt like a rock rattling around in a tin drum and he stopped very quickly. 'Anything before that night is mostly about my family.'

'Think!'

He screwed his eyes shut and concentrated. His mind skipped to a cramped bedroom with a toilet for a bedside table, and someone in the top bunk whose violent re-positionings kept shaking him awake. He remembered laughing during a riot, sitting somewhere and watching mayhem mirror the kaleidoscope of images in his mind.

There was another memory. Of people in blue shirts being kicked around like footballs. Of standing over one of the blue shirts and arguing with someone, being punched and coming back again. And later in his cell, sitting surrounded by people in blue shirts: some on the beds and one on the floor. And after that people in suits and ties patting him on the back - he remembered he didn't like that, that's the way he treated the dogs - and being nice to him.

'I don't think I liked prison,' he said.

There was an understanding laugh before the hard questioning continued. 'The politicians in London, when did you last see them? Did any of them contact you after that night?'

'No. As far as I know, no. But there's so much I've forgotten.'

'What about your wife, did they approach her for any reason? Did she ever mention their names?'

'No.' He struggled for accuracy. 'Again, they could have. She might have.'

The boys, which one of them?

He shouted, 'I can't remember. I can't remember.'

When they could get nothing there, they went back over the same ground, looking for something he had omitted to tell them. Again and again they put him over that night. And every time his mind closed up at the coffee stage.

They kept at him through the night. Until the cross he focused on came off the wall and hung in fiery drops before his eyes. Until Doc had to hold him with both hands to stop him from falling over. Until bile filled his mouth and slobbered his chin.

Chapter 97

They called in Arthur Anderson with his great strength to get Paul back upstairs. Paul was hardly aware of being lifted off the chair.

'Use your feet,' ordered Doc.

He did, in a rubbery-legged sort of way. They were on the stairs and taking him up sideways before he got his eyes open again.

He kept slobbering the question, 'The boys, are they okay? Do you believe me?'

No one answered him. Arthur threw him onto the bed. Paul rolled, his head hit the wall and he went silent.

'Easy,' said Doc.

'Hardly matters, he's done for anyway,' said Arthur.

Arthur stayed, Doc went back downstairs. He wanted to be handy if The Man had come to any sort of decision.

The Man had and he hadn't. He was sitting in the kitchen, drinking a cup of milky tea – no sugar, thank you – and talking to the men. All these men had thick police files, some had spent a decade in prison, yet they hung on The Man's every word as he described the future he envisioned for them and their families.

The Man acknowledged Doc's presence with a miniscule nod, which could mean anything or nothing. Doc would have loved a cup of tea, but that meant leaving his DNA on a cup. He hadn't taken off his rubber gloves since snatching Bradley. Bradley's DNA and fingerprints would be all over the house and the car, impossible to totally eradicate.

Jimmy's men were under instructions to wear gloves at all times and every beer bottle that touched their lips was put in a bin bag for later disposal. It hadn't occurred to Ronnie to give the same order.

The Man had a knife on the table beside him. He left it untouched so there were no specific orders for Doc, which in itself was a decision. The Man looked directly at Doc and tapped the breast pocket where he kept his wallet. *Use the phone number, make contact.*

The air in the kitchen became unpleasantly thick with cigarette smoke. Doc went into the sitting room and joined Jimmy and Ronnie. The two men were pointedly not talking to each other by pretending to listen to the television.

Doc took a chair at the back of the room, against the wall and just in the edge of Ronnie's vision. Doc noticed that Ronnie kept looking back, to check that he wasn't coming up behind him.

Someday I will be.

He did his usual listening. Normal traffic and pedestrians outside, so the police weren't on to them. Laughter as Ronnie's men worked at finishing the beer. Jimmy had laid on plenty, with orders to his own men to go easy.

Doc nodded at that. There's more than one way of incapacitating superior numbers.

Eventually he heard light footsteps running up the stairs, then heavier ones coming down. Doc stood up

'Do you want anything?' he asked Jimmy.

Jimmy looked around. 'No, things are fine as they are.'

'Ronnie?'

'Beer,' said Ronnie.

Doc slipped out of the room. Sam Gilliland, Jimmy's old driver, hung out in the hallway with one of his mates. Doc held up three fingers before slipping quietly up the stairs.

Chapter 98

Paul didn't want to die, but what about the boys, Rory and Shane? Which one? Will they be all right? He had tried to answer all the tribunal's questions, but the pain in his head had built up until he couldn't understand what more they wanted off him.

Other footsteps came into the room. He didn't mind who it was just so long as they didn't move him for a while.

It was RM. He said to Arthur, 'You go on, I'll take over.'

'I'm fine here.'

'The boss says.'

Arthur shrugged and got up, and pushed the chair well back. RM had to fetch it for himself. The floorboards creaked as Arthur clomped downstairs. Voices and the clink of bottles came from the kitchen.

Paul started to drift off into sleep. He realized what was happening and twisted violently onto his back. There would be enough time for sleep when he was dead. The pain had drained from his head leaving him feeling curiously detached. Every sinew and muscle from the center of his chest was stretched and contorted and his shoulders were on fire.

He forced his eyes open and focused on RM. His heart beat hard with a vague hope. Just one guard, the best chance he had. Probably the only one he'd ever get.

'Toilet,' he said. It came out funny and RM didn't understand. 'Toilet,' he said again, clearer this time.

RM said, 'Do it in your pants, you're not going nowhere.'

Then a smile replaced his surly expression. Paul didn't like the smile.

RM stood up and drew his gun. 'Come on,' he said.

Paul crawled out of the bed. It took him all his time to get onto his feet and stay there.

And I'm going to fight my way out?

He was too. Even if he had to crawl up the road he was going to make it.

Paul felt better once he started to move, though he hugged the wall and used the banister for support to get himself across the corridor. He kidded himself it was mostly for effect.

There were people walking about down below and he heard muffled laughter. He was sweating by the time he reached the bathroom. He grabbed the towel rail for support and turned to face RM who had followed him in.

'Do you mind?' he said, fiddling with his top button. RM turned away. Paul wasn't to know that RM was afraid of what Doc would do to him if he killed Bradley without reason. He intended to turn in the doorway and fire, and claim that Bradley had gone for the window.

All Paul saw was a turned back and a chance. He used the towel rail and the door handle for support as he drove his heel into the small of RM's back. RM pitched forward into the corridor. Paul slammed the door shut and palmed the bolt home.

His body was moving now, awkwardly and not very coordinated. He climbed onto the bath rather than the toilet because the toilet was directly across from the door and he expected bullets to tear through that at any second. It didn't happen nor did RM raise the alarm. All Paul heard was another small thud from the corridor, laughter still from the men in the hallway and the front door closing after someone.

The window swung open easily. The hinges squealed but not too loud. He knew he was being over cautious, taking too much time. He put his foot on the bath and launched himself through the opening headfirst. He jammed somewhere, got his arms down, wiggled this way and that, and folded onto the roof. There were people beneath him partying. He could smell beer through an open window.

Daylight already, he realized, and he had the yard to cross. He crawled to the edge of the roof at the gable end of the house, slithered over the edge and scraped down a rough-dashed wall.

Dear God, thank you God, I'm free.

Something touched the back of his neck, something hard and cold, and something soft, the breath of someone who had hurried

A voice said, 'Guess.'

'Don't do that, it's bad manners.' Paul turned to face Doc. 'Get it over with.'

He couldn't believe how calm he sounded, how inevitable everything suddenly seemed to him.

The gun wagged him on. He walked ahead and didn't bother putting his arms up. They probably wouldn't have gone anyway. He turned for the kitchen door but Doc aimed him for the garage. The kitchen blind was down and no one saw them pass. The fear started to come back again.

There were already three men in the garage. They didn't seem surprised to see him. Jimmy appeared and he was. 'Where are you're taking him?' he asked.

'I'd hate someone else to get the piecework,' said Doc, and pushed Paul on.

Chapter 99

The men grabbed Paul and held him while Doc put sticky tape over his mouth and pressed it home. A balaclava was pulled over his head, back to front. The frizzy strands tickled his nose and eyes and choked his breathing.

He tried to protest and struggled against them, but they threw him to the ground. A knee between his shoulder blades held him there while they plaited his arms together with plastic ties.

'You know what to do?' said Jimmy. He sounded uncertain as he asked, 'No mistakes, no bodies lying where they shouldn't be?'

Doc said, 'A nice clean job.' Something was shoved into Paul's pocket. 'There, that bit's done?'

'I'm going now. See you,' said Jimmy.

Paul heard his footsteps retreat. *Dear God*, he thought. Could only hope that his death would be quick and painless. And he hadn't asked about the boys.

Which one? Would they be okay?

Jimmy's footsteps stopped. A car door opened and closed. The car pulled away from the front door.

Doc said to the men, 'Come on, it's time.'

They got Paul to his feet, his legs worked though his knees couldn't lock, and they put him in the car. They were gentle with him, quiet and tense because of what they had to do in a town saturated with police. He and Doc sat in the back. Paul's heart thudded so fast there was no pause between beats. He found himself twisted round and down until his balaclavaed head rested on Doc's legs. Doc kept him there with a gentle hand on his head, the other held a cocked gun to his throat.

It was a short journey, in a car tense with men on the lookout for the police. The car stopped and Doc bundled him out onto the pavement. No gentleness now. A boot to the back of the legs knocked him to his knees and a hand forced his shoulders forward until his forehead touched the ground. The gun barrel rammed into the back of his neck.

Paul was crying. He couldn't help himself.

Dear God, Dear God, Dear God.

It was the only prayer he had time for.

The gun was withdrawn.

Dear God, Dear God, Dear God.

Did he shoot? Am I dead? He'd heard of people talking even as their brains spilled out of their heads.

He could hear cars in the distance. A bird singing nearby.

No way will I die sniveling.

He straightened up. No one said no. No gun barrel forced him back down again.

'Get on with it. Bastards!' The words were muffled by his tears and the tape over his mouth.

Paul continued to kneel and cry. Hard sobs tore through his body. He knelt there a long time. Birds sang around him.

Would they do that if there was people about?

He tried to see through the balaclava. There was the darkness of a high wall in front of him and the lightness of a street stretching away on either side.

They couldn't have gone.

He scraped around on his knees to see behind him. Sunlight in every direction. Not the dark shadow of a man standing over him or their car.

His heart was pumping again.

They're letting me live.

He stumbled to his feet and made it to the wall for support. It gave way before him and spiked his face. *A hedge?*

Paul was trembling. His teeth chattered and his sweat-saturated clothes felt cold against his skin. Which way? He couldn't be sure because the balaclava muffled his ears. To the right, the sun starred his vision. He turned left and used foot and shoulder to guide himself along the hedge. Stumbled as the footpath dipped for the entry. He found the hedge again and sensed it had turned a corner. He took a breather. A car passed but didn't stop.

He took another step and his shoulder hit something hard. A pillar? He turned into the supposed opening. Terrified. If he lost the hedge he could wander forever. Fall into the path of a lorry.

A voice shouted, 'Hi!'

He heard the pound of running feet and a hand steadying him while the other hand ripped at the balaclava, then the tape from his mouth.

And before him stood Ken.

Chapter 100

Kristie came running. 'My God! What have they done to you?' She flung her arms around Paul and held him, not fiercely, gently, and she crooned to him as she would to a baby. He slumped against her hardly knowing what was happening.

Ken ran for wire-cutters and snipped away the plastic ties. 'I'll ring for an ambulance,' he said.

Paul said, 'I'm fine, I'm fine.' Found himself unable to explain to them his horror of being confined again: of prisons and mental institutions. The smell of their echoing corridors was already working on his frayed nerves. He got stubborn and refused to go to hospital.

'What's our telephone number?' asked Kristie.

He gave it correctly. She looked into his eyes. He tried to stare her back, but hadn't the energy.

They helped him up the stairs into the granny flat and took him into the bedroom. Kristie wouldn't let him lie down, she was very positive about that, and she dismissed Ken. 'I'll take it from here.'

Ken tried to object, but he was used to obeying her orders and backed off. 'Go on,' she said, as he hesitated in the doorway. 'Do something useful, ring for the doctor.'

He left.

'Poor Paul,' whispered Kristie. She balanced him upright with a hand on his back and started to work at the buttons on his shirt. She stopped him from slipping sideways. 'Oh no you don't. You're not getting into my bed until you've had a shower. You smell like a manure pit.' She unpeeled the shirt from his body and caught her breath when she saw the extent of the bruising. His face was bad enough.

She let him flop back with a, 'Now don't you go asleep on me,' warning while she took off his shoes and socks. He moved in protest when she started on his trousers. 'Give over,' she said, impatiently.

Embarrassment brought him around a bit. She helped him to his feet and lent him a steadying arm as he walked to the bathroom, and deliberately put him in the shower before she switched it on.

The sudden smash of cold water popped his eyes wide open. She handed in a facecloth and soap. 'On you go and don't forget your hair.' He was holding the facecloth to shield his nakedness. She snorted. 'Huh! The last time I saw one that size it had nappy rash.'

But she turned away and left a towel handy before going into the bedroom to close the curtains and turn down the quilt. He followed a few minutes later with a bath towel held around his waist.

He slumped onto the bed. She rushed to get another towel to dry his hair and back properly. Then she rolled him into bed and pulled the quilt up before whipping off the wet towel. His eyes were closed again, his breathing already slowing into sleep.

She said, 'It's Tuesday, in case you've forgotten. Dinner's at seven, I'll call you before that.'

She brushed the hair from his eyes and stood watching him for a while. When she was sure he was asleep she collected the dirty clothes for the wash and went through his pockets. A piece of paper stuck fell out of his wallet. She scooped it up and read.

Stay in England.

It was unsigned. She placed it on the bedside table where Paul could see it when he woke up.

She said, 'While you were gallivanting across country Girl qualified for the final of the Rosebowl.' She bent and kissed him open-mouthed.

His eyes unglued themselves slowly. It took longer before a totally disinterested voice said, 'That's nice.' The eyelids slid shut.

Kristie patted him on the groin. 'You mightn't have much there, son, but what you've got is all balls.'

Chapter 101

The kennels were under siege by the media. In the yard and grounds was normality. A police detachment held chaos at bay at the front gate. A chip van had even turned up to feed the determined press core and the curious onlookers.

Kristie was having a ball. Gone were the old work-shirt and faded jeans. The wife of Kenneth Stockdale, leading greyhound trainer, now attended the dogs in a chaste cocktail dress. By mere chance she walked a double handful of dogs near the waiting photographers. The silk scarf fluttered beautifully in the breeze at just the right time.

There was no question of Paul being asked to leave. Not in his role as the owner of their currently most successful dog.

Paul stopped at the French windows leading into the living room. He held a tray in his hands. Only Ken was there, stretched out, dozing.

'Go on in,' shouted Kristie, from the kitchen.

Ken's eyes popped open and his face broadened into a smile of welcome. 'Great!' he exclaimed. 'Great! Welcome back. How do you feel?'

He got himself into a muddle trying to take the tray off Paul and shake his hand at the same time. Kristie rescued the tray before it and its contents could cascade to the ground.

Even with the table set for three Paul was still unsure of his welcome. 'You said seven. And thanks for the drinks and stuff when I woke up, I was ready for it.' The color around his damaged cheek heightened. 'And for everything else.'

Kristie was briskly practical. 'If there's anything you need, just say.'

'You're very good.'

'Me? Good? Ha!' She was bursting with mock fury. 'The newspapers reprinted those photographs, Mr. Goody-two-shoes Bradley making an arse of himself.' She slapped Ken on the back. 'Arse! Get it? Arse!'

Ken frowned at her.

'Sorry, sorry, sorry,' she said. 'Oh God but it had to come out. You here all this time and I never twigged.' She slapped her forehead with the palm of her hand. 'Aaah.'

Ken protested, 'Paul's a guest.'

Paul played along, the teasing was deliberate, making it easy for him to settle in again. 'I'm staff or I was, and easy bait for the missus' sharp tongue.'

'I should have known,' she said. 'Oh I should have known.' She danced a jig of mock rage around the room.

Paul tried to laugh with her, but his chest hurt too much. 'You can always invent some stories for your friends.'

An eyebrow arched up. 'I'll have to, won't I?'

He hoped not, not with Barbara's suspicious mind.

'What about Girl?' he asked Ken, to change the subject.

'Still yours,' said Ken. 'I didn't like to sell her without first discussing the price with you.'

Paul smiled his relief and was aware of them watching him as he walked stiffly across the room and worked at making his body mold into the curves of the chair. He kept his expression a studied blankness.

Ken asked, 'Did you hear the draw for the final?'

Paul shook his head. He, in his turn, was watching Ken, pleased that he looked much better and appeared stronger.

Ken said, 'Kid Carbine's in trap 2 and Bromide's in 3.' He allowed his joy to show. 'Girl's got the red jacket, number 1.'

'Will the inside suit her?'

'You've got to believe it.'

Kristie poured Paul a drink and then stood and surveyed the two of them. 'Nothing but walking wounded,' she complained. 'I'm doing the work of three and the housework as well. When this is all over I'm going to bed for a month and I expect to be tended hand and foot.'

Ken made conciliatory noises. Paul kept his face straight and continued to appreciate the pre-dinner whiskey.

'Stop crawling, Ken,' she ordered, eventually, and they burst out laughing. Her finger stabbed at Paul. 'I promised Barbara you'd ring as soon as you got up. Would you do it now please before dinner's ruined.'

'Yes ma'am,' said Paul, dutifully, and stretched for the phone near him. He grunted in pain as the muscles protested at having to do anything. Kristie was watching for the winch and he smiled at her. 'It could be worse.'

Chapter 102

Barbara answered the phone on the second ring. Her, 'Yes?' was wary. He could feel the tension subside and another one build when he identified himself.

She started with, 'Paul! Paul! Boy's, it's your daddy.'

He heard a remote duo, 'Hi, dad.'

'Hi, monsters,' he called back.

She asked, 'Are you all right?' She had been crying, was crying.

'I'm fine.' He could hardly get his hand up high enough to hold the receiver to his ear.

'You don't sound it.'

He shut his eyes bringing his family into the same room as himself. A private room with the door closed to strangers. He said something that had been on his mind for hours, something he thought he would never get to say again, 'I love you.' And added, 'You're the only girl for me, you always were.'

'I love you too,' she said.

The boys spoke to him, they sounded subdued. His eyes popped open. Dear God, which one? If I got it wrong, if they didn't believe me, if, if, if...

'I'm fine,' he assured them. 'Shaken but not stirred.' His worry for them hurt so much that he could hardly talk to them. 'Shouldn't you be studying or something?'

'Dad, you've got to stop sometime,' protested Rory.

'Slave driver,' accused Shane.

They sounded happier in the old slanging routine.

Shane wanted to know. 'Which plane are you catching?'

'I'll talk to your mother,' he said, wondering if he would ever see both of them again. Tears stood in his eyes.

'Paul?' Barbara sounded anxious. She'd said something and he hadn't replied.

'Sorry, I was thinking.' Thinking what it would be like for her to lose a child. She had built a protective shield around her family to keep further hurt at bay. The loss of one of the boys would rip her apart.

'I'm very tired,' he said.

Barbara's anxieties came boiling down the line. 'Are you really okay?'

'I'm fine.' he assured her. That was mostly true. Other than bruises, pain and a feeling that there wasn't a bone left intact in his body, he was fine.

'But what happened? We saw it on TV, the police nearly killed you.'

He had forgotten about the confrontation at the service station. 'It was some sort of mistake.'

'They could have killed you,' she repeated, and sobbed.

'Not one of my better days,' he agreed, and talked on until she had taken a tissue to the tears and blown her nose.

She didn't believe that he was all right. 'Kristie say's you've got some terrible bruises.' It came out as an order. 'You should be in hospital.'

'Thanks but no thanks.'

'Shouldn't you hide somewhere in case those people come back?'

He lied. 'If they'd any unfinished business with me I'd be lying in a ditch somewhere.'

'I want you home,' she said.

'I can't,' he blurted out.

The moment of harmony they were sharing started to fragment. 'Why not?'

He recovered rapidly. 'I don't want the boys involved, just in case. These people play rough.'

Rory said, 'Don't you worry, dad. They come near you and we'll sort them.'

'That's what I'm afraid off,' he said.

Barbara said, 'Maybe we should all move to England?'

He relaxed. He was over the hurdle of home.

Chapter 103

Ronnie Fetherton walked fast and furiously along Cromwell Road and ran up the steps into his hotel. Built for the down-at-heel coming up to London for the weekend, the hotel had long lost any pretensions to grandeur.

Everything about the place annoyed Ronnie, especially his new beard. A beard always brought him out in a rash but he needed it as a disguise for what he planned. Another few days and he could cut if off and get back to normal. Normal that is, except for a few changes. Jimmy and his friends eliminated, RM too, and a safe seat guaranteed for him as an MP at the next General Election.

He stomped over to the reception desk, put his finger on the buzzer and kept it there until a shadow of life appeared from a back room. 'Ere!'

'Key,' said Ronnie.

'What number?' asked the receptionist, after a pause.

'319. Any phone calls or messages?'

The receptionist took his time looking. He returned to the desk but stayed a step back out of arms reach. 'No.' He smirked, and wandered off.

Give me a fiver and I'd torch this place, thought Ronnie.

He'd love to burn the hotel to the ground and the smart-ass receptionist with it, but didn't dare. People were saying he'd made too many waves recently as it was. Those were the people talking to him. Other supposed friends were unavailable, or if he did get through said they couldn't speak to him just then.

They were available enough when they thought I was doing them a favor.

Favors like sorting Bradley and his anti-gangster campaign. The protection money was drying up. Those who paid were openly complaining, and many actually refused to pay knowing that the no one dared do anything about it. They'd paid later with their teeth, but that didn't help at the time. The only way to stop the rot was to silence Bradley, and not make a martyr of him in the process.

Of course I was the man everyone looked to. *Now they don't want to know.*

Ronnie took the lift to the third floor. The door to room 317 lay open. He stopped and looked in.

Four men played cards. RM and three others. Arthur Anderson lay on the bed, hands under his head. Only his eyes moved.

RM nodded at Ronnie's beard. 'Looking good, boss.'

RM had copied Ronnie by stopping shaving. He rubbed at his own beard, looking for a compliment. Ronnie thought it a disaster, more like an outbreak of black acne.

The television was on and right then featuring Bradley giving a live interview to the assembled press.

Bradley's face was colored with bruising and his walk had a hint of concealed suffering that drew sympathy from most of the interviewers. They accorded him the deference due to a Lazarus, a dead man come alive again. Paul, for his part, made light of his sufferings. Rumors about a miscarriage of justice had started to circulate and the press were hungry for details. Paul evaded all direct questions or referred the questioner to the Speaker of the House of Commons.

Bradley was international news, therefore RM was news, wanted for questioning in connection with the death of Nelson, the telephone engineer. A picture of RM was flashed up on the screen, followed by the picture of Nelson. The fact that the thug who forced Nelson to put a trace on Bradley's phone had managed to kill himself soon afterwards and the fact that the owner of the car had been brutally murdered, added spice to the story. Without actually saying it openly, the police assumed that the replacement RM had killed the car owner to ensure his silence.

'That picture doesn't do you justice,' said Arthur, making RM jump.

'Yeah,' he said, macho man.

Ronnie, struggled to conceal the distaste he felt for RM. He motioned for him and Arthur to follow him into room 319. He pointed to the dressing table as RM sidled in through the door. 'Whiskey, you'll have a whiskey.' Arthur slouched in after them. 'Arthur would you do the honors?'

'Coming up,' said Arthur. He swilled out a glass and poured in three fingers of whiskey and one of water. RM took a large gulp and choked. 'Too strong?' asked Arthur.

'No, no, no, not at all. Wonderful.'

Ronnie sipped his own three water to one whiskey drink and pretended friendliness even as he assessed RM. He thought RM down in weight and, according to the other men, not sleeping. He was too dangerous to keep, but handled right he might do a turn on Saturday night. Come Sunday at the latest, he would be dead.

Ronnie put an arm around RM's shoulders and made himself sound pleasant. 'Next week, I'm planning for the two of us to visit a French whore house.'

'Is there one of those in London?'

'No, Paris.' Ronnie had difficulty keeping his temper.

'It's supposed to be... anything goes?'

'Anything, any number, anyway.' He cut through RM's thoughts. 'But business before pleasure. I was talking to people today, they're not very pleased - RM started to sweat - Bradley, Doc, Jimmy, they think there's a fix going on there. Jimmy's out, I told them you would take care of things.'

RM took another drink, a sip this time. 'Yeah, yeah,' he said. He didn't sound very confident.

Ronnie said, 'If you don't mind, Jimmy's my pleasure.'

'Whatever, boss.'

'But Bradley's yours, you've got to establish your credentials with the politicians. Get this one right and you can forget all that nastiness about Nelson. In fact, you could walk into any police station and give them the finger and they wouldn't be able to touch you.'

'Wouldn't be the first time,' said RM.

Arthur said, 'It's easy to hide when no one's looking for you.'

Ronnie glared at him and offered RM a refill before continuing. 'Let's be honest, you need the experience and, come Saturday night, Bradley will be a sitting duck.'

RM asked, 'What's so special about Saturday night?'

'The dogs,' said Ronnie. 'Bradley's got one in the big final. There'll be thousands of people there, each and every one of them concentrating on the race. All my man has to do.' He smiled at RM as he said "my man". 'Is step up behind Bradley and use a pistol with a silencer. The crowd will be packed so tight that my man will be at the far end of the track before Bradley has room to fall.'

'Yeah,' said RM. 'Yeah.'

'Takes a man to do something like that,' said Arthur.

RM preened himself. Ronnie glared at Arthur for a second time.

'Right,' said Ronnie. 'From now on you're my official hit-man.'

'Well piss in my soup,' said Arthur.

Ronnie turned on him. 'Shut up!'

Arthur shrugged.

Ronnie's made his face carefully pleasant when he turned back to RM. 'Now you're an important man you've got to look the part. You've got to act like it and you've got to dress like it.' RM looked so down-at-heel in his mock-leather jacket that Ronnie didn't know where to start. RM needed a lot of things, especially a bit of backbone.

Ronnie threw RM out at that point. Told him to get ready, they were going shopping for new clothes.

Arthur freshened up their drinks. Arthur added mostly water to his own drink. Ronnie nodded in approval, getting the message. Arthur eased up on the drinking when a job had to be done. A price had still to be agreed, Ronnie shuddered at its likely cost, but Doc and Jimmy were as good as dead men.

The best way to start the negotiations, he decided, was to unsettle Arthur. He said, 'Arthur, you've been out to annoy recently.' Arthur shrugged as Ronnie continued. 'You stopped RM from shooting Bradley in Marston.'

'I never did.'

'Twice, he told me.'

Ronnie stretched out on the bed and lay staring at the ceiling. His face set in a deep frown as he planned his next moves. After five minutes he said, 'Jimmy's been getting at people, it's either him or me.'

Arthur shrugged. 'I've seem Jimmy and Doc in action. A job like that is bloody dangerous?'

Ronnie countered with. 'Why did you stop RM from killing Bradley?'

'Doc would've killed him.'

'So?'

'Then I would've killed Doc.'

'So?'

'I don't kill Doc for nothing.'

The men drank again before Ronnie asked, 'How much for him and Jimmy?'

Arthur had thought about it. 'Twenty thousand.'

Ronnie was shocked. 'You're getting dear.'

'Jimmy and Doc have a lot of friends.'

'But twenty?'

Arthur shrugged.

'Done,' said Ronnie, being in no position to argue. 'I want you and the other men to go home tomorrow and start setting things up.'

Arthur drained his drink and put the glass down. 'There'll be expenses, people to pay.'

'We can sort that out later,' said Ronnie, sourly.

He got an equally surly head-shake in return. 'A good lump sum up front. You're a hard man to get money out of when the job's done.'

'For god's sake, I don't keep that sort of money on me.' Arthur stood stubborn. Ronnie gave way with bad grace. 'All right, I'll have money waiting for you in Belfast.'

He sat up and swung his feet off the bed. 'For that sort of money I want a freebee job.'

'What?' asked Arthur.

'Saturday night, there's two ways of destroying Bradley. What if something happened to his family, slowly and nastily?'

Chapter 104

Jimmy was scowling at the television when Doc walked in. Outside tires squealed as a car fought its way around a skid pan. 'Have you any idea what this hanging around is costing me?' Jimmy demanded.

'No,' said Doc, and pulled up a chair to where he could watch out the window.

They were in the rest-room of a first floor office, with a large window overlooking the skid pan. Even as Doc settled, a car spun out of control and sideswiped a wall of tires. Derisory cheers went up from the onlookers.

Jimmy's scowl deepened. 'What has that cheer just cost me?'

Doc said, 'It was your idea, qualifying them to be...' His voice took on a formal, almost derisory note, '...mobile security escorts for the safe delivery of high value assets.'

Jimmy screwed around in his seat to have a good look at him. 'I remember a time when you just sat there with your mouth shut.'

Doc said nothing.

Jimmy said, 'I can't even moan in peace now.' He went back to watching the television.

Doc stood up. 'I'll see you at the dogs.'

That got Jimmy's attention. This time he increased the volume of the television before he turned. 'Doc, leave the woman...'

Ignoring the plea Doc asked, 'Do you plan to go armed.'

'What of it?'

'You haven't fired a gun in years. Even idiots like Ronnie can get lucky.'

'I can take care of myself,' said Jimmy, angry and aggressive because he knew Doc was right.

'Saturday night,' said Doc and walked out, leaving Jimmy telling himself that he felt nervous for having queried Doc's movements and intentions. It wasn't the first time he'd done that recently and Doc must be alert to his uncertainty. Especially when he'd doubly made it plain that he didn't want Paul Bradley lying with a bullet in the brain.

Chapter 105

Doc clattered down the stone stairs and out the open fire-escape door into the car-park. He took the Lexus, the car they'd used when kidnapping Paul, but now with different number plates. He liked the car, liked the way it handled. It seemed a pity to torch it after the weekend, and unfair on the owner, but with the police and DNA it couldn't be risked.

He gunned the car through the gates onto the road and headed for the motorway. Fetched a pair of glasses out of the glove compartment and put them on. They were plain glass but the heavy frames would attract attention to his eyes rather than to his general appearance.

Doc parked up the Lexus in what he hoped was a safe residential area near Heathrow airport and caught a bus to the airport itself. From there he flew under an alias to Dublin in the Irish Republic. Once in Dublin he went into the toilets and changed out of his suit into black trousers and a black polo-neck. He then took a flight in his own name back to Birmingham.

All a bit crude and, annoyingly, not his usual standard of evasion. However this time he hoped the police would trace his flight from Dublin to Birmingham. That would set up his alibi, and indirectly Jimmy's, for whatever happened at the racetrack on the Saturday night. He was banking on the police being more interested in proving that he was in Birmingham to kill his wife, than in trying to find out how he'd got to Dublin Airport in the first place.

Doc reached Birmingham at teatime and took a taxi to the Holiday Inn Express on the Coventry Road.

'I hope you enjoy your stay, Mr. Terence,' breathed a receptionist and Doc smiled back at her. Mr. Terence would stay in the hotel until Sunday morning, when he would settle his bill and check out before eleven. Someone would sleep in the room every night, but it wouldn't be Doc.

JP had been told that the girlfriend, whoever she was, had to take her own room and make sure that it appeared used. Restaurant bills were to be paid by credit card. The suitcase Doc carried up to the bedroom contained only his suit. The rest of the clothes belonged to JP. Doc made a point of leaving fingerprints on places unlikely to be touched by a cleaner's spray. With time to spare, he sat in a padded armchair and read the Gideon bible. He loved the cadence of the old-style words.

At near eight-thirty Doc's newly purchased mobile phone buzzed as a message came in. Doc got off the bed where he had been stretched out trying to rest, and went downstairs to meet JP.

As arranged, JP was at the bar, waiting for a pint of Guinness to settle. Doc took a seat two stools down and ordered a glass of white wine, Chablis. He took an instant dislike to the chrome decor and functionality of the bar-cum-restaurant, being more of a traditionalist himself.

On his way to a table, an old childhood game with JP came in useful. Doc palmed JP his room key and credit card as he passed. He sat and sipped his drink and had a think about a redhead just checking in at reception. When this is over, Doc thought, I'll check out JP's girlfriend and make sure she's safe.

Then he thought he should leave that to JP's parents. When it came to women he could trust Eleanor's instincts. She had warned him long before his first date with his future wife to "watch that one".

'You haven't a clue about women,' she'd told him. 'You're putty in their hands.'

'If I am, it's your fault from all that nagging,' he'd said back.

She'd given him a contemptuous look and gone off to make the tea. Leaving him to placate a screaming JP with a soggy nappy and colic.

Ronnie had given him the same look that day when he'd walked into his office.

Doc finished his wine in a gulp and paid for it in cash. Pulled on an anorak against the evening chill and headed out.

He walked down the road until he was out of sight of the hotel and its security cameras and then flagged down the first empty taxi passing. Once in the city center he paid off the taxi and made his way to the taxi firm he'd staked out on the previous visit. He arrived just as heavy dusk was settling over the city, found his doorway, and waited.

Drivers and passengers came and went. The lights in the taxi firm brightened as the evening deepened into night. Doc zipped up his anorak against an unexpected nip in the breeze. Kept his hands in his pockets, so that they wouldn't be cold and unresponsive when the time came.

The cold reminded him of how he and his wife used to lie into the other on a cold night. Even near the end, she'd still reach out for him in the dark just before dawn. He didn't know what was so special about those moments, other than she hadn't built up that day's spite and he didn't have to talk.

A taxi pulled up, a Volkswagen Bora, that he hadn't seen before. The driver got out. He was a big man with plenty of slack muscle on his shoulders and waist. He wore a crumpled jacket and an open-necked shirt. His hair gleamed with jell. Even at a distance Doc got a strong smell of aftershave and peppermint.

And she fell for him?

Doc watched as the driver went into the taxi firm and spoke to the Dispatcher. The Dispatcher looked pointedly at the clock and there appeared to be a heated discussion. The driver sat down and lit a cigarette. The Dispatcher pointed to a notice and the cigarette was stubbed out. Other drivers came and went, and still he sat.

Doc waited. Somehow his customary calm had deserted him. He kept thinking in terms of how he was going to handle things and struggled to make himself stop. He hadn't enough information to be that positive. His wife and that excuse of a man she had run off with could be living in a detached house or an apartment with thin walls.

The thicker the walls the louder the noise, was the nearest he allowed himself to a definite plan.

He tried to divert his mind by thinking of Connie, and veered quickly away from her. Connie would understand his need to protect Jimmy and his family, but she would never approve of his methods. JP was probably in his bed right then with the redhead. Doc nodded approval at that thought, because the continuance of the generations was what life was all about in the end.

Finally the Dispatcher seemed to relent and called the driver to the counter.

Now, thought Doc.

Doc slipped across the street and backed into a doorway just beyond the Volkswagen Bora. He held himself tight against the door as the driver came out and the central locking system clicked the car open. The driver got in. Doc slipped quickly up the pavement and got into the back seat.

'I'm on a call. You'll have to see the Dispatcher inside,' said the driver.

Doc put the tip of the knife against the driver's neck. Had to control the urge to stick it in deep and twist. This is business, he had to remind himself, letting the knife blade scratch a raw area on the driver's neck. 'Guess who, Rob.'

'Oh Jesus!'

'Drive,' said Doc.

Rob's breathing quickened. The sense of alcohol in the car increased. 'What do you want?'

'What do you think?'

'Listen... Please...'

Doc increased the pressure of the knife until it drew blood. Said nothing. Finally, reluctantly, Rob put the car in gear and they drove off. The radio was transmitting static-filled messages between the Dispatcher and other drivers.

'Turn that off,' said Doc.

'If I don't collect that fare, I'll lose my job,' stuttered Rob.

'Losing the job is the least of your problems.'

He loved the sweet, sickly smell of fear that streamed off Rob. It reminded him of honey and balsamic vinegar. Of the cold honey-roast and salad lunch he'd enjoyed that last day at Connie's. He forced Connie and her food out of his mind.

Rob did as he was told and turned off the radio. Doc removed the knife from his neck and sat back.

'Still the same old Rob,' he said. 'Working when he's not drinking, and in between shagging anything or anyone that comes handy.'

'It was her,' said Rob. 'She insisted on coming with me.'

Doc said nothing.

'Look, I'm sorry,' said Rob. 'Give me a chance. I'll keep driving. She'll never see me again.'

Still Doc said nothing. Watched out for police cars and made sure Rob stayed inside the speed limit.

The inner city streets changed to leafy sidewalks and semidetached houses with a front garden. Rob pulled into a driveway that sloped up from the street. Put the car in neutral, pulled on the handbrake. Dived out the door.

Doc was there before him, knife up and threatening. 'Now, Rob, you wouldn't be thinking of going somewhere, would you?'

'Please.'

'House.'

Chapter 106

Doc wanted to prick Rob with the tip of the knife, pinpoint every part of him with his own blood and then shake salt over the wounds. This was one useless bastard who should suffer. He'd driven him, Doc, to his wife's house without being told where to go.

'Into the house,' said Doc, and pushed Rob on.

Rob stumbled on the doorstep and fiddled forever with his keys until he found the right one. Before he could turn the key in the lock the door opened and Hillary, Doc's wife, stood there in her dressing gown. 'What's your excuse this time, Rob?'

She saw Doc, gasped and covered her mouth with her hand. Backed away.

Doc saw that Hillary had changed. She'd put on weight and her unkempt hair hung around her face in greasy ringlets. The tongue's still the same, he told himself as he shoved Rob ahead of him into the house. He closed the front door and put on the snib and then the chain to stop a quick escape.

Rob was crying. 'He made me come here, Hillary. You tell him, it wasn't my fault.'

Doc kept pushing Rob ahead of him. Hillary backed through the doorway into the kitchen and up against the units at the sink, her breath coming quickly.

'I knew you'd come,' she said.

Doc said nothing.

Rob said, 'What do you want? If it's your money, it's nearly all gone.'

The first tear trickled down Hillary's face. 'He's here to kill us.'

'Oh my God,' said Rob. He clasped his head and began to scream.

Doc chopped him across the throat. Rob collapsed onto the floor.

Now Doc could see Hillary clearly. She hadn't put on weight.

She's pregnant!

That complication hadn't occurred to him. Going by the way the baby bulged out the dressing gown it was well advanced.

If I cut it out afterwards, would it live?

Hillary flicked the hair back from around her face and he saw bruising along the cheekbone.

That's good.

That meant the neighbors on the other half of the semi-detached houses were used to screams and raised voices.

Doc started with Rob. He raked his foot along Rob's thigh. Really he wanted to sink his foot in the man's flabby stomach but was afraid of vomit pouring Rob's DNA over his shoes. With his injured throat Rob could barely cry out.

Doc said to Hillary, 'Even you could have done better than Rob.'

'You'd scared them off,' she said.

'Everyone except the local drunk, and you let him knock you up.'

He looked around the kitchen of the house that Jimmy had bought for her with the proceeds from the sale of their house. A new kitchen too, white with charcoal colored worktops, so Jimmy had been generous with what wasn't his. Formica rather than marble, he realized, so not that generous.

Jimmy shouldn't have interfered, he thought, then Jimmy was of the opinion that people deserved to live.

Doc looked at Hillary and wondered how many nights had he lain beside her and planned this moment. Cut out her tongue to shut her up. Burst her eardrums so he wouldn't have to listen to perpetual soaps.

Hillary started to cry and turned away, turned back.

A kitchen knife gleamed in her raised hand as she ran at him. 'You'll not kill my child.'

Doc blocked the blow. He stepped back to absorb the force of her charge, snagged a foot on Rob's leg and overbalanced. Doc went down, knocking his hand on a chair as he went and lost his knife. Hillary fell on top of him. Her knife was a vegetable cutter with a long, curved blade. Rob saw his chance and scrambled over them, trying for Doc's knife.

Doc's elbows were jammed outwards, taking away most of his strength to hold back Hillary. Hillary was using her weight to ram the knife into him. The point was close enough to tickle the hairs at his throat. He tried kneeing her but chairs got in the way and he cracked his knee as well. Rob had found Doc's own knife and was turning to attack. Doc strained his arms upwards, Hillary's teeth were gritted hard as she fought against his push. Her hair was falling over his face, getting into his mouth. It tasted rancid.

Hillary tried to move further up his chest, intending to use her whole bodyweight to drive the knife into his throat. For an instant her bodyweight pressing down on Doc eased. That easing allowed him to snap his elbows together and force her upwards. He rolled her sideways off him and twisted her hands until the knife sliced into Rob's thigh. Rob screamed and fell away.

Doc brought the knife-point back, driving it into the hollow of Hillary's bellybutton. 'I count three, then I straighten my arm.'

'No, please the baby.'

She scrambled away. He got to his feet, snatched back his own knife and sat against the kitchen table to catch his breath. Rubbed his sore knee. 'I'd forgotten you were good,' he said.

I taught her well.

Hillary crawled heavily to her feet. Her dressing gown gaped open. She wore a blue nightdress, it showed the shape of her pregnancy clearly. Like Doc she was out of breath, sweating as well. Rob lay on, his hands clamped around the cut, blood already staining the floor. Not arterial but still bad enough.

She cupped her hands around her coming baby. 'Your fight's with me, not the baby.'

'So?'

'Let me live until it's born.'

'You'd run.'

'Probably, but you'd find me again.'

She spoke without any great hope. Quiet and reasonable, not the shrill harridan he was used to.

Rob started to yell as pain replaced the numbness of shock. Doc got off the table, kicked him to shut him up, sat down again.

'You want me to let you have that useless bastard's child?'

'It could have been yours. You wouldn't even discuss it.'

'Who would want my genes in their child?'

'I did.'

He didn't reply, not wanting to get involved in the old argument. Instead he nodded at her face. 'How did that happen?'

'I walked into a door,' she said.

'That never happened in my house.'

'Ours,' she said.

He stood up. Flexed the knife in his hand.

'Look,' she said nervously. 'I've a bottle of sleeping pills, it's nearly full.' She glanced almost contemptuously at Rob. 'And there's some whisky left. You could watch me take them... It would be easier... I mean...'

'I want to kill you,' he said. 'The years I've dreamed of leaving your body parts in different rooms. Your guts in a bucket and that damned tongue of yours nailed to the wall.'

'You're no saint yourself,' she said, and pulled the dressing gown shut as if it could protect her against the coming stab.

'Killing you is business,' he said. 'It's about maintaining credibility with my principals.'

'Balls, you're jealous and you're pride's hurt.' She laughed contemptuously. 'I didn't think you had it in you. You've got the personality of paint drying.'

He looked at her for a long time. He'd been called many a worse thing, usually by people who feared him and their insults had been meaningless. Hillary had willingly shared his life as "Doc", so like Jimmy or Eleanor she had a right to criticize and be listened to.

What if I had shared something of Fredrick Robinson with her?

Finally he said, 'My row is with you and Rob. I'll give you...' He hesitated, trying to work out the time needed from the mound of her stomach.'

'Four months,' she said. Calm, now she was sure that the baby would be born.

More like two, he reckoned, so she intended to run again. He'd find her, he was certain of that. People always left a trail. Anyway, sometimes the chase was more fun than the killing itself.

He went across and kicked Rob to get his attention. 'She ever walks into a door again, she shows a bruise or a limp, I'll get to know about it.' He kicked again. 'Touch another drop of alcohol, a beer even, and you won't get the four months.'

For some reason he felt good about his decision to let her live. Not as good as he usually felt after an inventive killing, but in a way better. He knew Connie would approve.

At the kitchen door he stopped and looked back. A thin smile edged his lips. 'I pity that baby. I think you're just as mad as me, in your own sweet way.'

He walked out of the house.

Chapter 107

Mick's thumb hovered over the "Call" button. He sweated fear. The voice of cold glass mightn't like the way he'd found out. The hover became a tremble. He'd like it even less if he wasn't told.

Mick pressed the button.

Three rings and the voice said, 'Tell me.'

'She, Mrs. Taylor is going away for a few days.'

'When?'

'Tomorrow, Saturday. First thing in the morning.'

'How do you know that?'

'She changed her hair appointment and was asking about kennels for the dog.'

'Where's she going?'

'She didn't say, my wife said she evaded the answer. Just said she fancied dinner: starter, dessert, the works.'

'Your wife?'

Suddenly Mick desperately wanted the toilet. He hadn't intended to bring his wife into it.

'Your wife?' repeated the voice.

'No, Mrs. Taylor. I figured… you know, woman always get their hair done before they go somewhere… anywhere.'

'Good thinking.'

A *whee* of air whistled out of Mick. Air he hadn't been aware that he was holding.

The voice said, 'Delete the record of our calls in and out and the number itself.'

'Yes, sure.'

'Now!' said the voice and disconnected.

Sweat dripped off Mick's hair and down the back of his neck. *Hopefully this is the end of it.* At the same time his mouth went dry. From the papers he gathered that people in his profession were ending up dead. People who might, should, perhaps know something.

Dear God, don't let me be one of them.

Chapter 108

The Man had arranged to meet Doc on Saturday afternoon in Barkingside Park on the outskirts of London. On the phone he had sounded politely irritated at losing part of his valued weekend to business. No invitation for a meal this time, no quiet chat in a dark corner. Merely an order to be there, and on time.

Doc felt a chill at the tone. The Man was annoyed and someday their meeting would turn out to be a trap for one of them.

Doc waited for The Man at the Redbridge entrance to the park. The entrance was narrow and short, only the length of the adjoining houses and gardens. Children played in and out of the houses across the street. His only danger, Doc felt, was a drive-by shooting or for someone to be waiting for him in the park itself. He stayed tight against a weak spot in a hedge where he could dive into a neighboring garden if the need arose.

Doc wore a shirt and tie, no jacket. The weather had stayed sunny but the nip in the breeze had gone. He tensed when a car pulled up, then relaxed again when The Man got out and walked down the narrow path to join him. The Man wore a dark suit and silk tie, and was carrying an umbrella.

An umbrella for God's sake.

The sun was beating down and the park had enough trees spaced around its perimeter to start a forest fire in Doc's nose.

The Man acknowledged Doc with gracious nod. They went through the gate into the park. *No one close, no one loitering suspicious.* The Man led indicated for them to follow the high boundary hedge, keeping well away from a cricket match and its onlookers.

The Man got straight down to business. 'Mr. Kyle, there have been complaints.'

'Such as?' asked Doc.

'Bradley.'

Doc watched for The Man's reaction as he said, 'Perhaps I could complain about the representative who met me at Liverpool Street underground.'

He saw The Man's eyes flicker.

The Man asked, 'What representative? When?'

'The last day we met. He didn't say much, just kept going.'

The Man seemed uneasy, looking around as if hoping for a witness to be nearby. 'And you let him go?'

'He had a train to catch.' Doc smiled, it seemed to make The Man even more uneasy. 'You should be more careful whom you report to.'

'Mr. Kyle, I hope you don't think...'

'I don't think, I obey,' said Doc. 'Anyway, like Bradley, he's not important.'

Tension drained out of The Man who became testy. 'That's your opinion.'

Doc couldn't understand why The Man refused see the obvious, so he repeated it, 'Bradley's not important, he never was.'

'He could put you away for a lot of years.'

Doc found himself saying, 'He won't,' with confidence. Even without the photograph and the threats to his family, Bradley wouldn't name him. Bradley had given his word right at the start that nothing would go back to the police, and nothing would.

Doc did a silent count on his fingers. With Connie that made two people other than family that he trusted.

It's not like me.

The Man said, 'You're a fool to take a chance like that, I never have. Any loose ends I tidy away.' Doc remained silent. The Man gave an impatient grunt. 'You had your orders.'

'To tidy up.'

'I meant...'

Doc shook his head, it never paid to kowtow to the Man. 'You meant nothing.'

He knew that wasn't enough. With The Man you had to spell things out. Meetings with The Man often left him exhausted from talking.

He said, 'The last thing you did was to spin your knife, heads or tails. Ronnie tried and failed, after that it was Jimmy's turn.'

'Ronnie says you assaulted RM and spirited Bradley away.'

'Ronnie says a lot of things. I'll bet he didn't say we picked up Bradley in the yard with no one near him.'

The Man stopped, shocked. 'He escaped?'

'Out the bathroom window and away. RM was supposed to be guarding him.'

The Man was quiet for a while. Then he said, 'The dispute between

Jimmy and Ronnie is making things very unsettled at this end.'

Doc took it that The Man wasn't happy about the confrontation in the underground station. Someone The Man had confided in had betrayed his trust. All the same, The Man was a rat in a corner and could jump any way.

Doc kept spelling out the obvious. 'Ronnie's sloppy, if the police raid his premises they'll find things.'

'He'll never talk.'

'Do you remember the remark he made about drugs?'

'He's not an addict.'

'Are you willing to bet your freedom on it?'

They turned back at the far gate. The Man out of breath by then. He was ageing and unfit, so they walked more slowly.

The Man asked, 'If I told you to kill Jimmy and Bradley, would you do it?'

The Man's bluntness startled Doc. There had to be a lot more going on at the political end than people in Belfast suspected. The Man had to be worried, maybe even for himself.

Doc said, 'You have to ask?'

'Is that a yes?'

'Bradley's irrelevant. If you want him dead, he's dead.'

The Man became impatient. 'You keep saying that Bradley's unimportant, that he's irrelevant. What is important? What is relevant?'

Doc said, 'Someone took it upon themselves to destroy Bradley.'

'It's a bit late to be supporting democracy.'

'Not democracy,' said Doc. 'The Organization is supposed to act as a unit. No precipitous action.'

'Grouping,' The Man corrected him. 'A grouping of people from various political parties, with interests in common.'

They selected a bench and sat down, watched a struck cricket ball arc high in the air. A fielder ran in under the arc to catch the ball. Handclaps rippled around the ground.

'Mr. Kyle, you're not stupid,' The Man tapped his forehead. 'Not much up here, but you can read people like a book.'

Doc nodded. 'It takes me a while but I usually get there.'

The Man asked, 'What do you want to know?'

'Long ago I gave my word to you and Jimmy not to... engage in my profession without specific orders.'

The Man looked uneasy, glanced around in case anyone had strayed close enough to overhear. 'And?'

'No complaints, though things were quiet for a long period.'

'So no, shall we say, moonlighting?' asked The Man.

Doc stared into the distance for a while then he said, 'I need specific orders, not hints. That was the agreement.'

It was also is his quiet way a challenge. The Man had prevaricated long enough. Time for a decision.

The Man said, 'With the Speaker of the House now involved, things are rapidly coming to a head.'

Doc said nothing but felt good at work coming his way.

Someone had left a newspaper on the bench. The Man pulled out a pen and wrote down a figure. After that he put his pen on the seat and spun it.

The Man said, 'I need your assurance, Mr. Kyle, that whoever…'

'Whoever,' agreed Doc.

Finally The Man showed Doc the amount he'd written on the paper.

Doc barely glanced at the figure. The Man was always generous. 'Time schedule?'

The Man hesitated before saying, 'Tonight might be a good time.'

Chapter 109

'**A pox on Bradley,**' said Jimmy, 'and the same on Ronnie.'

Jimmy was in the offices above the skid pan and he'd just written a check for a week's training for mobile security escorts. The hotel bill was nearly as bad and then there was the 'overnight' allowance that had funded the men's bar bill.

He scowled at the men. 'Don't even think of a pay increase until next year.'

'We're not due one until then anyway, General,' said Sam Gilliland, the old driver. He had a cigarette in one hand and a walkie-talkie in the other. The other men grinned.

Once the walkie-talkies appeared the men had started to call Jimmy "General Jumbo" after the character in the *Beano* who was able to deploy an army of radio controlled miniature toy soldiers.

Jimmy's scowl deepened. He got nothing but lip from this particular bunch of men, no respect at home and Doc had started to answer back.

For heaven's sake, he was supposed to be the head of an organization that the police "took an interest in". They'd tried often enough to ensnare him, but all they and the Inland Revenue ever found was a legitimate taxi and dry cleaning business and a few rents coming in. No evidence of protection money or money laundering.

'Maybe because there isn't any,' Jimmy kept telling the authorities, but did it in a way that made them try harder to find something. The extra annoyance was worth it to see the frustration on their faces.

'You know where to go and you know what to do,' he told the men. 'Be there on time and lay off the drink until this is over.'

Sam Gilliland said, 'We wouldn't say no to a couple of guns.'

The other men nodded.

Jimmy shooed them out the door. 'This is the Peace Process. You're supposed to talk your enemies to death.'

He would be armed, the men knew that without being told. He was the one risking prison for being in the possession of an illegal weapon. Even so he understood their concern. Facing an unknown number of enemies without some personal protection was chilling. Jimmy hadn't given Doc a gun, partly because he operated best without one and partly because he and Doc were going to have it out. What bodies were due to him and why? And the answers had better be good. He touched the butt of his pistol. A gun against Doc's instincts? It didn't give him much of an advantage.

Jimmy saw the men off and then settled himself in a chair and turned on the television. Too early yet for the regional news and, anyway, Eleanor kept him informed of any developments at home. He looked up at the ceiling. 'Lord, if we're not in the news tomorrow, then things will have gone right at this end.' He clicked 503 on the remote and got the BBC 24 hours World News. He half listened as he rehashed his plans for the evening, in his head.

Bradley would be at the greyhound track, where he would be out in the open and vulnerable. Nothing would keep him away with his dog in a final. Ronnie knew that too and Ronnie was still in England, so he had something nasty planned for the evening.

Jimmy gave the ceiling another look-up. 'Lord, let's get this straight. I'm risking my neck to protect a politician, and a disgraced politician at that. It might make sense to you, but...'

What he was really thinking, he had no intention of sharing with the Good Lord. Somehow, for some reason, Bradley was the key. Bradley could name names, tell of dirty deeds done behind closed doors. Bradley, with his honor and reputation risen like Lazarus from the dead, would be believed. If Bradley lived then he, Jimmy, would live. If Bradley died... Ronnie didn't take prisoners and neither did his political friends.

Something a news reporter said caught Jimmy's attention. The man was standing on a bridge overlooking a motorway. The TV camera panned to a section land near the motorway that had been cordoned off by police tape.

The reporter continued talking. The body of a young girl, as yet unidentified, had been found by boys out rabbiting. The Police had released details of a photograph and a cuddly toy found near the scene.

The photograph was of a man and a woman and a young girl standing in the middle of Eurodisney. The couple looked like they'd come to marriage late in life. All three were smiling, the child and the woman had matching dimples.

Jimmy went white, thought he was going to faint.

260

Chapter 110

The Assistant brought through the last client of the day. 'Jerome, Mr. Evans is here.'

'Tom.'

'Jerome.'

Jerome used his professional smile as he indicated for Tom to take a seat. Really the man was impossible. Making an appointment, by the way to have his photograph taken, and then not bothering to wear something decent.

Why anyone employs him is beyond me.

He turned to the Assistant. 'You go on, I'll finish up here.'

She nodded and went out, closing the door behind her. Thirty seconds later the front door slammed shut. Just to be sure, Jerome checked the reception area. Confirmed that it was her leaving and not someone coming in.

He went back into the studio. Tom was wandering around, but at least he wasn't touching anything. Probably casing the place for a night time visit, thought Jerome.

Wouldn't that rag of a newspaper just love to get its hand on some of my images?

The backgrounds for portraits hung from the ceiling like window blinds. Jerome started to pull them down. 'What do you want for a background: library, kitchen, outdoors?'

'You've got to be joking,' said Tom.

'You made an appointment. First thing tomorrow she'll be looking to do the prints.'

Tom sat down and folded his arms. 'Whatever you want, but I'm damned if I'm paying you just to keep her books right.'

Jerome tapped his hip pocket. 'Cash job up front.'

He looked around the cramped studio wondering what to do with the man. Portrait? Not in that outfit. The get him to strip. Emphasize sagging muscles, beer belly, dirty hair and half a week's stubble. It was surprising how many women liked to buy a bit of rough on the internet.

He eyed Tom, imagining him naked. *Maybe men as well?*

'What's this all about?' asked Tom, bringing Jerome back to the real reason for him being there.

261

It's so like him to be blunt.

Jerome hated admitting that he knew nothing. 'I was told we could expect someone for a job on tonight.'

Tom smiled. 'I hope it pays as much as that last one we did.'

If only I could capture that leer, thought Jerome, and said, 'It paid well.'

'Well enough to renovate this dump,' said Tom, taking another look around.

Jerome shrugged, not willing to admit that most of his income came from the internet. People now used their mobile phones and iPads to catch those *intimate* moments.

Never children, one has standards.

He fiddled instead with lights and camera. 'Take off your coat and pullover, open your shirt down to the navel.'

'What?'

There was an old string vest lying around somewhere. If Tom put that on, had the hairs coming through?

So retro.

Realized he'd have to encourage the man a bit. 'You don't want this for your mother. It's for the women. You want to look...' He gestured upwards with his hands, 'You know.'

He didn't, but at least the coat was coming off.

Tom struggled through the layers. With his head covered by the girth-sagged pullover he mumbled, 'This reminds me of the night with that politician, Bradley.' His head popped into view. 'And we all had a go at the woman.'

'Well she had to look well served,' murmured Jerome.

'Except you of course.'

Annoying man.

Nearly as annoying as those photographs in the papers. The papers were full of them again this week. If only he dared claim reproduction rights, he was owed a fortune.

Tom was finally stripped down to his vest.

Not string unfortunately.

The tattoos on the arms are perfect, Jerome decided, crudely done and fading with age.

He put the discarded clothes aside and decided on a classy sitting room background for contrast. Tom sat stiffly. Jerome made him slouch back in the seat and open his trousers a couple of buttons.

'You'll have me naked next,' complained Tom.

So he's interested? Perhaps after a few drinks?

'It depends on whom you're trying to impress,' Jerome said.

He checked light and focus and tried a couple of experimental images.

Not bad, but I need that leer back.

He said, 'Have you seen Bradley on the television? He claims he never touched his secretary?'

Tom leered. Jerome took several quick shots. 'Nice one.'

A coin tapped on the glass of the front door. Jerome's stomach convulsed. 'He's here.'

Tom jumped up and rushed to get into his clothes. 'Wait until I'm dressed.'

Jerome didn't dare wait, no one kept Mr. Kyle waiting. Jerome opened the front door. Kyle wore a light shower coat and a slouch hat. Jerome thought he looked more like a self-supporting coat hanger than a man.

What about him standing in the far corner looking towards a naked Tom?

'Mr. Kyle, so nice to see you again.'

'Jerome,' said Kyle, and insisted on shaking hands. 'Is Tom here yet?' he asked as he led the way into the studio.

Kyle took the seat recently vacated by Tom and wanted to know how the men were doing and about their families. Jerome and Tom looked at each other in surprise. Having Kyle friendly and chatty was akin to winning the lottery when they hadn't even entered.

'What's the job tonight?' asked Jerome when Kyle let the conversation slacken.

Kyle said, 'A few photographs, with Tom accompanying you to ah… record the event.' He checked his watch. 'Plenty of time yet.' He slid a vanity mirror out from a pile of props. 'Do you mind?'

He put his hand in his left-hand pocket and pulled out a twist of tinfoil. Dribbled a line of white powder onto the mirror, resealed the tinfoil and put it back in his left-hand pocket. Used a comb to straighten the line of powder and sucked it up through a rolled-up twenty-pound note.

He sneezed and rubbed at his nose with the back of his hand. 'Wow! That's some stuff.'

Tom said, 'I didn't think you did…'

He quailed under Kyle's look and went silent.

Kyle said, 'Sorry, I'm forgetting my manners.' He handed the mirror to a surprised Tom. 'Do you fancy a line?'

'Yeah... well...'

Kyle put a generous line of powder on the mirror. Gave Tom the rolled-up note as well. 'Think of it as a bonus.'

Tom looked at Jerome who shrugged back, equally startled at Kyle's sociability. Tom snorted up the coke, Jerome had a line afterwards. Immediately his head started to roll off his shoulders and float somewhere around the ceiling. It seemed funny because he was lying on the ground looking up at his head, so his eyes must have stayed below as well.

He didn't see Kyle go into the little kitchen off the studio and take a twist of tinfoil from both his right-hand and left-hand pockets and empty them down the sink. Run water for a long time to make sure the powder had flushed away. Nor did he see Kyle light the gas stove and put on the frying pan. Throw lots of cooking oil into the pan and spill the rest onto the work-surfaces. Nor hear him go into the fridge and take slices of bacon and flick them into the pan.

He was aware of Kyle coming back and sitting in the chair, with his feet stretched out on Tom's stomach for comfort. After a while there was a whoosh and a bright light from the kitchen. Jerome knew that it wasn't good, that he should do something about it. He couldn't make his body move.

Kyle tipped his hat to both men and left.

Chapter 111

Ronnie left London in that gap when all, but the most dedicated Saturday shoppers had gone home.

They travelled mostly in silence. RM was nervous of what lay ahead and compensated by being boastful of his abilities. Ronnie quickly silenced him and suggested some music. RM's fingers were as nervous as his mind and, after listing to twenty stations in nearly as many minutes, Ronnie told him to leave it where it was. They spent the rest of the journey tuned in to Classic FM. RM fell into a stupor, neither asleep nor awake.

The Arena was easier got to than they originally thought. The last stretch of road ran tight against a continuous rise on the left. Bushes grew to the very edge of the road itself. On the other side the ground was more level. The undergrowth had been cutback to contain a series of the most incredible houses. Ronnie began to consider diversification into kidnapping and extortion. Once he had stung the owners often enough, he could use their money to buy one of these little palaces for himself. He chuckled at the thought.

RM's new coat, this time made of real leather, creaked when he stirred. 'What, boss?'

'Go back to sleep.'

They came to a halt sign. The gates of the Arena were straight across the road from them, on the T-junction. Ronnie turned left and accelerated away.

'Hey, boss.'

Ronnie said, savagely, 'There's about six cars there, do you want to stand out like a sore thumb?'

By the time he found a lay-by to turn in he had worked out what to do. He headed back to the Arena and turned up the side road they had come down only a few minutes before. He travelled slowly along it until he spotted a rutted track leading up the hill. He turned onto it.

The car lurched sickenly in the ruts. RM grabbed the door for support. 'Where are we going? We'll get stuck.'

'I've taken a forty foot rig over worse,' said Ronnie.

'A lorry, on a road like this, what for?'

'Depends what you're delivering.' Ronnie tapped his nose.

RM looked impressed.

The track twisted and contorted as it climbed and ended suddenly in a clearing large enough to turn the car in.

'Hey!' said RM, appreciatively.

'Nothing to it,' said Ronnie, taking an undeserved plaudit. He could have reversed back down anyway, but this saved him the bother.

Impatient now, he unlocked the boot and flung out cases to get at the long, flat one buried under the rest. RM had to retrieve them.

Ronnie placed the long, flat case on the ground and opened it. RM's eyes widened. 'That's the...'

'Yeah,' said Ronnie. 'And it's not just any Lee-Enfield.' He held it lovingly while RM inspected it from a distance. 'This is a 1914 Snipers Pattern with the original P/18 Aldis Sight. The magazine only holds five rounds, more than ample for any real marksman.' It sounded good. The hastily acquired book knowledge came out pat, and RM looked suitably impressed.

Ronnie clipped the magazine in place. 'Lock up and follow me,' he said, and headed off towards the main road.

They found it hard work pushing through the undergrowth. The bushes grew close together and the young shoots came back against their skin like the tip of a whip.

'Frig,' said Ronnie. 'I wouldn't like to do this in the dark.'

RM wisely said nothing. His leather jacket was taking a pounding but he himself was all right.

They came out onto the crest overlooking the Arena and worked along it until they were at the junction of the two roads. The first cars and vans were starting to pull into the car park; they held the doggy men bringing in that night's runners. Ronnie stared across the open ground and selected the main entrance to the stands as his aiming point.

'How far do you think that is?' he asked.

'Do'no.'

Ronnie sighed and re-calibrated the telescopic sights.

'What are you doing, boss?'

'Setting the sights for four hundred yards.'

'Why?'

Ronnie could have told RM to shut up. Instead he decided to impress him with his knowledge. He said, 'A bullet reaches its maximum velocity as it exits the muzzle. Thereafter it slows, and as it slows gravity - you know, Newton and the apple - begins to take effect and the bullet's trajectory becomes a curve

266

instead of a straight line. If I set the sights for four hundred yards the gun will automatically aim high to allow for the downward curve of the bullet over that distance. Also, this is an old weapon and it's not as powerful as it once was so I've got to allow a bit for that as well.'

'Gee.' RM was tactful enough to let a few seconds pass before he asked. 'I meant, what are we doing here?'

'Watching for Bradley. When he turns up.' Ronnie put a finger to his temple. 'Bang.'

'What about me? I'm supposed to do it.'

'Don't worry, we'll say it was you.'

Ronnie turned his attention back to the car park. If he could get Bradley from the hill it would save a lot of bother. His mouth went dry at the thought of killing and maybe being found out. But this was far less risky than actually doing it close-up at the track itself. He glanced at RM. *That stupid bugger couldn't hold his water.*

Anyone else who could get him jail over the Bradley affair was being taken care of, which made him determined. When he left, RM was staying. Maybe he could arrange things to make it look like murder and suicide.

Either here or at home in Glenlish, tonight Bradley was as good as a dead man.

Preferably both.

And if that didn't make any doubters in the Organization sit up and take notice, nothing would. They'd be queueing up to take pot-shots at Jimmy and Doc, on his behalf. And after Jimmy and Doc? He was sure The Man whose name must not be spoken would take care of Arthur as well.

Hopefully before Arthur comes looking for the rest of his money.

Chapter 112

One of the early arrivals at the track was a tall, grey haired man driving a Mercedes estate. He parked close to a side entrance used by all the doggy men and took two dogs, a brindle and a smaller fawn, out of the back.

Ronnie was practicing his aim on the tall man's forehead when the shock of recognition made him pull the trigger. Luckily he hadn't worked a round into the breach. The hammer snapped home on an empty chamber.

'Shit and damn,' he roared. 'No Bradley.'

'Damn,' agreed RM. He looked relieved.

They watched Ken walk the dogs to the side entrance. They knew it was him from his picture in the papers. Just before he disappeared from view Ken looked towards the main gate and then at his watch. Hope soared again.

'He's expecting someone,' said Ronnie.

'Bradley?'

'How the hell would I know?'

They waited until people were pouring in. Twenty Bradley look-alikes had teetered on the edge of extinction before Ronnie gave up and reverted to their original plan. A rage of frustration built up in him. If RM had spoken he'd probably have killed him there and then just to relieve the pressure on his brain.

Before they left Ronnie checked his own beard in the wing mirror for length and thickness, and thought it fine. Better than that, darned good looking. He tried on a pair of horn-rim glasses, and nodded, satisfied. Not even his mother would know him. RM's beard on the other hand? Ronnie looked at him in distaste. It was the sort of beard that made people wonder what the wearer was trying to hide.

They found the bar and had a couple of doubles – to stiffen RM's spine, Ronnie told himself. RM was afraid of being recognized in spite of the money spent on him. Gone was the slightly grubby man. The dripping hair had been replaced by sideburns and an expensive razor cut. In addition to the begrudged cost of the leather jacket, RM now wore black jeans and matching silk shirt.

They gulped down their drinks and took position on the open terracing near the main gate. No matter where Bradley went he had to pass them first.

Ronnie hadn't been to the dogs in years, it wasn't in the same class as horse racing. He was surprised at the number of men wearing suits and ties, particularly thin men. He sighed in relief when he spotted Bradley come through the entrance. The 40X binoculars Ronnie carried brought Bradley in close. So close he felt he could grab Bradley, pull him into a quiet corner and kick his head in. Rather than dwell on the impossible, he concentrated on what could be done.

He swung his binoculars onto the stands at the far side of the track and thought of the rifle in the boot of the car. But he knew it wasn't just a case of walking, cold eyed, into a strange place, taking your target out and strolling away again. These things had to be pre-planned and gone over in detail.

He nudged RM and they watched Bradley stroll the line of bookies before disappearing up the stairs into the restaurant. Ronnie convinced himself that his way was best. Bradley was a hands-on man, he did his own dogs and was bound to go to the paddock to see the bitch. All he had to do was to aim RM in the right direction and keep well back. If it worked, fine. If it didn't, he pressed his arm against the legally held Smith & Wesson in his shoulder holster. He'd make damn sure RM wasn't captured alive. In the meantime he kept his binoculars focused on the door leading to the restaurant. Occasionally he swept them over the people crowding the rails, looking for Jimmy or Doc. Not that he expected them to be there, but one could never be too careful.

Chapter 113

Inspector Ian Patterson led the way into the Glenlish Arms, his men were to follow in two minutes. This was his party and he honored it by wearing his best uniform. As an added insult to the hard-men clientele, he had come unarmed.

The bar was crowded with early evening drinkers. The bursts of laughter and the talk died at his appearance. Grit from the street cracked under his feet as he marched across the wooden floor. He thought the place grotty and in need of a good clean.

Except for the padded seating, the fruit machines and the lighting, it could have been something out of the Wild West. Some people never grow up, he thought, as he swaggered up to the bar.

The barman tried to ignore him and continued serving someone else. Patterson slapped the bar with his swagger stick and the crack echoed in the silence. 'Bush and water.'

The barman forgot about the other customer and turned towards the optics. The customers watched Patterson and he watched them back in the mirror. The men along the bar edged away.

The drink was brought and fresh water served up in a jug.

'And a clean dishcloth - if you've got one.' He liked that.

Two men got up to leave, he spotted them in the mirror. 'Just sit, boys,' he said without turning. He continued drinking.

The door opened and his men came in. The first two in were handpicked, men he suspected of drinking in the Arms itself. They wouldn't do that again. They wouldn't be welcome back. DC Green wore a bullet-proof vest and carried a Heckler & Koch submachine gun for emphasis.

Patterson took the dishcloth, unfolded it and draped it over the beer handles. He turned to face his audience. 'This bar is closed until further notice. Every man will stay where he is until called forward to identify himself and be searched. After that you can go home – most of you.' He sensed the barman move, and said, 'Keep your hands where I can see them.' And thought, John Wayne, eat your heart out.

His men knew their jobs and they swung into action. He nodded to the three detailed as his flankers. They closed in on him as he headed for the

270

rooms at the back. The room they wanted was upstairs and to the rear: the window boarded over to stop light from showing out and a stack of clean glasses set on the window ledge.

'Handy for after-hours drinking,' commented DC Green.

The room itself was fairly large. It had a few chairs, a camp bed and a microwave oven. Again the floor was bare wood. Patterson sniffed around while the men searched. He felt vaguely cheated. He had only got permission for the raid because the Assistant Chief Constable owed him for connecting Ronnie Fetherton, albeit indirectly through RM, to organized crime.

A pile of magazines lay in a corner. He poked through them: gun magazines, girlie magazines and an ancient copy of *The Anarchist Cookbook*.

'Oh Lord, how pathetic,' he said out loud to the picture of the queen above the fireplace. He touched his cap with his swagger stick. 'Sorry missus,' and walked to the door, feeling he would be better employed downstairs.

Just before he left he glanced back. Something caught his eye. What exactly he couldn't say. He stopped and looked around carefully and realized that some of the floorboards under the chairs were a lighter color along their edges. He walked over and examined them. They appeared to be well nailed down yet they moved under his foot. He looked closer. The boards had crush marks along the sides as if they had been pulled up several times.

'Good man,' said Patterson when Green lifted the chairs clear and produced a screwdriver. Green slotted the screwdriver into the largest crush mark and heaved. The board came up as easy as turning the page of a book.

The first thing they saw was white powder in clear plastic bags. Hardly more than a generous personal supply, but cocaine nevertheless. They photographed the drugs, then bagged and labelled them. Lying beside the cocaine was a GPS tracker and the tracking device.

'That's one way of keeping tabs on your shipment,' said Green.

Patterson shrugged. That seemed too neat an explanation of Mick going electronic.

The next board up uncovered a police issue revolver. The revolver was well greased and covered in fingerprints. Someone chuckled and they all started to laugh, especially Patterson. He reckoned that this was the gun his man had lost two years before. Amnesia wouldn't help Big Mick this time. Those fingerprints on the revolver could be, almost certainly were his. The barman they'd do as well. The team searching downstairs had found a supply of Rohypnol tablets at the back of the cash register. They might explain a recent outbreak of date rape in the area.

Chapter 114

It was one of the most talked about Rosebowls in years. Last year's winner, Kid Carbine, was running like a dream machine and the fact that disgraced MP and kidnap victim, Paul Bradley, had a dog in the final didn't hurt either.

Paul stood in front of the main stand, and breathed in the sight and smells of jostling humanity. He and Kristie had stayed back to feed and settle the rest of the dogs, and then travelled together in the Audi. He parked the car while she went on to secure their table in the restaurant. He was anxious to get there himself before the pressmen recognized him and came running, yet he found it difficult to hurry. There was something special about a final night that he wanted to savor. Girl's chance of winning the big race was none to a miracle.

All the same...

He could let himself dream for another hour or so.

The bell sounded announcing the departure of the dogs from the paddock for the first race, and the bustle of people intensified. A bookie, Jim Neeson according to his board, shouted his opening bid. 'Even money the field.' Neeson got some interest but no takers. He wiped the electronic board and started again. Four of the dogs came up at twos, but Neeson hesitated over the others. Eventually Number Five became a reluctant three to one. However the price for Number One remained stubbornly elusive. The depth of would-be punters thickened down the line of bookies as odds were tendered on the boards and then hastily deleted.

The price of the four dogs drifted out to threes and Number Five became four-to-one. Neeson still had nothing against Number One. 'Two-to-one the favorite,' shouted someone. Neeson put up six-to-four against Number One, but a rush of money at the other "book" made him change his mind. He hastily changed the six-to-four to a diagonal line, *evens*. He caught Paul watching and winked. Serious betting wouldn't start until the two-minute bell.

Paul headed for the restaurant. He didn't see a stout, ageing man lift a walkie-talkie to his lips and say. 'This is #3, Bradley's here.'

The restaurant ran the length of the main stand, the dining area tiered so that people could watch the racing without having to move from their tables. It was crowded, and Paul was just asking the *maître d'* for Ken's table when he spotted it. Not just Kristie but – a thrill equal to his hopes for Girl - Barbara was there as well.

The two women could have dressed to compete. Kristie wore a powder blue skirt and a white blouse embroidered down its front. The gold in her ears and at: neck, lapel and wrist was all the more impressive for being understated and very old. Barbara competed with a cocktail dress in muted red and black, diamond stud earrings and a choker of bling pearls.

'It's all right,' Paul told *maître d'*, and walked across to join them. Barbara saw him come and stood up. Her kiss of greeting was polite and neutral, but she had a sparkle in her eyes that he hadn't seen there in a long time. Kristie's social kiss just happened to leave a smear of lipstick on the side of his mouth. Barbara hurt him scrubbing it away with a moistened tissue. He took the hot seat separating the two women.

'What are you doing here?' He asked Barbara.

Totally tactless, he knew, but that's what was what he was wondering.

Her fingers touched the bruising on his face. She was controlled, but tears trembled very close. 'I really can't say.'

He saw her eyes harden as she looked between him and Kristie.

That suspicion again.

He asked, to change the subject in her head, 'Did you bring the boys?'

She shook her head, and didn't tell him that the boys wanted their dad home and normal, so much so that they were afraid to come. He for his part knew that she had come to bring him home, and he couldn't go. This time he'd have to be honest with her. No more Glenlish, no more home.

He gripped her hand under the table, she locked her leg around his. He ached to take her somewhere private and hold her naked in his arms. Impossible here, difficult at times even at home. Which made him think again of the boys.

He asked, 'Is it safe to leave them on their own?'

She shook her head. 'If last weekend's anything to go by, no. But, Paul, you've lost nearly two years, we've got to trust them now.'

He was silent, hurt.

She said, 'They promised faithfully to be in before dark and not to overnight this time at a friend's house.' She sniffed and fished a handkerchief out of her bag and blew her nose. 'All this flying, I think I'm catching something.'

Paul smiled at this little moan of normality.

Ken wound his way through the tables to join them. They watched the first race while they ordered their meal.

Chapter 115

Across the track, in the Sixpenny Stand another man reported. 'This is #5. He's in the dining room, third row back and sitting sideways onto the window. It could be done but it would be a hell of a shot.'

Without giving his call sign, Doc asked, 'Is it still the two?' He meant Ronnie and RM.

Jimmy replied, rather pointedly, 'This is #1.' Then he said, 'Still two.'

'What about the ones left in the kennels?' Doc meant Ronnie's men who had gone back to Belfast.

'This is #1. They were in a pub at lunchtime getting tanked up, and we've people watching the airports.'

'No sign of a ringer in the race?' Doc meant an outside contractor.

'This is #1. None that we know off.' Jimmy waited, Doc didn't reply. Jimmy sighed, 'And use your bloody call sign.'

Chapter 116

Ken went off to see the second race from the rails, indicating for Paul to follow. Paul shook his head, Barbara would be hurt if he rushed off. 'The final,' he promised.

Ken was back in ten minutes. He gulped down his prawn cocktail, told the waiter to hold his main course and made a permanent break for freedom before the third. The big brindle was running in the fourth race and he had to get him ready.

Paul sat on and suffered death by a thousand tongues. Kristie and Barbara's polite dislike for each other nearly killed him. He lifted the atmosphere by suggesting a pool on each race at a pound a time. The winner was the person whose dog came closest to being last. They upped the ante by actually betting the three pounds on their highest priced choice at the two-minute bell.

Paul got it disastrously wrong in the third race. He picked the actual winner and they won nearly sixty pounds on the tote. The women were agreed on one thing, he was no true greyhound man if he couldn't even pick a loser. They bet nothing on the fourth, their hearts were with the big brindle.

Paul excused himself and went to the windows to watch the dogs parading.

The stout, ageing man was standing at the edge of the track. He took a practice sighting and said, into his radio, 'If he stays there, he's a sitting duck.'

'This is #1. Use your call sign #3.'

'#2 doesn't,' said Sam Gilliland, and smirked in Jimmy's direction.

The kennel boy walked the big brindle in the parade while Ken waited with the starter. The big brindle had only one foible. He fought with the strength of a claustrophobe if anybody, other than Ken, tried to put him in into the box. Yet Ken only had to point and pet and he went in like a lamb.

Paul looked over at the TV screen showing the betting. The big brindle was two-to-one favorite, a good price in the circumstances.

They loaded the dogs, 1,3,5 first; 2,4,6 last. The big brindle was in trap four. When his turn came he strolled forward on Ken's pat, stopped to check that the starter was holding the door correctly and entered to a cheer from the crowd. Ken hurried to the center of the field. Kristie and Barbara joined Paul at the window as the hare started its run.

The race was over before it began. Five dogs came out in a line together. The sixth, the big brindle, bombed out a length ahead of the rest and quickly made it two lengths. From there on he was never in any real danger of being caught, though he started to fade in the final stretch for the line. The results board quickly said: First, Number 4. Time, 28.22. The crowd's gasp and cheer acknowledged a fantastic run - one point outside the track record.

Paul, Kristie and Barbara were still celebrating with laughter as they turned away from the window. The women's good humor continued for the rest of the meal. Paul was on eggs until it was time to slip away for the final.

Chapter 117

Ronnie saw Bradley come out of the door that led to the restaurant, and turn to the right. He sighed in relief. 'At long last.' He nudged RM. 'Come on.'

RM was silent. He had been for a long time.

'Come on,' said Ronnie, again, and pulled him on.

Bradley got well ahead of them as they pushed through the crowd and down the steps. At home Ronnie would have shoved and threatened, his heart was beating hard enough to push a ton of people out of the way. Here he didn't want to be noticed. He had to drag RM along after him.

'Come on, come on,' he kept saying.

They lost sight of Bradley once they were on the level. Ronnie cursed himself for not staying closer to the door. He walked on tiptoe, giving himself a two-inch viewing platform.

Bradley had walked with purpose. Bet you he's going to the top bend, he thought, and felt better. They had plenty of time.

Chapter 118

The dogs were coming out for the parade when Paul and his butterfly nerves neared the top bend.

Girl will win. She hasn't a chance. I should have sold her when I could. Tomorrow she'll be worth jujubes, and that's not fair on Barbara.

The press were waiting for him.

A battery of lights came on, jerking him into the present. A microphone was shoved under his nose and someone muttered "BBC News" before the questioning started.

Paul ran with them for a while and gave all the standard answers. 'It is an eventful night.' And, 'Yes, it's great having a dog in the final.' He felt alive and euphoric. Questions of a more personal nature followed and he started to twist the answers to bring the questions he wanted.

A rumor that the Speaker was to make a statement in the House on Monday?

A shrug, 'I can only guess.'

The microphone edged even closer, 'Guess what?'

'Ahh...'

It was just enough. Enough to tease them along, to let two young boys see their father in full, confidant flight again.

Ken grabbed him by the arm and hauled him through the crowd to the rails. 'Would you stop that tomfoolery, and come and wave at the bitch.' His impatience carried over to the reporters, 'Kill those lights before they put the dogs off.'

The lights faded and died behind them.

Chapter 119

Ronnie stood at the back of the crowd and watched the interview take place. He was suspicious of RM. The wimp stood too straight and too steady, as if he had psyched himself up for something.

'Boss,' said RM. 'I could get him from here, right on prime time television.'

Ronnie thought RM was a genius. People were again starting to kick against paying protection money. Killing Bradley on live television would encourage them to keep paying. 'Just don't miss,' he said, delighted.

RM pulled out his gun, a .22 revolver with a silencer attached. Ronnie stepped back and away, apparently uninvolved, as RM cocked the trigger. The lights went out and Bradley's outline disappeared into the crowd.

RM stood holding the gun, looking stupid.

Ronnie's head was light with relief. *It's going to work.*

He said, 'On your bike, do it my way.' He grabbed RM by the arm. 'Remember, the front entrance immediately afterwards. I'll be there with the car.'

In face he'd be right behind RM ready to kill him. No way could he risk him being caught.

RM cradled the gun under his leather coat, nodded and walked towards the rails.

Ronnie watched him go, anxious now in case his nerve would break. But RM worked his way forward at a slow, deliberate pace and disappeared into the crowd. Ronnie was about to follow when someone brushed past him. A scruffy man with a hearing aid and several day's growth of beard.

'Watch it!' said Ronnie.

The scruffy man walked on. From the rear, his dark hair was neat and trim, his collar properly turned down.

Doc! Dear God in heaven, Doc!

Ronnie started to run.

Chapter 120

Girl, as number one, led the parade. She hauled ahead like a husky, her body arched against the kennel boy's restraining hold. She glanced in Paul's direction as she passed and he shouted, 'Would you take it easy.' Immediately a battery of flashes went off around him. He had to close his eyes and shake his head before he could see properly again. By that time Girl was well past him. The crush of the crowd was fierce and the press of the cameramen wriggling into position didn't help. He ignored the lot of them and concentrated on keeping his heartbeat down to a reasonable rate.

Girl fought going into the box. They could see the kennel boy struggle with her. Paul sighed in relief when the kennel boy stepped back and wiped his forehead. Girl scrabbled at the flooring and howled her temper while the other dogs were being put in. The bell rang and the famous Arena roar started with the hare, drowning out the noise of its coming. It was almost on top of Girl before she ducked down and pressed her nose hard against the lid.

The hare came rattling around the bend. Paul leaned out to watch the start and a flash went off in his face. He jerked back startled, 'For heaven's sake, lay off,' he snapped. Another flash recorded his protest. He gave up and turned back to the rail as the dogs went past. Kid Carbine was in the lead, Bromide on his outside, three quarters of a length back in second place. The rest of the pack passed in a shoving scrambling bunch. Girl was in amongst them, though he didn't see her. She had to be because she wasn't down the track and she wasn't stuck in the box.

Ken was still hyped. 'Look at her go! Look at her go!' he shouted. He was wasting his breath. Only one dog in the country could come from behind to head Kid Carbine, the big brindle, and he wasn't running. Paul felt disappointed as he settled back to enjoy the race for its own sake.

The virtual rear-view of the dogs started to stretch into profile as they came around the second bend. The roar of the crowd intensified as they watched the leaders fight for glory.

Ken grabbed at Paul and repeated, 'Look at her go!'

A photographer saw something worth recording in that and, again, a flash exploded in Paul's face.

'Quit it!' he snapped, and cupped his hands around his eyes to protect them from any further glare. His vision was full of black floaters and at that distance and in the relatively poor evening light he could make out very little of what was going on in the race. He thought Girl was lying about fifth but couldn't be sure. Ken had gone very quiet, which confirmed that, for them, the final was over.

All down the track people were hanging over the rails to watch the closing stages. Their shouts crescendoed as the dogs turned into the home straight. Paul stood straight rather than give the photographers something else to record and could see nothing of the race for a sea of heads and shoulders. The rim of a hat or something, touched the back of his neck. It irritated. He shook his head and twitched his shoulders at its cold touch.

Chapter 121

RM dream-walked forward. He could have got Bradley under the lights but he'd been too careful, trying to be sure of his aim. From here on he was someone in his own right, hit man for the Organization. Let people dare laugh at him now.

He kept his gun concealed in his folded arms as he wriggled through the press of people. Bradley's head only appeared occasionally as he straightened to say something to the reporters and then disappeared again. RM was two rows behind Bradley and jammed in tight. One more row in would have been better for a clear shot. The roar of the crowd increased, they were all looking to their left. Bradley stood upright and stared ahead.

Now!

RM brought the pistol up and laced it between the heads of the people in front of him until the muzzle was inches away from Bradley's neck. No one seemed to notice that it was a gun. He got shoved from behind. An elbow – it felt like an elbow – hit his neck. The elbow felt sharp. Now the gun was actually touching Bradley. No way could he miss.

RM remembered how something dangerous happening, no matter how fast, seemed slow to the people involved. It was taking his finger a long time to pull the trigger. For some reason his aim was off. His arm had fallen onto the shoulders of the man in front, the man wriggled in protest. A man with a hearing aid reached forward and took the gun from RM's fingers. RM saw it happen but didn't feel it. He could feel nothing.

What's happening to me?

People around him had grown. Now his head was at their shoulders, their waist. He was on the ground and could feel nothing.

Darkness.

Chapter 122

People shuffled clear of RM's fallen body.

'Are you all right, mate?' said a voice.

'Bloody drunk,' said another.

The movement of people gave Doc a chance to ease out of the crowd. A nice kill, he thought, right on the cusp. Tomorrow he'd go over it, move by move. There was always something to be learned from every killing, even a simple one like this. After that he'd savor the memory of the kill itself: the stalk through the crowd, the press of bodies around him, the heft of the little Swiss army knife with the dark carbon blade. Someone's breath on his neck, a muttered "sorry mate" as someone else bumped him. Saying back, 'don't worry about it,' as the point touched RM's neck. The same voice saying to him, 'This is some final,' and his 'You've got to believe it,' as the blade sliced into RM.

RM's body had stiffened as the knife went in, but he'd allowed for that with the angle of entry. The grating feeling as gristle gave way. The tingle of satisfaction of a job well done as the blade slid between RM's third and fourth vertebrae to slice his spinal cord. RM folding to the ground even as he eased the gun from his fingers. Walking away with the gun shoved under his jacket.

Doc spoke into a hidden microphone, 'The odds have dropped to evens.'

He went back the way he had come, looking for Ronnie.

Chapter 123

It suddenly occurred to Paul to worry about Ken and he looked over at him. Ken was exulting, 'What a race! What a race!' He gave Paul a friendly bang on the shoulder - more flashes - before he headed off to see to Girl.

A reporter asked, 'What did you think of the race, Mr. Bradley?'

'It would have been nice to it,' snapped Paul, and turned away.

There was a swirl of people behind him. 'Watch out,' someone was saying.

'Heart attack,' said someone else.

The concerned voices drew the reporters and the photographers. Paul edged sideways along the rail and away.

He looked up at the Results Board to confirm that Kid Carbine had won. Instead of the number of the winning dog there was a P - A photo finish.

Bromide must have run his guts out.

And the time 28.57. He reckoned it had to be one of the fastest finals ever.

The crowd stayed static. Their hushed expectancy was filled with, 'Did you ever see anything like it?' or, 'This is one for the record books.' And the bookies were shouting. 'Evens Kid Carbine,' or, 'Six to four Bromide.'

Barbara waited for him on the bottom steps. He waved to her twice before her searching eyes spotted him. She waved back, ran down into the crowd and forced her way through to him. He thought of the argument to come, about him going home, and his hand lifted to the scar.

Barbara caught his hand and held it to her lips.

'Please don't,' she pleaded. 'It makes me feel guilty whenever you do that.'

He said, 'There's nothing to forgive.'

She threw herself into his arms and half squeezed the life out of him. He kissed her, she responded.

An onlooker said, 'Don't you two get enough of that at home?'

Barbara clung on to Paul, she was highly excited, 'You must be so proud.'

'Proud?'

'I think we've won,' she burst out.

'Won?'

Something about the bookies registered at last. They were giving prices on Kid Carbine and Bromide. In a photo finish they only gave prices on the dogs they thought had lost.

He ignored her protests and dragged her through the crowd to the nearest monitor. The tape was reversing for the umpteenth time. The dogs blurred back into their boxes pursued by the hare. The tape stopped and came into focus. After a moment's delay the hare came back around the bend and the dogs surged out of their boxes in hot pursuit.

Girl, Kid Carbine and Bromide came out in a line together. Daisy Away in trap five led the second group. Paul gasped as he watched Girl match her peers stride for stride to the bend. Kid Carbine was a short head in front, Bromide slightly in arrears of him and Girl was the jam between them and the fencing.

Kid Carbine stretched for the turn. Bromide, for once held his line and Girl refused to give an inch. Paul could almost feel the planking brush her shoulder as she fought back. She held them, denying Kid Carbine the inside slot, and the three of them went around the bottom bends matching stride for stride. The second group of dogs crunched on the first bend. Daisy Away was the worst affected and had to fight back to take fifth place. In her dark jacket, Paul had mixed her up with Girl during the race itself.

Kid Carbine unleashed his famous charge down the back straight. He pulled half a length ahead of Girl, but she clawed him back. Bromide finally found his overdrive. The three dogs were neck and neck going into the third bend and out of the fourth, and they fought a see-saw battle for the lead up the home straight. The video stopped them two strides short of the line and inched them forward.

Barbara was squeezing Paul to death. 'Look! Look!' she was saying.

It was close. The camera wasn't quite on the line so it was impossible to say. And it was taking the judges a long time.

'What do you think?' she demanded.

He smiled down at her. 'It's looking good.'

She stared into his eyes, all humor gone. 'I want it - to replace our other cup.'

He said, 'Even if someone else gets it, it will still be our cup.'

He bent down and kissed her. She responded. For a moment they forgot where they were.

Suddenly she broke the kiss and looked at him. 'When did that happen?'

'Right now,' he said, embarrassed.

A tight packed crowd was no place to have a hard-on.

'Hell!' she said, 'There'll be no sleep tonight.'

Paul gripped her to him, felt Barbara match his fierceness. Everything was coming together at last: his life, his marriage. For some reason he wanted to cry.

The loudspeaker stuttered static as it was switched on.

The talk, the shouts and the laughter faded away, and the dark under the lights became a sea of washed pink as faces were raised to the speakers. Unnoticed, a stray raindrop fell among the crowd. Barbara buried her head in Paul's shoulder.

A voice said, 'Here is the full result of tonight's seventh race...'

A sheet of paper crackled over the air as the announcer pulled it closer.

'First...'

The Announcer knew how to draw the last ounce of expectancy out of the crowd. It was so quiet a cough disturbed and brought glares from those nearby.

Chapter 124

Jimmy stood in the glassed-in public area, his heart still palpitating from Bradley's close call. Bradley was proving a hard man to keep alive.

I'll bloody kill, Doc, he thought, he runs it to the line, every time. Every bastarding time.

He caught a grip of himself and looked around. There was no one near him so he took the two-way radio out of his pocket and said, 'Unit check call.' His men were giving him funny looks and talking among themselves. *That training I gave them on handling on two-way radios.* A couple of pints at home, and the word would be halfway across Belfast that Thicko Jim wasn't quite as stupid as he let on. The tag "General Jumbo" would only make things worse.

I'm breaking cover for a politician?

Jimmy nearly spat the word, yet he knew that Paul Bradley was right. Things had to change, and properly this time, especially about the protection rackets. The cash he sent The Man quarterly were little better than that. Ten percent of profits, allegedly for The Man's share of the business. Actually, they bought protection from prosecution for past mistakes. With that money he could have other wee businesses running, found jobs for the unemployed kids of his men.

More than half the working people in Northern Ireland depended on government hand-outs to make ends meet. What the Province needed were men who used their profits to create new work. Not act like absentee landlords, draining the Province of its wealth.

Jimmy started back to the present when his earpiece gave three static clicks as radios were switched on and off. The fourth didn't come, Doc never answered.

Jimmy spoke again. 'This is #1. Anybody, what's going on?'

A voice crackled in his ear. 'This is #4. I can see Ronnie. He's near the front entrance. I think he's heading for his car.'

'Keep an eye.' Jimmy got a click in return. He then said, 'Anybody else. Anything?' There was no reply and he called up #3, Sam Gilliland. 'Listen, Stockdale's car, immobilize it.'

He put the radio back in his pocket. The two-way radio and his first-ever mobile phone were stretching the material of his new jacket. The wife wouldn't be pleased, but there was nothing he could do about it. The Walkman and a holstered gun were clipped onto his belt. Their weight wasn't exactly comfortable either.

'Bugger, bugger, bugger,' he said.

'I know, mate,' said a passer-by. 'That wee bitch blew my Triella as well.'

Jimmy laughed and fished a betting slip out of his pocket. 'I had a hundred on her.'

'So what's the problem?' said the passer-by and walked on.

Jimmy made himself think. The problem was Ronnie who had kept only RM with him and sent the rest of the men home. Now RM was out of it, which left Ronnie on his own and running scared. It was a dangerous game when a rat turned.

He knew he was taking a chance that Ronnie hadn't shipped in some outside help. He had done it before, but nothing showed this time. He and Doc were as much at risk as Bradley until this was over. He supposed he could always tell Bradley of the danger. That would wipe the smile off his gob and stop him from snogging his old woman in public. He hoped Bradley was worth breaking cover for. He felt naked without the thick-but-willing image that had helped protect him for half a lifetime.

They were calling the winning owner and trainer for the presentation. Jimmy stayed on in the glassed-in public area. It would be so much easier being down there, kidding himself that he was actually doing something.

The presentation party came into view: the track management in their white shirts and classy suits, Ken Stockton and his wife, and Barbara. No Bradley, for that Jimmy was grateful. And even more grateful that Bradley's kids were still at home and safe. Two less to worry about.

Which left Bradley on his own, presumably in the restaurant.

Jimmy hoisted his radio once more. He said, 'Moving to restaurant,' and got three clicks in return.

The restaurant looked half empty but that was deceptive because people were coming and going all the time. The *maître d'* was quick to recognize Jimmy as a newcomer and even quicker to recognize the £50 note slipped into his hand.

Jimmy indicated a small serving table near the door. 'If I might sit there?'

'It's a bit late for dinner, Sir, but perhaps…?

'A steak and all the trimmings,' said Jimmy. 'Go hard on the onions and lay off the greens.'

The cloth was changed and a chair found for him. He set it against the wall where he could protect his back and keep an eye on Paul at the same time. Paul was at a table halfway across the room, constantly half-standing as people came up to shake his hand. Jimmy put the Walkman on the table, plugged in the earphones and settled them over his free ear. This was a special Walkman, KGB modified to do more than play tapes. It could pick out individual voices at a surprising distance.

Paul's voice came over loud and clear. He sounded confident as he accepted the congratulations. A complete sea change from the broken man of a few days before. More people joined the group around him and few left as he drew them in to his circle, making instant friends. Jimmy wished him well, and buried himself behind a menu as Paul came to meet the honor party carrying the trophy. It was processed to the table and filled with champagne amidst loud applause. The Yuppies liked a winner and the true greyhound people knew that moments of achievement were rare.

The party was going well and there was no way Jimmy could protect Paul if someone decided to get up close. It was dark outside now and the brightness of the room would allow a sniper to work from a distance. Hopefully his men could prevent that from happening.

He unplugged the Walkman. The laughter hurt, and his ears were still sore from that evening in Marston when the lorry driver had blasted his air horn outside the house. A buzzing noise from somewhere plagued Jimmy. He looked around, wondering what it was. Realized it was his mobile phone. Probably Eleanor, still new-fangled at being able to talk to him anytime. She could wait, the action was all here.

Thinking of Eleanor and of home and, indirectly of his own children, he remembered the Shaw child, wee Elaine. Of all the kids, she was the one who always remembered to say 'Thank you, Uncle Jimmy,' after every school run.

Wasting her like that in case the kid knew something.

Jimmy checked his watch, near ten o'clock and the evening news. Hopefully they'd catch her murderer and if they didn't, he would.

He caught the *maître d's* eye and asked for the nearest television screen to be switched to the ten o'clock news. Anyway, he was sick of the sight of greyhounds going perpetually around the track. The first part of the news was politics. Jimmy loaded the fork with meat and onion and chips. At the price of a steak, he thought, this had better be good.

The television image changed to the murder scene. The reporter was still on the bridge overlooking the motorway. Jimmy ate as he listened to Elaine's slutty aunt try to explain how she'd been bluffed into handing over "the sweetest, kindest, most thoughtful, child". She finished by saying, 'Closer to me than one of my own.'

Jimmy grunted, disbelieving, and went white faced when the police said they were looking for a man who had introduced himself as Mr. Kyle. An artist's impression followed of Mr. Kyle. He was described as medium height, gaunt faced and thin. Wearing a suit and tie and driving a blue car, make unknown.

Jimmy knew that sometimes Doc passed himself off as Mr. Kyle. Knew that he was in England the weekend the little girl had disappeared. And he knew that sometimes Doc did work for The Man that he didn't want to know about.

But if Doc's started to pick on children...

Sickened by the sight of food on his plate, and anxious to keep things moving, he slipped out of the restaurant and stood in a windy hallway while he called up Sam Gilliland by name.

To hell with all this #1, #2 stuff.

'What's Ronnie up to?'

Sam said, 'Ronnie took his car and left. Funny thing, #1,' the #1 said with emphasis, 'He didn't go far down the road. I watched.'

Jimmy ordered, 'Go to emergency routine.' The mobile phone buzzed again, an annoying bumblebee noise that became loud enough for people at the next table to glance his way. Jimmy cursed. Eleanor was going to get an earful for annoying him when he was working. The buzzing stopped and he counted three clicks come through his earpiece.

No Doc as usual.

He said, impatiently, 'Did you get that Doc?'

Doc replied, 'I'll go look-see.'

A woman came out of the restaurant. She was tall and shapely, her face burnished by the weather. She wore a cream skirt and white top and had a piece of bling around her neck. In other circumstances Jimmy might have fancied his chances. Right then the last thing he needed was her approaching him. 'You're Jimmy, aren't you?'

'Might be.'

She said, 'Eleanor's been trying to get you. Please call her back, it could be important.'

290

He had her accent pinned down to North Irish, country rather than town.

'Who the hell are you?'

'Back-up in case you get too involved,' she said, and went into the ladies toilets where he couldn't follow her.

'Bloody hell! Bloody Eleanor and who's that bloody bitch?'

Jimmy stormed back into the restaurant and his dinner. Rather than ring Eleanor and have a row in public that he couldn't win he checked his mobile phone. Eleanor had forwarded on a message she'd received from Ronnie's secretary.

Mrs. ronnie envelope arthur collect @4 thousands glenlish excited

'Bloody rubbish,' muttered Jimmy and loaded his fork.

This steak is to die for.

Then he remembered Doc's worry about Arthur Anderson and the other men in Belfast.

He rang a Belfast number. 'Where are they now?' he asked without any preamble.

'Got in a car and gone off, boss.'

'Where to?'

'Don't know, boss.' The voice became defensive, 'But we've got the airports covered.'

Jimmy brought up the text again and forwarded a copy to Doc.

Doc called straight back. Jimmy heard him breathing deeply as if he'd been hurrying.

'Jimmy, one question. Who have we got covering Bradley's kids?'

Chapter 125

It was after dark and the boys were cycling like mad as they crested the hill.

Shane was trying to imitate the rhythm of a train, 'She'll killus, she'll killus, she'll bloody well killus.'

'Oh shut up,' said Rory.

They curved out onto the middle of the road to get the turn, chopper-jumped the pavement and stopped at the garage, stymied by the closed door.

Rory wanted to know, 'What did you close the door for?'

'I didn't.'

'Did.'

'Didn't.'

'Well it wasn't me, I never close anything.'

They dumped their bikes on the grass and ran for the house. Shane started to hunt for the key buried deep in one of his pockets. Rory was impatient and, out of habit because mother was always home, depressed the handle and gave the door a push.

It opened.

They looked at each other, this was serious.

They stepped into the hall. A pile of bedclothes lay on the floor. They hadn't been there that morning. The drawers of the hall table and its contents were strewn over the bedclothes. Leaked petrol from a five gallon can stank the air. The boys looked carefully to make sure they were in the right house.

Shane said, 'She will kill us.'

The door to the sitting room was open. The television was on low, the glow from its screen cast weird ripples of light over the walls. They might have left it on, but never on low. The boys slid their hurley sticks out of the hall-stand and hefted them, grimacing at the other to be silent.

'Do something about that draft,' said someone with a Belfast accent.

They heard a chair creak and a man appeared in the doorway. The man and the boys looked at each other.

'Arthur!' said the man, and jumped forward to grab them.

They still weren't sure what was going on, but no way was that man going to touch them. They swung their sticks and cracked him on his knees, just enough to hurt. He yelled, tripped over the bedclothes and went down with a crash on the wooden floor.

'What the hell,' said a voice from the living room.

The boys looked at each other again. The man on the floor grabbed at their legs. They hit his hands and this time they meant it. He roared and rolled away. A man, Arthur Anderson, appeared in the doorway. They saw the gun come up. Panicked, Rory took a swipe, caught the gun on the barrel and knocked it out of Arthur's hand.

Then they ran.

They tried to retrieve their bikes, but a third man pushed the living room window open and leaned out. Again they saw a gun. Shane threw his stick. It missed the man but slammed into the glass and cracked it. The stick rattled around the man as it fell to the ground.

'Mother'll kill you for that,' said Rory.

'That I'd be so lucky.'

They abandoned the bikes, cut across the lawn, hurdled the wall and hared down the road. A bullet whipped past them and the noise of the shot followed. They doubled over and kept running. The next bullet screamed off the coping-stone of the wall beside them. Arthur took his time with the third shot and tracked Rory's upper spine. He fired, just as Rory disappeared behind a pillar.

The other two men joined Arthur.

He pointed to one. 'You, get the car.' And to the other. 'Come on.'

He needed a hand on the wall to hurdle it, but he was light on his feet and downhill his bulk worked to his advantage. The second man ran with him. He was already wheezing. Behind them the garage door banged open. Seconds later Arthur heard their hidden car start up.

The boys were about twenty yards ahead of them. Arthur tried a snap shot, all he had to do was wing. He missed again and they swerved into a gateway.

That particular garden was full of flowerbeds and clinging roses. The hedge was mature Castlewellen Gold conifers, twenty foot high and thick. The boys ran the paths to get to the back. Arthur took a short cut over the flowerbeds and gained ground.

The high hedging continued the whole way around the perimeter. The boys threw their hands over their faces and dived into a gap between the trees. The branches tore at their faces and clothes and the dust from dead needles made them sneeze. Rory's hurley stick caught and had to be jerked free. Arthur came around the corner of the house, saw the branches waving about wildly and fired twice. The first bulled scorched past Rory's face making him flinch. The second thudded into a solid tree trunk.

If it was possible, the boys ran even faster.

They came to the boundary with a rail fence. They rolled over it and kept going. This garden was all grass and they felt naked as they tore across it and hurdled the fence into the next garden down. Arthur snagged in the high hedging, but managed a snap shot. It winged over their heads.

'Doesn't he ever run out?' complained Rory.

'It ain't no six shooter anyway,' said Shane.

They were too frightened to even smile at the forced jokes.

The garden they were now in was long and full of obstructions. They ducked and weaved around gnomes, jumped sunken paths and split to run the opposite sides of a large ornamental pool. They came together again on a stretch of grass before a high, narrow hedge.

A bullet burned between them and tore through the hedge.

'Bugger it,' said Shane, and lead the way through. Snagging branches pushed him off balance and he wasn't expecting the long drop on the other side. He landed awkwardly and his ankle gave way. He cried out and fell.

Rory got through safely. He tried to haul him to his feet. 'Come on. Come on.'

Shane took one step and fell again. They could hear the pound of feet of the men on the other side.

'Go on,' he said. 'Go on.'

'The hell I will,' said Rory.

He put himself between his brother and the hedge. Hefted the hurley stick in his hands and waited.

Far away, at the opposite end of town, the fire siren began to wail.

Chapter 126

Inspector Patterson could have done cartwheels all the way back to the police station. The Glenlish Arms was sealed off tight. The Technical boys were going to give it the once-over in daylight.

Patterson loosened his jacket and stretched luxuriously in his chair. His wife, Imelda, was on her way to pick him up. It didn't matter that she was busy and it didn't suit, and just for once it didn't matter about the children's homeworks. He'd give them a note for the teacher in the morning. The family were going to the pub in Donaghmore for dinner.

He looked at the reports already piled on his desk and patted them fondly. The Glenlish Arms, and all nefarious activities that went on there, was out of business, and the Detective Sergeant was confident that this time he could break Big Mick. For some reason the man seemed anxious to talk but couldn't bring himself to start.

The Assistant Chief Constable phoned, full of congratulations. He also confirmed that the liaison job at St Andrews was guaranteed.

I'll not forget this day in a hurry.

Imelda should come as well, thought Patterson. We'll get someone to mind the kids.

The phone rang again. He reached for it and was still sufficiently relaxed to wonder who was ringing to congratulate him this time.

It was the Desk Sergeant. 'Sir, there's a man on the phone. He says he wants to talk to you personally about the Bradley family.'

'Put him on to DC Green.'

'Sir, he says he's Jimmy Terence.'

Patterson snapped upright. According to the files, Doc was a psychotic killer but, allegedly, Jimmy Terence gave him his targets. 'Put him on. Record and trace the call.'

'Mr. Patterson... I have reason to believe... They're going to murder the Bradleys...'

Patterson bought time. 'Mr. Terence, I'd need you to be more specific.'

If this really is Jimmy Terence, Patterson thought. But if he's not Jimmy Terence if he's bluffing, he's a good actor. The inflection of panic was perfect.

Jimmy said, 'Arthur Anderson and probably some friends. They left

Belfast hours ago. The boys are on their own.'

Patterson was on his feet and running before he thought to let go of the receiver.

He burned rubber stopping at the main desk. There was only the sergeant there and DC Green. Green was reliving the raid on the Glenlish Arms and making the most of it.

The sergeant looked more relieved to see Patterson than surprised at the speed of his arrival.

'Sergeant, maximum alert.' He took a breath to steady his thoughts. 'Everyone of our men on duty, everyone. Order them to head for Sperrin Manor, there's a gang in town to kill the Bradleys. I want maximum noise, alert the fire-brigade and ambulance service as well. Any men off duty, tell them to put their car across the road at the nearest speed limit. I want this town sealed tighter than a duck's ass.' He hauled at Green's jacket. 'Come on.'

Imelda was just pulling up at the kerb as they ran down the steps.

'In,' said Patterson, and ordered Imelda, 'Drive,' as he jumped into the front seat.

She looked at Green getting in the back. 'Darling, we're past the gooseberry stage.'

'Bloody go,' roared Patterson. 'This is for real. Belfast road.'

'Yes, dear,' she said meekly. Too meekly. He knew he'd pay for his outburst later. The road was clear, she swung out briskly and hit thirty in minimum time.

The traffic lights ahead turned red.

'Crash them,' he ordered.

'This is our car,' she reminded him.

He had never trusted her driving, she seemed to concentrate on everything but the road ahead. He closed his eyes and hoped for the best. He was thrown about when the car swerved, there was a squeal of tires from elsewhere and they were through. He clicked on his seat belt.

Dear Lord, no gun.

He sneaked a look at Imelda. If she spotted that she would insist on going back to the station for it. He settled his hands over his tummy and tried to conceal the lack of a weapon with his elbows.

Imelda was being the Station Inspector's wife, sticking strictly to the speed limit. He said, 'Bugger the speed limit, there's a murder gang on the loose.'

Her foot hit the boards. 'Who?' she wanted to know.

296

'The Bradleys?'

'Haven't they suffered enough?'

They were up to seventy. The street was narrow, cars were parked on both sides and there were pedestrians everywhere.

She looked at him. 'Don't you take any chances.'

He started to get palpitations. 'Would you look where you're going.'

They were getting a clear run until a car pulled out of a side street without stopping. A quick swerve and duck and they were past.

Green was impressed. He said, 'Mrs. Patterson, you must have done our advanced driving test.'

'I failed,' she said. 'Worst score ever.'

That silenced him.

One of Patterson's own prowl cars was ahead, cruising gently into the night. He wound down his window, stuck his head out and waved at them as they passed. Immediately their blue strobe came on and their siren wailed.

There was an L driver hesitating to go at the roundabout. Imelda took him on the inside. The police car followed and the L driver lost control. He shot across the road and impacted on the directional arrows sign.

Patterson tried not to think what the paper-pushers at HQ would make of that bill.

They were on the Belfast road now. The police car tried to pass and Imelda fought them off. Patterson hear sharp cracks from somewhere. Shooting.

There's still a chance.

He pointed, 'Turn up Mullough Avenue.'

There was an oncoming car. Imelda ignored it, took the center of the road to get the swing and cut the corner doing fifty. The tires burned rubber and the car took up all the road. Her hands were everywhere, but she kept control. The police car went on, heading for the other entrance.

Good man, thought Patterson, and immediately changed his mind. There was a car coming down the hill on the wrong side. It was travelling slowly as if the driver was trying to pace an invisible runner. There was more gunfire. It was close. Green said he'd seen the flash of gunfire from a garden.

Patterson pointed at the car. 'Ram him.'

'This is our car,' she reminded him again.

He was brutal. 'If it was our children you'd do it.'

She slowed. 'Would twenty be fast enough?'

'Yes.'

297

The other car stopped to let them pass. Imelda changed down into third gear and pulled her legs off the pedals. Patterson had an impression of cardboard folding in on itself as the noses of both cars crumpled. The noise was more a crunch than a bang. The car lights flared and then died. He was flung forward until the seat belt pulled him up short. It dug into his shoulder and chest. He saw the driver of the other car slam forward and his head impact the window.

Imelda turned off the ignition and they sat a moment in the near dark. Patterson saw her rub her breast. Concern for her got him going again.

'Take cover,' he shouted.

The door needed a good shoulder push before he could roll out. Green was more uncoordinated and was a bit behind him.

Imelda grabbed for the nearest weapon and headed for the other car. She was frightened.

What if we rammed the wrong car?

There was only one person in the car, the driver. She pulled open his door, saw the gun in his hand and attacked. The first uniformed policeman to arrive managed to drag her and her handbag away before the injuries could become serious.

Patterson pounded through the nearest gateway and cut left to pass the house on its downhill side. Green was soon level with him and going like a gazelle. Patterson found some extra speed to keep the lead as he turned the gable corner.

Two men were running down the garden: one big and bulky, one light.

'Police!' shouted Patterson.

Flames stabbed from both of the men. He felt something tug at his open jacket.

Bugger it, no gun.

He was in the open and travelling fast, it was his only chance. He went for the bigger man. Green seemed to have disappeared. There was a bang from just behind Patterson. One of the gunmen folded onto his knees and knelt with his head resting on the ground.

The other gunman, the bigger of the two, was taking his time with his next shot. There was a click. Out of bullets or a misfire Patterson didn't know which. He turned his shoulder and hit the man, Arthur, hard. It was like hitting concrete. Patterson bounced off and sideways.

It gave Green the chance of a clear shot and he took it. His first bullet caught Arthur on the sternum. The second blew away his aorta artery.

Patterson was totally off balance, he spun and half fell, half jumped through a gap in the hedge.

Chapter 127

Fear made Ronnie sweat gallons as he forced his way through the crowd. There were others like him, rushing to get a viewpoint before the big race started. Eventually he found the gap between the bottom step of the stand and the rails where no one lingered, and fled along that. At one point he thought he was being followed because a man in a trilby kept pace with him.

Ronnie gripped the butt of his Smith & Weston, ready to draw and shoot, but the man turned away waving twenty-pound notes at a bookie.

The one man he might have recognized, Sam Gilliland, stepped back into the crowd as Ronnie approached and kept his face buried in his race card until he had gone by.

The doorman asked Ronnie, 'Are you not waiting for the big one?'

Ronnie ignored him and passed from the brightness of the buildings into the dimly lit car park. He felt vulnerable in the open and drew back, seeing a threat in a group of latecomers hurrying towards him. He retreated into a corner. This time he drew his gun and held it behind his back, ready for action. The crowd roared as the hare began its run and he started at the noise. His breath came in quick jerks.

The latecomers came in, rushing. They were friends because they tussled good-humoredly through the turnstiles. Ronnie stiffened and cocked his gun when one of them looked his way, but it was a casual look. The group disappeared out of sight as the roar of the crowd crescendoed then faded quickly to a murmur of intense noise.

With the big race over, people started to leave. Footsteps and voices came towards the exit. Ronnie had his panic under control by then and knew he must move. RM was dead, that he was sure of, and Bradley still alive. He felt anger and frustration through his fear. Jimmy had interfered once too often.

And for the last time.

Arthur would see to that.

He held the gun stiffly along his leg and walked out into the car park.

This time there was no one in sight and he felt there was no immediate danger unless Jimmy had positioned a sniper on the ridge. *That would take intelligence.* Ronnie ducked down, and kept close to the cars themselves, and twice spun on his heel to see if he was being followed. By now a trickle of people were coming out of the exit, but they were hanging about, talking among themselves.

The announcer gave the result of the race. First... Number one. The roar of the crowd drowned out the rest of the announcement. Ronnie was furious.

Bradley's bitch.

He wanted to shout, 'Wait until you hear from Glenlish, that'll wipe the smile from your face.'

He made it to his car safely and settled into its enclosed interior, with a prayer of thanks. He got a clear run and hardly slowed through the lanes of parked cars until he was pulling out of the gate onto the main road. He kept his eyes on the hill.

The gate was the crucial point. No one fired at him, no one was there to block his escape. Suddenly he changed from being the cringing hunted to the hunter. He had a sniper's rifle in the boot.

Why not?

Bradley's allegations might spoil his chances of a political career but Jimmy wanted him dead. Jimmy and Doc tended to travel together. If he got Jimmy there was no reason why he couldn't get Doc at the same time.

'Yes,' said Ronnie to himself. 'Yes,' and thumped the steering wheel for emphasis.

He turned off the main road and took the winding track back to the small clearing. Before he got out of the car he turned it and left it facing downhill for a quick exit.

The gun case was on top of the luggage. He was trembling again, this time with eagerness, as he pulled it out of the boot and set it on the front seat. He turned on the light to see what he was doing and ran his hand along the rifle barrel and the stock. It felt different somehow now that he was using it for the purpose intended. He clipped on the telescopic sights and made sure the magazine was full before he shoved it home with the heel of his hand. He stepped back from the car and worked the bolt to bring a round into the firing chamber.

Moving cautiously, he went back to the vantage point he had chosen earlier and tried various sightings to get his eye in. The image intensifier really worked, everything had a luminous glow about it and people's faces stood out clearly. He picked out Ken's car.

Maybe Bradley will go home in that?

If he could get all three men at the one time, great.

He aimed at the gate and the security guard standing there. The guard was so close his face filled the scope.

Fifty yards, fifty five.

Jimmy was as good as dead.

There was now a constant stream of people drifting towards their cars. Ronnie watched the exit from the stadium. There were plenty of light there. Jimmy was no greyhound man so he was likely to leave early. And if he did he could be picked out handy enough.

Doubt niggled Ronnie's mind. What if he shot Jimmy but wasn't quick enough to shoot Doc at the same time? Long term Doc on his own would be a loose cannon that no one in the Organization would dare let live. Ronnie knew that he wouldn't be safe from a vengeful Doc until he was back among his own people in Belfast.

Maybe making sure of Bradley would be best?

Ronnie focused in on the Mercedes.

Chapter 128

The party in the restaurant was in full swing. The piano had been requisitioned for a singsong and the diners were collected into several impromptu groups.

The night was heady for Paul. With no more props than a slack stance and a fixed smile he was giving a passable imitation of the Prime Minister at Question Time answering, or rather not answering, questions on the alleged fixing of a greyhound race.

The *maître d'* caught Kristie's eye and beckoned her over. She saw a security man with him and went immediately. 'Yes?'

The *maître d'* said, 'I'm afraid, madam, your car…'

'What about it?'

'The Mercedes, someone has slashed all the tires.'

'Bugger!' said Jimmy, who was using the Walkman to listen in. 'Wrong car. I wanted to get Paul in my car, not the dogs.'

Ken had joined them. He said, 'Only the tires?' in a "that's not so bad" tone.

The security man nodded.

'Easy fixed,' said Ken. He turned to Kristie. 'It's some sore loser, don't let them spoil your night.'

The security man went off relieved.

Kristie asked, 'How are you going to get home?'

'Your car, you can get a taxi.'

'Good idea,' said Jimmy, from the far corner.

She was indignant. 'You're not putting the dogs in my car.'

Ken stuck his face close to hers. 'They paid for it, didn't they?' He kissed her and she responded.

Jimmy thought, I should bring the wife, they're sex mad around here.

Kristie pulled back. 'Tomorrow first thing, I want my car valeted.' She wagged a warning finger under his nose. 'And if I find so much as one dog hair there'll be...' She thought about the punishment. 'No nothing for a month.'

Ken said, 'I've got news for you. I'm in arrears at the minute.'

303

Chapter 129

Jimmy watched the Bradleys celebrate their win, with a heavy heart. He held out no hope for the two boys in Glenlish. He could only pray that it had been mercifully quick, and he didn't believe that either. His left his dinner virtually untouched.

His mobile phone rang. A number that he didn't recognize. He stood up as the *maître d'* approached. 'I'm finished,' said Jimmy pointing to the virtually untasted meal. 'You can take it away.' He went into the hallway to take the call. 'Hallo.'

A man said, 'Is that Jimmy Terence?'

'Yes?' He'd didn't recognize the voice, definitely North Irish. It could be some sort of trap. He slipped his hand into his pocket and clicked the radio transmit button twice, with a gap between each press. Once for Jimmy, once for "Immediate danger".

'Sir, Detective Constable Green here. Mr. Patterson wants to know about Mr. and Mrs. Bradley, are they okay?'

Jimmy felt Patterson could have spoken to him himself. 'Let me speak to him.'

'I'm afraid Mr. Patterson sustained a head injury during the rescue. He's on his way to hospital.'

Rescue! Jimmy loved that word. The boys were okay, he was told, but shaken and very contrite at hitting Patterson as he burst through the hedge. The Bradley's, Jimmy informed Green back, with a touch of disinformation, were safe in England.

Even the police know I have a mobile phone.

First thing tomorrow morning he'd buy a new sim card.

He got back in just in time to stop the waiter from lifting his plate. Cold and greasy as it was, he ate his steak and onions with gusto and had a double dessert to celebrate.

Eleanor rang again. This time he took the call, he didn't dare not. She wanted a chat, all excited at the evenings events. He'd nothing better to do so he let her talk on, actually started to enjoy her titbits of gossip and information.

Just when he thought he would have to move the Stockdale party himself they started to organize lifts home. Jimmy disconnected from Eleanor and gave

Doc a quick call even as he raised his glass with the rest and drank a final toast to Paul and Girl.

The man had more guts than sense, Jimmy reckoned. He'd soon be back on the political scene, fighting cronyism and self-interest and all the crooked deals that were destroying the country let alone the Province.

Chapter 130

Ken insisted on organizing things. 'The dogs and me in the Audi, the rest of you can get a taxi.'

Kristie was horrified for her Audi. 'Don't you dare let those brutes make a mess of my car.'

Ken said, 'What if we got them nappies?'

Kristie looked at his smiling face and gave up. She held out her hand. 'Money.'

Paul pulled their £60 back-the-loser winnings out of his pocket and put it on the table. 'Use this.'

He looked at Ken, trying to bring him back to earth. 'After all, you only won two hundred thousand tonight. You still have another three hundred thousand to go.

Ken trumped the sixty pounds with a check. They all gasped at the amount. £452,000.

'What have you been up to?' demanded Kristie.

'Simple,' said Ken. 'The big brindle was a penalty kick and the prize money was £2,000 to the winner. So I bet it on him at fives and that gave me £12,000 to put on Girl at twenty to one. That came to £240,000. Add in the original credit bet of two thousand at a hundred to one, and Bobs-your-uncle. The bank's off my back bigtime.'

He looked from one to the other, at their stunned faces. 'It was so obvious a bet I'm surprised the rest of you didn't think of it.'

Paul said, 'There's a fault somewhere in your logic.'

Kristie smiled, this was Ken as his best, being logically illogical. She scooped both check and money into her handbag.

Jimmy caught the *maître d's* eye and he came over immediately. Another large note passed hands. He said, 'The Stockdale party will be ordering a taxi. Tell them it's waiting for them at the door where the dogs come out.'

He left and walked slowly out of the building. The life was draining out of the place now because the racing was over and the people were leaving. He saw one man he recognized, one of his own, and passed without a look. Exiting into the car park was a sweat because he knew that Ronnie was out there somewhere and tonight would finish one of them. He hung back until a group clattered down the steps and followed close on their heels.

Once on his own in the dark Jimmy activated his transmitter, and said, 'Bradley is moving.'

Chapter 131

Doc barely heard the message "Bradley is moving". Doc had his receiver turned down in case its electronic hiss would carry in the stillness of the undergrowth. He had a lot to do and now very little time to do it in.

Getting out of the stadium had been difficult because Ronnie, presumably with the Lee Enfield, dominated the exit. It had to be the Lee Enfield, the rifle that he'd left in the warehouse. He doubted if Ronnie had a better long-range weapon in his armory. It added a new element of danger to the evening. He'd known that when he'd left the rifle for Ronnie to find in the first place.

Isn't that what life's about in the end, taking risks?

Eventually Doc found a gap in the boundary wire. There was always one, made by local kids, if you knew where to look for it. It had taken time because the gap was to the rear of the enclosure and he had to move well away from the track lighting before he dared approach the main road where he now crouched.

Doc pulled on a black mask and gloves and waited until there was only one car on the road, going towards the track. He broke cover as it drew level with him and sprinted across the tarmac, trusting that the car lights would blind Ronnie to his dark shadow in its rear. He made it safely without a bullet coming his way.

The problem now was passing cars on the main road. People were bound to notice a masked man running along the verge. It only took one to report him to get the police involved. Doc cut through the undergrowth itself, heading for the houses and gardens he knew lay up the side road ahead.

The undergrowth was nasty stuff and the harsh darkness created by the light from the Arena concealed all sorts of snags for clothes and feet. He angled well away from the road and found the going much easier because he was now travelling with the reflected light from the stadium instead of trying to travel into it.

Doc walked quickly with his hands up to protect his eyes and was soon breathing hard. He hated the thought of the pollen he was stirring up and breathing in.

In one step, he was still in the maze of bushes and wondering if he had cut things too fine. The next he was among trees, standing in a dark garden with a pile of an unlit house looming over him. The pollen from the trees irritated his sinuses. He fought down a sneeze.

Doc stepped onto the lawn and ran along its edge until he was at the gravel drive leading to the road. The grass continued as a verge, and he kept to it until he reached the gate. He crouched down at the pillars and checked up and down the side road. No matter when he broke cover it was always going to be dangerous. He had to cross the road, and Ronnie or an unknown henchman could be on the lookout for such a move. The road was dark, with no cars coming or going. He sprinted across the dark tarmac, then he stopped and re-orientated himself while he drew breath.

He had come too far through the undergrowth. The lights from the Arena were a fair distance away. The chances were that Ronnie now had his back to him.

Or maybe not?

Ronnie with a rifle and expecting him, against Doc's knife and RM's .22, was always going to be interesting. He couldn't remember when he'd last had so much fun.

Doc started to run along the road, back towards the Arena. He kept hard against the bushes for cover. After a hundred yards he found the track. He was nearly past it when he realized that the bushes had stopped brushing his arm. He experimented with the toe of his shoe and found the stoned path. It was the only lead he had so he followed it.

It was a fair climb and the track curved to and fro as it fought the gradient. After a little, Doc became aware of a sensation of light ahead of him. He stopped and focused in on the light. Whatever, wherever that light dominated his approach. He drew his knife and took to the bushes. The light grew into an awareness as he crept forward, though it was never strong. He found himself on the edge of a clearing, looking at a parked car with its interior light left on.

Doc shook his head in despair. 'Ronnie, Ronnie, will you never learn?'

Chapter 132

At home Connie strode the fields in the pitch dark, with confidence. In the badly lit car park she walked cautiously, eyes and ears alert to people coming close. She didn't know whether to give up on Doc and go home, or to stick to his precise instructions. Charlie, her husband, had introduced her to a sleazy way of life: of dogs and drugs and dishonesty. Not all the greyhound men were like Charlie, in fact very few, but no matter what he did, Charlie always gravitated to the lowest level. With that baggage, to spend a night at the dogs, on her own without her host even having the manners to see her to her table let alone join her for dinner…

Connie knew she was storming at the unimportant things. That phone call she'd got, the message that message she'd passed on. That made her complicit in God only knew what crime. She'd watched Jimmy afterwards, saw him almost age with worry until another phone call made him sag with relief. Somebody somewhere had got hurt. That was the sort of men Jimmy and Doc were and yet…

Love was too strong a word. Life with Charlie had beaten that sort of hope out of her. Doc was… Doc – and the dog liked him. That thought made her smile as she worked through the lines of cars to Doc's. Or at least the Lexus he'd given her to use. Doc was kind and a good listener. She knew she rattled on a bit but after half a lifetime of Charlie she had a lot of silences to make up for.

As for his nickname "Doc". God alone knew why he'd got that, and she'd rather not speculate. Even so she preferred it to the name he called himself. "Fredrick Robinson". He was no more a Fredrick Robinson than she was the man in the moon.

And his manners! Socially Doc was totally inept. Inviting a lady out to dinner and then not joining her. Not thinking of flowers or phone calls until she'd demanded them off him. Now at nights she found herself planning to be in bed before he rang. Naked, pretending the heat of the receiver against her ear was his body beside her. He knew when to lie close, when to give her space. Things like that he was sensitive to her needs.

That phone call!

The thought of somebody injured or – *oh my God* – dead because of her made her shudder.

She was at her car at last. Made sure it was the right car by checking the number plate against the registration number on the key-ring.

The last of Doc's instructions were easy. Drive to Marston, park up at the railway station and wait for him to join her. The thought of the possibly dead man back home made her hesitate. Go to Marston, yes, but grab her case and take the first train to London and the plane home. She had already risked jail for him. Risked years spent in an airless building, in crushing proximity to other people. Without her fields and the ability to breathe she'd go mad.

And yet Doc had said "bring a case full of clothes" like he planned them spending more than one night together. She'd packed fragrant massage oils, could imagine lying stretched out on the bed while he...

'Mrs. Taylor.'

'Yes?'

She turned, expecting to find someone bringing a message from Doc. Like *"see you at Land's End"*. In the near darkness it took her a few moments to recognize the man who had called at the farm. The man the dog didn't like.

He straight fingered her under the rib cage. All the air gasped out of her lungs, none replaced it. She doubled over, giving breathless screams. Couldn't do anything to resist when he pushed her against the car, grabbed her wrists and bound them behind her back with plastic ties.

Her mind was screaming 'Doc! Doc!' as he threw her into the backseat and secured her legs as well. Tape went over her mouth, a hood over her head. A pause then a needle went into the back of her thigh.

'Doc! Do...'

Chapter 133

There was now a chill in the night air that dug in under Ronnie's shoulder blades. He was hardly aware of it, his whole being was concentrated on watching for Bradley or Doc and Jimmy.

Take out who I can here and deal with any survivor once I'm home.

The car park quickly emptied after the last race. The few cars left stood out like a beacon in his night sights. Ronnie aimed at each car in turn. At that distance he could hardly miss. End of Bradley. Followed by the end of Jimmy and Doc, courtesy of Arthur. But the price? Twenty thousand!

I might just kill Arthur myself.

He focused in on people coming out of public entrance, and recognized no one. He stiffened and whispered, 'Yes,' when he spotted a car travelling towards the side door where the dogs came out. The car had no lights on, so someone was stupid or Jimmy was running scared.

Jimmy running scared, decided Ronnie, and his confidence built. He rested the butt of the rifle on his foot and rubbed his hands together to take the chill out of them and flexed his shoulders. He felt like an All-American footballer winding up for the big one.

The car stopped and its side-lights come on as people approached it from a small doorway. The shape of Jimmy behind the wheel was clearly outlined against the lights. Ronnie brought the sights to bear. He had him dead to rights, but hesitated. It was an angled shot, and no matter what Jimmy did he had to come out the front gate. The closer he was the less chance of a miss.

Ronnie steadied himself against a tree and looked along the sights, making sure he had an unobstructed view of the front gates. He was confident that he had worked a round into the breach ready to fire, but maybe, just to be sure...

Further back among the trees Doc heard the scrape of metal on metal as Ronnie worked a fresh round into the breach.

Chapter 134

Jimmy was uptight and ready to scream. What's to decide? Who cares who takes the cup? Sweat stood on him.

The women knew one thing, they weren't travelling in the back of the Audi with the dogs. The approached the car. Jimmy leaned across and swung the passenger door open.

Kristie leaned in. 'Are you waiting for the Stockdale party?'

'Yes, madam.'

They got in: Barbara first, Kristie next. Paul left Ken and joined them. Both Barbara and Kristie edged towards the middle of the seat to keep him on their side.

Paul's eyes flicked between the two women. He said, 'I'll ride up front.'

Jimmy didn't miss a beat. He was shocked.

Goody-goody-two-shoes Bradley and that woman?

He didn't believe it. Fought her off more like. He looked at Kristie in the mirror.

Try me darling.

Kristie teased Paul with knowing smile before winding down the window and shouting at Ken. 'Cup or no cup, the dogs come second to the kettle if you're in before us.'

Paul got in. The taxi was already moving when he looked at the driver and recognized Jimmy. At the same time first two then one electronic click sounded in Jimmy's earpiece. #2, Doc's call sign, and one for immediate danger.

Paul looked ready to jump out. Jimmy stared straight ahead and cursed Doc for cutting everything fine as usual. He drove in sidelights to make things as difficult for Ronnie as possible.

Paul's voice shook as he asked, 'Where are you taking us?'

'Marston, to drop off your woman there, then on to Heathrow. They're holding the last flight for you.'

'Flight?'

Jimmy said, 'You know, planes, Belfast. Home? Give me a call next week, my number's in the book.' At the same time he wondered if there would be a "next week" for any of them. He felt he shouldn't be there at all. He should be in hiding until the all clear sounded, but someone had to draw

Ronnie out and god curse Doc for taking his time.

The cars in front of them pulled out onto the main road. Jimmy eased forward to the white line and waited. There was a lorry coming, a forty-footer from its Christmas tree lighting.

Paul asked, 'What do I have to do to be clear of you and yours?'

Ronnie steadied himself against the tree and aimed carefully. He could see little, just the shape of Jimmy's head behind the glass. Even that became vague as other cars set up a haze of light around him. The taxi was at an angle to Ronnie, it would have to be a shot through the side window. The lights dimmed and he could see clearly again. It was definitely Jimmy, and a black haired man was sitting beside him. Bradley. With a bit of luck he could get the two of them. He sighted carefully on Jimmy's forehead and fired.

Even as he did so, he remembered that the sights were still set for four hundred yards.

The bullet tore open the roof and exited through the side window. Paul and the women froze, shocked. Jimmy killed the lights and sank the boot. There was a metallic clang as a second bullet hit the rear wing.

The car shot out the gate and tore across the road under the wheels of the oncoming lorry. First the lorry's lights surrounded them and drained the color from their world, then the bulk of the huge vehicle itself loomed over them. The lorry driver braked hard, Jimmy kept his foot to the floor and, somehow, the car squeezed out from under crushing death. It rocked wildly in the displaced airwaves as it shot up the side-road, pursued by an indignant blast from a powerful horn.

Paul shouted at Barbara, 'Get down!' He threw off his seat-belt ready to climb back and protect her with his body. 'Get down,' he repeated, just as a staccato of clicks sounded in Jimmy's ear. Danger over.

Jimmy switched on the lights. It was a relief to see the road ahead again. He restrained Paul with a hand. 'Relax Sir Galahad, we're in the clear.'

The two women were clutching each other for mutual comfort. They separated and worked at straightening their clothes. Jimmy watched Kristie in the mirror. There's a woman I wouldn't mind having, he told himself, the euphoria of being alive making him randy.

Kristi saw him watching her and posed while she ran fingers through her hair.

Jimmy smiled. *Maybe not this week, darling, but I'll be back unless Doc gets there first.*

He scowled, what women saw in that excuse for a man was beyond him. Look at that strange woman telling him to phone home. That had to be one of Doc's floozies.

Paul put his hand back between the seats and clutched Barbara's hand, she was sobbing in fear. 'It's all right,' he told her. 'We're safe now.'

Jimmy flicked a look in the rear mirror. Way back he could see the lights of a car. He clicked on the radio. 'Sam, where are you all?'

'This is #3. Just exiting the car park – and use your call sign,' came back the reply.

'I need one of you to take over,' said Jimmy and indicated to pull in.

'What's going on?' asked Kristie. She sounded frightened but composed.

Jimmy forced a laugh. 'Business, missus, Northern Ireland style.'

He stopped laughing and felt apprehensive. Now was the time to sort Doc out. He daren't leave it any longer.

Chapter 135

Doc used his knife to pin Ronnie against a tree while he relieved him of his .38. Things had quietened down again at the Arena. Jimmy and all the men were safely away and the lorry had gone on. No one else seemed to have noticed anything.

Doc said to Ronnie, 'I didn't like it when someone tried to set me up for Winston Shaw's killing. But trying to kill my big brother?' The point of the knife pricked Ronnie's throat with every word. 'Now that's personal.'

Ronnie's breath was coming in wheezing gasps. Doc knew he would start screaming soon, but he wasn't worried. The knife was in the right place, it only needed a shove and a twist to cut out the voice box. Time might be short, but Ronnie wasn't going to die easy.

Doc didn't mind Ronnie sweating a bit. The truth was, he was short on time. What if he told Ronnie he was going to torture him first, threaten to start between his legs and work up? He didn't think it would make any difference to the panic Ronnie was displaying. And there was a smell. It didn't need a second sniff to be certain. Ronnie had wet his pants.

'Not such a big man now,' he said. 'And you'll be pleased to know that the Bradley boys are unharmed. Arthur Anderson and one of his mates are dead. The other one is singing like a canary.'

Really he didn't want to waste his breath talking to an idiot like Ronnie. Just do the job as neatly as possible to minimize the danger of a DNA transfer and go. Part of him was hearing Ronnie's ragged breathing. The greater part was concentrated on a roll of stone on the path leading from the road.

'You always do, or should I say did, things on the cheap, Ronnie. Now The Man, he knows how to pay well.'

Someone was near the car. He could hear the swish of grass as feet made their way around it.

'Tomorrow the police will impound your business records and your computers. It will be interesting to see what they find. Little things that implicate important men. Embarrassing things that'll take some explaining. They'll be queuing up to castrate you.'

Nearby drying leaves rustled where there was no wind.

'Imagine them burying you alive, with your privates shoved up your ass.

316

You might be glad you're already dead. They certainly will be.'

Still with his knife to Ronnie's throat, Doc aimed the Smith & Weston into the darkness. 'Are you coming out, Jimmy, or are you going to stand there all night?'

The rustle of leaves intensified. Jimmy stepped out of the intense darkness of the trees. He held his gun pointed at Doc. 'We need to talk.'

'Help me, please,' pleaded Ronnie, his Adam's apple flexing against the point of the knife as he spoke.

'Talk about what?' asked Doc.

He knew he sounded totally relaxed. He was. This was living, gun on gun, one pointed directly at his heart.

How far can I push it and who'll fire first?

'Wives and families,' said Jimmy.

'You bought her a nice house,' he said.

'So you found her. What did you do?'

'Rob was a bit messy and he squealed like a pig. I thought the neighbors might hear.'

'For God's sake, Doc, she gave you nearly twenty years.'

'Of hell,' said Doc.

'You would marry her, you wouldn't be told.'

Doc wished Jimmy's would stop moving. His restless feet kept rustling dry bracken. Doc loved it, being here, deep in the country, listening to the silence of the night after the constant background noises of the city.

Doc said, 'She volunteered to do it herself, drink and drugs.' Realized his eyes had adjusted well to the dark because he could now see individual shapes. Saw Jimmy hold out his gun that bit further.

'You bastard, she was pregnant.'

'Not mine.'

Doc realized that some anger other than the wife was driving Jimmy. Wondered how far he could push things before it came to shooting. Without realizing it he brought his knife hand away from Ronnie to be properly balanced for the shot.

Ronnie sensed his lack of concentration. He pushed the knife arm up and away and punched Doc in the head. Doc stumbled and went down, taking the fall hard rather than risk the aim of the gun stray off target. Ronnie turned to flee into the darkness. Doc's foot caught his leg and Ronnie's head bashed against a tree on his way down.

'Naughty, naughty, Ronnie,' said Doc, still on the ground. He had the knife close enough to Ronnie to be a threat, his eyes and gun aimed in Jimmy's direction. Doc got to his feet and motioned with the knife for Ronnie to do the same. Got him hard up against the original tree, knife firmly fixed to his throat.

Ronnie pleaded with Jimmy, 'I didn't want to go against you. These people at the top, they made me.'

'I believe you,' said Jimmy. 'Thousands wouldn't'

Ronnie was crying openly. 'Jimmy, I'll give you the protection rackets. You couldn't believe the money they bring in.'

Somehow in talking the point of Jimmy's gun had moved on to Ronnie. Jimmy brought it back to Doc. 'Tell me about Elaine.'

Doc asked, 'What about her?'

'It's on the news. They found her body and they're looking for a man just like you.'

Doc said nothing.

'For God's sake, Doc, you're out of control.'

Jimmy's arm tensed for the shot.

Doc's mobile phone rang.

Chapter 136

Teasing Jimmy to the point where he'd be tempted to shoot was one thing. Doc's mobile phone ringing had to be serious. He knew that if he used his knife-hand to take the call Ronnie would run, and if he used his gun-hand, Jimmy might shoot.

Now this is living.

The mobile continued to ring.

Even if Jimmy shot him, he wouldn't let Ronnie get away. *And that's what it's all about.*

'I'll take the call,' said Doc.

He stuck the gun in his pocket. In the near darkness he saw Jimmy take aim at his forehead. Jimmy wouldn't want his little brother to suffer.

'Hold your trigger finger, this could be important,' said Doc.

He tried to balance himself so that if Jimmy shot, his knife would rip through Ronnie's carotid artery as he went down. Doc's heart beat hard from the anticipation of the bullet tearing though his skull.

Not that he'll shoot. He'll give me every chance until he's dead himself.

Doc pulled the mobile from his pocket. Only four people had his number. Jimmy, and it wasn't him ringing, Eleanor at home, Gunner Smith and …

Connie's name showed on the screen. He was almost surprised she hadn't phoned earlier.

He put the mobile to his ear. 'Hi, I'm on my way,' he said.

Instead of Connie, a man's voice, Belfast, educated and with an English inflexion said, 'Bring Ronnie Fetherton with you – intact.'

'And if he's already dead?' asked Doc.

His mouth was moving, saying things, buying time. His brain seemed to have frozen. The last time he'd felt like this was the day his mother died choking on asthma. He'd wanted to kill her to put her out of her agony. He'd wanted to give her his own lungs.

'That would be unfortunate for all concerned,' said the man known as Kyle.

'Believe me, it would,' said Doc's mouth.

What he could see of Jimmy and his gun was blurred by moisture in his eyes.

'I'm proposing an exchange,' said Kyle.

'I'm listening.'

'The large car park in Marston, one hour.'

Marston, Doc knew, was at least forty minutes away.

'That's too tight a time frame.'

Kyle had disconnected.

Doc stood on, breathing through clenched teeth, hard, shaky breaths.

'What's going on?' asked Jimmy.

He was closer now, the gun pointed at Ronnie rather than Doc.

'They've got Connie,' said Doc. It took all the breath in his body to get the words out.

The darkness was no longer welcome. It was a threat, holding him back from reaching Marston on time.

Jimmy asked, 'Connie, is that the woman in the restaurant, the one who spoke to me?'

Doc ignored him he was ringing one of his pre-saved numbers.

Jimmy kept asking. 'Who is she anyway and what's she got to do with us?'

The mobile at the other end was answered. 'Gunner, listen, Kyle's got Connie. He said he'd exchange her for Ronnie. The big car park in Marston in one hour.'

Gunner said, 'We're more than that away.'

'Do your best.'

Doc hadn't time for even a quick breath. He could only be grateful that Jimmy's distracting questions had stopped. He threw a spare pair of gloves at Jimmy and when he'd put them on, the Lee Enfield.

Then he hauled at Ronnie. 'Come on, you.'

Chapter 137

Doc held Ronnie by the collar and forced Ronnie ahead of him through the bushes. Even with his hand up to protect his face from whipping branches, Ronnie walked proud and confident. Things, he'd gathered, were going his way again.

'I warned you I have friends in high places. Good friends,' he boasted.

The last thing Doc needed was someone shooting off their mouth when he was trying to plan ahead. He said, 'One more word out of you, and your good friends will have a coming politician minus a voice-box.'

After that there was only the sound of their feet crackling through the dry leaves and the hiss of branches whipping back into place. Even so Doc found that he couldn't plan. Every nerve-end in his body wanted him to charge in gun blazing and kill Kyle and as many of his backup men as he could before he himself went down. No one would dare take-on him and Jimmy on their own, particularly in a prisoner exchange. There had to be backup men, probably other "Kyles" run by The Man.

How many of us are there anyway?

Doc didn't think there was many "Kyles" still around. The Peace Process had left the market oversupplied with contract killers. In the years following the Good Friday Agreement that brought the Troubles in Ireland to an end, several "Kyles" he knew off had died or become the new "Disappeared".

They came to the clearing where Ronnie had parked his car. The interior light still glowed.

Doc opened the back door and threw Ronnie in. Made sure his head slammed off something hard as he landed. Ronnie yelled in pain, Doc told him to shut up.

Jimmy was standing, the rifle held under one arm, his pistol aimed at Ronnie and his eyes on Doc.

Doc said, 'Get in and if he makes another sound shoot him somewhere fleshy. We only need him alive, not intact.'

They got in. Doc started the engine and turned the car, not worrying about the enclosing bushes scraping Ronnie's paintwork. He freewheeled down the slope, foot on the brake, when he wanted to slam the car into top gear and speed towards Marston. The last thing he needed was a broken spring.

Jimmy was on his mobile to his men. 'What do you mean you're halfway to Cornwall?'

He disconnected in disgust. 'Sam Gilliland is on his way to Heathrow with the Bradleys and the rest of them are too far away. They've hired a boat for a day's fishing. With my money!'

He sounded mad enough to shoot someone.

He leaned forward and tapped Doc's shoulder. 'Who's Connie?'

'None of your business.'

'Kyle?'

'The cover name for people who do jobs for the men at the top of the Organization.' Doc knew one bit of forward planning that he needed. 'Find out who ordered wee Elaine killed.'

'So you didn't do it?'

Doc didn't answer. He was trying to remember the shape of the car park in Marston and what surrounded it. Where people could hide. If only he hadn't been so focused on catching Bradley that time.

Jimmy prodded again. 'And your wife?'

Doc supposed he'd only get peace to think when Jimmy irrelevant questions were answered. He waited until the car finally came out of the bushes onto the road. Then he whipped through the gears and had the car at ninety miles an hour before he said, 'She offered to kill herself. I told her not to bother.'

'And Robbie?'

'Still squealing for all I know.'

Jimmy sat back with a sigh of relief. 'I don't know why I ever doubted you, you've never harmed a woman yet.' He prodded for a final time 'In fact, I wouldn't trust you to drown a female cat.'

'Now can I think?' said Doc.

Short of a disaster they could make Marston in an hour. Drive into the car park, hand over Ronnie in exchange for Connie and then… There was no way he could get Connie clear before the shooting started. Doc glanced at the dark shape of Jimmy in the rear-view mirror. Nor him. Jimmy always hesitated to shoot. He'd be standing there trying to figure a non-violent solution while a Kyle riddled him with bullets.

Doc said, 'Jimmy, I'll drop you just short of the car park, on the street side of the small river.'

'I'm coming in with you.'

'You'll have the railings to steady your aim and an overall view of the car park. Look for heads appearing over the tops of cars.'

'And when I do?'

'Shoot Ronnie.'

Chapter 138

There was a time when Doc wouldn't have minded going down in a mayhem of bloodletting. Take on the army, the police, any group of men for the sheer joy of letting his body do what his mind always wanted to do. Rampage.

If Ronnie was dead, Jimmy would be safe so long as he escaped the planned ambush. More than safe in fact. The Man had made it clear that the survivor of Jimmy and Ronnie would have enhanced status in the Organization.

Doc wished he had paid more attention to The Man's offer of an indecent sum of money for him to kill Jimmy. The Man was generous, but not that generous. It was really a warning to be on guard against more than Ronnie's botched attempts on Jimmy's life.

Doc thought about the sum of money offered by The Man. It was a lot more than the going rate for killing someone. Allow something for costs and a bonus for the higher than usual status of the people to be killed – Jimmy and himself... Doc thought he was up against three Kyles.

Once Connie's clear the rest will be fun.

And yet he knew that the only "clear" Connie would get would be for her to be lying flat on the ground when the bullets flew.

The car was doing over a hundred on a good road and the glow off Marston curved over the darkness on the horizon. They could make it with time to spare. Gunner would be late. Doc slowed the car to seventy. He hated the thought of Connie being in the hands of Kyle for one second longer than needed. However, her best chance of living was for Gunner and his friends to arrive before the surviving Kyles moved in to make sure there were no survivors.

Doc said, to Jimmy, 'Ronnie's got spare clips for the Lee Enfield in his pocket. Just keep shooting, keeping heads down until Gunner and his old army friends arrive.

Doc's shoulder was starting to hurt from Jimmy's prods. 'What do you mean Gunner? He's at home.'

Doc said, 'Gunner's specialty in the army was the extraction of friendly forces when things went wrong.'

'So?'

'He's on his way in to extract you.'

Jimmy shouted so close to Doc's ear it hurt. 'That woman and now Gunner. You might have told me all this before.'

'And you might have planned things better.'

Jimmy paused for thought rather than snarl back. Then he asked, 'When you say Gunner's old friends?'

'Yes.'

'I didn't get to ask what sort.'

'And I'm not saying.'

Mercifully, after that Jimmy went quiet.

At the outskirts of Marston, Doc slowed to thirty miles per hour. This was no time to be pulled for speeding. He kept a wary eye out for parked cars with people in them, though figures were hard to make out in the orange-tinted street lighting. There was little traffic at this time of night and Kyle knew he'd be heading into town from this direction.

Nothing showed and no cars followed them. Even so Doc stayed alert, if only because he was counting down the final minutes of his life. Jimmy would, should, must survive this ambush. He held no great hope for himself, but if he could save Connie. Die doing one good thing in his life… He put that sort of maudlin thought out of his mind. Dying, killing or being killed was his job. This time it was his turn to die.

Doc's plan was simple if brutal. The night was dark and the street lighting poor, worse probably in the car park. Kyle wouldn't dare risk a distant shot as he drove into the car park. If the shot missed or if Doc was only wounded then Ronnie would die, and Kyle's job was to keep Ronnie alive. No Kyle would wait until after the handover.

Way ahead Doc saw the aerials of the police station stretching above the surrounding rooftops. Kyle would be expecting him to come in from the right. Doc turned left, aiming to come up behind the police station and do a drive-past down the left side of the car park. With a bit of luck they'd spot where at least one of Kyle's friends lurked

Doc found Marston easy to drive through: wide streets running parallel to each other and no one way system to throw him off course. He kept an image in his mind of where the police station should be, drove beyond that point then looped back, driving past the police station itself.

He saw lights in the windows and cars at the door but the place had an air of the officers on duty enjoying a peaceful shift.

That's likely to change.

Doc rang Gunner. 'ETA?' he asked.

'Better than expected, one of my mates knew a shortcut,' yelled Gunner over pounding music thundering out of his speakers. The music became muted. 'Can you buy us a few minutes?'

Doc said, 'If I was Kyle I wouldn't wait either.'

'What would you do?'

Doc hated the thought of listening in on the phone while Connie lost a finger.

Or a lip.

Chapter 139

The street running the left side of the car park held three-story Georgian buildings, some obviously in apartments, going by the lights in the windows. Most were offices and closed up for the night.

Doc told Jimmy to look that way and to watch, in particular, for dark windows that lay open. In the car park, a cluster of cars grouped around a pedestrian entrance, obviously they belonged to the residents of the apartments. Doc concentrated on the cars beyond that. He noted a discouraging number scattered throughout the car park. Kyle's backup team could be hiding anywhere and almost impossible to spot until they popped up shooting.

One car was parked near the exit, its lights on. Doc assumed that was Kyle with Connie He didn't dare slow the car, an obvious giveaway that he was reconnoitering the area, but he managed to pinpoint a group of three cars. *That's where I would stand.*

Kyle at the car with Connie, one man at the cluster of cars. That left one to spot.

He reached the end of the car park and drove on, turned left when he could, which took him to the road running along the right side of the car park. Near the turn he stopped. 'Right Jimmy, out.'

'I don't like this,' said Jimmy.

'And I don't like you even thinking that I'd kill wee Elaine.'

'Stop trying to pick a fight to make me feel better.'

Doc jerked a thumb at Ronnie. 'Put that low life in the front passenger seat before you go.'

A draft of chill air wafted into the car as Jimmy's door opened and closed. Doc watched as he crossed behind the car and Ronnie's door opened. The car lurched as Ronnie got out. Lurched again as Jimmy manhandled him into the front passenger seat.

Jimmy reached across and rested his hand on Doc's shoulder. 'Take care little brother.'

Doc said, 'Remember, Ronnie first.'

Ronnie's door closed. Jimmy's dark shadow merged into a doorway, and he was gone.

Not much of a goodbye, thought Doc. Though how he could find the words to thank someone who had struggled to give him a home and normality after their parents died, was beyond him.

He looked at Ronnie sitting, apparently cowed. For emphasis he rested his knife on his thighs. 'Kyle wants you alive. You try anything and you'll be carrying parts of yourself in a bucket.'

'I won't.'

As safe as a trapped rat, thought Doc, but left it at that as he put the car in gear and drove over the bridge spanning the stream and then went straight across at the junction. He checked his watch. *Barely time.* It was all a question of bluff.

The shortest route from the dog track would have Doc heading towards the car park from the south. Kyle would expect Doc to try and do the unexpected by approaching the car park from the north. Then Kyle would assume that Doc knew he was expected to arrive from the north and approach the car park from the south. Then Kyle would know...

All this bluff and counter bluff was giving Doc a headache. *The way I'm headed, from the north.* He checked his watch. *Seventy-two seconds and I'm out of time.*

He increased speed, took the first turn leading towards the car park, passed an old church and a graveyard with headstones hanging like a crone's teeth.

'I hope you've picked your plot,' he told Ronnie.

'For you,' said Ronnie, suddenly brave when help was nearby.

The street ended opposite the "EXIT" of the car park. Doc switched off his lights and powered straight across the road and under the raised barrier. Turned towards the car with the lights on and the four doors open.

Doc felt that driving in by the "EXIT" set the right impression of wariness, but Kyle standing waiting in the open for him, with the four car doors hanging open seemed too obliging. Doc had to force his eyes away from the dark shape lying across the backseat of Kyle's car.

The four doors meant he could clearly see that no one waited in the car to ambush him. At the same time when he went to close those doors, with the street lighting behind him, somebody would have a clear target. Doc glanced to his right. *From the cluster of cars.*

Which still left one man unaccounted for.

Chapter 140

Kyle was a dark figure standing between the headlights of the car. *I could always bull straight at him and crush him between the two cars.*

That, Doc knew, wouldn't work. He would be clearly illuminated in the headlights as he came. Kyle could shoot him straight through the windscreen long before he could be sure of a clear shot himself. Neither could he risk parking his car parallel with the other one, to block the see-through light from the street. That meant risking a head shot from the waiting Kyle as he drove past.

Doc wasn't afraid, at least he didn't think that what he felt was fear. More like regret: at not making a better job of his marriage; failing to save the innocents, like wee Elaine; and for not enjoying a life that suddenly had endless possibilities, instead of always being on business. Even so, Doc struggled to keep his heartbeat down. Every beat was a jerk of his body as he aimed, when every shot had to be right on target.

Instead of going directly to the waiting Kyle, Doc turned away and drove in an elliptical curve around the car park, looking to see if he could spot hidden gunmen. *That Kyle would expect.* Yes, he was sure he saw a shadow duck down at the cluster of cars and *that van at the bottom of the car park?*

The van's dark color allowed it to mold into the night. *I should have seen that straight off.* A sniper in the back of that van would have a clear view up the drive-through to the waiting Kyle and his car.

That's the three of them, thought Doc.

Kyle still stood between the lights, waiting for Doc to finish his cautious tour around the car park. Close up, Doc recognized the car with the open doors. His own hire car, he realized. He braked and came to a halt on the street side of the car. The meant that Ronnie's car blocked the see-through street lighting in the hire car. It also blocked the man in the van from getting a clear shot.

He selected RM's gun with the silencer attached, cocked and pointed it at Ronnie. 'I'm getting out of the car now. You follow me out my side.'

Kyle waited, apparently politely, at the other car, so he wasn't an immediate threat. *Giving the other men a clear shot.* Even so, Doc didn't dare glance Connie's way. He swallowed hard, knowing that she lay helpless almost within reach.

Doc opened the car door and eased partly out, the gun never wavered from Ronnie's head.

He kept his head below car-roof level to deny anyone a clear shot. 'Now you.'

Ronnie made an apparent try to get his foot around the gear stick. The heel of his shoe appeared to catch on something. 'I can't. It's impossible.'

His back was hard against his door. Ronnie was ready, once his foot came free, to piston a kick into Doc's face. Doc knew he would be off balance and vulnerable before he could hope to pull the trigger unless...

Doc rested the muzzle of the silencer against Ronnie's kneecap. 'Make it possible.'

Ronnie wrestled the foot free and slid out of the car feet first. Once enough of his bulk was out Doc hauled him upright and used his body for cover. The gun he kept pressed against Ronnie's lower spine.

Connie hadn't moved, hadn't spoken to acknowledge his arrival. If she was already dead, rather than kill Ronnie he'd leave him a paralytic and in constant pain for the rest of his life.

He looked across at Kyle. He thought he recognized him from years back. Doc didn't even try to remember the name. Somebody would know it for his tombstone.

Doc said, 'Your turn.'

'She's sleeping, like Sleeping Beauty,' said Kyle.

Doc noted that the polite-part-of-Belfast accent had developed an English intonation.

'Wake her up.'

Kyle walked out of the headlight beam and down the far side of the hire car. Doc's eyes wanted to fix on Kyle as he bent into the back of the car. Instead he made himself watch the cluster of cars and the van. Jimmy was down that way and knowing Jimmy he'd be so focused on Ronnie he wouldn't notice anything else.

From the car, Doc heard a ripping sound followed by Connie's voice giving a confused cry of pain.

Alive! Drugged. He didn't have to rip like that.

Doc made himself stand where he was, his heart stretched into that car. *I'm here my love.* Somewhere in the distance he could hear the pound of music. Somewhere close a stone turned.

Kyle made himself busy hauling Connie out of the car, cutting the ties around her hands and feet, helping her support herself. A good act. A man anxious to complete a done-deal and head away.

'You'll have to help her, she's still groggy,' said Kyle.

'What did you give her?'

'Nothing dangerous.'

Now Doc had a choice. Walk Ronnie to the front of the cars and be illuminated in the headlights or to the back and be dark shadows against them. He went to the back, knowing that was what Kyle wanted, but the darkness did help preserve his night vision. He still held the gun against Ronnie, but now pointing outwards. Lights were working for Doc as well as against him. He was against the lights, but in turn he saw a dark shadow move against the far street lights. *Close but not close enough.*

So was the music, getting louder, hard metal pounding through the night air.

Kyle man-handled the disjointed Connie out of the car and joined Doc at the back of the cars. One arm held Connie around the waist, the other had a gun pushed in under her left breast. Doc tightened his grip on Ronnie in case he tried to break free.

The dark shadow was closer now, the pounding music much louder.

Still apparently out to placate, Kyle asked, 'How do you want to do this?'

Doc tried not to ignore on Connie's unfocused smile at seeing him, her hand out to take his. 'You put the lady down and step back.'

'I think not,' said Kyle.

Doc said, 'We're professionals. Professionals walk away from events.'

He loosened his grip on Ronnie. Ronnie immediately tried to break free. Kyle's gun came away from Connie and swung towards Doc. His grip had loosened on Connie who fell sideways against the car and started a slide towards the ground.

Doc let Ronnie go, helped him along with a push and a hook of his leg. Ronnie stumbled against Kyle and Connie. The three of them crashed to the ground. Doc was there before them, a bullet from the shadow whipping over his head. Doc fired back. The shadow doubled over. A second bullet sent it flying backwards.

Kyle had rolled away, under the wheels of surrounding cars and disappeared. Ronnie was on his feet and running for the safety of the street. Connie lay crying with pain and from shock.

Something hissed past Doc. The tire of Ronnie's car exploded. Doc heard the delayed crack of rifle fire. *The man in the van.*

Doc was in the firefight he had dreamed off, but he wasn't enjoying it. All he wanted was to go to Connie. Ached to hold her and assure her that everything would be okay. He didn't dare. Wherever Kyle lay hidden, he'd have Connie in his sights.

If Doc moved away, took cover from the rifle fire, Kyle would kill Connie and come after him. And if he didn't the man in the van would kill him.

A second bullet sizzled into the ground near Doc's head, followed by the sound of the rifle shot. Doc realized that stretched out the way he was, to the gunman he was just a dark shadow among dark shadows. The man was quartering the area with his bullets. If the third shot didn't hit Doc, the fourth would.

Another rifle shot, this time no bullet. Instead the sound of metal punching metal.

Jimmy!

Jimmy taking on a professional gunman. Doc worried for Jimmy even as he felt mad at him. *That bullet should have been for Ronnie.*

A dark shadow rolled out of the van, took cover behind the wheel arch. Both rifles flared light as the two men fired at each other. Rifle shots echoed and re-echoed around the car park. Lights came on in the surrounding apartments, people hung out windows.

Doc didn't dare help Jimmy by snapping a shot at the gunman. The flare from the muzzle of his gun would give away his position to Kyle, then both he and Connie would die. Equally, Kyle couldn't shoot Connie without giving away his position.

Illogically he thought of the police station and the officers on duty enjoying a nice quiet night. *Into every life a little rain must fall.*

Chapter 141

Suddenly lights of a car swept the car park as a car turned in. A yahoo was leaning out the window of the car, beating on the door panel in time to the music. Doc had been concentrating so hard on saving Connie that he had tuned out all extraneous sounds, including the thunder of heavy metal music. The car came in through the "Exit" and curved around the far side of the car park.

Gunner and his mates!

Doc didn't have to think that. It was in his head, already part of his planning. Kyle didn't know if it was a pack of Saturday night drunks or danger. He turned to check as the car passed behind him. Doc saw the movement. Even as he took his shot, he launched himself over Connie's body to protect her from any return fire.

Somehow over the pound of the music he heard the crackle of bone as his bullet struck home. He sent two more into Kyle just to be sure then, still shielding Connie he looked Jimmy's way.

The lights of Gunner's car illuminated the last gunman against the van. The man was on his feet, preparing to run. A rifle shot rang out. Dark matter spurted from the man's head. He spun and fell. Jimmy had finally got his shooting eye back.

The music died away, Gunner's car stopped and its lights died. Doc was aware of men spreading out swiftly through the car park. He stayed with Connie, lay with her and held her tight. She was struggling into consciousness, not really taking things in.

Gunner appeared out of the darkness. 'Doc?'

'Yes.'

'Is she hurt?'

'No.'

'I need you out of here now.'

Doc got to his feet and hauled Connie into his arms. He eased her into the backseat of the hire car. She clung to him when he tried to leave her.

'Stay with me.'

'I can't.'

Much as he wanted to he couldn't, not with Ronnie running loose. Tonight had to finish everything. They'd been lucky so far. Next time things might not fall there way, so there mustn't be a next time.

Gunner was like a teenager as he relived the excitements of his old life. His friends held back in the darkness so they could never be identified. He had bags ready held out and opened. Gunner wiped the gun with a cloth smelling strongly of industrial cleaner, to remove fingerprints and DNA traces before dropping it into one bag, Doc's gloves went into the other.

Jimmy came up. He said, 'I should have shot Ronnie.'

'You should, but you did save Connie,' said Doc.

'And you.' Jimmy pretended disgust. 'You're supposed to protect me, not the other way around.'

Doc gave Jimmy's arm a friendly squeeze. For some reason Jimmy wouldn't sleep properly for a few nights. Even ordering people killed got between him and his sleep, no matter how deserving.

A quiet shout, almost a hiss of sound came across the car park. 'Over here.'

The way Gunner tensed it had to be one of his friends, possibly in trouble. Doc took to his heels, drawing his remaining gun as he did so. Ronnie's own .35.

Gunner's friend stood at the railings separating the car park from the stream. When Doc arrived he pointed down. Ronnie lay in the water, the only movement from him was the bottom of his jacket bobbing in the current.

Gunner's friend flicked a torch light onto the body. In jumping into the stream to get away Ronnie's foot had gone through the side of a drowned shopping trolley. From there he's pitched head forward into stones. Unconscious or trapped he'd drowned where he lay.

Gunner came up. Doc took the cloth off him. He wiped down Ronnie's gun and threw it into the water.

'Il est terminé,' he said.

It went totally against his normal behavior but for some reason he liked the dramatic gesture.

He went back and climbed into the car beside Connie. She clung sleepily to him – warm and alive, her heartbeat matching his – as Jimmy drove them off into the night.

ACKNOWLDEGEMENTS

A writer only thinks that he writes alone, that the finished work is all theirs. The truth is that any work of fiction takes if not a committee then a crowd of helpers, who give of their time and experience, to bring it to fruition.

The first pages of *Pursuit* were written during a creative writing course at Ty Newydd, Criccieth, Wales. Various versions of the novel as it developed were critiqued by the Writers in Residence and the students of the Queen's University, Belfast, Creative Writing Group at the Seamus Heaney Centre. Thanks Guys.

A special thanks to Mike Shaw of Curtiss Brown who believed in Jimmy and Doc long before the book was anywhere ready for publication. Glenn Patterson who gave me the title. Ian Samson for reminding us that writing is fun and should be reflected in our work and to Professor Ciaran Carson for his insightful critiques and his insistence on us checking the exact meaning of words before we use them.

Thanks also to Sammy Gillespie (the real life template for the argumentative Constable Gillespie of the Barlow books) for permission to use the name of his dog, Mullinure.

"Arrant Beauty" also had a real-life counterpart whose favorite game was to run straight towards me at full speed. At the last moment, jerking a shoulder to the side so that she merely brushed my trouser leg instead of shattering a kneecap.

Thanks also to my constant mentor, Kevin Hart. And to Hillary H, who wanted me to use her name for one of my most awful characters. I hope I've done you proud.

To Consultant Neurologist Stella Hughes for all medical advice, which, like any good patient, I don't always follow. My extended family and all my friends for their constant encouragement. My daughter, Lucie, for her enthusiastic promoting of her father's books and my son, Daniel, who hunts the internet for useful facts and sorts my computer problems.

Lastly but not least, my wife, Patricia. I'm not always there when she needs me. Especially on a winter's morning when her "hot-water bottle" is away writing instead of keeping her warm.

ABOUT THE AUTHOR

John is married with two children. He is one of the "doggy" McAllisters from Ballymena, Northern Ireland. For almost three decades he worked weekends and holidays on his uncle's farm, which had eighteen cattle and 70 greyhounds. His uncle's trophy cabinet contained every major cup, including the English Derby.

John's "real" job was that as an Accountant in Practice in Northern Ireland through all of the recent Troubles. He lost count of the number of times his own premises were bombed – from a 'good rattle' to total wipe-out.

In 1998 John took a sabbatical one year to read for an MPhil in Creative Writing at the Oscar Wilde Centre, Trinity College, Dublin.

People used laughter to get them through those darkest of times, a humor that is reflected in John's writing.

Other Books by John McAllister

(Barlow #1) The Station Sergeant

When local farmer, Stoop Taylor, is found dead, Station Sergeant Barlow has the sinking feeling his comfortable life is about to be turned upside down. While local hoods, the Dunlops, are stealing cattle to order, a traumatized German soldier escapes and roams the countryside. Barlow's personal problems multiply as well. He falls in love with another woman, his schizophrenic wife turns violent, his daughter is growing up too fast and the new Inspector wants him demoted. The Station Sergeant faces a battle to find a killer and save his career.

(Barlow #2) Barlow by the Book

Station Sergeant Barlow is back, but if he thought life was going to return to normal after his last case, he couldn't have been more wrong. Barlow's house is bombed, and he is suspended from duty on suspicion of Perverting the Course of Justice. His problems mount when his schizophrenic wife is released unexpectedly from the mental institution and he learns the truth about her traumatic childhood; while his daughter, Vera, is shot during a robbery. Barlow is under strict orders not to interfere in the ongoing investigations, but shooting Vera has made it personal.

(Barlow #3) Barlow Laid Bare

Barlow needs every ignorant bone in his body to survive against an unknown enemy who is using witchcraft to bring him down. An old adversary of Barlow's murdered during a witchcraft ceremony and a second man is killed with Barlow's own pistol. All of which delights District Inspector Harvey, because if Barlow doesn't hang he'll spend the rest of his life in jail.

(Barlow #4) Barlow Goes Forth

Barlow has to risk his life and his career to protect a Russian spy from the ruthless agents of the British Government. One of his officers is murdered, a vicious bull tries to kill him and Barlow has left a trail that could implicate him in the death of at least one man. Unless Barlow can find a mysterious package destined for Moscow, the spy will be killed and he will face a charge of triple murder.

(Barlow #5) Barlow at Christmas
Due out December 1st, 2019

It's the days leading up to Christmas Barlow has contend with an aggressive ghost and big city crooks determined to extend their protection rackets into Ballymena. A few murders and a new Woman Police Sergeant with a reputation for being *difficult*.

(Jimmy & Doc #1) Fight or Flight

Jimmy and Doc grew up "hard", then the Troubles come to Belfast. Enemies on both sides want them dead and their friends are even more dangerous.

(Jimmy & Doc #3) Line of Flight

Jimmy Terence, doesn't know who is killing his men, but he intends to find those responsible and sort them.

Jimmy himself is shot, someone tries to assassinate his family and his son's pregnant girlfriend is kidnapped.

Things get more complicated when Republican Activist, Mick Quinn, goes rogue in England with mortar bombs; and old enemies come together, determined to defend their Protection Rackets by bringing terror back to the streets of Belfast.

Jimmy finds himself fighting not only for the Irish Peace Process and the life of the Queen of England, but for the very existence of his own family.

Printed in Poland
by Amazon Fulfillment
Poland Sp. z o.o., Wrocław